Out of Control

ALSO BY SALLY JENKINS

STANDALONES
Little Museum Of Hope
Waiting For A Bright New Future
Out Of Control

out of control

SALLY JENKINS

Choc Lit
A JOFFE BOOKS COMPANY

Choc Lit
A Joffe Books company
www.choc-lit.com

First published in Great Britain in 2025

© Sally Jenkins

Cover art by Jarmila Takač

ISBN: 978-1781898468

PROLOGUE

Christmas Eve
30 Years Earlier

Fiona placed a hand on her belly and smiled. This time next year Amber would be here. She'd be six months old, smiling, possibly sitting up, and enjoying all the fuss of a first Christmas. And before that, she and Rob had the pleasure of 'the announcement'. Both sets of parents were invited for lunch on New Year's Day. Rob planned to uncork the champagne and share the news that there would be a new family member towards the end of June. Fiona would have only a tiny glass of fizz, heavily diluted with orange juice. There would be applause and excited chatter — Amber would be the first grandchild on both sides.

Rob had bounced around the house with excitement for a full five minutes when she'd told him. Then they'd decided to be cautious and wait until Fiona had reached twelve weeks before telling anyone else. This magical shared secret had pulled them closer after a rocky patch in their marriage, during which Rob had developed a habit of staying up when she went to bed, making hurried, muffled phone calls and often arriving home late without explanation. Fiona had been wary of asking too many questions for fear of making things worse. But after she told him about Amber, he became a homebird.

"How can you be sure it's a girl," he'd said, caressing her still-flat belly.

"Just a feeling I get. Pregnant women have special powers, you know." Then she'd kissed him, long and deep, and they'd gone upstairs without Rob making excuses to stay up alone.

But this week he'd relapsed and had been home late from work every day. And now, on Christmas Eve, he hadn't even phoned to say where he was.

She opened her notebook at the 'Christmas Dinner' section again and checked for the umpteenth time that she had everything required and had done as much preparation as possible in advance: red cabbage made — tick; turkey defrosting in garage — tick; two dozen homemade mince pies in cake tin — tick; melon just ripe for their starter — tick. There would be ten of them, all adults, and the largest number she'd ever cooked for: four parents plus Rob's brother and sister and their spouses. Working as a computer programmer had finally come in useful — Fiona was good at logical thinking and could use her skills to ensure everything would be ready at the right time. There would be no gnashing of teeth because the bread sauce was still a pile of crumbs, or the scarlet and gold crackers had been omitted from the place settings, or the brandy butter was still in the freezer. Rob had wanted to make the baby announcement during Christmas dinner, but Fiona had argued that their parents deserved preferential treatment and she would feel more confident telling them at thirteen rather than twelve weeks.

A sharp knock at the door made her jump. Had Rob forgotten his key? No, he tapped gently on the window on those occasions and then presented himself on the doorstep with a woeful expression. There was another impatient knock before she'd reached the hall.

"I'm coming!" There was rapping on the window as well now — and much harder than Rob would do.

A burly man had his foot over the threshold as soon as she opened the door. Taken by surprise, Fiona stepped backwards into the hall, allowing him to enter. He was wearing a dark suit, a pristine white shirt and a neatly knotted tie. The word 'gangster' jumped into Fiona's mind. Another, even broader, man stood beside a white unmarked van in their driveway. Something was wrong. Fiona vacillated. Should she ask them to leave? Tell them her husband would be home any minute? Call the police?

"I'm looking for Mr Robert Washington." The man waved an official-looking piece of paper at her. "Your husband?"

She nodded, heart racing, blood pounding in her ears. She rested her hand on her stomach.

"He bought a brown leather three-piece suite on hire purchase." The man's voice was brusque. "He stopped payments six months ago and ignored all subsequent correspondence. We are here to repossess said suite. Is this the lounge?" He went into the room she'd just vacated, swiftly followed by the second man.

Adrenaline flooded her body but shock rooted her to the spot. The bills came addressed to Rob and she had trusted him to deal with them. Now the men were manhandling the settee down the hallway and out to their van. The settee she'd been sitting on only a few minutes ago.

Fiona sank onto the bottom stair, her fists clenched with restrained anger. Anger at the two men who were violating her house, and anger at her husband who had somehow got them into a financial mess. How, she had no idea; with two salaries going into their joint account, they could easily afford the repayments on the suite. She'd wanted to save for a few months before buying it and then pay cash because the shop and the salesman gave her the creeps; the last thing she wanted was a long-term relationship with them. But Rob had insisted that the interest rate on the loan was less than they were getting on their savings and therefore the HP was a good deal. In the spirit of trusting her husband to do his best for them, Fiona hadn't checked. Now she was rigid down her spine and across her shoulders. Her breath was coming in shallow gasps. She opened out her hands and tried to breathe normally for Amber's sake. But it was impossible to let go of the fear and her fingers curled again. She was dimly aware of her nails digging into the palms of her hands as the two armchairs followed the settee outside.

The second man climbed into the driver's seat of the van while the first came back into the hall with his piece of paper and a clipboard. "Thank you for your cooperation, Mrs—" he referred to his piece of paper — "Washington. You made things very civil for all concerned. Now, if you could just sign here."

Like an automaton, she stood up and signed without reading the form. She became aware of tension in her belly. Tension that turned to cramping, and for a moment she forgot about being pregnant and wondered if she was getting her period. But only for a moment. Then she was terrified. There was wetness between her legs and she didn't dare look down for fear of discovering the truth.

"Hey! You're bleeding." For the first time there was a sign of emotion on the man's face.

"My baby." The pain was increasing and Fiona doubled over, crying out from physical and emotional agony. Her daughter was dying. She was dimly aware of the man gently pushing her back into a sitting position on the bottom step and using the phone under the stairs. It seemed like hours until she was in the hospital, but in reality, Rob told her later, it was only thirty minutes. He'd arrived home just as the man put the phone down.

A scan confirmed that Amber was lost. Rob cried as much as she did. Then, after several mugs of sweet tea provided by the nursing staff, he told her about the gambling. How it had

4

started in a low-key fashion with wins in the office Grand National sweepstake and a works night out at the greyhound track. He got a taste for the 'high' of winning and started following form for horse racing. A string of wins showed he was skilled in picking successful runners. These wins had paid for their first-ever cruise holiday the previous year — Fiona had been so trusting that she'd believed him when he told her about a 'bonus' from work. But then it had all turned on its head and he'd had to chase his losses — using the money put aside for bills and the mortgage.

"It's only a matter of time before I get my eye in again and win the money back. If that stupid shop had given us another couple of months, I'd have been flush and there would've been more than enough cash to go round for everyone."

"Everyone?" Emotionally and physically fragile after losing her baby, Fiona's brain struggled to comprehend. "Not just the furniture people?"

Her husband's head was in his hands and he mumbled something about the mortgage, gas and council tax.

"We owe all those people money?"

He nodded, still looking down into his lap.

"Are we going to lose the house?" She would've willingly let the house go over Amber, but losing both, she couldn't contemplate. Rob didn't look at her. That was when Fiona knew their marriage was over and she became hysterical.

CHAPTER 1

The last day of her old world. The ducks Fiona had carefully placed in a row over the past three decades now needed judicious rearranging. Just over three months ago, immediately after her sixtieth birthday, she'd had yet another retirement planning meeting with her financial advisor. He'd given her the green light to hand in her notice and start accessing her pension pots and savings.

"The Monte Carlo analysis of your funds shows no risk of you running out of money before you're ninety," Frederick had explained.

"Even if we have another stock market crash like in 2008 or 2020?" As a single woman, with only herself to rely on for possibly the next thirty years, she had to be certain that retirement seven years before her state pension kicked in was financially viable.

"Even if that happens. And you have substantial assets in cash which won't be directly affected by a crash." He paused. "Together, over the years, we've made sure you've got a good spread of investments."

Fiona had nodded. She'd tracked her finances as closely as any of the IT projects she'd managed. She and Rob had come out of the divorce and subsequent house sale with very little, and she'd panicked about building from a standing start and having enough to retire. That was why she'd become a client of Chingworth Wealth Management Consultants, and Frederick in particular, even though at that point she'd had no wealth to manage. Frederick had joined the firm on the very day she'd plucked up the courage to trust a professional with her money. He'd immediately understood that money, trust and men weren't easy bedfellows for Fiona, and always took care to give her absolute clarity and full involvement in what was going on and what fees she was being charged. When the state pension age for Fiona's cohort jumped to sixty-seven it felt as though the rug had been pulled from beneath her again, but Frederick had been on hand to explain how the situation could be managed and mitigated.

At the end of the summer, Fiona had spent a couple of weeks studying Frederick's report and her own spreadsheets before she was comfortable that everything she'd worked for over the years had now fallen into place. When she'd handed in her notice, a ripple of shock had run through her team and the management layer above her.

"You can't leave us!" her deputy had wailed. "And you love your job — so why go?"

Good question. She did love her job, and she was good at it. But watching her octogenarian mother struggle in the family home after the death of Fiona's father, and then the months spent helping her downsize into the retirement complex, had crystallised something in Fiona's mind: there wouldn't always be a healthy, confident future stretching in front of her. If she wanted to do anything with her life, other than sit in front of a computer and get blinded by spreadsheets, she had to seize the day. And that day was now.

"Because none of us know how long we've got before our bodies start to age or we drop dead."

So here she was, the day after her leaving party. They'd given her a send-off to remember and sent her home in a taxi with a huge bouquet and a generous gift card for her favourite store. Today there were a few sore heads in the office — something Fiona had avoided by the disciplined use of water between each red wine that came her way. Her professional image was not going to be sullied on her last evening.

"What are you going to do with your time?" asked her deputy, who would soon cease to be a deputy and become a fully-fledged project manager.

"Get more involved with what goes on in this town. There's a retired business persons' club that I've already joined. We combine our various skills and raise money for local charities."

"You mean swapping one kind of project plan for another that you don't get paid for? It sounds heady stuff."

"Don't be sarcastic." Fiona took a playful punch at her grinning colleague. "It's more relaxed than work, and we do fun things too. There's a Christmas dinner coming up and a couple of weekends away next year." It sounded tame, but that was how Fiona liked things — well ordered and under control. "I'll have more than enough on my plate."

"I must up my pension contributions so that I can join this excitement ASAP!"

"I'll be doing more running and yoga as well." Fiona grinned to herself at the thought of spending more time in yoga instructor Meeko's company — he always sent the class away feeling good. Over the years the two of them had become close, and now she counted him as her best friend.

"And tonight, at five p.m., when you are officially freed from this prison, will there be a celebration? Is there a special person?"

Her project team were continually fishing into her private life and Fiona always fielded them successfully. She and Joe were each other's secret and would remain so. She simply smiled enigmatically. "Let's just say, I have plans for the evening."

"Oooh! And will you miss having us lot to keep in check?" The words were said in jest, but the loss of her work 'family' had played on Fiona's mind. Her current life was carefully engineered but might need some well-planned reworking to avoid future emptiness.

The personal contents of her desk filled only half a cardboard box. She had no family photos on display or mugs declaring her to be 'A Special Mother' or 'A Genius at Work' or even 'A Best Friend'. Fiona didn't do close relationships — Meeko excluded — unless under exceptional, controlled circumstances. Once bitten, twice shy.

She started her round of goodbyes at 4 p.m. and finally handed over her keys and car park pass an hour later.

Tonight was the first time she'd asked Joe to vary their schedule and come round on a Friday rather than their customary Thursday. For two reasons: her leaving do had been the previous night, but more importantly, she didn't want to make her first step into a new and daunting life alone. This latter feeling, plus the removal of her 'family' of work colleagues, made her wonder whether it was time to allow life to become more free-flowing, more 'normal', as other people might describe it. But letting go even a tiny bit was a scary prospect that Fiona didn't know if she could achieve.

CHAPTER 2

By the time Fiona had negotiated the Friday rush-hour traffic, unloaded her box and started cooking their celebration meal, she felt in a party mood. Bridget Jones had it all wrong. Forget envying the 'smug marrieds', it was being the 'smug occasional girlfriend' that the rest of the world should aspire to. The thought popped into Fiona's head and the joy of it made her twirl between cooker and fridge. The skirt of her dress rose and danced in wave-like anticipation of Joe's arrival. She got all the romance and excitement without having to share a curry-smelly bed after his evenings with mates, or having to put up with adult children continually boomeranging back and forth. As soon as a man moved in, everything good went out of the window. More absence than presence makes a relationship work.

The oven-timer pinged. Fiona retrieved the stroganoff, stirred in the cream cheese and put it back to finish cooking. Joe wouldn't complain about the beef being replaced by a plethora of exotic mushrooms — even though at heart he was a carnivore.

She scrolled through Spotify and selected 'Classic Romance' as tonight's background. Obvious, commercial, in-your-face, lovey-dovey tunes were for people insecure in the arms of their lover or those too young to know better. She prepped the broccoli and sugar snap peas to the 'Love Theme from Romeo and Juliet'. The veg would go into cook while Joe was pouring the wine. He always brought a half-bottle of expensive, quality red, which made Fiona feel spoiled and special, just one large glass each so that Joe could still drive home at the end of the evening. If they lived together or saw each other more than one night a week the romance and excitement would disappear. Plus, she didn't want his presence to impinge on the other carefully curated areas of her life.

When the doorbell went, Joe's face on the camera was obscured by roses. Without counting, she knew there'd be twelve. Unoriginal but forgivable. His grin was bigger than usual when she opened the door and, after depositing the roses on the kitchen worktop, his arms went around her. He smelled faintly of soap and toothpaste and spicy aftershave. She ran her fingers down his back and over his still-firm bum. Kissed the start of his chest hair, which was just visible in the 'V' of his open-necked shirt, and attractively dark despite the classic silver peppering on his head.

His breath tickled her ear as he pulled her closer. "I've missed you. Once a week is not enough. And I had to wait an extra day this time."

Fiona didn't reply, she just melded into him. There was no point in spoiling the moment by saying once a week still suited her just fine. In the beginning, when he was getting over the rawness of his divorce, it had suited him just fine too. But recently, after almost a year together, she was getting the feeling that he wanted more from her, and she wasn't sure that she had more to give. Now he pulled back and looked her in the face. He was frowning slightly, and his eyes were silently questioning, as though he was judging the situation before announcing something she might not react well to. Fiona felt her shoulders tense. Saved by the ping of the timer, she rushed to rescue the stroganoff and sent Joe into the dining room with wine glasses and corkscrew.

11

"I brought roses because this is a celebration." He picked up his conversational thread when she'd served the vegetables. It was then that she noticed he'd brought a whole bottle of wine this time.

"Thank you." Fiona looked up from the creamy mushrooms and smiled. She assumed he was referring to her retirement.

"Depending on what you think, this could be a brand-new start for both of us."

"Both of us?"

"The stars have aligned. Or rather, the pipes have corroded."

Fiona put down her knife and fork and looked at him. "What?"

"I got woken early this morning by the ceiling coming down in the kitchen and part of the lounge."

"Oh no!"

"Oh yes. Apparently, the pipe to the hot water tank has given way. I don't know all the details, I had to go to work before the letting agency got a plumber there."

"Have they fixed it?"

He shook his head. "The house is uninhabitable. I need somewhere to live." He put his cutlery down for a moment. "My brother's agreed to put me up tonight but he's not keen on an open-ended arrangement. And then I thought, after twelve months together, this is the perfect time for us to move our relationship on to the next stage. What do you think?"

Heat engulfed her. *He wanted to live here! Seeing him once a week suited her just fine.* "Doesn't the landlord have to rehouse you?"

His knife and fork were on their way to retrieve his final few mouthfuls of mushrooms. "No."

Fiona suddenly felt suffocated. She stood up and, without waiting for him to finish, took both plates into the kitchen. She needed space to think.

"Hey!" he shouted after her.

She grabbed a spatula and scraped the remnants of their meals into the organic waste caddy. When she looked up, he was there, handing her a refilled glass of wine.

"Sorry. I've surprised you, landing like this. But I didn't want to call earlier and interrupt your last day at work."

Fiona's brain wouldn't calm down and find the words to speak coherently. "I . . ."

"I know we agreed to take things slowly, but that was months ago. The ink on my divorce papers wasn't dry and you wanted to get used to having a man in your life again. That's all in the past now, and we get on great, don't we?"

Joe was right, they did get on great — for one evening a week, not 24/7. "Are you sure there isn't alternative accommodation insurance or something?"

"The landlord didn't have insurance and the repairs could take months. I'll pay my way; I'm not looking for a free ride."

"What about a hotel until you can find somewhere else to rent? What we have together is special and I don't want to spoil it by rushing to live together." She was trying to let him down gently and preserve the relationship they already had at the same time.

"This isn't rushing, Fiona." He took her hands in his. "And Rose's tenure in the family home ends next year when Adele turns twenty-one, so then I'll have capital to use towards us buying somewhere together."

Buying together was definitely not going to happen, but turning Joe away now could mean losing him completely. And she didn't want that either. "OK." She spoke slowly; only a few hours earlier she'd recognised life might have to become more free-flowing to fill the black hole left where her career had been. "Let's see how it goes."

She wouldn't be able to please herself; she'd have to bend and compromise to accommodate his wishes. She'd heard her colleagues whinge about their partners and she didn't want that to happen to her and Joe. But as long as she recognised all of that as a possibility, she could make sure it didn't happen.

"Thank you." He pulled her gently towards him and kissed her. "We can properly share our lives now, meet each other's family and friends . . ."

Fiona didn't want Joe overlapping into all parts of her life. It was easier and safer to keep things separate, but she couldn't say that yet.

"My stuff's in the car. You put the coffee on while I fetch it. And I've got a present for us."

Fiona covered the fruit salad she'd made for dessert; her appetite had gone.

Joe came back into the hallway with two huge suitcases and a long, chilly draught of late November air.

"We have to have ground rules. I'm not taking on the role of a wife or housekeeper," she said. "No dirty underwear or wet towels on the floor. There is a laundry basket in the bathroom. You do your share of housework — I'll make a rota."

"Stop panicking! I am housetrained, you know."

"And no boomerangs. Definitely no boomerangs."

Joe grinned at her use of their private nickname for his son and daughter. "Dan's just started renting with a mate. And Adele's uni term doesn't finish for another fortnight but she's totally wrapped up in this boyfriend of hers anyway. She was mostly at his in the summer. I haven't spoken to her for weeks but she said back then that she'd been offered waitressing work over Christmas so not to expect her back."

Joe knelt and unfastened the larger suitcase. Then he stood up and, with a flourish, presented her with a large, flat cardboard box patterned with scarlet Christmas roses, plump pink hearts and white mistletoe berries. It was perforated with little numbered doors.

"Allow me." Joe pressed open the door marked '1' and retrieved a chocolate.

"But it's only the twenty-ninth. We should wait until Sunday — delayed gratification and all that."

"Let's start the way we mean to go on," he said. "Life is for living. And that means we can break the rules if we want to. You've retired today and I've moved in. Two brand-new starts that need celebrating. Half each." Instead of snapping the chocolate in half and handing her a piece, he held it in his mouth, pulled her close and kissed her.

The act was sensual, toe curling, and Joe was working his usual seductive magic on her. Slowly and gently they shared the dark chocolate between their tongues. Maybe, just maybe, with a fair wind, a housework rota and no boomerangs, they could make this work.

CHAPTER 3

They ended up in the bedroom before Fiona could formulate any thoughts about clearing away and washing up. Slowly, they undressed one another, and it was as though Joe's bombshell about moving in had never happened. She luxuriated in the gentle touch of his fingers, lips and tongue. Simply being next to each other, bare skin alongside bare skin, was what she liked best about making love. And Joe was happy to give her all the time she needed until she couldn't bear the anticipation of them coming together any longer.

Afterwards he wrapped his arms and legs around her and held her close. For a while, sated, they both dozed. Then, through habit, Fiona forced herself back to consciousness. "Joe?"

"Shhh! There is no more leaping out of bed to drive home. We can fall asleep together. I don't know why we ever had that rule anyway."

Fiona knew why — she hadn't wanted to share her bed or have the two of them tripping over each other to shower and get off to work the next day, or Joe stealing precious time out of a weekend morning that she wanted to use for running or yoga. She attempted to push past these inconveniences and relax into the warmth and security of another body beside her — instead of the cold air that used to leap in and tease her vulnerability when Joe threw back the duvet and leaped out.

"Find yourself someone special," her mother had nagged for years.

Now Fiona began to understand why — there was a certain contentment about settling down to sleep together that she hadn't experienced for a long time. Joe moving in was a shock, but it had the potential to turn into a pleasant surprise — especially if they invested in a king-size bed. Even when she was married, Fiona had felt a double bed was not big enough for two to actually sleep in. It was impossible to get far enough away from the other person to give the illusion of privacy or to have sufficient space to sprawl and spread as much as necessary.

At this moment, Joe's presence felt right, but she couldn't sleep wrapped in someone else's arms, feeling their breath on her skin and the faint tremble of their heartbeat. He was already asleep. Carefully, she shifted herself away from him. The ideal position, back-to-back with as large a gap as possible between them, wasn't achievable without waking him. Joe didn't snore but he did breathe heavily and audibly. And he insisted on sleeping facing her. She turned away to face the bedside table but could feel his breath on her neck and hear each inhale and exhale. The more she thought about it, the more audible and annoying his presence became. That novelty of 'warmth and security' didn't sufficiently make up for losing her own private sleeping space. Fiona had two spare bedrooms, the smallest filled with a desk and computer and the larger with a double bed for guests. That bed wasn't made up and the prospect of getting out into the cold to find sheets and a duvet didn't appeal, especially not since she'd gone without her usual fleecy winter pyjamas in favour of nakedness for Joe.

At 2 a.m. she pulled a tissue from her bedside box, tore off a couple of small strips and screwed them into balls to act as ear plugs. Then she shuffled as near to her side of the bed as she could without falling out. It must have done the trick because the next thing she knew, Joe was getting out of bed.

"Is it morning?" she muttered.

"No. It's three fifteen and I'm going to the loo. Sorry, but I've got to put the light on. I can't manage in the pitch dark in an unfamiliar room."

The sudden bright glare from the other side of the bed made Fiona's muscles jump. She pulled the quilt over her head and focused on breathing slowly and deeply. Breath in, breath out. Breath in, breath out. She could feel her heart rate calming.

Then there was a bang and a vibration through the bed frame and mattress. "Aaah! Bloody hell! It's like negotiating an obstacle course."

Fiona flung the quilt back. "For God's sake, Joe. How can you walk into the bed with that spotlight on?"

From his jerky movements she could see that he was now hopping rather than walking back round to his side of the bed.

"I didn't put my glasses on. Everything's blurry."

He got back into bed. She felt some tugging on the quilt, he went still and then started breathing heavily again. Now all Fiona could think about was going to the toilet herself. Breath in, breath out. Breath in, breath out. The more she tried to ignore her bladder, the more it dominated her thoughts. Breath in, breath out.

She pushed back the covers and made her way to the bathroom in the dark, shivering and cursing her lack of nightwear. Joe didn't stir. No need to put the light on in the bathroom, she knew exactly where the toilet was. She sat down and immediately stood up again. "Damn him!"

Joe had failed to put the toilet seat down and now the backs of Fiona's thighs felt slightly damp from whatever residue he'd left behind. She remembered his glasses abandoned by the bed and tried not to let her mind veer towards his accuracy of aim. She scrubbed at the back of her legs with toilet paper, put the seat down, did what she had to do and then deliberately washed her hands for a long time under the running tap and flushed the toilet. He'd inconvenienced her so she had the right to wake him up, accidentally on purpose.

She got back into bed, wriggled around and pulled on the quilt for as long as she could without it seeming deliberate. None of it worked. He continued to breath rhythmically and loudly onto her neck.

* * *

"Wakey-wakey!"

Joe was standing over her with a tray. How, given his nocturnal noises, had he managed to get up, get dressed for work, boil the kettle, which sounded like a rocket taking off, and then bring in a breakfast tray — all without waking her?

"Sit up! You don't want to fritter your retirement away in the land of nod."

Obediently, she pushed herself up to a sitting position and shrugged on the dressing gown that Joe was offering. She rearranged the pillows behind her and Joe placed the tray across her lap.

"Coffee, toast and a bowl of that fruit salad, which I assume we should have eaten last night."

"Thanks."

"No problem. You deserve it for taking me in."

Fiona smiled at him. It was nice to be pampered and not have to go downstairs and make her own breakfast in a kitchen still chilly before the central heating properly kicked in.

Joe sat down on the edge of the bed, leaned over and kissed her. "I've got to go. It's my Saturday to work and the first patient is at eight thirty a.m. Don't worry about cooking tonight. We're going out — it's the practice Christmas do and the first chance I have to show you off. And I am going to make the most of it!"

Then he was gone, leaving Fiona blinking her gritty, sleep-deprived eyes and trying to imbibe coffee quickly enough to enable her brain to compute the full impact of what Joe had just said.

CHAPTER 4

Joe's overriding feeling as he drove away from the house was relief. Relief that Fiona hadn't said 'no' to his plea for somewhere to stay. Fiona was self-contained, confident, happy in her own skin, and appeared to have no special need for him or anyone else in her life. She'd never demanded anything from him, meaning he was free to carry on with his own life without the complication of wondering when or if to introduce her to his young adult children or wider family. Their weekly dates had been spent in a desert oasis reserved for just the two of them and that had suited them both. But his mates were getting curious about 'this Fiona'. He suspected they thought he was making her up. And he was frustrated with making excuses for not taking her along to things and appearing like a Billy No-Mates.

As he drove, he hoped it wasn't too late to add Fiona as his 'plus one' to the practice Christmas do that evening. He was looking forward to his colleagues' reactions when he turned up with 'this Fiona', who was more attractive than his ex-wife, even though she was ten years older.

"Carol." He leaned conspiratorially on the reception desk and spoke to the woman who kept the whole physio practice in check. "I'll be bringing someone with me tonight — is that OK?"

"Fiona, at last!" Carol exclaimed. "That is fabulous. But why now?"

He didn't elaborate any further, despite Carol clearly being desperate to know more. Fiona would look stunning this evening and everyone would be impressed. The anticipation thrilled him. How would he introduce her? His partner? Cohabitee? Girlfriend? Or just by her name?

Joe made himself a mug of instant coffee in the grimy cubbyhole that passed for a kitchen in the staffroom. Not as good as the coffee served at Fiona's but on a par with the stuff his ex-wife Rose had always seemed happy with. Rose accepted the mundane and didn't strive for anything better in the way that he did. Unfortunately, he still had to tolerate the mundaneness of work. His state pension was seven years away and the divorce meant that leaving the petty stresses of his career behind was not an option. He should have started a practice of his own as a young man instead of making money for someone else. He couldn't even say he'd devoted himself to the NHS and received all that Covid-clapping back in 2020. He blamed Rose's love of the ordinary for the failure of his marriage — more of the same had no longer been enough for him. With the kids leaving home they should have been doing something out of the ordinary.

He pulled himself back to the present. Tonight wouldn't be mundane at all with Fiona shining at his side. He couldn't wait.

Carol poked her head around the staffroom door. "Your first patient's here, Joe."

He gave her a wink and headed to his treatment room.

CHAPTER 5

The toast Joe had made her was cold and covered in massive amounts of marmalade — he hadn't listened when she'd told him a few weeks ago that she'd switched to sugar-free peanut butter. The banana in the fruit salad had gone soggy overnight. The breakfast reminded Fiona of the Mother's Day trays her colleagues described in minute, loving detail, made by their young children. The difference was that a child could be genuinely praised for putting such a meal together; it was harder when the chef was a grown man.

"Don't be such a perfectionist, Fiona." That's what her mother would say of this situation. "You can't expect everyone to meet your high standards."

To be fair, Joe couldn't have rectified the banana situation without travelling back to the previous evening and not making his bombshell announcement and then not dragging his suitcases in from the car, thus allowing them to eat the fruit salad at the correct time. But it wasn't difficult to put some logical thought into breakfast, especially when he, unlike her, had had the luxury of a full night's sleep. He could've brought the coffee and fruit salad first and then gone to make fresh, HOT toast instead of staring at her and talking about showing her off to his work colleagues this evening. The magnitude of that last thought made her worry again. Would they mistakenly think she'd been the catalyst for his marriage break-up? She couldn't bear to be branded 'the other woman'. They'd want to know why he'd been keeping her hidden away for so long. People loved to gossip and they'd put two and two together and make five.

How would he introduce her? She cringed at the thought of him calling her his 'other half' or 'partner'. Anything like that made them seem more of an item than they actually were. She wanted him just to use her name.

Fiona moved the tray onto the empty side of the bed. As she did so the plate holding the cold toast slid to one side revealing an advent chocolate nestled on a yellow Post-it note from the pad beside her landline in the hallway. He'd scribbled, *Jumping the gun again with the calendar but I want you to know how much I love and appreciate you. XXX.*

It was like giving someone your last Rolo. Fiona's heart filled. She felt wanted. The inedible toast was forgiven. Joe might not be the world's best breakfast chef but he was a romantic at heart. That was just one of the reasons why the relationship they'd had over the past year had worked so well. Smiling, she was about to pop the chocolate in her mouth when she had a better thought. She placed it on one of her lace handkerchiefs on his pillow for him to find later.

In the shower some of her tiredness slipped away. But as she towelled herself dry, her mind wouldn't relinquish its journey around this new version of her relationship with Joe. She'd always looked forward to and enjoyed their weekly dates, but having him turn up with his suitcases or meeting his work colleagues had never been on her agenda. She'd been retired from work less than twenty-four hours, and it was a Saturday, but she felt a longing for the office, where everything would be as she expected and the day would proceed in an orderly fashion. Without surprises. She gazed at her work suits hanging in the wardrobe, each one protected by a dry cleaner's polythene sheath and ready to wear. Next year's electronic calendar had a reminder set for the end of May. If the suits hadn't been worn by then, they would be donated to charity, one a month, until there were just two remaining: her favourite navy one for funerals and her only beige one for christenings and weddings. Fiona wasn't a hoarder. Her garage was the only one in the road that housed a car instead of cardboard boxes. Similarly with the loft — Fiona's held only the small Christmas tree that Joe had bought for her at the beginning of their relationship.

She pulled one of the suits from the wardrobe and stroked the few inches of caramel-coloured fabric hanging below the reach of the plastic cover. At work her mind was focused and it was easy to keep any demons or overthinking at bay. In the early days, after losing Amber and then the divorce from Rob, it had been a relief to have the ordered thought process of computer programming and later the endless spreadsheets of IT project management forced upon her. Now, as well as taming retirement, she faced the additional unknown of life with Joe.

Her phone buzzed and flashed up the warden's name from her mother's sheltered housing complex.

"Oh, Fiona! I'm glad I've caught you. I know it isn't your usual day for visiting but could you pop in and see your mum? I just did my morning check on all the residents and she sounded down in the dumps. You know how she gets sometimes — lonely like everyone else here. I don't know why they find it so hard to confide in each other. When I asked her what the problem was, she said something about not knowing what was happening at Christmas."

Fiona sighed. As the date of her retirement had got closer, these last-minute requests from her mum, via the complex manager, had become more frequent — it was as though the old lady wanted to lay claim to a significant part of her daughter's retirement. Fiona didn't mind visiting but she liked to do it according to the timetable they'd agreed, and Saturday wasn't her day. Before Joe had turned up, today had been earmarked for trying out a new Pilates class and then a spot of Christmas shopping. Joe and the breakfast and the job of washing up last night's dinner stuff, a task which he had ignored, meant she was running too late for the class and her day had become annoyingly skew whiff before it had started.

"Do you think a phone call would do the trick?" That would only take ten minutes out of the already spoiled day.

There was a hesitation before Mrs Fairchild replied. "No. I think she was up really early baking and she mentioned having a delicious sponge cake all ready and waiting."

Fiona sighed. Her mum's reaction to any woe was to bake. Which then made the old lady even more fed up because there was no one to eat her baking. "OK. I'll be there, but don't give her a time otherwise she'll sit and watch the clock."

On the drive over to the sheltered housing complex, Fiona braced herself for an inquisition into her love life and for the criticisms that had been part of their relationship for as long as she could remember. An only child, she carried all her mother's hopes and expectations single-handedly. One expectation that Dorothea had been voicing more regularly was to spend more time with Fiona when she retired. Which was now. This visit would be an opportunity to ensure those expectations were managed realistically for both of them.

Her mum's sheltered flat was like a dolls' house with an open-plan lounge/kitchen, a bathroom with an accessible shower, a bedroom which just fitted a double bed pushed up hard against the wall, plus a 'dining room/second bedroom'. This latter space wasn't big enough for either purpose and had become Dorothea's jigsaw room, with a camp bed folded up under the window 'just in case'. Fiona had had a joiner fix shelving to two of the walls to hold the old lady's extensive jigsaw collection, and in the centre of the room was the old family dining table covered in a mat, specifically for doing jigsaws. A radio sat on the windowsill so that Dorothea could listen to Radio 4 as she worked.

"So," her mother said when Fiona was settled in an armchair, "have you got yourself a nice young man yet who's willing to settle down? Or is it still that one-night-a-week chap who I'm not allowed to meet? Has he got three heads or something?"

"His name's Joe. And . . ." she paused for dramatic effect, wishing she could have a drum roll to accompany her announcement, "he moved in with me last night." There was no point muddying the waters on the technicality that the situation was forced by a burst pipe, or mentioning that Fiona wasn't sure if she wanted him there.

"About time too. Are you getting married?"

Married? Fiona's stomach lurched and she felt like a horse shying away from a sudden hole in the road. "We . . . haven't discussed that."

"But you'd say 'yes', if he proposed?"

Fiona wished she'd kept her mouth shut on the Joe situation.

"Hmmm." Dorothea set her lips in a thin line when Fiona didn't respond. "Growing old alone isn't much fun, and I should know." She pointed to the slices of Victoria sandwich, liberally dusted with icing sugar and thickly filled with buttercream, on the plate between them. "Eat your cake. I've cut you an extra-large piece — I don't get many visitors to share it with."

The cake was twice the size of a standard piece. "Mum — I can't eat all that." Fiona patted her stomach.

Dorothea waved a hand dismissively. "For heaven's sake just tuck in. You're far too skinny."

Her mother's cakes were the best; Dorothea hadn't won the WI Christmas Cake Competition seven years in a row for no good reason.

"How about I wrap my piece in a serviette and take it home for Joe? He's got a very sweet tooth. And he appreciates his food."

"Well, that's a point in his favour." The old lady smiled. "Remind me before you go and I'll get him some of the flapjack I made yesterday. I could make extra for next time you call?"

"No, Mum. It's fine, really. And I did want to talk about my future visits." Fiona took an orange felt tip from her bag. "I'm going to mark more dates on your new calendar for next year. OK?"

The old lady beamed as Fiona circled an extra day per fortnight and added the dates to her phone calendar. She'd chosen times when she'd have an hour to spare en route to the Retired Means Active club meetings.

Then Dorothea diverted back to her favourite topic: her daughter's inability to sustain a relationship with a suitable man. She seemed to have forgotten about her anxiety over the Christmas arrangements which had brought Fiona here in the first place. "Even if he likes my cake, this Joe-person still sounds dodgy. He keeps you at arm's length for months and months and then, all of a sudden, he moves in. It's your pension lump sum he's after. Mark my words, this won't end well."

"Mum! You can't judge a person you've never met. And he didn't keep me at arm's length, it was the other way around."

"And why are you so cagey when I ask how the pair of you met in the first place?"

Her mother had decided that today was the day for awkward questions. If Fiona admitted to internet dating, her mother would voice a less than positive opinion on it. *Keep it vague.* "Mutual interests. But it's really not important!"

"If it was a normal relationship, you would have introduced us already." Dorothea had a mouthful of cake and tea before continuing. "Now Rob, he was a nice lad. You never gave him a proper chance to put things right and show that he could change. You can be an unforgiving woman, Fiona."

Fiona choked on her tea. In one breath her mother was saying, with no proof at all, that Joe should be avoided because he was after her money. And in the next she was saying that Rob, who had gambled away everything they had plus some, should be given another chance.

"The thing is, Fiona—" her mother leaned forward as though she was letting her daughter into one of life's biggest secrets — "you are sixty. Your life is at least two-thirds finished. Your ability to attract a man is probably limited to the next five years; by then everything will have sagged and wrinkled beyond repair. Unless you want to turn into an old maid — and, as I've already said, growing infirm on your own is no walk in the park — you need to get your act together. Stop letting things that have gone wrong in the past, like your marriage to Rob, frighten you off trying them again. Learn to trust again."

"Mum, it's my life."

"Exactly. That's why you don't see it objectively." Dorothea dropped her voice to a dramatic stage whisper. "I've heard on the maternal grapevine that Rob is back in town." Dorothea sat back in her chair with a satisfied look. "Single. Available. He's looking to meet new people. I told his mother about that retired business club thing you've joined."

"Mum!"

"Rob is a lovely lad. He worshipped the ground you walked on. Me and your dad thought you were a match made in heaven. It's a shame you never got as far as producing kiddies, but he always treated you well."

"Except for when we lost everything through his gambling addiction." *Including your unborn granddaughter.*

Over the intervening years Dorothea had never mentioned the miscarriage. Immediately afterwards Rob had insisted, against Fiona's wishes, on telling both sets of parents about it, even though they hadn't known she was pregnant in the first place. "They have a right to know. And you need your mother's help to get through it." Fiona swore she didn't need help. She wanted to stay in her black hole out of respect to Amber. But eventually she had accepted Dorothea shopping and cleaning for them until she could face domestic activity and the outside world again.

"People change," Dorothea said. "Apparently after all that business he went cold turkey and hasn't gambled again."

"Hmmm." Whether he was a reformed character or not, Fiona had no intention of getting involved with her ex-husband again.

As Fiona put her coat on to leave, Dorothea pushed a foil-wrapped package on her. "Flapjack. For Joe."

CHAPTER 6

"I don't know why you're so nervous," Joe said, as Fiona stood in front of the mirror and tried to decide whether her floor-skimming scarlet sheath dress was too over the top. "Stop examining yourself. I will feel a million dollars with you on my arm."

When she'd pressed him for more details about what to expect of his colleagues, he'd described a mix of other physios, podiatrists, a chiropractor, an osteopath, a couple of receptionists and someone who did Botox. Thoughts of the latter made her lean closer to the glass and examine her face. As her mother had forewarned, things were sagging, and she lacked those wonderful high cheek bones that act as scaffolding to keep everything in check. Joe eased her back from the mirror and kissed her.

She pulled away and looked at herself again. The phrase 'scarlet woman' came into her head. Conclusions would be jumped to that she had been instrumental in the break-up of Joe and Rose's marriage. Had Joe emphatically told his workmates that he hadn't met Fiona until after the divorce? A subtle outfit would be better, unless she wanted to star in the workplace gossip that would surely follow the party. She changed into her ubiquitous, knee-length little black dress, which went anywhere without problem.

Joe looked disappointed. "I preferred the other one. It made a statement."

"I don't want to make a statement. Let's focus on us before worrying about how we appear to others."

"That sounds like fun." He pulled her close and kissed her again. Her toes curled and she warmed inside at the memory of the rationed evenings they'd spent together, making the most of every minute. Then she gently pushed him away. Now they had all the time in the world to do that sort of thing, it wasn't so important to take every opportunity.

"Talking of the future . . ." Joe produced a small black box from his trouser pocket. Fiona's heart went cold. *Please don't go down on one knee. Please don't ask the question. Please make that box disappear.* "I got you this. Wear it tonight." She closed her eyes and tried to concoct a neutral reply. She couldn't agree to a marriage proposal. He opened the box. "It's a pendant," he said.

Her chest deflated like a balloon. The relief was overwhelming.

"You always wear that old amber thing and I thought it was time for a change. And since we're going to paint the town red, a ruby seemed most appropriate. Let me." His hands went to the back of her neck to unfasten the pendant she'd had specially made three decades earlier in memory of her lost baby daughter.

Fiona's hand immediately went to the stone. "No. I . . ."

"Don't be silly. Amber and ruby together will look out of place."

She wanted to tell him to return the ruby to the shop. She would never wear it because the amber pendant only came off when she was in water. But he'd undone the catch and the chain cascaded into her hand, making a curled shiny nest around the bespoke mustard-coloured stone. He fastened the new gold chain at the back of her neck. It was just the right length and the red stone nestled neatly in her collar bone. Joe stood back to admire his choice. "That looks much better than the old yellow one. You are keeping those red heels on, aren't you?"

That had been her intention but she disliked the way he was toying with her outfit and the impression he wanted her to project. Had this sort of interference been instrumental in his divorce from Rose?

"Joe, I am going to wear the amber pendant. It has sentimental value to me." She fiddled with the fastener on the ruby's chain and then handed it back to him.

"What sentimental value?"

"Just something from . . . it was a long time ago." Her fingers were rubbing the smooth surface of the amber stone. She couldn't talk about it now, casually, when they were in a hurry to go out.

He frowned but didn't pursue it. Only in the car did the cost of the ruby occur to her.

"I appreciate the thought behind the pendant." She tried to be diplomatic. "But I thought all your capital was tied up until the house can be sold next year? And you're paying an arm and a leg to keep Adele at uni."

He glanced across at her. "My house is uninhabitable so I've stopped the standing order for my rent. Fiona — for once just relax and enjoy. Let someone else be in control. You don't have to be the boss all the time. And it's not your money I'm spending." His sharp voice was a shock. They'd never argued because they each had their own space and their own private lives to return to, and they both knew where the line was drawn. They'd been sharing their domestic lives for only twenty-four hours and already it had become difficult not to challenge where the new line now sat.

Fiona took a breath. She wasn't ready to tell Joe the whole story around her divorce and reveal her vulnerability. But she wouldn't allow herself to be treated like 'the little woman' who didn't understand finance. "When I was married there were . . . money issues. That makes me want to know the ins and outs of where any cash is coming from."

He patted her knee, his eyes still on the road, and then spoke flippantly. "Thanks for telling me. But don't worry. I won't bring the bailiffs to your door."

Fiona went cold inside. "Don't treat it as a joke."

The practice had two reserved tables at Moorcroft Hotel's Christmas Dinner and Disco evening. As they walked into the large function room, hands from a far table were up in the air and waving madly in their direction.

"They do know I wasn't involved in your marriage break-up?"

"It will all be fine." He squeezed her hand.

Fiona felt her stomach clench with nerves as they approached the table.

"Joe, my mate! My fellow, fizzy physio!"

"Evening, Mark, I think you've already been on the pop." Joe went round greeting his colleagues with play pushes, back slaps and warm hugs. "A quick introduction everyone. This is Fiona, the significant other in my life."

Fiona gave an acknowledging nod around the two tables, relieved that she was not expected to listen to or remember the names of the people gathered there. *Significant other.* It was less clinical than partner and didn't give the impression they were joined at the hip. It would do.

Joe located the seats with their names and poured them both a glass of red wine. Fiona drank gratefully and tried to get her bearings. The tables were round and already littered with bottles and spent Christmas cracker debris. The background music was too loud to allow natural conversation and raised voices were batting back and forth across the table.

"Cracker?" Joe turned towards her and brandished the shiny red paper cylinder from his place setting.

Fiona angled herself so that she could take a grip of both the open end and the snap hidden by the frippery.

The cracker snapped, spilling its contents in front of Fiona. "You have them." She pushed them sideways to her 'significant other'; reading out jokes and brandishing a cheap plastic water pistol in front of curious strangers didn't appeal.

Joe picked out the scarlet paper crown. "Here." He indicated she should lower her head.

Fiona glanced around the tables. Everyone else was wearing the spoils from their cracker. Refusing would bring more attention to her than just putting up with the thing. She bent her head and Joe placed the crown gently on her carefully blow-dried hair.

"What happened to the pendant?" Mark's words fell into the lull between two tracks of music and everyone heard. "The one you were showing off in the staffroom this afternoon?"

Fiona's gaze was on her cracker debris. Her cheeks went hot and she slid her eyes to the left in an attempt to see Joe's reaction. His initial frown turned into a forced grin.

"It cost an arm and a leg, didn't it?" Mark continued, oblivious to the discomfort he was causing.

"You know women." Joe gave a little laugh. "Always fickle. Lucky I kept the receipt."

Fiona was grateful for the sudden return of the loud music and the appearance of waitresses with plates at some of the other tables. Their own food couldn't be far away. A woman she took to be the party's organiser came over from the adjacent table. "Sorry, Fiona, but because you were a very late addition, you're stuck with the menu choices that the hotel has a surplus of. I hope you're not vegetarian or anything?"

She'd become the centre of attention. Carol was waiting for a response and the rest of the table had fallen silent again. "No allergies?" Carol prompted.

"No. It'll be fine. I eat anything and everything." *Please go away and let people stare at their soup and their goat's cheese tarts and their garlic mushrooms instead of at me.*

* * *

Once the Christmas pudding, strawberry trifle and cheeseboard plates had been cleared, Fiona excused herself and went to the ladies. It had been the right decision to leave the scarlet dress at home. And that's where she ought to be right now.

"Remind me how long you two have been together?" Carol emerged from one of the cubicles as Fiona was tearing the paper crown into tiny strips over the waste bin. "And why have we never met you before?"

Here was her chance to stop any gossip. "We've been seeing each other about a year, but not seriously."

Carol smiled into the mirror. "Joe can be a sly old fox. Did you know Rose? No, of course you didn't. I liked her. She was completely different to you. The divorce surprised me."

Fiona escaped into a cubicle before there were any further questions. For the rest of the evening she alternated between trying and failing to get Joe on his own so she could suggest they leave early, and making sure he didn't drink any more than the two glasses of wine he'd had with the meal. It had been his suggestion that he drive rather than booking a taxi, but she was worried it would slip his mind the longer he spent in the company of Mark. She wasn't familiar with the version of Joe heavily under the influence; previously they'd had that wonderful rule about him driving home every night, so alcohol had never been a major part of their time together.

It was much later that he pulled carefully out of the car park onto the dual carriageway. "That was a success. They liked you. It was a good night, wasn't it?"

"It . . ." She had to tell him that his attitude towards her had been the problem with the evening, from trying to influence her choice of dress to the debacle over the pendant. It was an attitude she couldn't live with and, therefore, he had to find somewhere else to stay.

But she was too tired for a showdown tonight. In the morning she would ask Joe to leave. As a temporary compromise, he could have the spare room for a couple of weeks until he got himself sorted with non-flooded accommodation, but they could no longer be a couple. He hadn't made a positive decision to be with her, it had arisen out of necessity, but it definitely wasn't a necessity on her part. Over the past twenty-four hours she'd had her belief that a part-time man suited her needs best confirmed.

CHAPTER 7

Fiona's head was thumping when she woke. Two consecutive nights with another person in her bed wasn't good. The searing night sweats and general insomnia of the menopause had receded over the past couple of years but she still remembered the advice her female GP, also of a certain age, had given her at the time: "Sleep alone in a double bed if you possibly can. Believe me, it works wonders." Fiona had merely smiled and nodded; sleeping alone had been her default situation and at that time she'd had no intention of changing it. Now, with the forced proximity of the man with whom she'd thought she had the perfect relationship, Fiona understood exactly where her GP had been coming from and also why royalty so often chose to sleep in separate bedrooms.

Joe's breathing was loud, heavy and far too intimate as it gusted over the base of her neck, causing her shoulders to knot. The gap between the curtains showed only a wisp of greyish light. Somewhere out there, Sunday was beginning to happen. The thought of early morning fresh air made the fug of shared breathing feel like a pillow over her head. On her back, she slid sideways away from Joe. If he woke there'd be expectations and she didn't want to talk, make love or even eat breakfast with him, either in or out of bed. She needed time alone to sort her thoughts out. Her own company — that was what she liked. Especially after the fiasco of the previous evening. In his enthusiasm to introduce her to his colleagues, Joe had tried to influence what she wore and the impression she made. But she had stuck to her guns and worn what she wanted. She doubted he would try the same thing again. Perhaps he'd been as apprehensive about the evening as her and this had fed into his behaviour.

There was other stuff in her head too, such as her mother's advice about growing infirm alone not being fun. That was well evidenced from the other residents in her mother's complex. And, unlike many of them, an elderly Fiona would have no family to visit her. And there was what her mother had said about not allowing past failures to cloud her future. And giving people another chance and learning to trust them. Her mother had meant Rob — the one man in the whole world that Fiona could *never* again have confidence in. But maybe it was Joe she shouldn't write off too quickly? He was trying to make this work; he'd bought her jewellery, made her breakfast in bed, stayed sober so he could drive her home, been lavish with his compliments. She postponed her hasty decision about asking him to leave. She'd go for a run, clear her head and see how things panned out over the next few days.

Ferreting in the drawers for clean running gear would be too noisy, so instead she raided the laundry basket in the bathroom. The last time she'd run had been before work on the day Joe turned up, homeless. If she'd known it would be her last day of freedom she'd have run further and faster, or maybe slower so that she could enjoy every moment — a sort of 'last meal' for the condemned woman.

Fiona pulled on luminous yellow leggings and a matching stretchy top, keeping her nose averted from the lurking odour of her previous exertions. She bypassed the reflective running jacket hanging in the hall; cold air was needed this morning.

A gentle jog took her half a mile down the road where she paused, moving her feet on the spot, until the lights changed and let her cross the traffic into the wild natural park — out-door 'green' exercise made her feel better than anything done in a gym or studio. Fiona's feet knew the way. She tried to empty her mind of the constant background buzz that had plagued her since Joe, plus suitcases, had arrived. But within a few seconds her current situation catapulted back to her.

An only child, Fiona knew she had been spoiled and could be selfish. Her mother had drilled that into her. "Other children have to share," she was told every time she received sweets or presents. These 'other' children were invited to tea parties by Dorothea, "To help you learn." For five-year-old Fiona, sharing was an over-rated experience. It meant giving away what you wanted to keep for yourself. But eventually she'd learned to tolerate, and even, with the right people, enjoy sharing — as long as it wasn't everything, all the time.

Now, as she felt the satisfactory 'thud, thud' of turf beneath her trainers, she realised that she would have to share her whole life. Her every action would have to be rethought from Joe's perspective. What would he be thinking right now when he woke and found her gone? Would he enjoy some time to himself or would he think her selfish for needing these moments alone? She had no idea what he was like in an 'off' mood. If he didn't like something she did, would that be his problem or hers? She feared it might be hers. Maybe Rose had always made her life fit Joe's schedule — until she reached breaking point.

Fiona slowed from a run to a jog to a walk. She had to pass the edge of a small pond, more like a puddle in the summer but growing to a lake at this time of year, turning the footpath to mud and requiring eyes on feet to navigate it successfully. Then she opened the throttle again and picked up pace as the footpath emerged from the wooded area and re-joined the tarmac. This was the bit where she built up to a sprint, well, as much of a sprint as a sixty-year-old woman could manage. The tarmac led to the northern exit of the park, and opposite the gate was the Birnside Hotel. It was a nondescript, four-storey concrete building and part of a hotel chain that stretched across the country. It didn't promise four-poster beds or roaring fires but it had a leisure club with a postage-stamp-size swimming pool and it also had Meeko, yoga teacher extraordinaire and her best friend. He break-fasted in the hotel every day, in between his early morning and mid-morning classes — a free breakfast was his only perk of the job. Somehow, he'd persuaded the staff to turn a blind eye to Fiona joining him, and now she was such a fixture that they just waved her in too, even if she appeared alone, too early or too late for Meeko. It was over these breakfasts that she and Meeko had become close. A closeness only allowed to grow by Fiona because the existence of Meeko's live-in 'almost-fiancée', Lynn, had meant there was no danger of a romantic relationship developing between the two of them. Fiona had introduced Meeko and Joe only once, two months earlier, breaking her own compartmentalised-life rule at the insistence of Meeko. It had been a strained couple of hours followed by separate, awkward conversations with both men. Not helped by the fact that Meeko had dropped the bomb-shell at that meeting that he had broken up with Lynn. Joe had immediately offered to introduce Meeko to a couple of his female acquaintances who were recently single.

"No thanks." Meeko had raised the palm of his right hand and thrown Fiona a weird look. "I'm not open to meet-ing new women."

"Platonic friendships only work in books," Joe had said to Fiona later. "Now that he's finished with his girlfriend, he'll be after something more from you. That's why he doesn't want to meet anyone new."

"He just doesn't seem your type," Meeko had said about Joe, without expanding on what he thought Fiona's type of man was. "Be careful."

These comments had left Fiona having to justify herself to each man, and emphasised, in her mind, that life worked better when everybody was kept in separate compartments.

Now, as she walked past the hotel's leisure complex, she caught sight of Meeko waving off his first class, covering his slim, Lycra-clad figure with a baggy orange hoody and then sitting to tie his trainers. He ran his fingers through his spiky silver hair and grinned at the young woman in charge of towels and signing people in at the leisure club reception.

Usually, Fiona's heart rose at this point. Meeko's company over coffee, fruit, yoghurt, eggs and the best granary bread she'd ever tasted was a great start to the day. Meeko never stressed over anything. He was calm, laid-back and, unlike her, he didn't sweat the small stuff — or even the big stuff for that matter.

She'd first met him ten years ago when she'd joined the hotel leisure club and attended her very first yoga class. It was Meeko's first session too and they'd both lurked on their mats at the back of the studio for fear of making fools of themselves nearer the front. At the end, Fiona had decided yoga wasn't 'her thing', but Meeko, with a twinkle in his eye, had persuaded her the class needed another chance. He'd turned out to be naturally supple while Fiona's joints and muscles constantly complained. In the early weeks it was Meeko's supportive smiles and winks that maintained her attendance.

"I'm going to train to be an instructor." he'd announced after a couple of months.

He qualified, resigned from his job as a classroom assistant and stepped into the shoes of the club's existing yoga teacher, who was moving on. Fiona had attended his classes ever since.

Meeko wasn't motivated by money but was careful with what he had. While his contemporaries had gained degrees and built careers, he had done voluntary work overseas. Then he'd got paid work with a children's charity in the UK before deciding to move into schools. Over the years he'd moved through a series of bad landlords, but each time he'd just shrugged and moved on. "Where I live is one of the things that I can change in life and so I do — no point in getting uptight about it."

When he was told his mother's breast cancer was terminal, he lost his smile and his shoulders sagged but then he righted himself. "I can't change this," he said, "but it doesn't have to define my attitude to the whole of my life. It doesn't change who I am or who Mum is." His grin returned, he continued to care about his class members, he still dressed in bright colours and he always took his mum a feminine treat on his daily visit — a new lipstick, one of the tiny complimentary body lotions from the hotel, or a sample of perfume from the waitress who held cosmetic parties in her spare time. In Fiona's opinion, Meeko was a prince among men. He loved everyone. His break-up with Lynn, a former receptionist at the hotel, after eleven years, worried her because he'd been unable to explain why he'd suddenly decided the relationship had run its course; she hoped he wasn't throwing his future away over a minor disagreement that could have been easily fixed.

She'd tried to suggest that instead of removing Lynn from his life completely, they just see a little less of each other for a while. That was when she'd been more open with him about Joe and how it was the greatest arrangement ever. "It works because we only see the best of each other," she'd said. "Sometimes relationships fail when, side by side, you have to deal with all the annoying flotsam and jetsam of life. We get all of the pleasure and none of the aggro."

He'd looked disapproving. "Working together to solve things can make relationships stronger," he'd countered. "For me it's all or nothing."

After that they'd never again discussed the rights and wrongs of her relationship with Joe or his break-up with Lynn. Their respective love lives remained in closed boxes, alongside the details and tragedy of Fiona's failed marriage — some things were just too painful to reveal, no matter how close the friendship.

They arrived at the entrance to the restaurant at the same time. Meeko hugged her, kissed her on both cheeks and then grinned. "I missed you yesterday."

She hesitated, not sure how he'd react to the news of Joe moving in. "Food first and then I'll explain."

Since Fiona's last visit a couple of days earlier, the hotel restaurant had been transformed with giant gold and scarlet baubles hanging from the ceiling and ropes of shiny tinsel clinging to the walls. Advertisements for a series of December tribute band party nights stood proud in the middle of each table.

Meeko chased the last of the Greek yoghurt and blueberries from his dish. Fiona took the first spoonful of hers; she'd done the talking while Meeko ate. Now he appeared to consider her plight.

"The perfect situation is no more," he pronounced eventually.

"Yes and no." She licked the smear of yoghurt she could feel on her lips. Then she spoke quickly before he could brand her a hussy who only wanted Joe for weekly sex. "I really looked forward to our weekly dates and loved his company."

"But you enjoyed his absence as well?"

"I guess so. I didn't like the way he seemed to be showing me off last night, and having him in my space all the time, it's . . ." It would be disloyal to Joe for her to say anymore. If they did stay together, he would meet Meeko again and it would be embarrassing if Meeko knew too much.

"Claustrophobic?"

She nodded. The chef shouted and Fiona jumped up to fetch their boiled eggs. She walked slowly back with the egg cups, pausing to gather her thoughts by the coffee machine. Why was what Meeko thought of her changed relationship with Joe so important to her? The two of them could still enjoy their breakfast together and he would continue to gently adjust her hips and back to improve her downward-facing dog and plank positions in his classes.

Meeko cracked his egg with a spoon and peeled off the top of the shell. He'd already buttered his toast and chopped it into soldiers. She watched him dip and saw the satisfaction on his face when the yolk was just the right consistency. She tried to push thoughts of Joe away and concentrate on slow, mindful eating. She focused her mind on the feel of the velvet yolk on her tongue. It didn't work; her shoulders remained tense and her brain felt as though it was in chains, being dragged in a direction it didn't want to go.

"What will you do about him?" Meeko's eyes met hers as she looked up from the half-empty shell. "Don't just shrug. This is something that you can change. If you want to."

Fiona watched the light catch the green Christmas-tree-shaped studs in Meeko's ears. Her mind was clearing, as it often did in his presence. A thought was emerging that she'd never consciously been aware of before. "What Joe and I had together was good. If I ask him to leave that will be the end of us forever. And I'm not ready for that. We're just having teething problems."

There was no affirming or negative expression on the yoga instructor's face. He was totally blank. Fiona had the weird feeling that she was on a psychiatrist's couch.

"But also, it feels like I'm sitting in a trap waiting for vicious metal jaws to close around me and make me a prisoner for life."

"Does recognising those feelings help you decide what to do?" The neutrality remained. Fiona wanted him to grin or at least smile. She wanted some credit for this great insight she'd just produced. She wanted to be told whether she was right or wrong.

"I don't want to throw him out. Yet. But I do want to lay some ground rules. And maybe some timescales for how long the situation is going to last and what he might do as a permanent solution."

Now Meeko's lips did form a smile. "You had me worried for a minute, but the real Fiona-I-am-in-control-of-my-life has just re-emerged."

Fiona grinned back. The dimples that appeared around the corners of Meeko's mouth always made her smile. A braver woman than her would reach out and touch them.

Meeko looked at his watch. "I've got to love you and leave you. I want to grab the PC in the leisure club office to do some emails before my next class." They hugged again and for a few seconds Fiona luxuriated in his warm male smell, unadulterated by aftershave or scented deodorant. He gave her a squeeze that told her he'd always be there for her. Then he was striding out of the dining room.

Fiona power-walked home — running on a part-full stomach didn't aid her digestion. There was a note from Joe indicating he'd gone football training and wouldn't be back until later in the afternoon. She felt relieved.

CHAPTER 8

Fiona drafted the ground rules for their cohabitation in long-hand. She was itching to type them up with space at the bottom of the page for each of them to sign and date the agreement. But even she could see that was too formal. Perhaps she'd produce an 'official' document when she'd talked him through the draft. She stuck to the practicalities that would give this unplanned life as a couple a fighting chance. Since Rob had destroyed her trust in men, she'd created her own structure for living, which at times had been lonely, but the prospect of sharing her life again had always been too scary. It still was scary. However, stuff happens and you have to adapt or walk away. She could say goodbye to Joe or she could give their relationship a proper chance. She wasn't ready to say goodbye, so devising the ground rules felt like building essential scaffolding to keep everything in its place:

> *Separate bedrooms except for 'date nights' (this is proven to give each person a better night's sleep).*
>
> *Finances kept completely apart. NO joint accounts of any kind (probably not an issue for now but a rule for the future should this turn into a long-term living-together arrangement).*

> *Joe to pick up the extra costs of him being here, e.g. extra*
> *council tax because the single person discount will disappear,*
> *fuel and water bills (I will pay the standing charge and the*
> *broadband because they will be unchanged) and food.*

> *Housework to be shared — we need to discuss a rota.*

She put the list to one side to 'settle' and then turned her mind to Christmas and the tasks it demanded, even from a non-religious person who had little in the way of family.

* * *

Fiona was updating the Christmas card spreadsheet on her laptop when she first noticed the girl. The little digital numbers in the bottom right of her screen said it was 15.03. It was a crisp, clear afternoon — one of those days that make you prefer the clarity of winter to the heat exhaustion of midsummer. The girl didn't appear to share those feelings. It was impossible to see her facial expression — she was walking on the opposite side of the road — but the silhouette of her body sagged. Only the girl would know whether this was with tiredness or depression, or perhaps it was the effort of keeping a steady gait when loaded with a large rucksack at the back and an obviously pregnant stomach at the front. Fiona contemplated the figure for a few seconds, hoping she didn't have far to go. Then the list of cards received last year reclaimed her.

She made a little test scribble with the gold gel pen on a piece of scrap paper. Then she tried the silver and the scarlet. She smiled and remembered her favourite childhood treat — a brand-new pack of felt tip pens and a colouring book. Not one of those cheap books with absorbent paper that encouraged the ink from felt tips to bleed outside the lines or go right through to the picture on the other side of the page. When she had one of those books, Fiona had always checked both pictures to make sure she chose the best one to colour in — invariably the one with the most scope for using a range of bright colours, for example, a girl in a striped party dress would always win over a picture of a fox or a badger in woodland.

She wrote the first five cards on her list. On the left-hand side of each card she wrote a couple of personal sentences. Something that had happened in the last twelve months which would amuse that person, or asking after their family. Then she laid them open for a couple of minutes for the ink to dry.

As she reached for the envelopes, the girl walked back down the road in the opposite direction and on Fiona's side. This time, because she was nearer, the girl's face was more visible. Tiredness was reflected in her face and the way she walked. Black leggings were visible beneath the coat, along with heavy black shoes that were probably fashionable but added weight to every step. The girl glanced at each house as she passed. Her eyes lingered on Fiona's front door. The young woman was looking at the numbers. Suddenly on her guard, Fiona stared at the girl, willing her to carry on walking. She didn't want to be picked out as a burglary target. The girl looked directly at her. Fiona leaned back in her chair, trying to put herself and her laptop out of sight. The girl carried on slowly down the road, but now she was continually glancing back at Fiona's window. Fiona drew the curtains even though it wasn't quite dark.

Fifteen minutes later there were voices outside the front door and then the key in the lock. She tensed; Joe had said nothing about bringing a friend home with him. She bundled the Christmas cards back into their box and closed the laptop. The rest of the room was tidy.

"Fiona! We've got a visitor." She went into the hallway and Joe kissed her cheek. His skin felt cold from the December air. The pregnant girl had dumped her rucksack inside the front door. She was looking around and frowning.

"I'm sorry, Joe," Fiona said. "You've caught me on the hop. I don't remember . . ."

"Fiona, this is my daughter, Adele. Adele, this is . . . Fiona. I'm staying with her at the moment."

Masking her shock with a smile, Fiona offered her hand, keeping her eyes on the girl's face and not her bump. Adele shook hands briefly and then turned to her dad. "Why has Mum disappeared? And where am I supposed to go?"

Joe glanced over at Fiona and she caught his unspoken plea. He wanted her to take control. She didn't know what was going on, but order was better than chaos.

"I'll put the kettle on." It was a cliché used by generations of women to wave magic wands over the calamities brought home by their families.

"I only drink coffee," the pregnant girl declared, then she hesitated and touched her belly. "Decaffeinated."

"I can do that."

Joe ushered his daughter into the lounge, and the pair were sitting in an awkward silence when Fiona carried in three mugs. "Sorry, I've got no biscuits." She attempted an apologetic laugh but no one smiled.

Adele took a sip of coffee. "I need answers, Dad. I've been trying Mum on her mobile ever since I got on the train from uni this morning. It goes straight to voicemail. It says she won't be picking up messages for an indefinite time." She stared at her father. "Then when I get home there's someone else in the house. They said it's on Airbnb and shut the door in my face. By that time, and with this to look after—" she pointed at her stomach — "I'm having a nervous breakdown."

"Your mother shouldn't have let you find out like that." Joe pushed his glasses up his nose.

"How did you know where your dad was?" There was something going on with Rose that Joe hadn't told Fiona about. Early on in their relationship they'd decided not to spoil their evenings together with any mention of Joe's ex-wife or his children or any other domestic minutiae relating to either of them. But this sounded like something that Fiona needed to know about. Something that might have an impact on her. "And what's going on with Rose?"

"I tried to phone him, but as usual he didn't pick up."

"I was on the football pitch!"

"I went to his house and there was a skinny man with a beard just getting out of a car."

"The letting agent — he'd have been there to see the damage."

"He said you'd left this house as a forwarding address." Adele took another mouthful of coffee. "Where's Mum?"

"India."

"India!" Fiona and Adele spoke in unison.

"She sent me an email from the airport on Friday just as she was leaving. What with the flood and everything else going on, I never got chance to tell you. Either of you."

He swiped at his phone and handed it to Adele. She read aloud, "Hi Joe. In thirty minutes I will be on a plane to India for a Gap However-Long-I-Choose-To-Stay. I have informed no one else and have left it so close to departure because I don't want you, or anyone else, to persuade me not to go. After years at the beck and call of others, now it is MY time. I'm going to find the real ME. Please deal with anything that arises in my absence. The children are adults and wrapped up in their own lives — they will be OK. Adele told us ages ago she wouldn't be home for Christmas and Dan only turns up when he wants something. Don't try to contact me — we have to hand our phones in on arrival at the retreat. Digital detox and all that. Rose."

Adele handed the phone back. Her hand was shaking and her voice cracked as she spoke. "What happens to me now?"

There was an awkward silence. Joe glanced questioningly at Fiona. She kept her face blank; this was his family's mess, not hers. He looked over at his daughter. "When's it due? And what's the story?"

"January fifth," Adele mumbled, and shuffled in her seat. "You met Nicholas in the summer."

"Briefly, and only because your mother insisted we check on you when you said you were staying in Sheffield for the holiday." Fiona could see Joe mentally counting the months. "Why didn't you tell us then?"

Adele picked up the coffee mug again and kept her head facing down. "I suspected then, but I wasn't brave enough to find out definitely until it was obvious I was getting fat. Two months ago I told Nicholas and he finished with me." She pulled a tissue from her jumper sleeve and blew her nose. "Then I didn't know what to do. I did nothing until almost the end of term and then I came home." Joe took the full force of a venomous glare. "At least I thought I was coming home."

Joe stood up and paced the distance between the window and his chair. He picked up the advent calendar and offered it to his daughter. "We've jumped ahead on this. But you and er . . . my grandbaby can have the next chocolate. I'm losing track of days." He was out of his depth and casting around for anything that might make the situation better. His small gesture touched Fiona.

"Do you want to be a granddad?" Adele was looking at him hopefully. Fiona willed him to say the right words.

Adele hadn't taken the chocolate from the calendar. Joe gently opened the door numbered '3' and put the chocolate on the table in front of his daughter. "Of course I do!" The atmosphere in the room went down a notch. "And your mum will love being a grandma, I'm sure."

"Can we tell her? I want her to come home." The rest of Adele's words were lost in sobs — a tsunami of tears that appeared to have been held back for months. "I'm . . . scared . . . look after me."

Joe perched on the arm of Adele's chair and held her close. The two of them rocked in silence. Fiona was superfluous. Unwanted. She went upstairs and sat in her office. It was now fully dark outside. She pulled down the blind and switched on the desk lamp. The yellow glow and the sound of rain outside made her feel cosy and safe. Unlike how Adele must be feeling. A vulnerable pregnant woman couldn't go cap in hand to her friends and ask to sleep on their sofa. She couldn't give birth with no home for the new baby. There was no convenient stable with a hay-lined manger.

Back in the day, she and Rob had had plans for Amber's nursery. They'd taken meandering walks around Mothercare and The Early Learning Centre, each pointing out what they would buy as soon as Fiona tipped past the twelve-week danger line. None of it had come to pass — she'd been naive and oblivious to the financial catastrophe around the corner. Unaware that her husband was gambling at all, never mind chasing his losses with increasingly large bets in a vain attempt to secure his family's future.

There was no other option. She had to offer Adele a home, at least until Joe got his own place back or found somewhere else. This office-cum-spare-room was too crowded with desk and filing cabinet to fit a bed. Adele would have to take the guest room. The one that Fiona had been about to ask Joe to sleep in.

Her mixed-up feelings about her lover were ebbing and flowing as each new happening buffeted her closer to him or highlighted a less attractive personality trait. Last night she'd been sure they had no future together. Then she'd switched to thinking that, with compromise, they could make things work. Even before the burst pipe, she'd recognised he was ready for more than just their weekly dates. Once, he'd suggested a holiday together, and another time that she accompany him to a friend's birthday party. Fiona was sure he wanted something deeper and more long-term than their previous relationship, and talking to Meeko had helped her make sense of her own feelings. She wasn't ready to completely give up on what she and Joe had together, especially now she'd seen his tenderness with his daughter. Fiona did want to be part of his circle of love. If, later, she felt the metal jaws close around her, she would deal with it then. She went to make her offer.

Joe looked up from his phone when she came into the room. "I've just booked a week at the Holiday Lodge. After that I'll try and get us an Airbnb."

"No need. You can both stay here."

Joe looked shocked. "Are you sure? It was different when it was just me, but you'll be swamped with both of us, especially if the baby comes early."

Images of a newborn baby in this room blurred with emotional thoughts of what might have been with Amber. Fiona hadn't factored in the baby arriving early. She nearly retracted the offer and then realised it was impossible without explanation. "I'm sure we can make it work for the time being." She hoped she sounded positive and upbeat.

Joe flashed her a look of gratitude and Fiona tried to quash her anxiety. How difficult could it be to share her home with a pregnant young woman over the Christmas period? The painful memories of losing Amber would never go away but that was no excuse to turn away a desperate young mum-to-be. Despite the nerves, she had a feeling of easing open a long-closed compartment and letting light in. It was a new but not unpleasant feeling.

Besides, first babies were always late; there would be time for Joe to sort out alternative accommodation before the birth.

CHAPTER 9

Meeko waited for his knock on the leisure club manager's door to be answered. There were two ways this meeting could go: more classes or fewer classes. Given the cut in the opening hours of the hotel's pool, it was probably fewer. Meeko couldn't afford that. His monthly budget was already stretched since Lynn had moved out, leaving him to juggle all the expenses alone. He hadn't told Fiona that his finances were a balancing act because she'd insist on helping him out and he didn't want to be beholden to anyone, least of all his closest friend.

To Meeko, Fiona was a pauper too, but in a different way. She didn't lack material comforts but she was so closed in, and focused on remaining so, that she missed the riches life had to offer. Fiona couldn't go with the flow. Everything had to be choreographed to the nth degree and also have a Plan B. When he'd challenged her, she'd put it down to her career in IT project management, where attention to detail and timing was essential. Meeko thought it more likely to be due to something in her past. A catastrophe that had gone beyond the bounds of a normal calamity and wrecked any trust she might have had in fate or other people. He knew there'd been a divorce, but the way she lived her life was out of proportion to that. Some bond of trust had been so deeply severed that, from that point on, the only person she trusted was herself. And that was sad. Several times he'd tried to ask about her past, but she always looked as though she was about to cry and then clammed up. He was sure that, one day, when she was ready, she would tell him.

There was a muffled "Come in" from behind the door. Meeko crossed his fingers and entered. Frank pushed his laptop to one side, stood up briefly and then gestured at the guest chair in front of the desk. The manager couldn't be more than forty. He was dressed in a hotel polo shirt and close-fitting jeans and had the sort of physique that Meeko, on the cusp of his seventh decade, was having to work harder and harder to maintain. Broad-shouldered but slim and muscular everywhere else. Meeko's mind flitted to Joe. He'd been wearing chinos and a long-sleeved shirt when they'd met, but as a physio, Meeko guessed he'd be no slouch in the gym either. 'Joe the toad' was how Meeko preferred to think of him.

Frank and Joe even had better, more solid names than Meeko. Meeko's real name was Michael but in junior school his friends had labelled him 'Mickey'. His mother had thought that was common and that her son deserved a better class of nickname. She came up with Meeko, after a friend went on a package holiday to Italy, when such excursions were rare, and came back with photos of a handsome waiter. The nickname had caught on with his friends and he'd been stuck with the label ever since. If he had the guts he'd revert back to 'Michael' or the more macho 'Mick'.

"The feedback from your yoga classes is consistently excellent and they're always fully booked. Your regulars turn up four or five times a week and get great value for money from their monthly fee." Frank leaned forward and smiled, despite his voice indicating there was a 'but' on the way. "But we need to diversify our timetable to attract new members to the leisure club as a whole. We need more people to set up that monthly direct debit, and the best way is to cash in on the January dieters with a slogan like 'Burn fat the Birnside Way'. That means reducing the number of holistic classes and increasing those that burn calories."

Meeko felt a rug starting to be eased from under him. "You can't penalise me for being successful!" There was an awkward silence. It seemed that Frank could indeed punish success. Meeko hadn't seen this coming. He had to invent something quickly to maintain his claim on the gym time-table. He couldn't be a one-trick pony. "What about a Legs, Bums and Tums class, including some brisk moving about the room to raise the heart rate?"

"Still sounds like a session for the ladies-that-lunch. Those are the people *already* attending your classes. We need something hardcore. Something to attract *new* people to the club. Something that really raises a sweat for our members. I've already hired a new instructor." There was another awkward silence before Frank found his flow again. "We want to appeal to the younger gym user."

Frank hadn't said it in so many words but it was obvious that he felt Meeko, due to his age, was no longer an asset to the club. This wasn't just a kick in the teeth, it was a full-on, knock-out blow and Meeko felt physically winded. His classes weren't the right type and he was too old. There was nothing he could do about his age and Frank didn't want to give him a chance on trying a different class.

"Of course, you've still got your loyal followers." Frank smiled. "And we don't want to alienate them. So, to start with, I'm only dropping your early Saturday and Sunday classes — those are peak times for younger people who are working during the week."

"My regulars are going to be disappointed. There'll be angry people at your door." A lot of Meeko's attendees relied on his classes to keep their joints mobile, improve their balance and guard against falls. Others, like Fiona, came along to maintain flexibility and strength, and to keep all the muscles toned and strong. In Meeko's classes everyone worked at their own level of ability. "You're going to lose members."

Frank shrugged and stood up to indicate the meeting was at an end.

"I've grown the holistic offering at the club massively and there is still a demand for it," Meeko tried.

Frank shrugged again.

Someone with a quicker brain would have thought up a clever response to that shrug. Instead, Meeko walked out of Frank's office and joined that scrap heap dedicated to those aged sixty-plus. He cursed the day he'd decided to be self-employed rather than a hotel employee when he was first offered the role. He'd thought keeping his independence would allow him to teach elsewhere as well, but in reality he'd done very little of that because his Leisure Club classes had easily filled all his time. And now Frank could wave goodbye to him at the drop of a hat. No mention had been made of the glowing emails that his class attendees occasionally sent to Frank, praising Meeko's classes and the time he took afterwards to answer questions. No mention had been made of Meeko's innovative monthly 'Relax and Restore' afternoons, which were slowly growing in popularity, or the way that Meeko had responded to demand and taken an additional, self-funded, course in order to offer a Yin yoga class. Frank's mind had been made up, possibly by head office, before he even spoke to Meeko.

The breakfast waitresses were clearing away as the last of the late-risers strolled from the dining room.

"Meeko!" one of the waitresses called him over. "You look like death. Sit in that corner, out of sight, and I'll get you coffee and one of the left-over Danish pastries."

"Make that two," he said, "and a couple of serviettes." He'd had his free breakfast hours earlier, but this additional dip in his finances, on top of Lynn moving out, meant he needed to make preparations for a free lunch too whenever he could. A diet of pastries wasn't great, especially for a yoga teacher, but needs must.

He ran his fingers through the silver spikes of his hair and added sugar to the coffee. He felt shaky as Frank's words hit home. The loss of the two classes meant fifteen percent of his income had disappeared overnight. And it wasn't just money that was getting him down. At breakfast with Fiona the previous day, he'd felt he was finally breaking through that carefully controlled electric fence she'd constructed around herself. But then she'd told him about the toad moving in. In Meeko's head Joe hadn't properly got over his divorce and still carried a candle for his ex-wife. Now the toad would have a claim on the time that Fiona had previously spent with Meeko.

Couple that with learning he was too old and not attracting the right sort of people to his classes and Meeko's confidence was at rock bottom. He'd been pushed off a cliff. At the end of November, he'd decided on his new year resolution. After the success of his Yin yoga class and the 'Relax and Restore' afternoons, he was going to investigate the possibility of teaching barre yoga — but the instructor course had a cost attached and Frank would have had to be talked into supplying the additional equipment. That was now going to be a non-starter. Meeko was left with the prospect of a bleak Christmas and an even bleaker new year.

CHAPTER 10

"Fiona! Where've you been? I was worried. You didn't leave a note and I wasn't sure how you really felt about Adele turning up out of the blue like that." Joe looked genuinely concerned and wrapped his arms around her as soon as she stepped into the kitchen after her morning run the next day. She'd resentfully given breakfast with Meeko a miss because of the chaos at home. Joe smelled of soapy artificial lemons and spicy aftershave; there was no smell of man there at all. Fiona thought wistfully of Meeko and his plain maleness. Then she pulled herself together; he was her platonic best friend, who was taking a break from romantic entanglements.

Adele was at the kitchen table with an overflowing bowl of Shredded Wheat and milk. An open bag of sugar was in front of her and she'd obviously been making liberal use of it due to the lack of frosted cereals in Fiona's cupboards. Eating for two. Fiona's pregnancy had never got far enough for that. *Don't dwell on Amber. Joe, Adele and retirement are offering you a fresh start — grab it now before it's too late.*

Escaped white grains had created a pathway between sugar packet and cereal dish. Fiona folded down the top of the bag, secured it with an elastic band and put it away. She'd decant some into the sugar caddy later.

The atmosphere was strained, as though she'd walked in on a quarrel between father and daughter.

"How about a supermarket trip for you girls?" Joe wore a mask of false jollity. "I'll pay. We're not going to be a financial burden to you, Fiona."

"I—" He silenced her with a look before she could explain it was easier and quicker to go on her own. Fiona wasn't into girly shopping trips. Perhaps she would have been if Amber . . .

Adele kept her head down over the Shredded Wheat. The tender relationship between father and daughter from last night had dissipated.

Joe stumbled on with his one-sided conversation. "Two women sharing a kitchen can be difficult. So, I was thinking, spending some time together and deciding on what food we need . . . it might break the ice, help you understand one another . . ."

"It would be easier for me to do the food shopping on my own." Fiona finished the sentence Joe had tried to silence.

Adele was swiping at her phone with her left hand, the right one still being in charge of a spoon that was tipping slightly and in danger of dumping its soggy load on the table top.

"Adele!" Joe spoke sharply. "Watch what you're doing."

His daughter threw him a look of annoyance. Fiona wasn't the only one struggling in this mismatched household. Adele was used to the autonomy of her life at uni. Joe had regressed to being 'Dad' and dictating her behaviour, which, in turn, was making Adele regress to being an awkward teenager again. Fiona felt for this girl, caught somewhere between the child and adult world and on the cusp of becoming a mother herself. And without her own mum to help smooth things along. The food shopping would be better done on her own, but maybe it would help the bigger picture if she was more flexible on this point — albeit in a controlled way.

She backpedalled just a little bit. "We need to compromise and become a team in order to make this situation work." Treat it like an IT project and everything will be OK. "The supermarket's a good idea. I don't know what food you like, Adele. But when I was—" She closed her mouth quickly, discovered an old tissue in the tiny key pocket of her leggings and blew her nose. She kept the crumpled scrap over her face for longer than necessary while she recomposed herself after almost revealing the secret of Amber. "There's no rush. Take your time. Have a shower and then we'll go for a mooch. There's no harm in finding out if we've got the same taste in food."

Adele frowned at the Shredded Wheat. Then she stared Fiona in the face. "I can tell when someone's offering charity and trying to be a false friend. You're not my mother and you're not going to be my best mate either. Both of those positions are already taken." Adele pushed the bowl of cereal away. "You're simply my dad's girlfriend."

Fiona's proffered dish of kindness had been upended. "I'm trying to make the best of the situation."

Adele stalked upstairs.

"Apologise immediately," Joe shouted after her. "Stop behaving like a stroppy teenager. Act like the adult you are, the adult you'll need to be if you're going to be a good mother." He turned towards Fiona. "I'm sorry. Hormones?"

Fiona shrugged. She could understand Adele's reaction. "How else can she behave? She's still hurting from your marriage breakdown, and I'm the obvious target."

"But you had nothing to do with that!"

"That's not how she chooses to see it. And now, when the going has got tough, her mother has disappeared and she has to share her father with another woman. If I was her, I'd hate me too."

"It's impossible to hate you. You've offered her a home. I don't understand. Last night she seemed accepting of the situation." Joe pulled her close into the warmth of his body. Fiona pushed away a fleeting image of Meeko and relaxed into Joe. "I love you so much, Fiona Ormeroyd," he said, "you are so big-hearted. Being cramped like this is only temporary. As soon as Rose reappears, Adele will be off to her like a shot. Next year the house will be sold, I'll get my share of the capital and we can buy a place together."

No! She pulled away from him. After Rob, she couldn't combine her finances and home with someone else. Joe was suffocating her by jumping too quickly into what *he* wanted from their joint future. She needed baby steps, but he was used to being the leader of a couple, the leader of a whole family. For Fiona, a couple was a partnership of equals, and she needed to experience that equality with Joe before committing to anything. Fiona's freedom had been too hard won. The pain of trying to extricate herself from Rob's debts would never leave her. Except, hadn't she, over the last few days, already relinquished part of that freedom?

Then she realised that Joe had just declared his undying love for her, despite her being sweaty from her run, with no make-up and drizzle-dampened hair sticking out at odd angles. In their previous one-day-a-week existence he'd only ever seen her looking perfect. Confused, she grabbed herself a bowl and filled it with breakfast berries and walnuts.

An hour later Adele stood in the hallway, trying and failing to make the edges of her jacket meet across her bump. Her lower half was clad in stretchy blue denim and the bottom of a baggy sweatshirt hung just below the hem of the jacket. "Are we going or what?"

In the supermarket Fiona took charge of the trolley. Neither of them made a move for any of the aisles and Fiona realised she'd made a faux pas. Never had she arrived at the supermarket without previously creating a meal plan for the week and an associated shopping list, with the items ordered according to their place in the store. She never deviated from that list. Now she had to make the best of a bad job by planning in real time while trying to build an adult relationship with Joe's resentful and abandoned daughter.

"Any preferences for where we start or what we buy?" She tried to sound as though she were willing to be totally flexible, like a blade of grass in the wind.

"Biscuits. Chocolate. Crisps." Adele's words were like bullets.

Don't lecture about what the baby needs. Don't mention the unhealthy calories. "OK. The confectionery aisle is our starting point."

Fiona expressed no opinion as Adele loaded the trolley. She merely hoped that it was at least a month's supply and not for the single coming week. "And what about breakfast and main meals?"

"Frosties, honey-nut cornflakes, pizza, sausages, baked beans."

"Cereal aisle." She let Adele have free rein here too, but added a box of her own favourite porridge oats with added seeds.

"I thought we could eat together in the evenings when your dad gets home from work. We could share the cooking." Fiona paused, waiting for Adele to offer an opinion, but the girl merely picked up another cereal box and started reading the special offer on the back. "I don't mind starting us off with a few of my own dinner ideas but feel free to butt in if there's a meal you'd like to cook for the three of us." She'd nearly inserted the word 'proper' in front of 'meal' and then thought better of it. "Chicken casserole and jacket potatoes, lentil curry, fish pie and chilli. Are you OK with all of those?" Adele merely shrugged and followed Fiona up and down the aisles as she collected the ingredients.

Then Adele spoke as if she'd been building up to this request. "Could we get pizza for today? I feel like I really need it."

Pepperoni pizza went into the trolley and Fiona balanced it out with a couple of bags of salad leaves and a pack of vine tomatoes.

"I think we're done," she said, and mentally patted herself on the back for accomplishing the trip with compromise and without argument. Joe would be glad to get a positive report. "Anything else you can think of while we're here?"

"The baby section." Adele's words were barely more than a whisper. "I'm going to need stuff. And if Dad's paying . . ."

"OK."

The baby aisle was quieter than the rest and its basic contents hadn't changed in the thirty years since Fiona had daydreamed her way through it, a perfect vision of motherhood in her mind. She tailed Adele past the tiny jars of weaning food, tins of formula milk and bulky packs of nappies. The girl was headed for the little outfits on miniature hangers. She picked them up, caressed them and put them down again. Fiona's heart ached for her own younger self who had done exactly the same thing and had planned to run riot in the department as soon as January came and the world knew that Amber was on her way.

"Do you know the sex?"

"Girl." Adele's eyes were suddenly alive. "And I'm going to dress her in pink."

Pink for a girl. Fiona hadn't expected that from a young woman in today's swing away from gender stereotyping. She wished Adele's baby was a boy; it would be less painful. The mum-to-be also selected toys in all the colours of the rainbow, a small teddy and cot bedding. Fiona blinked her eyes and swallowed. This was the fun that had been torn from her by Rob. Watching someone else enjoy what she'd missed was more than she could bear.

"Adele, I'm feeling bushed. Take your time. I'm going to grab a coffee in the café." She managed to keep her voice and face composed until she'd turned round and was heading away from that maternal fairytale land.

She added a sachet of brown sugar to her latte — sometimes you just needed that comfort. The power of the emotion she'd felt in the baby aisle had shocked her. How could she, the master of self-control, let her feelings overwhelm her like that? The sweetness of the liquid and the warmth of the cup in her hand were comforting and brought her back from the brink of becoming a quivering wreck in public.

You are over-reacting, Fiona. Lots of people lose babies but they don't go around being jealous of anyone with a baby bump or blubbing in baby departments. Especially not thirty years after the event. Why wasn't she coping? She was an independent, financially secure, mature woman. But those other women who'd lost children hadn't also lost their trust in men on the same day. They hadn't been betrayed by the one person they thought had their best interests at heart. If Rob hadn't been the man he was, maybe she wouldn't have been destined to remain childless and single. Perhaps she would have married again and had a whole brood of youngsters. Perhaps she would have had grandchildren by now.

Why couldn't Adele have done the typical young person thing and ordered everything online so that Fiona didn't have to have the plaster ripped off her wounds yet again?

"Fiona!" Adele was waving to her from the café entrance. The trolley looked significantly fuller than when Fiona had left her. She swallowed, blew her nose and walked over slowly.

"I've got a few things. Can we go through the checkout now?"

The girl's mood had soared as Fiona's had crashed. Fiona had to look away as the cashier scanned the little pink items. And this wouldn't be the only baby shopping trip. Adele had only chosen the fripperies; lots of practical things were going to have to be purchased as well: cot, steriliser, nappies, et cetera.

The cashier was smiling and congratulating Adele. Then she looked at Fiona. "Is it a first grandchild?"

Fiona tried to smile, waiting for Adele to butt in and explain venomously that Fiona was not her mother. But for once the girl stayed silent.

CHAPTER 11

The atmosphere over the pizza and salad wasn't good, even though the meal was Adele's choice and Fiona forced herself to remain quiet about the pizza's unhealthy stuffed crust and feign enjoyment. The green salad, grated carrot and dish of vine tomatoes were ignored by Adele as she went for a second helping of pizza. Fiona longed to advocate for the baby's wellbeing and vitamin needs. Instead, she had more salad herself and mentioned how increasing her plant intake had done wonders for her energy levels. Adele speared a piece of pizza crust with her fork and chased a lump of melted cheese around her plate.

"Can't beat a pepperoni stuffed crust," Joe said.

Fiona wanted to talk about processed meat and the link to bowel cancer. She tried to catch his eye. As a physio he should know better than to encourage the consumption of junk food. He looked her way and she deepened her frown.

"But all things in moderation," he said quickly, and dropped a tomato onto his daughter's plate.

The possibility of a scene like this had never entered Fiona's head when she'd first clicked on Joe's profile just over a year ago. His picture had shown him to be attractive. In fact, she had wondered whether he'd used an old photo because he looked younger than his date of birth indicated. But then she'd enlarged the picture and noted there were laughter lines, silver hairs and the ruggedness that indicated a life well lived. He was muscular, broad-shouldered and five feet ten inches tall, which would make him a few comfortable inches taller than her. In the photo he was wearing a polo shirt branded with the logo of the clinic where he worked as a physio, and tracksuit bottoms. This had enabled her to double-check that he was who he said he was.

She'd narrowed down his profile because they shared an interest in fitness, books and music and, unlike many of the profiles she'd skipped over, he hadn't ticked the box to indicate he was looking for a life partner. His 'About' information stated that he was newly divorced and dating for the first time in decades. He described himself as 'dipping a toe in the water'. All of this was true for Fiona as well. Except that it had taken her nearly thirty years from her divorce to actively dip a toe in the water. She certainly wasn't looking for or expecting a great romance, but with retirement on the horizon, it would be pleasant to have someone to share activities with. Especially if that person wasn't expecting to muscle in on all areas of her life.

When they met for a drink for the first time, she immediately confirmed there was no ring on his left hand — just a faint white line to show there'd been one sometime in the past. His face was weathered in a good way, indicating that he actually was, as mentioned in his profile, a fan of the outdoor life. She liked that he didn't have the vanity to cover the initial grey in his hair with stuff from a bottle.

He'd asked her why she'd left it so long before dating again. Without details, she'd explained that it had been a case of once bitten, twice shy. That she'd had a demanding career and simply hadn't felt the need to add complications to her life. Which was all true. She didn't tell him that, for years, when her path had accidentally crossed with a handsome unattached man, she used to think of Rob, the rat she'd married. She remembered the way he'd covertly robbed her of the savings she'd brought to their marriage, the way he'd faked her signature, and his superb ability at cloak-and-dagger subterfuge. At that point she could almost feel the cramping in her stomach and the wetness between her legs as the bleeding started. Having mentally relived the worst time in her life, there was no danger that her body would betray her and accidentally give out any 'I fancy you like hell' signals. Time had dulled this reaction to the point where there was now pleasure from having a man in her life — as long as that person understood the strict boundaries she placed on their relationship. It had been no surprise to Fiona that this stipulation alienated most men. Online dating was attractive because she could easily make any possible dates aware of the situation from the outset. But this narrowed down the type of men who made contact to either married men looking for a weekly dalliance or those who would not be immediately attractive to women, for reasons including body odour, an obvious mismatch to their profile picture, and conversational technique based solely around football, their ex-wife or their career 'success'.

When she first spoke to Joe he immediately understood. "That suits me, too. It's not long since I got divorced so I'm still feeling my way about how I want my life to be."

And, until the day of the flood, he had never tried to break through her safety barriers.

But now the basis of their relationship had changed. She was on a bullet train to an unknown destination, her hand hovering over the communication cord.

"Blueberries and extra thick Greek yoghurt for pudding," she pulled herself back to the present. "Are we all up for it?"

"Not for me." Adele took the last piece of pizza from the serving plate and left the room before Fiona had chance to mention that blueberries were supposed to be a 'superfood', or to suggest the use of a plate to avoid greasy, cheesy crumbs being trodden into the stair carpet.

Joe shrugged his shoulders and his expression said, *What can you do?*

When Fiona came back into the room with their desserts the fourth advent calendar chocolate was sitting in the bowl of her spoon.

"My way of apologising for her," Joe said.

Fiona bit the chocolate in half and shared it. Joe rewarded her with a grin that reminded her of the pleasure of their weekly date nights. Maybe there was a reason to stay on that bullet train. Adele wouldn't be here forever.

CHAPTER 12

Tuesday morning brought a welcome stillness to the house. Joe had gone to work after taking Monday off in lieu of his monthly working Saturday. Adele had gone to the GP's surgery to register and, hopefully, access some antenatal care. Fiona surveyed her home. The place felt and looked as though it had been invaded by aliens. The bed in the guest room was a dishevelled mess. Adele's rucksack spewed crumpled clothes on the floor, and the open wardrobe showed a half-hearted attempt at unpacking — presumably symbolic of the fact that Adele didn't want to be there. A feeling of compassion for this disorientated young woman, heavy with child and hormones, made Fiona start tidying. If her own daughter had lived and found herself in this situation, Fiona would want some other woman to show her understanding and make her welcome. She fully emptied the rucksack, filling the bedside drawers and the wardrobe. Then she remembered the scented drawer liners, an unwanted raffle prize from the summer fayre at her mother's retirement complex. She emptied the drawers again and carefully cut the violet-scented paper sheets to size. The smell wasn't the most attractive in the universe but it was a touch of luxury that she hoped the girl would appreciate. She wanted Adele to get the message that Fiona was doing her best.

Afterwards she cleaned the bathroom, which was suffering under triple the usage it normally saw, and then her own bedroom. That was the room that felt most violated. Until a few days ago it had been her private sanctuary, with Fiona able to control who went in and how frequently — i.e. Joe, but only at pre-arranged and rationed times. Now it almost felt as though it was open to the public.

She boiled the kettle and dwelt again on the previous day's supermarket trip and her inability to cope with the baby department. She was counting on Adele having left before the baby came in a month's time. Or six weeks if it was late. The thought of having to handle a newborn, to see its detritus everywhere, or at the very least hear it cry and possibly feel a ghostly tingle in her nipples, made her hands shake as she poured a mug of tea. She couldn't do it. She could pay for Adele to decamp to a hotel. A newspaper headline appeared in her mind: 'Selfish girlfriend evicts lover's pregnant daughter at Christmas time'. Not good.

The tea calmed her temporarily. She had to do it. She had to cope with a baby in her home or explain why not. And she couldn't explain because of the pity tsunami. Pity would open the chute back into that big black hole and remind her that the only person you can properly trust in this world is yourself. Telling her story to Joe, Adele, or even Meeko, would cause them to hover and fuss and treat her like someone who didn't know her own mind. Just like thirty years ago when Rob had insisted that she needed her mother's care and had phoned Dorothea without his wife's permission. Regardless of the pleas from her mother, father, husband, GP and relationship counsellor to let the hormones and grief settle and give Rob a second chance, she'd ploughed on with the divorce. She'd wanted to show them that she *did* know her own mind, and that meant shedding her skin like a snake and starting afresh, in a new job and free from old relationships. Her friendship circle had eventually got the message and drifted away. Her parents were the only ones she'd felt obliged to provide with her new address and phone number when the marital home was sold and she was forced to rent until she could afford the deposit on a house solely in her name. Consequently, her mother was the only person still in her life today who knew everything that had happened back then.

Without pausing to think, she pulled on a jacket and drove to her mum's flat. She didn't want to talk to the old lady about the past or its impact on her current situation — she just wanted to be with someone who knew her completely. Even if the two of them rarely agreed on anything.

"Fiona! I was hoping you'd pop by but I didn't like to ring because I know what you're like for sticking to a schedule."

Despite Fiona's protestations that she'd only just had a cup of tea, the kettle went on, two homemade scones were warmed and a lacy cloth went over the teak coffee table.

"It's not your usual day — is something wrong?"

"No." She didn't need her mother offering solutions to a problem the old lady couldn't fully understand.

"So why have you come today?"

That rigid visit schedule was backfiring on her. At the beginning of the year Fiona had annotated her mother's calendar with all the dates that she could expect to see her only child. This was as much to set expectations on her mother's side as to give Fiona a sense of order and control in her own life. Dorothea was struggling with loneliness and Fiona wanted her to be heartened by the sight of regular bright orange circles on the calendar, in the same way that yellow circles of sunshine on the weather forecast can make you feel the warmth of the sun on your back. She didn't want her mum sitting in the flat wondering when or if Fiona might come. This meant she now had to provide a reason for turning up, or run the risk that her mother would expect multiple ad hoc visits in the future — and then suffer disappointment on top of her loneliness.

"The sale of your house." The letter had arrived on Saturday and ideally Fiona had wanted more time to put plans in place before presenting a fully formed timetable to her mother, but it was the best reason for her visit that she could come up with.

"Am I going to be rich soon?"

"Not exactly. The buyer's survey has shown some damp in the cellar and a fault with the electrics. They're asking for a ten-thousand reduction in the price."

"You do know that your dad and I paid under three thousand for it when we got married in 1960? Let's not look a gift horse in the mouth."

Fiona had long ago stopped trying to explain that the price her mother had had to pay for the retirement flat, the bridging loan plus the ongoing, sky-high service charge, meant there was no profit from the house sale and her mother's savings had taken a hit.

"I wouldn't call it a gift horse but we'll take the offer because you need that cash now — we can't wait for another buyer to come along." It grieved her but it was a financial necessity.

"Have a scone." Her mother had spread butter and jam thickly on them both. "It's so nice to have company to eat them. I miss having someone to bake for."

"I'm not hungry, Mum."

"I told you before, my freezer's full of baking and no one to eat it."

"Could you ask the complex manager to organise a coffee morning and you'll supply the eats?"

"I don't know about that. They all keep themselves to themselves around here. Probably no one would come. Go on — have one now. You've not an ounce of fat on you."

And I want to keep it that way. "Can I wrap a couple up and take them home for Joe?"

The old lady beamed. "Take four — men always have a good appetite."

There were definite benefits to Joe's presence. Fiona wrapped the scones and dropped them into a plastic carrier bag that Dorothea produced from a kitchen drawer. Then she felt the need to continue justifying her presence at her mother's flat on an unscheduled day. It was difficult because she didn't understand herself why she'd suddenly had to come. "I'm clearing out the last few bits in the house," she said. "There are boxes and boxes full of letters and cards."

The older lady sat back in her armchair and pressed a button. Silently the foot rest rose and Fiona's mother's eyes closed. "Keep the ones that mean something to me. Bin the rest. Most people don't mean those flowery words, exaggerated kisses and scrawls of 'with love'. Don't trust anything that people write in cards."

True. Fiona thought about her unwritten Christmas cards. But sometimes you had to toe the line of societal norms — in the same way that you couldn't make a pregnant woman homeless. *Write Christmas cards* was still sitting on Fiona's 'To-Do' list, the task rudely interrupted by the arrival of Adele. If Fiona's world hadn't imploded this weekend, those cards would now be in envelopes, expensively stamped in the top right corner with the over-colourful wings of an angel. "How do I know which mean something to you? Shall I bring them over so you can sort through them?"

"Dear God, no! That would take longer than I've got left on this earth. You go through them and pick what I should keep. You've got a better analytical eye than me."

Rare praise! Or emotional blackmail to get a job done. "It won't be soon, Mum. I've got a lot on my plate at the moment . . ."

"I thought you'd retired and had all the time in the world?" Dorothea suddenly sat upright, pressing the button to retract the foot rest. She leaned eagerly towards Fiona. "I've just remembered what I was going to ask you last time you came. Christmas! Last year we went to that lovely restaurant. Have you remembered to book it again? I know it's a bit pricey but I'll pay my share. It would be different if there were going to be babies and children and family around." A fleeting look of disappointment crossed her mother's face and then she looked eager again. "But we need to make the best of a . . ."

Bad job. Fiona mentally finished the sentence which her mother had left hanging in the air. The restaurant was booked. She'd done that weeks ago because it was so popular, plus she wanted to avoid the two of them feeling like Billy No-Mates at her dining table with only a game of Scrabble to look forward to. That was before the arrival of Joe and Adele. The expectations of seasonal jollity and inclusion meant that she couldn't leave them home alone, but in order to do anything else she would have to tell her mother about Adele and the imminent baby. And she had to do it now in order to give her time to get used to the idea so she didn't go wading into the conversation with size ten boots on.

"I'm glad you brought that up, Mum." How to phrase what came next in the best possible light?

"Don't tell me that my ultra-efficient daughter forgot to get our lives organised six months in advance?"

"I hadn't forgotten. It is booked. But things have changed." She took a breath. "There will be four of us on Christmas Day." *Technically four and a half.*

A smile played around her mother's lips. "Go on. I'm guessing I'm finally going to meet jolly Joe. You've kept him so well hidden, I was beginning to think there must be something wrong with him."

Fiona sighed. Even though her mum knew all about Rob and the baby, Dorothea still wouldn't grasp that it was safer for Fiona to keep everyone in their little box and to only have relationships that could never, ever send everything out of control again. "We just don't live in each other's pockets, that's all."

This time Dorothea sighed, and then suddenly realised exactly what Fiona had said. "What do you mean by *four* of us?"

"Joe's daughter, Adele, she's staying with us as well. And she's eight months pregnant." Done. That was all she needed to say. The bare facts were out there and her mother could make of them what she wanted. She didn't need to explain that there was no baby's father on the scene. Her mother would make her own skewed judgements on that. "She'll be with us on Christmas Day."

There was a moment's silence while Dorothea computed the facts. Then the old lady's face shone with sudden delight. "A new baby on the way! Can I call myself a granny-by-proxy? That would be one in the eye for my neighbours — they pity me for not having a phone full of grandchildren photos. It'd better be beautiful, bouncy and hit all its development milestones before any other baby that's ever lived."

This wasn't the reaction Fiona had expected and suddenly she felt sad. Over all these years she'd been consumed by her own grief, her own inability to trust again and therefore to create a family. She'd never thought how this might have affected her mother. By allowing Adele to stay, she was finally doing something right in her mother's eyes. She smiled. "I think it makes you a *great*-granny-by-proxy."

Dorothea looked content. "I think we should eat at your house, not the restaurant. Adele might appreciate being able to have a lie-down — you know how tiring it is being pregnant."

Fiona put her hand on the yellow stone hanging from the chain around her neck. She only knew the emotions of early pregnancy, not how tiring being heavily pregnant might be.

"Does he know?" Her mother had intuited what she was thinking about Amber.

Fiona shook her head, the lump in her throat blocking her voice.

"If you're going to be a couple, he needs to know."

Fiona shrugged again and reached for her coat. Thoughts of Amber had brought her here, but now the subject was out in the open, she couldn't stay. And she couldn't countenance telling Joe about her lost daughter.

"I'll bring the cards and stuff when I've been through them all."

Her mother touched Fiona's arm. "I've got my misgivings but I do hope it works out with Joe. The baby might help banish your demons for good."

A sudden thought halted Fiona at the door. "You mentioned Rob's return last time I was here. You and his mum won't encourage anything, will you? I can't . . ."

"Thank goodness you reminded me. There's a card for you on the mantlepiece from him. I think it's got a letter inside."

Fiona's heart dropped like a stone. She stuffed the envelope into her handbag.

"Aren't you going to open it?"

"Later." *Or I might just bin it. I have to look to the future, not the past.*

"Just one more thing — with all this excitement at home, you won't abandon me, will you?"

Fiona gave her mum a quick hug. "Of course I won't. All those bright orange days are still on the calendar."

"Hmmmm." Her mother didn't look convinced, and then her face suddenly came to life. "Take four more scones. That girl . . . Adele, was it? She'll be eating for two now."

CHAPTER 13

The next morning, a voice called to Fiona from the office just to the right of the hotel's reception desk as she was on her way to catch Meeko at breakfast at the end of her run. She looked round. The receptionist grinned and inclined her head towards the door, which was ajar. The familiar voice called again in a loud whisper, but the voice didn't match the face which was cautiously peering out. Was her mind too wrapped up in its own mire of problems to process what was in front of her eyes? Or was this a hallucination from a continued lack of sleep in a shared bed?

"Ho ho ho," the voice repeated, and the grin on the attached face grew broader as each syllable was enunciated. It had become less artificially deep and now included some barely suppressed laughter.

Fiona moved over to the door and was hastily pulled inside. "Hey!" she protested. She touched the figure's red jacket and then ran her fingers over the white beard, which descended like a foaming waterfall from his chin to his mid-chest. "Meeko?"

"No. Ho ho ho. Santa Claus."

"What's going on?"

"Ho ho ho. Isn't that explanation enough?"

"I get who you're trying to be, but why?"

Meeko pulled the beard to one side before taking a breath of air. "You wouldn't believe how hot it is having this on your face for more than a couple of minutes. God knows how I'm going to survive it all day."

"But why?" She glanced down at the rest of his body. Gone was his usual slim figure, which was made for skinny jeans or yoga leggings. Instead, his stomach had expanded into an unhealthy paunch, soft and cushion-like when she gave it a gentle punch. It was encased in velvety scarlet fabric. A wide black belt marked the spot where his waist should be.

"Hey! Stop prodding," he objected. "You'd be the first to complain on the grounds of an invasion of personal space and fat shaming. I'm expecting it from the kids but not the grown-ups, who should know better."

She was about to remove her hand from his fake belly when he gently took it in his. For a second before he let it go, a shiver ran through her, followed swiftly by a current of disappointment. Then she pulled herself together and motioned with a finger that he should give her a twirl.

"Not bad. But your bum is no longer in proportion to your belly. Father Christmas doesn't have a bottom like yours." It took physical effort to stop herself touching the piece of Meeko's anatomy that she found particularly attractive. "You need padding in there too if you're aiming for authenticity."

"That's why I'm glad you're here. I want to be the most believable Father Christmas there's ever been."

"Why? This isn't going to improve your teaching of yoga, unless you're going to get the class into a deer pose and then choose the best six, or is it eight, to pull your sleigh. Don't forget to reward the best one with a red nose."

"Ha bloody ha."

"So, explain to me, Saint Nicholas, what is going on?"

Her friend took a breath and paused before speaking, as though he was about to admit something that pride meant he would rather keep to himself. "I've got a temporary job at the garden centre — as the rotund gentleman himself." Meeko took a step, flung his arms out wide and pushed his chest and stomach forward. "Ho ho ho!"

"Be serious!" Something wasn't adding up. "Is this new career supposed to enhance your standing as the best yoga and meditation instructor in town?"

"No." He sat down heavily on one of the wheeled office chairs. "Call it a safety net in case of a fall from the high trapeze — which is absolutely, bloody certainly on the cards now."

Fiona pushed away the mess of her own problems. "I thought you had a faithful following and classes that are fully booked?"

"Unfortunately, business isn't just about satisfied customers. There are bigger factors at play. Things I can't control."

"Such as?" Fiona took the chair next to him.

"Management. They want to attract a younger clientele and, apparently, youngsters want to leap about, damaging their joints and building up a sweat. Some of my classes are being cut to make room." Meeko stood up, puffed his cheeks out, repositioned his beard and gave a huge fake grin. "This is an interim solution — earn money elsewhere. The situation is what it is. Worse things happen at sea and all that. Ho ho ho! Will I pass muster with the kids?"

"Absolutely."

He looked at his watch. "Got to be off. I've a morning's training session at the garden centre — health and safety, store layout and other boring stuff."

She left him changing back into his ordinary clothes and, not for the first time, wondered about the real reason he'd suddenly decided that his relationship with Lynn had 'run its course', and why he'd said that he didn't want to meet anyone new. It grieved her. Meeko had such a lot to offer the right person. But on the plus side, it meant that she got to see more of him without worrying that she was stepping on anyone else's toes.

Meeko made her feel good about herself. But since Lynn had left there'd been something else too — disconcerting but extremely pleasant sparks when they accidentally touched. There'd been no reaction from him to indicate he'd shared the sensation. Perhaps it was just her mind playing tricks. And it was better that way — things got messy when sexual attraction was introduced to a relationship. The risk of losing a good friendship was huge, and being friends with Meeko was different to being friends with a woman. Fiona had never had a lot of close female friends, but those she'd had had made her feel excluded because her life hadn't followed the same traditional family path as theirs. Meeko's journey had been anything but traditional, so he and Fiona were well matched. All would be well — as long as she ignored the sparks.

On the way home Fiona's mind jumped ahead to Adele and what sort of reception might be waiting. Joe was still treating his daughter like a moody teenager and, when he was around, she acted that way. But occasionally, and mostly when they were alone together, Fiona got to see Adele's potential as a caring young woman. She had read somewhere that you should treat people in the way you would like to be treated yourself. That had to be the way forward. And, inadvertently, Meeko had given her the perfect idea for showing that she empathised with Adele.

"Hi, Fiona." Adele's greeting when she unlocked her front door made her jump. The mum-to-be usually stayed hidden away in the spare room unless Joe forced her downstairs at mealtimes. "Sorry if I startled you. You look like your head is in a different world."

"Hi." Fiona smiled. Adele was making an effort; this was a good start. "I just bumped into a friend and discovered he's got himself a new job. As Father Christmas."

"Cool." Adele sat down on the bottom stair as Fiona removed her trainers. The young girl seemed to want some company.

Fiona studied her laces. She had to be sure she wanted to do this before opening her mouth. It had the potential to turn her house upside down. There would be an invasion of people, plus a lot of work and organisation. She would be stepping completely out of her comfort zone and it would be impossible to backtrack once she'd floated the idea. Since the divorce she hadn't hosted more than a handful of people in her house at any one time.

No, she couldn't do it. Adele would be gone by the new year; it was pointless to make such a grand gesture for such a short-term relationship.

Then the girl spoke hesitantly. "It's tough, you know? Coming back home, like this." She stroked her belly. "Everyone staring at me and not knowing what to say if they bump into me in the street."

Fiona placed her trainers on the shoe rack, desperate not to say the wrong thing and spoil this moment of connection. She could still make the offer.

"Even your old school friends?"

"Most of them aren't back from uni yet. It's their mothers, mostly. Judging me and trying not to be obviously relieved that it's not their daughter who's got herself into this mess."

Fiona needed to put the message across that an unplanned pregnancy could be as much of a positive as a planned and longed-for baby. Her stomach tightened as she remembered how very wanted Amber had been. Then she remembered how good it had felt to offer Adele a place to stay, and the subsequent sensation of allowing light into one of those tightly controlled compartments of her life. Would making another offer be too much too soon? Could she cope with it, on top of retiring and Joe moving in? She looked at Adele's down-beat expression. A mum-to-be should be looking forward to a bright new future. She shouldn't be feeling ashamed of her condition.

"Adele, we are going to celebrate this baby." Fiona surprised herself with the determination in her voice.

"We are?"

"How do you fancy a baby shower? Here. With all your friends. No more shame. You and your baby deserve as good a start as anyone else."

Adele was looking at her open-mouthed.

"A baby shower with a real, live Father Christmas in attendance," Fiona went on. This would help Meeko and ensure that she had an ally in attendance as well.

"Yes, please." Adele's face was glowing.

CHAPTER 14

The hurried conversation with Father Christmas meant that Fiona had missed her hotel breakfast. She made tea and toast while Adele was upstairs making initial baby shower plans. Then she reached for her handbag — receipts, shopping lists and other detritus were gathering there. The mess did things to her brain. And she couldn't do with anything else tangling her mind. It had to be tidied.

But first out of the bag was the envelope from Rob. Even if she hadn't known it was from him, the handwriting was instantly recognisable from all those years ago. She turned it over in her hands. The flap was properly sealed rather than simply tucked. It was slightly thicker than a simple Christmas card, indicating her mother was right when she said there was a letter in there as well.

"You're not just telling me you're in town, are you, Rob?" she said in a whisper. "There's more to it than that."

She left the envelope on the table with her name facing upwards and made more tea. Her mouth had gone dry and her stomach no longer wanted the last piece of toast left on her plate. She should tear up the envelope without looking inside. Whatever he had written would bring everything back and push her once again into that big black hole. She'd pushed him away once and she had to stick to her guns.

Whenever she thought about her ex-husband the word 'betrayal' jumped into her mind. And it wasn't just the betrayal of gambling away their financial future. It was the way he'd gone against her wishes in the days that followed too. She'd expressly told him not to inform their parents about the miscarriage, but it had been water off a duck's back.

The hospital had discharged her early on Christmas morning.

"You're in no fit state to cook Christmas dinner for our families," he'd said. "Our mums will be happy to do it between them. I'll tell them why."

"No! They don't need to know. I don't want other people in my kitchen using my stuff. I'll manage with your help. You can tell them I've got a stomach upset but will be doing the best I can."

"But why?"

"I don't want people to see me differently to the way they did yesterday." It had been hard trying to put into words exactly how she felt. "I don't want everyone to know I failed at pregnancy as well as at being a wife."

"You haven't failed at either."

"Yes, I have. If this was a good marriage, why would you gamble away our future? And for now, we say the suite had a fault and has gone back for repair. Bring down the two armchairs from the bedroom and fetch the padded garden chairs from the garage."

Christmas Day had been a masterclass in acting. There were several times when Rob had looked on the verge of blurting out the truth but, each time, she managed to either steer him into the kitchen or change the subject. Fiona went to bed as soon as their guests left. Rob stayed up to finish clearing away and then he followed her instructions to sleep in the spare room. But the next morning her parents turned up on the doorstep with food and sympathy, plus a demand from her mother to know why she hadn't been told about the pregnancy sooner. Rob had phoned both parents with the news after he was sure Fiona had fallen asleep, exhausted after spending the previous night on a noisy ward and then faking festive smiles all day.

"It was a massive thing to have happened." He'd tried to defend his actions later. "Our parents needed to know why the two of us will never be the same again."

He was right when he said that neither of them would ever be the same again but he was wrong to have gone against her wishes. Just as he was wrong to have sent this note which could only rake up the past.

For a couple of minutes she took comfort from holding the hot mug in her cupped hands. Then she put it down, took a deep breath and carefully eased open the flap of the envelope.

The card was a generic snow scene but the letter was handwritten. Immediately it felt emotionally invasive. Why hadn't he hidden behind a typescript? The address at the top of the letter was a new luxury block of flats at the other end of town. Rob had done well for himself.

Dear Fiona,

I hope this letter reaches you via our mothers who have recently become reacquainted. Through their catching up I've learned the basic facts about your life and what I've learned makes me feel able to contact you without fear of upsetting your apple cart too much.

I don't know how much of my situation has worked its way through to you. Like you, I've never found another life partner and have struggled to come to terms with the loss of our baby. The latter has been made more difficult because I know the miscarriage was my fault and for that I am deeply, deeply sorry. Of course, I acknowledged my guilt at the time but now I realise the immediate trauma of that episode made it difficult for you to process much of what I said or promised.

*I admit that, at the time, I thought you were being unreasona-
ble but the passage of the years plus counselling has made me
better understand how it must have been for you back then.*

*Counselling. I bet that's shocked you, hasn't it? It was
recommended to me recently by someone I met at Gamblers'
Anonymous (I haven't gambled since shortly after the divorce
but still attend meetings to keep me on the straight and narrow
and to help others) and I wish I'd done it years ago instead of
carrying a head full of spaghetti emotions for half a lifetime.*

*Anyway, the counsellor suggested that reparation could
be the final step in putting the loss of our baby to rest. And,
God knows, I need to do that if I'm to have any sort of peace
as I head into retirement.*

*Why am I contacting you? Because I want you to be part
of my journey to reparation. Please will you join me?*

Fingers crossed,

Rob

Fiona screwed up the letter and dropped it in the pedal
bin. She didn't want to be part of his 'journey to reparation'
— why on earth did he think she would want that? She had
no intention of pandering to his conscience or making him
feel better about what he did or offering him any sort of forgiveness. When he gambled away their possessions, he also
killed their daughter and stole Fiona's future. Absolutely no
way could she assist her ex-husband on his search for redemp-
tion. And she needed to instruct her mother that under no
circumstances should she pass on any further information
about Fiona's life. Except to emphasise that she was now living with Joe and therefore any further communication from
Rob would be unwelcome.

On second thoughts Fiona retrieved the letter from the
bin, unscrewed it and tore it into shreds. A paper snowstorm
drifted down and coated the existing rubbish. She exhaled the
breath unconsciously trapped in her chest. Obliterating his
missive increased her sense of control and determination. And

that was what she needed in the current upside-down mess of her life. Then she forced Rob to the back of her mind and returned to tidying her handbag and wondering if she could follow through and be completely positive about the baby shower; Fiona had wet blanket and party-pooper tendencies very near the surface of her personality.

CHAPTER 15

Dorothea checked for the third time that she had Tony's clutch of letters and his two photographs in her handbag. She patted her hair in the mirror; her stylist had used so much hairspray that it now felt like she was wearing a crash helmet, but it was better than arriving at her lunch date looking like Worzel Gummidge. *Date. Date.* The word sent a shiver of excitement to her stomach and caused it to somersault. She hadn't been on an actual date for at least sixty years, since she and Arthur started courting. But Arthur had been dead two years. The initial grief had been so all-consuming that Dorothea hadn't wanted to even poke her head outside the front door. Then Fiona had helped her to move to this flat and Dorothea had realised that she had to make a new life for herself or drown in the never-ending loneliness. Fiona visited when she could, but one daughter couldn't be expected to fill every hour of every day. Responding to Tony's advert in the free newspaper had felt like a betrayal of her marriage vows, but gradually the pleasure she'd gained from their corresponderce had dimmed her guilt; she was the one left behind when Arthur died and she had to get through it as best she could. Tony used a PO Box number instead of his address, which had seemed a bit cloak-and-dagger. Her first instinct had been to respond with her actual address, but then she'd read the advice at the bottom of the lonely hearts column about divulging only a minimum of personal details and meeting in public places until you could be sure that a prospective partner was genuine. So she'd gone to the main post office in town, somewhere that she wouldn't be recognised, and taken out a three-month PO Box subscription. It wasn't cheap but Fiona would never forgive her if she got burned playing with fire. As it was, Fiona would never find out about this lonely-hearts foray. If it worked out, she and Tony would cook up some imaginary way that they'd met, and if it didn't work, well, her ultra-efficient and controlling daughter would be none the wiser.

The bus was five minutes late and then it got held up by temporary traffic lights. Dorothea was flustered by the time she entered the café and scanned the room for a good-looking, older man with silver hair, large black-framed spectacles and holding a copy of the *Daily Mail*. Tony spotted her first and waved from a table in the corner. As soon as she reached him, he stood up and kissed her full on the lips. Before she could react, he pulled her close for a hug and then kissed her on the lips again.

"Oh!" Dorothea staggered backwards as soon as she was released.

Tony hurried round to her side of the table, pulled out the chair for her and helped her off with her coat. "It's so lovely to finally meet you in the flesh, Dorrie." He put his arm around her shoulders and gave her a squeeze before taking his own seat opposite her.

"Dorrie?"

"Lovers always have nicknames. *Dot* sounds common. *Dotty* sounds like a dog's name. So, Dorrie it is, darling."

Dorrie. Darling. Kissing on the lips. None of this fitted with the Tony she'd imagined from his letter. Was this how the dating scene was in the twenty-first century? Even for oldies like themselves?

"Aren't you going to say anything, Dorrie?" He reached across the table and squeezed her hand. "I'm feeling a bit emotional and over-awed as well. Meeting you in the flesh and taking our relationship to the next level is fantastic."

He must think she was a tongue-tied numpty. She had to respond in some way. "It's lovely to meet you, Tony." She looked around for inspiration to get the conversation onto a more neutral footing. "Is that the menu? I could eat a horse." It was a lie. Tony's greeting had robbed her of what little appetite first-date nerves had left her with.

"I like a woman with a healthy appetite." His eyes glinted unnervingly as he passed her a menu. He leaned across the table and she felt his breath on her face. He'd eaten garlic the night before. "Have whatever you like, this is my treat."

He was too effusive and overpowering. She looked at the menu. Tony wasn't pushing the boat out to impress her. The most expensive thing was a jacket potato with a smoked salmon, scrambled egg and mayonnaise filling. She ordered it. Tony had the same. "We're a match made in heaven," he said, winking at the waitress. Dorothea thought how different, in a slimy way, Tony was from her late husband.

"Tell me about where you live?" he asked between large mouthfuls of potato. "You mentioned a flat but you didn't say where it was. I'm in a bungalow in Gleneagles Road."

The growing line of tension across her shoulders pulled taut. She spent some time dissecting bits of pink salmon and remembering the advice in the newspaper. "Just a small flat in an anonymous block. Nothing special."

"Everything is special about you. I loved the way your hips shimmied as you walked over to me. You are fragrant, with a face at least a decade younger than your years."

In her letters she'd already knocked ten years off her age but, even with the thickest layer of foundation and under-eye concealer, there was no way she could pass for sixty-five — that was only five years older than Fiona. He was coming on too strong. But she should give him the benefit of the doubt. It could be nerves. Men got nervous about meeting women just as much as the other way around. She needed to show some interest in him. "You mentioned the U3A History Group in your letters. What period are you studying?"

He looked awkward and mumbled something about Henry VIII. "But we don't want to be young ones discussing school. Shall we skip dessert and cut to the chase?" The waitress was clearing their plates. "Can we have the bill, please?"

"What do you mean? I could pay for pudding." Dorothea had had her eye on the giant pieces of carrot cake inside the glass counter. She could never indulge when Fiona took her out because of her daughter's unbelievable self-control. Eating such treats in front of Fiona took away the enjoyment. The waitress hovered, looking from Tony and back to Dorothea.

"We'll have cake to take away." Tony gave Dorothea a meaningful look. "Add two pieces of that red velvet cake to the bill."

Surely he didn't intend them to sit on a park bench in the biting December wind to eat the cake? It was sunny, but not sunny enough for a picnic — however romantic that might be. And it would have been polite to ask which cake she preferred. He carried the white cardboard box as they left the café.

"Where are we going?"

"I suspected you might be reticent about giving me your address on our first meeting, and . . . there are reasons we can't go to mine. I've booked a room at the Birnside Hotel."

"The Birnside Hotel?" Dorothea was totally flummoxed.

"It's walking distance." Tony offered his arm. Feeling unsteady on her feet after all that had happened, she took it. "And very discreet."

Discreet. Suddenly the alarm bells jangled. She extricated herself from his arm and they both stopped walking. How had she not realised before? There was only one reason for a man to take a woman to a hotel room in the afternoon.

"No thank you, Tony."

"What?"

"There's been a misunderstanding. Thank you for the lunch but I'm not going to the hotel. Please don't contact me again."

"Wait a minute! You can't lead a man on and then scarper. I've taken the Viagra and paid for the room."

Trembling, Dorothea turned and walked towards the centre of the town. She was aware of Tony following her. She couldn't go straight home; he mustn't know where she lived. Loneliness had made her let down her guard. She had been incredibly stupid. Please God, don't let Fiona find out. Something like this would never happen in Fiona's ultra-controlled life. She went into the library and straight to the ladies' toilets. She didn't come out of the cubicle for thirty minutes. Then she asked the library staff to call her daughter because she wasn't feeling well. Tony could easily follow her onto a bus but, unless he was hovering outside in a car, it would be impossible for him to tail Fiona.

For a panicky few minutes, she'd half expected her daughter to refuse to come because it wasn't one of those days marked in bright orange on the calendar. But Fiona didn't let her down. And her face was full of concern when she arrived.

Dorothea had intended to plead a headache but as soon as she was safely in Fiona's car she couldn't stop shaking and sobbing. The whole story came out and Fiona was more understanding than Dorothea had dared to hope. There was no reprimand, just consolation.

"Don't worry, Mum. You did all the right things, using a PO number and meeting in a public place. When Joe and I met . . ."

"When you and Joe met, what?" Had she ever asked how Fiona and Joe met?

"Need to concentrate." Fiona clammed up and gestured at the lorry in front of them, which had suddenly decided to stop and reverse.

Later, Dorothea tore all of Tony's letters into tiny strips and sobbed for a full half-hour for the companionship she thought she'd found with a new man, for the naivety she'd shown in believing it was possible to find a second life partner, and for all that she'd lost when Arthur died. She even began, very vaguely, to understand Fiona's philosophy on staying in control of each and every relationship. It wasn't right under all circumstances, but it was now obvious to Dorothea that there were certain men who couldn't be trusted. Then she broke her own rule about not drinking alone and had two glasses of brandy to help her sleep.

CHAPTER 16

Dorothea played on Fiona's mind while she was cooking the evening meal. She hadn't truly understood the gap her father's death had left in the old lady's life. Guilt seeped around her as she realised that, even though she knew Dorothea was struggling to make friends in the sheltered complex, she rarely opened the compartment in her life labelled 'Mum', except on orange days. It didn't mean there was no love there; it was just the best way of ensuring that there was a time and a place for everything in her life.

She stirred the pan, tasted and added more black pepper to the bolognaise. She'd thought this need for control had started after Amber, but, if she was totally honest with herself, she'd always been a private person, preferring to cope alone rather than being fussed over. Evidenced by the fact that she had wanted to delay announcing her pregnancy until at least twelve weeks, and by not wanting her mum to know about the miscarriage because Fiona knew it would lead to an influx of parental attention, which would only increase her emotional pain.

She dropped spaghetti into the pan of boiling water. Earlier this afternoon she'd seen her mother at her most vulnerable. And she'd been glad that her mother had called her and told her the truth about what had happened. She wished that Dorothea had told her weeks ago that she had started corresponding with Tony. Perhaps Fiona would've put more orange sunshine on the calendar or opened her mother's compartment wider and discovered that, as with Adele, she enjoyed letting more light in. Now she understood the pain her mother must have felt over the years when Fiona had kept things hidden from her. Was it time to build a better relationship with her mum? Did she even know how to do that?

Fiona's phone vibrated with a text message:

> *Feeling a bit queasy. Staying up here for a nap instead of eating dinner. Please can you tell Dad for me. He'll likely go ballistic and think I'm doing it on purpose.*

Fiona sensed fireworks ahead but did as she was asked, pleased that now Adele, as well as her mum, had felt able to confide in her.

"Adele! You are expected downstairs at mealtimes." From the bottom of the stairs Joe hollered into the empty space above him. "We are causing Fiona enough trouble without also refusing to eat what she has gone to the trouble of cooking for us."

"Leave her." Fiona tugged at his arm. None of them would enjoy the meal with one of the diners there under duress and, after realising how broken her relationship with her mother had actually become, Fiona couldn't cope with any further upset. "I'll save her dinner and she can have it when she fancies."

Joe shook his head and shouted upwards again, "Adele, I'm warning you!"

"I insist." Fiona took his hands and made him look at her. "She's not ten years old anymore. She'll soon be a mother herself. We have to give her some leeway to make her own decisions."

But even without Adele at the table the mood was awkward. Joe was furious with his daughter. Fiona hoped that Rose would reappear before too long to provide a better home for the pregnant girl.

"Are either of you going to let Rose know that very soon she'll become a grandmother for the first time?"

"What?" It took a second for Joe to come back from wherever his thoughts had taken him. "We can't. You saw Rose's email. All devices are handed in on arrival and she's left no physical address or landline number for wherever it is she's staying."

"She really was serious about this being her 'me' time."

Joe stared at the half-eaten bolognaise on his plate. "She found the divorce difficult. Even though she instigated it, on the grounds that we'd drifted apart since the children had grown up. I still had my job but she didn't know who she was anymore. It's just a shame that Adele's the one who's suffering now."

Fiona pushed the remainder of her spaghetti to the side of the plate and set her cutlery in a straight line. She could see something in common between herself and Rose and, after this afternoon, her mother as well. They were all struggling to move forward following the removal of purpose from their lives. They'd each gone from a situation of being needed to one of being superfluous. After years of bowing to the expectations of motherhood and marriage, Rose was in an empty house. After almost six decades, Dorothea had been widowed. And, following an all-consuming career, Fiona had to find purpose outside of the workplace. She understood Rose's quest to find herself — in another life they might have gone together. She hoped the other woman wouldn't regret the decision, which might mean her, unknowingly, missing the first weeks of her first grandchild's life, and maybe alienating her daughter for a very long time to come.

"What about post? She must have had to leave a forwarding address somewhere for bills, bank stuff and so on?" Was it possible to disappear into the ether?

"Everything's on direct debit. It's possible she left a friend in charge of the Airbnb stuff. Rose is like you — very thorough."

Was that a compliment or did it say something about the sort of woman Joe was attracted to? Did he prefer someone organised and in control because it meant he could be the laid-back, relaxed partner in a relationship? Fiona wasn't sure she liked the idea of a partner who was willing to coast his way through life on the back of whoever he could find.

"But she couldn't control your house being flooded or Adele turning up with her unborn grandchild."

"And I'm grateful to you for picking up the pieces." He squeezed her hand.

She looked at his plate; the knife and fork were splayed at an obtuse angle even though he'd finished his meal. Until he moved in, the fact that he didn't set his cutlery at 12 o'clock hadn't bothered Fiona. Now, after a few days of his continued presence, the habit was annoying her.

"Have you finished eating?" It was a superfluous question but she wanted to make a point.

"Yes. Thank you."

She cleared both plates and scraped her leftovers into the organic waste caddy.

CHAPTER 17

Meeko was already in the hotel restaurant when Fiona arrived the next morning. The temperature in the room felt too hot after the fresh outdoor winter air. Beads of sweat began to form on her forehead and trickle into her eyes, the salty sting making her blink vigorously. He was surrounded by empty dishes and a plate which showed signs of grease and baked beans. She pointed at it as she sat down. "I thought the cooked stuff was a heart attack on a plate and only for greedy fools?"

He shrugged. "Needs must. The more I fill up here, the less I need to put in my supermarket trolley."

"They've cut another class?"

He nodded. "The ten a.m. class is now only three times a week instead of every weekday. At least on the days when it isn't, I can really pig out — I don't need to worry about trying to do a forward fold on a tight stomach."

"Every cloud . . ."

Meeko piled up all the used crockery, leaving a plate of three croissants and some slices of cheese, which he wrapped in serviettes and placed in his holdall. "Tonight's supper."

For a few seconds Fiona's problems shrank as she imagined the anguish of not being able to afford enough food.

She offered him the blueberries and yoghurt in her bowl. He shook his head and patted his stomach. Then he added the croissant plate to the pile on his right, leaving a rectangle of empty table in front of him.

"What about the Father Christmas job? Isn't that helping the finances?"

"The living wage for only a few hours on a few days a week for three weeks in the lead-up to Christmas doesn't go very far. It's temporarily helping towards the electricity bill but that's it."

The Father Christmas gig at Adele's baby shower wouldn't go far towards improving Meeko's income but it was better than nothing. Before Fiona could tell him about it, he spoke again.

"However," he said, "I am not one for sitting around and letting fate march in and steal my life. I am being proactive and learning a new skill that will earn me money." He produced a box of playing cards from his bag and a library book: *Easy Ways to Read the Cards*.

Fiona was momentarily silenced. This didn't fit with the calm, grounded, 'in the moment' personality of Meeko. He couldn't be serious. "Do you really believe that rectangles of thin cardboard can predict our futures?"

"This might not fit with the way your brain works, but it helps some people focus on their goals, personal or professional. Using playing cards in this way is called cartomancy and it's seen as a simpler form of Tarot. It's been around since the fourteenth century — there must be something in it or it wouldn't have lasted this long."

Fiona held her hands up in mock surrender; things must be really bad for Meeko to have stooped this low. She should keep an open mind and be there for him. "OK. How does it work?"

"You ask the cards a question, take a card and allow the subconscious to guide you. It won't tell you about tall, dark, handsome strangers or the likelihood of you walking under a bus tomorrow."

"And how do you intend to monetise this?" She was trying hard to be open to the positive possibilities of cartomancy.

"On the internet using video meeting apps. Loads of people are already doing it. Are you on board with me?"

"What?" For a second, she had a vision of herself as a glamorous magician's assistant in a sparkly leotard assisting with card tricks. It wasn't a good look.

"The expression on your face!" Meeko's eyes lit up with the mischievous sparkle she loved him for; she realised now that spark had been absent for some time. "I need somebody to practise on and you'd be ideal, given all the upheaval and decision-making going on in your life right now."

She hesitated. Airy-fairy mumbo jumbo wasn't her thing. Even her own gut instinct was hard to follow without logic backing it up. If there wasn't a project plan embedded in a spreadsheet or, at least, a typed list of pros and cons, then she couldn't make a significant decision. "Even if I don't believe?"

"It's not a religion but it might make you think differently."

The decision to let Joe and Adele stay felt as though it had been forced upon her, and look how that was teetering with no pre-planned ground rules. How was the random turning over of cards going to help? But Meeko was a friend in need and she could disregard whatever the cards said. "OK, but I probably won't act on the outcome. Do you want to do it now?"

Meeko glanced around. The guests in the hotel restaurant had thinned out and there was a thick red, white and blue rope across the doorway, indicating breakfast hours had finished. The staff were collecting empty plates, wiping tables and resetting them with napkins, wine glasses, cutlery and lunch menus.

"They won't appreciate us taking up table space any longer. Come to mine for breakfast tomorrow."

"I'll bring the food." Fiona emphasised her words and made a mental note to bring far too much — buying food was obviously a big issue for Meeko.

CHAPTER 18

Meeko's plight lingered in Fiona's mind as she walked home. She'd wanted to envelop him in a hug but couldn't risk a repeat of the unrequited sparks that would generate. Sparks that had flared only since he'd split with Lynn. Had her subconscious put up a barrier while Meeko was spoken for, then let that barrier tumble as soon as he was available, even if he'd indicated that he wasn't looking to meet anyone new? Her new-found attraction to her best friend was just something else that she couldn't control and which, for the sake of her sanity, had to be pushed to the back of her mind.

Her shoulders sagged with relief at finding the house empty and her private space private again. She could put things back to how she liked them, but first she needed tea to power her through the next part of the day.

"What the . . ." Fiona's muscles quivered as she reached the threshold of the kitchen. A chimps' tea party couldn't have left a worse mess. As a single person who liked to clear and clean immediately, she didn't possess a dishwasher. A mug left neatly beside the sink was the most she could bear. The state of the kitchen told her that Adele and Joe preferred someone else to clean up after them. Poor Rose must have spent years doing that.

On the table, under a half-full bowl of milk-saturated Weetabix, was a scribbled note:

Adele — please wash up after breakfast. Remember we are guests here!!!! Destroy this note after reading. Dad.

A smiley face inside a wonky heart shape followed the word '*Dad*'. The cereal packet was on its side, with one of the white inner packages ripped to allow the crumbly biscuits to escape onto the table. A knife, glazed with marmalade, was planted in the open carton of low-fat spread. A second bowl exhibited artwork in the medium of dried-on porridge, and a glass measuring jug in the middle of the table contained evidence of how the oats and milk had been cooked. The crusty edges from a slice of toast and jam sat on a plate in the bottom of the sink. Fiona followed scarlet splodges to find the unlidded jam jar nestling in the cupboard alongside her tins of tomatoes, kidney beans and coconut milk.

Gritting her teeth, Fiona donned rubber gloves and filled the bowl — she couldn't settle to anything, not even tea, until everything was clean and back in its place. She put the radio on. Swore under her breath as loud, thumping music with no distinguishable words filled the room. She felt like an interloper into a teenager's lair or a squatter's den. Adele was an adult, an almost-mother, she should have more consideration and empathy for the woman whose house she was in. And the porridge stuff meant Joe didn't get off scot-free either. Fiona saw an image of Rose sprinting down the road with a suitcase and no backward glance. In another world they might have been friends.

Thirty minutes later, with the teapot full and her favourite mug warming, she heard noises above. Fiona's perceived privacy had been an illusion. Footsteps on the stairs. Had Adele deliberately waited until she'd heard the sink fill and empty again and the kettle boil before she decided to show her face?

The girl did have the grace to look ashamed as she shambled into the kitchen. Her hair was unbrushed and she was wearing leggings and a baggy top that looked like they'd been slept in.

"Adele, I'd really appreciate it if you could clear up after eating."

"Oh, Fiona! I'm really, really sorry." Adele spoke with sincerity and sheepishly screwed up the note that Fiona had pointedly left on the table. "I thought I had plenty of time before you'd be back. I must have fallen asleep again."

Fiona wanted to point out that she wasn't running a hotel and that she wasn't an unpaid housekeeper, but she bit her tongue. Adele looked genuinely contrite and pale with tiredness. Fiona needed to cut her some slack. "Don't worry, it's done now."

"I promise I'll do it next time. You haven't got children, have you?"

Fiona shook her head. "No." There was a familiar prickle in her eyes and she had to look away. Adele didn't know she was being tactless.

"Being pregnant is like having an alien inside of you trying to punch its way out." She rubbed her extended belly. "It uses up your energy so that all you can do is sleep or flop. Dad doesn't understand — he still thinks I should function like the old me. But I think the old me might be gone forever."

Fiona reached out and squeezed Adele's hand. The girl was spot on with that last sentence. Whatever the outcome of a pregnancy, the mother's outlook on life was never the same again. "Don't grieve; you might love the new you better."

She wanted to tell Adele that she knew exactly what it felt like to be pregnant and how tiring it could be. Fiona had found the first trimester tough. She hadn't had the option of lounging about while someone else cleared up after her, though. She'd had a house and husband to maintain and a job to hold down. Rob had kept saying that he was more than willing to help, but his offers were of no use because by the time he got home there was only time to eat and go to bed. Fiona, believing he was working late every night, had felt it was her duty to do everything — after all, a marriage is about teamwork, and he was earning more than her. If only she'd known back then that he wasn't doing overtime to provide a secure home for his wife and child but was in the bookies or playing the slot machines chasing a quick win to keep the bailiffs at bay. If she'd known, maybe she wouldn't have pushed herself so hard and, just possibly, she might not have lost Amber. Mostly, she tried not to reflect on that period, but when she did, guilt descended. The miscarriage might not have been solely down to the shock of the bailiffs. If she hadn't insisted on doing more than her share at home as well as working full-time, even though she was suffering from first trimester exhaustion and sickness, there might have been a better outcome. The medical staff had said it was just 'one of those things', but Fiona felt they had been trying to stop her from blaming herself. Losing Amber had been the biggest failure of her life — of course she was going to blame herself.

She looked at Adele but voiced none of her thoughts out loud. The girl was wan-faced, with more shadow under her eyes than a girl her age should have.

"Go sit down and put your feet up. Or relax in the bath. Just don't tell your dad."

Adele grinned at her. "Thank you." Then she mimed zipping her lips closed. "If you really don't mind, I'd love to have a bath."

Fiona waved her away with a smile and felt a little bud of brightness inside her.

When Joe returned from work the house was pristine. Adele was dressed in maternity jeans and an oversized sky-blue sweatshirt stretched snuggly over her bump. She'd made an effort with some make-up and looked a lot brighter.

"You're blooming!" Joe held his daughter at arm's length for a moment and then kissed her on the forehead.

"Impending motherhood suits you." He touched her belly. "But don't make a habit of it."

Fiona served homemade fish pie and broccoli. Adele accepted only a little bit of the broccoli onto her plate and bypassed Fiona's specially prepared tartar sauce, but was liberal with the tomato ketchup. Joe frowned as she squirted from the bottle onto her plate for a third time. Fiona caught his eye and give a little shake of her head. His face relaxed and he let it pass.

"Fiona has offered to host a baby shower for me," Adele spoke tentatively when they'd all finished eating. "Is that still OK, Fiona?"

"Absolutely." Damn, she'd forgotten to mention the Father Christmas gig to Meeko. Her organisational skills seemed to be escaping through the cracks as light seeped into the controlled areas of her life.

"I haven't a clue what a baby shower is," Joe said immediately, "but I'm behind it all the way." He was looking eagerly from one woman to the other as though pleased to see them bonding over whatever this unknown female ritual might turn out to be.

"It's a sort of party," Adele explained, "to celebrate the forthcoming birth of a baby."

"And you're happy to host this party, here in your house?" Joe was looking at Fiona as though this offer was totally out of character for her. He was right. Each time she thought of the impending event, her heart speeded up and anxiety settled in the pit of her stomach. Only the expectation that Meeko would be there on the night, as a supporting act, made her feel that this was something that she could actually get through.

"Yes. I wouldn't have offered otherwise."

Joe squeezed her hand. "Are you sure?"

"Yes." *No. Through choice, I'd have nothing to do with pregnant women, baby showers, et cetera, et cetera, but I'm finding that sometimes it feels good to open up those dark compartments. However, when it comes to it, this one might not feel quite so good.* "I'm sure Adele will keep everyone under control and it won't be too wild."

"What do you think, Adele?"

"I want it to go ahead. Obviously. But . . ." There was a silence and then the words came hesitantly. "It's just . . . everyone will see . . . it should be Mum . . . not . . ."

Joe looked confused but Fiona understood immediately. "Introducing me as your dad's girlfriend is embarrassing?"

Adele nodded but had the decency to look ashamed.

"Then tell them I'm a family friend; one of those friends of your parents who get called 'Aunty' even though there's no blood relationship. Will that work?"

Adele nodded again.

Joe looked satisfied with the outcome. "And we'll both help you with the catering, Fiona. I'll pay."

"There'd need to be a big cake. With pink icing." Adele glanced down at her empty plate, which had held one of Fiona's homemade sugarless flapjacks. "And with proper sugar in it."

"Sugar," Fiona repeated, "is not a problem." *At least not compared to the emotional strain of celebrating someone else's as yet unborn baby daughter.*

Joe had pulled a diary from his briefcase, turned to the back, headed the page 'Baby Shower' and was starting a list. "You're the expert, Adele, what do we need?"

"Let me!" Fiona held her hand out for the diary. She didn't trust someone else to do the organising. "I'll make the notes."

Relief flooded Joe's face as he handed the diary over, and Fiona's shoulders relaxed once she was in the driving seat.

"Pink balloons, prosecco, all sorts of nibbles, and there's a Baby Bingo game I've seen online. And, Dad, you do know it's women only?"

Joe's face fell and then recomposed itself quickly into an expression of positivity.

"First things first." Fiona opened the Calendar app on her phone. "What date are we aiming for?"

"What about the seventeenth?" Joe suggested. "It gives us time to prepare but there's still a week to go before Christmas."

"Entertainment," Adele said. "Your Father Christmas friend . . ."

"Meeko? I'm sure he'll be amenable, for a small fee." Fiona smiled. This was killing three birds with one stone: she was offering a helping hand to both Adele and Meeko. And she'd have her best friend present if her courage turned turtle and she couldn't cope. "And I'll pay his fee — my contribution to the party."

Joe frowned. "You said I was banished from the actual party because I'm a man. Why is Meeko allowed to be there?"

"As the entertainment, he's fine to be there," Adele confirmed.

Fiona went back through her list. "We've made a good start."

Joe leaned over and kissed his daughter on the forehead. "This baby shower will run like a dream. Even if I'm not there to oil the wheels."

It was the first time since Adele's arrival on her doorstep that Fiona went to bed feeling there was harmony in the house. And she felt satisfaction and pride that, despite her ongoing sadness over Amber, she was able to offer Adele help. She used these positive emotions to quash the anxiety that was rising and falling within her whenever she thought about the shower and its emphasis on babies and new life.

Joe must have picked up on the household's good vibes too. That night they made love for the first time since Adele had moved in — albeit as quietly and unenergetically as they could.

CHAPTER 19

Fiona had only been to Meeko's flat once before. That had been during lockdown when they'd met on the pavement outside to go for a walk. Meeko had suffered financially during the pandemic and had had to dip deep into his savings to pay his rent. Fiona counted herself as one of the lucky ones — being in IT, she'd been able to work at home, and most days had featured several online meetings. By the time evening came she'd been glad to escape the laptop and take her prescribed daily exercise.

Meeko's flat was in the attic space of a tall Victorian house. Fiona picked out his bell at the bottom of a column of four and pressed. A minute later a slightly breathless Meeko appeared, gave her a hug and gestured her through an inner door leading to a stairwell.

His flat was tiny. Washing hung drying on a rack, a slight smell of garlic tinged the air, and the door to a tiny bathroom was wide open, showing the toilet with a raised seat. The kitchen took up the back third of the living area and had a window over the sink which, she guessed, must look down into the garden. The window at the front, in the sitting area, had a view over the road she'd just walked up.

"Sit down." He gestured at a settee draped with a burnt-orange tie-dyed throw. Fiona wondered whether it was left over from Lynn's occupancy.

"Breakfast." She made a show of handing over a small brown paper carrier from the delicatessen containing croissants (for him), a perfectly ripe avocado plus a tub of prawns (for her) and a cardboard tray holding two takeaway lattes, one normal (for him) and one decaffeinated oat milk (for her). "Plate, bowl and spoons only are required." Surreptitiously, although Meeko couldn't have failed to notice, she placed a supermarket bag-for-life behind the kitchen counter containing muesli, bran flakes, a loaf of bread and a premium lasagne ready meal.

Meeko provided the crockery and Fiona decanted the foodstuffs, adding paper serviettes with an exaggerated flourish.

"Sorry about . . ." He licked croissant crumbs from his lips and gestured around the flat. "It's cheap and, well, there's only me now . . ."

"I like it." It wasn't a lie; the flat had a lived-in, cosy feel. There were full bookshelves and only a tiny TV — signs of someone who has their priorities right. It was just a bit chaotic for her. And there was nowhere to store or hide the chaos. "So, how does this card thing work?"

"You're going to ask me simple questions about your future and I'm going to answer them using an ordinary deck of cards." He pointed to a pack of playing cards on the windowsill. "But first, we finish eating."

Fiona scraped the inside of the avocado skin and double-checked the prawn container was empty. Meeko had nearly finished his second croissant, spread thickly with jam that he'd produced from the kitchen. After the third and final croissant was gone, he gestured that he needed to wash his hands.

A few minutes later they were seated across the table from each other with only the takeaway coffee cups and deck of

110

cards on the surface. Fiona felt a seed of apprehension in the pit of her stomach. She reached for the coffee. Was she going to learn something she'd rather not know?

"First we need to calm our minds and release all that inner chatter." Meeko closed his eyes and took deep breaths. Fiona followed suit, imagining it was the introduction to one of his yoga sessions. After a couple of minutes Meeko opened his eyes and repeated his earlier instruction. "You need to ask the cards a question."

Fiona chewed the inside of her cheek and then rubbed her arms. Logic told her this was all mumbo jumbo but still a swirl of nerves mixed with the prawns and avocado. Meeko looked at her intently and for a second their eyes locked. Something sudden, awesome, tingly and infinitely more pleasurable replaced her fear. She looked away from him, confused.

"There must be something you're curious about," Meeko persisted. "Your life is upside down at the moment and you hate it. Don't you want to know if you're ever going to be its ringmaster again?"

He didn't need cards in order to read her like a book.

"OK." She took a breath. It had only been a week since she'd finished work and Joe had moved in, but it felt like years. During that time, the tight rein she'd kept on her life had begun to slip. Did she want to pull it tight again? Yes, and no. She remembered the warmth of opening up and letting Adele have the spare room. And then the painful memories of Amber triggered by the pregnant girl's presence. She remembered the shock and shame of discovering exactly how lonely her mother was. And the relief that the old lady had finally felt able to open up to her. Fiona didn't want to strangle these two fledgling relationships by pulling too hard and clanging doors shut. But the presence of Adele meant Fiona and Joe had no privacy and she missed the fun they used to have on their weekly date nights. And father and daughter weren't getting on well — which fed into the disquiet between Fiona and Joe. It would get worse when the baby arrived. If Rose didn't reappear from India, Fiona's precious home office sanctuary would have to be converted into a nursery. She couldn't bear that. Such a conversion had almost happened once before. In another house. A long time ago. That had been a welcome conversion, but bar the paint buying, it had never taken place. Which relationship should she prioritise? Adele would disappear when her mother returned but, now the teething problems were sorted out, she and Joe might make it in the long-term. It might be kinder all round if she plucked up the courage to ask Adele to leave now. Joe's brother, Adele's uncle, lived nearby in a big house with empty bedrooms. That would keep the new baby at a more tolerable arm's length and leave her and Joe free to concentrate on each other.

"Should I ask Adele to leave before the baby is born?" She spoke slowly and deliberately, addressing her question to the pack of cards, not directly to Meeko. Looking at Meeko might cause that awkward tingling inside her again and there was no future in such a tingle.

"Good. That's exactly the sort of yes/no question that the cards can answer." He shuffled the cards, cut the deck and then merged the two piles back into one. "Red cards mean *yes*, and black cards mean *no*." He asked Fiona to turn over the top card. The three of spades.

She stared down at the black card and the answer she didn't want.

"You can ask another question, if you want?"

"Will Joe and I be happy together?"

Meeko shifted in his chair and cleared his throat. He looked uncomfortable but gestured that she should take a card.

The next card was the six of clubs. Another *no*. The cards were talking rubbish.

Fiona asked no further questions and turned over no more cards. "There's no science behind this. I could go home now, ask Adele to leave and build a happy love nest with Joe. My free will is more powerful than anything the cards might say."

"But you won't, will you? Nobody could be that heartless to a heavily pregnant woman."

He was right. But any one of a hundred scenarios might also happen.

"Adele has free will too. The father of the baby might turn up and whisk her away. Or her mother might return."

"Possible, and the cards might give a different answer tomorrow. Today's answer is unique to you and this moment in time."

Fiona picked up the cards and shuffled them again. "I'd rather play *Snap!* and make my own decisions about the future."

Meeko shrugged and took the pack from her. Their fingers touched and that weird feeling fizzed in the pit of her stomach again. Did Meeko feel it as well? His face gave no indication.

"Changing the subject." She averted her eyes from his and stared at the wall behind him, alighting on a wedding picture. He'd told her about it. He'd acted as best man at the wedding of two of his closest friends, just after gay marriage had become legal. Apparently, after waiting for so long to be able to tie the knot, the couple had pushed the boat out and the wedding had been an extremely joyful occasion, full of family and community. The sight of Meeko in his top hat and tails made her catch her breath and then look away. She softened her gaze so that she was looking at nothing in particular when she next spoke. "I've offered to host a baby shower for Adele and she'd like a real-life Father Christmas to be there. Can you take bookings on the side? I'll pay you the going rate." She made a mental note to add a big tip — today's visit had shown her how precarious her friend's financial situation was.

Meeko didn't hesitate. "I'd love to. It sounds like fun. And don't worry about payment. At mates' rates it will cost you nothing."

She brought her eyes back to his face. It was impossible to converse properly looking over someone's shoulder. His face was twinkly and enthusiastic. She loved him for his zest for life and his generosity. For his inability to hold a grudge or remain in a black mood. She wanted his secret to seeing the joy and positivity in anything and everything. And his ability to go through life so unselfishly.

Her mind jumped forward to the practicalities of his appearance at the baby shower: the Santa outfit belonged to the garden centre — should Meeko ask their permission? Did Adele simply want a few ho-ho-hos or would there be gifts to distribute? Gifts would help her back into Adele's good books; Fiona would fund them. Then she took a breath — it could all be sorted out in the coming days. It didn't have to be done this very moment. Learn to go more slowly and give others a chance to catch up. "All you have to do is turn up. And it will be all women — no men allowed apparently."

"I'm looking forward to it." His eyes twinkled again.

"And I nearly forgot — Mum and I are no longer eating out on Christmas Day; it makes no sense now that Joe and Adele have landed. We'd all love it if you could join us?" With Lynn no longer on the scene, Fiona couldn't bear to think of her best friend sitting alone in this flat, and she was already mentally preparing the doggy bag of food she'd give him to take home.

"Try keeping me away from a free dinner plus the company of three ladies!"

114

CHAPTER 20

On the way home, Fiona's head buzzed with anxiety and over-whelm. The prospect of sharing her home with Adele and a baby for months and months was suffocating. Please come home soon, Rose! The potential for her retirement to be a time of self-indulgence and joy had gone. She had responsibility for a young woman she barely knew, an unborn baby she was not biologically related to, and a mother who was permanently disappointed in her only child and so lonely that she had resorted to picking up men from the lonely hearts column. Plus, a confusing transition to make from passionate affair to domestic cohabitation with Joe.

And then Rob's grinning face sprang to the forefront of her mind. Fiona gasped and blinked hard to obliterate his image. He wouldn't side-swipe her off life's track again. "Go away! Go away! Go away!" she muttered, until home was in sight. Then she called on her ability to focus on the task in hand.

There were the details of the baby shower to work out and safeguards to put in place to ensure it wasn't an uncon-trollable nightmare in her own home. Joe was enthusiastic but didn't have a clue how to arrange even the smallest event, and Adele seemed like all the young people Fiona had worked with — totally last minute in the organisation of anything, from a simple night out to a holiday abroad. Fiona needed to take control. By the time she walked into her house she was itching to start. *Fail to plan, plan to fail.* A 'normal' person would be happy with a simple paper and pen list, but only a spreadsheet would make Fiona feel really in control.

She stopped in the kitchen doorway. Adele was at the sink, washing up. The kitchen table and all the surfaces were clear and damp, indicating they'd recently been wiped down.

"Wow! This is great. Thank you."

"I felt bad about the other morning, and Dad said . . ." Adele halted, as though realising any words might make her look less than willing.

"It doesn't matter whose idea it was. *You've* done the job." It did matter that this hadn't been Adele's idea. But Fiona remembered something Meeko had once told her, along the lines of: If we create an atmosphere of acceptance, gratitude and welcome to others, then they are more likely to follow our example and treat us that way in return.

Stepping further into the kitchen, it was obvious the surface wiping down hadn't been done properly. The main large areas were clean, but the toast crumbs had been carelessly pushed against the silicone sealant running between the horizontal surface of the worktop and the vertical surface of the tiled wall. And there were further crumbs and blobs of jam on the vinyl flooring immediately below. It took immense willpower not to criticise. Fiona took the cloth from Adele's hand, scooped up the jam and handed the cloth back. "Sorry, I just didn't want that to get trodden out of here and into the hall carpet."

Adele frowned and then turned back to the sink without speaking.

Fiona pursed her lips. She'd done the wrong thing. But anyone else would have acted the same. And she was still going to have to sneak back later and clear up all the crumbs now lurking in half-sight.

"I'll dry for you." She picked up a tea towel. This way she could ensure that everything had been washed properly. "Afterwards shall we dot the I's and cross the T's of the baby shower? What do you think — a paper list or a spreadsheet?"

"It's a group of friends, not a military exercise."

Fiona felt a flush burn her cheeks. It seemed their relationship was taking a step backwards. "Once an IT project manager, always an IT project manager." She tried to keep her voice light. "Planning carefully came with the territory; everything always had to be belt and braces. But paper it is." She picked up a plate with a smear of butter still clinging to the edge, was about to hand it back to Adele, then thought better of it, gritted her teeth, wiped the mark away with the tea towel and made a mental note to put the tea towel straight in the laundry basket. "The good news is that Meeko has agreed to come along and play Father Christmas. There will be a small gift in his sack for each guest."

Adele turned her head and grinned. "Brilliant — people will be able to get some great photos."

And social media will be bombarded with images of my living room. Not good but there is no way back now.

Afterwards they sat in the lounge and Fiona tried to be 'less military' by writing on the back of a flyer which had dropped through the letterbox, rather than using the A4 hard-backed notebook that sat upstairs on her office desk and contained the map of how to run her life.

"Guests." She underlined it as the first subheading. "How many? Do we send proper invitations and collect RSVPs — in which case there's very little time? Or do you do all that electronically these days?"

Adele's eyes glanced heavenward. "I'll put something out there. It's mostly old school friends. They're all back from uni for Christmas. It'll be a big reveal — most of them won't even know about this." She patted her swollen belly. "Unless word has spread among the mothers."

"Oh?" Fiona had assumed the girl would've told everyone via endless social media posts — isn't that how people lived their lives these days? But if she hadn't even told her parents, maybe that wasn't the case?

Adele looked awkward. "At first I didn't realise. And then I wondered about . . ." She looked down and stroked her belly again. "And then I hoped . . . the father and I . . . that it could be a joint announcement . . . and then, here we are."

The gaps said more than the words. Fiona patted Adele's knee. "It's OK, I get it." For a few seconds it felt as though a confidence had been shared. "Back to the guests." Fiona didn't want to wade back in with her big, flat military boots, but this party couldn't happen without preparation. "You do the inviting and collate responses. But I could do with a rough idea of numbers now, for food, drink and Santa's pressies. Err on the generous side — better to have too much than too little."

Adele rolled her eyes again. Fiona ignored the girl's irritated expression. It was essential to know whether to expect five or twenty-five guests. Adele mouthed names and counted on her fingers. There was a frustrated expulsion of breath and she appeared to start all over again, presumably having lost count when she got past ten.

"Here." Fiona passed her the pen and paper. "Write them down — it's a lot easier."

Resting the flyer on the coffee table, Adele filled the page with a list of names and handed it back. Fiona counted them. Thirty. She wrote the number down and drew a circle around it for clarity and emphasis. More guests than she would like but they probably wouldn't all come.

"They'll all be up for it. We haven't all been together for months. Probably since last Christmas."

Fiona tried to smile. "I'll have to fetch my . . ." She gestured at the ceiling with her pen. "You've filled my page."

On her way upstairs she remembered her mum's happiness at becoming a great-granny-by-proxy. The old lady would love to come to the baby shower — and not only because it would provide a wonderful one-upmanship conversation with her neighbours.

A few minutes later she had the red hardback book open in front of her with the title 'Baby Shower' underlined twice. She stapled the list of guests into the book alongside two pages torn from the back of Joe's diary containing the initial ideas from the previous evening.

"Adele, would you mind if I invited someone along?"

"Who?" There was a hint of suspicion in the girl's voice.

"My mother. When I told her about you and the baby she was over the moon. She hasn't got any proper grandchildren and she'd love to be involved in some way. She bakes wicked scones."

Adele appeared to weigh up this suggestion for a few seconds. "Yeah, OK." Then she added, "Is *wicked* usually in your vocabulary or are you trying to be down with the kids?"

Fiona blushed at her botched attempt to narrow the gap between her and the girl who, following her mum's logic, could be described as Fiona's 'daughter-by-proxy' — a term which had a much better, less wicked, ring to it than 'stepdaughter'. Then she looked down at her notebook and wrote the subheading 'Food'. After some argument about sandwiches and sausages on sticks, followed by an explanation of what a vol-au-vent was, Adele was firm: Fiona's suggested menu sounded like a children's birthday party. All that was needed were takeaway pizzas. They were easy and exact numbers plus vegetarian and vegan preferences could be sorted out on the night.

"Salad?" Fiona asked the question, even though she already knew the answer.

A discussion on drink followed, resulting in the requirement for at least ten bottles of prosecco, one of gin, several flavoured tonics plus a few beers. Fiona silently added fruit juices to the end of the list.

"Just Santa's gifts now."

"Do I get one?"

"Absolutely."

"In that case I want them to be a surprise. And . . ." A mischievous grin settled on Adele's lips. "Do we get to sit on Santa's knee?"

Fiona waved the comment away. She was starting to learn when Adele was winding her up. "Ah! I almost forgot. Does Santa need a grotto or can he just walk around the room with his sack?"

"A grotto — definitely!" Adele's eyes lit up like a child's.

Fiona kicked herself. She'd just increased her work by a multiple of ten. How do you create a grotto in a three-bedroomed semi-detached house? She turned the page in her notebook, wrote the heading 'Grotto' and underlined it three times.

CHAPTER 21

Fiona gave herself a pat on the back. Things were settling down at home and an acceptable, if not yet wonderful, atmosphere had descended. Most of the time Joe was remembering to treat his daughter like an adult instead of a child and, most of the time, Adele responded well. There also seemed to be an understanding developing between Fiona and Adele, brought about, at least in part, by their joint project of The Baby Shower. Fiona controlled the reins but consulted the mum-to-be on all aspects. Adele was laid-back and mostly able to go with the flow.

She poured a second cup of tea in the morning quiet of the kitchen. Joe had left for work and Adele was yet to surface. Fiona congratulated herself on her flexibility in adapting to a new lifestyle, her generosity in opening her house without argument, and her gradual success in morphing from girl-friend to cohabitee. This might actually be a situation she could live with until Rose returned and gave Adele a new home.

She jumped as her phone pinged and vibrated on the table alongside her cup. She picked it up and swiped.

"The club Christmas dinner! Damn! I forgot." The self-congratulation was misplaced. In normal times any date that she put in her electronic calendar automatically lodged itself in her brain and she barely needed the phone alerts. But now that her familiar scaffolding of work and routine was gone, she was struggling to hold disparate things in her head.

In the months before finishing work, she'd made an effort to organise the best use of her coming free time. She'd drawn up a list of new things to try, old interests to resurrect and travel destinations she wanted to visit. Most of the stuff, like dipping a toe into the U3A, investigating behind-the-scenes opportunities at the amateur dramatic society, and joining a Bridge club would be best tackled in January when they restarted after the Christmas break. Stand-up paddleboarding on the local lake would benefit from waiting until the spring. Before finishing work she'd already tried a few sessions of the Retired Means Active club for ex-professionals and it was the reminder for their Christmas dinner that was pinging her now. Did she still want to go? It seemed a lifetime ago that she'd been in the meeting room above the Red Lion and had signed up and paid her deposit. Could she still go? Joe had got into the habit of expecting a meal on the table when he got home from work. Adele wouldn't eat properly unless it was provided for her. Fiona felt obliged to make sure the baby got the best possible start in life. And wasn't part of this 'life partner' thing doing your bit at home while the other was out working?

Then the truth hit home: this was not how she wanted her life with Joe to pan out. If Amber had lived it would have been different. Making a home for your own child and its father would have been a worthwhile mission. She would have ensured that when Amber reached eighteen and went off to university she had all the skills to be independent. Amber would have known how to look after herself, and Fiona and Rob would have been free to enjoy themselves in the knowledge that their daughter was equipped to deal with whatever life threw at her. Of course they would've helped her in an absolute emergency but not in this constant drip, drip way that younger adults required these days. Now it seemed that the apron strings were never quite cut and parents never regained their freedom.

She drained her mug and stood up. Yes, she would go to the Retired Means Active dinner tonight. She looked at the notes in her calendar; she'd pre-ordered a mini Caesar salad, turkey with seasonal vegetables, followed by raspberry roulade. She started to look forward to it. The dinner and new people would be a breath of fresh air.

Adele wandered into the kitchen in a dressing gown. Fiona tried to picture how she might have handled this situation with her own daughter.

"I'll be eating out this evening, Adele."

"OK."

"Will you be able to do a meal for you and your dad?"

"OK."

This easy agreement didn't seem right. "What will you cook?"

The question seemed to wake Adele up properly. "Cook? I think you have Deliveroo around here."

"That's going to be expensive." *And unhealthy.*

"One takeaway isn't going to break the bank."

Says she who's not contributing a single penny to the household budget. It wasn't Fiona's problem but she couldn't leave it. And she didn't fancy returning home to the smell of chips, curry or garlic with the wrappings discarded haphazardly in the kitchen bin rather than taken straight out to the wheelie bin.

"I'll take some frozen bolognaise out of the freezer," Fiona said. "You can defrost that, cook some spaghetti and there's a bag of salad leaves in the bottom of the fridge."

"Whatever. But Dad will probably prefer a takeaway too — it's what we always did if Mum went out. Not that she went out often. Dad gave her too much hassle about it."

"Hassle?" A drip of anxiety started in her stomach. This wasn't something she'd have expected of Joe — given that he often had evenings out with his football or work buddies. Was this a case of one rule for the man but a different rule for everyone else? "What sort of hassle?"

"Just the usual stuff that he nags me about. Where are you going? Who will be there? What time are you coming home? How will you get home? I ignore it but it spoiled the whole prospect of going out for Mum. And his last question always used to be—" Adele switched to a whiny voice — "do you have to go out? It would be much nicer if we spent the evening together."

Joe wouldn't act like that with her — their relationship had always been one of equals with no dependency on her part. In fact, he was now dependent on her. Pushing those thoughts aside, she wrote detailed instructions about the bolognaise, spaghetti and salad. And then cursed as she realised she'd just placed herself in a wifely role. But it was her kitchen and she wanted to be in control.

Fiona was showered, dressed, made-up and ready to go when Joe got home.

"Would you mind giving me a lift," she asked. "And collecting me? I'd quite like to have some wine with my meal."

"Where are you going?"

She answered and he followed up with more questions, exactly fitting the pattern that Adele had said he followed with Rose.

"Joe, I don't need this inquisition. Look at me. I'm not Rose." He had the decency to blush. "Taxiing me there and back is the least you can do for the woman who you profess to love and who has given you a roof over your head." She managed to keep most of the anger out of her voice and also to push away the doubts about their relationship that this inquisition was feeding.

"Sorry, you're right. Let's go." Then he paused and looked at her neckline. "You're not wearing my ruby."

Fiona touched the amber pendant. "I . . . it didn't seem appropriate . . . too showy for this occasion." Why was she making up excuses? "And I've already told you, this one has sentimental value."

A frown lingered on Joe's forehead and then he called into the lounge, "Adele, what takeaway do you want tonight?"

His daughter came into the hallway. "Indian." Then she raised her eyebrows and silently said 'I told you so' to Fiona.

It was his money and she wasn't going to spoil her evening by leaving the house with an argument hanging. The bolognaise had hardly started to thaw. She pushed it back in the freezer and threw the note in the bin. They were trying to control each other, she by dictating what Joe should eat and, therefore, how he should spend his money, and he by wanting to know every detail of her forthcoming evening. She needed to treat Joe how she would like to be treated herself.

CHAPTER 22

Fiona was missing her usual confidence when Joe left her in the car park of the pub. Confidence went hand in hand with control and there were people and situations in her life now that she couldn't control. People who, even though they didn't say so directly, disapproved of tonight's outing and felt she was neglecting some sort of duty that she owed to them. It was this sensation of doing wrong that was sapping her confidence. She was about to phone Joe and ask him to come back for her when she heard her name.

"Fiona, isn't it? You're new to the group?"

Fiona nodded, trying to conjure up a name for the short, silver-haired woman in front of her. She might be the club treasurer. "I'm sorry, I've had to miss a couple meetings and I can't remember your name." It was always best to be brutally honest.

"Alison. I'm the programme secretary."

"Of course, I remember now." They went through the door together and someone else waved a greeting and pointed the way to the function room.

"Can I get you a drink, Alison?" Queuing at the bar would give Fiona a few minutes to pull herself together, gather some topics of conversation and see if she could spot any vaguely familiar faces. She didn't want Alison to think that she had to nursemaid her all evening.

The function room was heavy with the drone of voices. Fiona glanced from her place in the bar queue to the closed groups and huddles of friends catching up; none of them looked sufficiently open for her to gatecrash. She let her eyes rest on the Christmas tree, dressed in red and gold ribbons with a waterfall of tiny scarlet lights trickling from top to bottom by the magic of a microchip and electricity. The staff behind the bar were sporting matching Santa hats and scarlet T-shirts emblazoned with 'Merry Christmas'. The piped music was cycling all the seasonal classics. As she shouted her order she was in competition with Slade's 'Merry Xmas Everybody'.

"Two medium glasses of house red, please." She swiped her credit card, picked up the glasses and tried to find a pathway through the growing throng of people in the room. Then she saw him. At first, she wasn't sure. His face was fuller and his hair thinner but the height was right. He was broader in the torso but, in full conversational flow, his gestures and facial expressions were unmistakable. It was Rob. She felt like someone had punched her in the gut. She looked around wildly, not sure whether she wanted an escape route, a quiet corner or to actually go up to him. Did he remember that this Christmas Eve would be their thirtieth anniversary? Pearl, in wedding speak. Pearl — she liked that thought: a gentle white gem for the loveliest, most innocent baby. Had he written the letter about reparation because he knew it was a big anniversary?

"Fiona, are you all right?" Alison arrived by her side and claimed one of the glasses. "You look dazed. Do you need to sit down? The place cards are all out, so feel free to find where you've been plonked. It's all random, so don't take it personally if you end up next to the biggest bore in the room." The programme secretary moved away.

Fiona felt too blindsided to approach Rob immediately. She needed to decide on her opening gambit and what she wanted to get out of the meeting. Did she want to speak to him at all? There was nothing to be gained by going over old ground. They hadn't been able to help each other back then and it was highly unlikely he could offer her any empathy or understanding now, despite his apologies in the letter.

Fiona turned away and found the place card with her name in stylish black italic handwriting. She put down her wine next to an unlit scarlet candle embedded with glitter, its base encircled by a miniature wreath of fresh green leaves. She fiddled with a cracker and then noticed her glass was already half-empty. She drank more when she was nervous, and talked more too. She was at the very end of the table, which would give her fewer conversation options, either the person opposite her or the person on her right. She tried to decipher the name card opposite in order to determine whether it was a man or a woman but it was impossible to read the fancy writing upside down. Then she saw the name on the card to her right: Robert Washington. No! Her heart thudded and then missed a beat. It must be someone else with the same name as her ex-husband. But she couldn't risk being trapped for the whole meal. She took Rob's card, meaning to swap it with another one further down the table.

"Not allowed!" Alison had reappeared. Her voice was jokey and she was smiling. She meant no harm but Fiona still felt chastised and immediately put the name card back down in its original position. "Ah! This is unfortunate," Alison continued. "The lady who was supposed to sit opposite you has cancelled. Upset stomach. But I'm sure Rob will look after you. He's fairly new to the club as well. And here's the gentleman himself! I'll leave you to introduce yourselves."

Now he was next to her. His mouth dropped open in the same way as when she'd told him she was pregnant.

"Hello, Rob."

"Fiona! I heard via our mothers that you were a member here."

"And that's why you joined?"

"Not the whole reason. Did you get my note?"

She nodded.

"I had to send it via your mother because she was very cagey about giving your address or mobile number to my mum."

Thank you, Mum. At least you do have my interests at heart some of the time.

"I've recently moved back to the area, obviously. Joining Retired Means Active is partly a way to get to know people — and partly I hoped to see you too." He paused and looked across the table at the empty seat opposite Fiona. "Where's your significant other?" He'd chosen his words carefully, she realised, because her bare left hand was laid in full view on the table. She moved it to her lap, her empty fourth finger making her feel vulnerable.

Acknowledging a significant other existed was a new experience for Fiona. Although, given Joe's performance over her outing tonight, he might not be forever. "At home. I've only just joined and I didn't realise bringing partners was a thing. The lady who was supposed to sit there is ill."

Fiona took a sip of wine while she waited for Rob's reaction to the news that she had a partner; she was sure her mother wouldn't have divulged this. Rob picked up his pint. The silence seemed to elongate awkwardly, though it was probably only a few seconds. Then they were saved from any further explanation by the arrival of their starters. Unsurprisingly, Rob had gone for the chicken wings; he'd been an avid carnivore when they were together.

"Still on the healthy stuff?" He gestured to her salad. "You always did have more self-discipline than me."

There was nothing to add to that; he was the compulsive gambler.

The seat opposite Rob remained empty as well. After the last wing he wiped his greasy fingers on the napkin. "It looks like we'll have to chat between ourselves. What do you think of the club so far?"

He was making small talk as if everything they'd been through together had never happened. No — 'been through together' wasn't the right phrase. Fiona had gone through it alone. Rob had closed up after the loss of Amber. She'd wanted to talk. She'd wanted them to comfort one another. She'd wanted them to acknowledge their feelings. And she'd wanted apologies and explanations about the bailiffs and the debt and, ultimately, the gambling. Rob had wept huge sobs beside her hospital bed after an ultrasound scan had confirmed the miscarriage, but after that there'd been hardly any emotion at all. For Fiona the burden of grief had sometimes been too heavy for her even to lift her head from the pillow.

"Too early to say. I haven't been a member for long." If he wanted small talk, he could have small talk.

"The food's good, isn't it?" He paused. "Do you remember me bringing you here for your birthday, about six months after we started going out?"

Fiona frowned. So much of their early relationship had been forgotten in the blackness of what came later. It was possible they'd been here.

"It's been remodelled since then," Rob continued. "It was August, obviously, and we sat close to those French windows. They were open and you started flapping around because a wasp landed in your wine."

Fiona stared at the curtained doors and tried to imagine them open and full of evening sunshine. She pictured the room devoid of tinsel, garlands and Christmas cracker detritus. Yes, she did remember. It was like a mist clearing in her mind. "It was the first time you said *I love you*. To me." The first sentence was out before she could censor it and the second had to be added to dilute any meaning that he might read in to it.

"I didn't think you'd remember."

She shrugged. "You know me, Little Miss Attention to Detail."

They'd both gone traditional over the choice of main course and it was a relief to focus on requesting the bread sauce and redcurrant jelly from further up the table rather than on any more details of that long-ago birthday. Fiona didn't want Rob to remind her that it had also been the first night they'd slept together. She unwound the bacon blankets from her two sausage pigs and placed them at the edge of her plate. Bacon made her thirsty.

"Do you mind if I . . . ?" Rob was gesturing at the two rashers. "You always used to plonk them straight on my plate." He paused. "Not that we actually spent that many Christmases together. And for that I am truly sorry."

Fiona ignored his last sentence and transferred the slivers of cured meat to him. In return, and without asking, he tipped his plate and scraped red cabbage onto her slices of turkey. She felt heat rise in her cheeks. Swapping food like this after a gap of so many years felt like an act too intimate to be done in public.

By the time the raspberry roulade arrived, Fiona's stomach was suffering not only from food overload but also from the emotional tightness of being in such close proximity to her ex-husband and the memories he evoked. He'd released the cork by mentioning that birthday, and now past images were overflowing in her mind like the magic porridge pot: paddling in the sea at Blackpool on their first weekend away together, a visit to the zoo the day after she discovered she was pregnant, massive ice cream sundaes on their Lake Garda honeymoon because there was no more worrying about fitting into their wedding outfits. She took two mouthfuls of the roulade and put her spoon down.

"May I?" Rob gestured at her plate.

She nodded. He gave her his well-scraped Christmas pudding and custard bowl and started on the roulade, using her spoon.

"I run marathons now," he said when he'd finished the soft pink and white roll. "It keeps the weight down and helps the mental health."

"Wow!" The old Rob had derided any exercise other than football, and the term 'mental health' would never have passed his lips.

"I thought that would surprise you. The mental health bit anyway. Back then, it would have been seen as a weakness. Society always gave the message that the man had to be strong to care for his woman. That didn't work for us, did it?"

There was no answer to that.

"But times have changed. My last job before I retired was with a big multi-national organisation who bombarded us with emails about mental health and the things they offered to help us achieve a healthy mind. I had nothing to lose except the baggage from that dreadful time. So, I took up a personal recommendation from someone in my support group and went to counselling."

Rob was metamorphosing into a new man before her eyes. Fiona was seeing a part of him that he'd kept well hidden. Physically, he was little changed. His dark hair was now verging on silver but it was still all there. He was a little stockier than in his youth but she could imagine him pounding the streets in Lycra. She had a new respect for him.

"It's pearl, this year," he said. "Thirty years on Christmas Eve."

A sharp little arrow hit the bullseye in her heart. "I think about her every day."

"Me too. And the woman she might have become. The counselling doesn't take away the memories and the love but it goes some way towards managing the guilt. Not that you've got any guilt to manage."

Their chairs were now angled towards each other, shutting out the rest of the room.

"Coffee? Tea?" The interruption from the waitress brought Fiona to her senses. Getting too close to Rob was dangerous, but on the other hand it was a luxury to be with someone who had shared that awful time thirty years ago.

He still drank his coffee black with one sugar. On request the waitress fetched Fiona an individual pot of decaffeinated tea. Rob laughed. "On your birthday they didn't do anything decaffeinated. Now it's as common as vegan options on the menu."

"I just came to check that you two newbies were OK." Alison had slipped into the empty seat opposite Rob. "But you seem to have hit it off."

"We used to know each other back in the day," Rob explained lightly.

"Well, don't hog each other all evening. There's dancing and mingling to be done."

"We should meet up again, for old time's sake." He handed Fiona a business card. "Just in case you binned my letter. Most of the information's not relevant now I'm retired but the mobile number's still the same — give me a call and we'll go for coffee. Please." There was a barely discernible note of pleading in his voice.

Fiona looked at the card. He'd written *reparation* and underlined it twice. She slipped the card into her handbag. She'd think about whether to act on it later. Coming face to face with her ex-husband hadn't been the emotional catastrophe she'd feared; it had left her with a surprisingly positive feeling and a reminder of the closeness they'd shared early in their relationship. But taking the decision to actually instigate future contact was a big step and probably a further complication her life didn't need right now. He appeared to be a new man wanting to make amends for the past, but what would that demand of her? If she opened up the compartment labelled 'Rob', would she enjoy increased warmth and light or would she release the evils of Pandora's box?

Alison was serious about getting everyone to mingle after the meal. She made a point of introducing Fiona and Rob to different sets of people and there was no further chance for them to converse with each other that evening.

Joe texted to say he was outside in the car thirty minutes earlier than they'd arranged. Fiona bristled as she apologised and said goodbye to the group who were discussing setting up a book club within the Retired Means Active membership. Getting her teeth into organising something like that would have embedded her into the club. She wondered whether Joe didn't trust her to be out on her own.

In bed he reached for her but she pleaded a headache from the wine — in reality, she wanted to be alone in her head to process the re-emergence of Rob and whether she should bin his business card or dial the number.

CHAPTER 23

This time Fiona's sleepless night wasn't Joe's fault. It was her indecision over Rob. If she contacted him again to find out more about his reparation idea there was the risk of spotlighting difficult memories and plunging herself back to that dark place she'd inhabited thirty years ago. And there was the risk of releasing additional complications into her relationship with Joe: he accepted, but wasn't over the moon about, her close platonic friendship with Meeko, so how would he feel about a friendship with her ex-husband? To turn it the other way, how would she feel if Joe was choosing to meet with Rose even if there were no children to keep them close? She would definitely be wary of such a friendship. But if she resisted Rob's pull then she wasn't opening up new compartments to see where they might lead her. As dawn broke, she determined the only way to get some proper perspective on the previous evening was to go for a run and catch Meeko at breakfast. Joe was still breathing heavily at her side. Fiona crept downstairs and took her phone from the charger. There was a text from her mother, sent at 4 a.m.:

The days are long and empty. The nights are even worse. Would really appreciate a visit?

The guilt was like a brick wall toppling onto her. She'd got so wrapped up in her own life that she'd hardly spared a thought for her mother, who, in contrast, had so little in her life. If only it was possible to transplant half of her complicated situation to her mother. The old lady would love to get her teeth into the web of problematic people and connections that was fastening itself tightly around Fiona.

She sidelined the run and went straight into the shower instead. Beneath the pummelling of hot water, she remembered Adele's agreement to extending a baby shower invitation to her grandmother-by-proxy. That would earn Fiona brownie points. Her mum would be delighted and, as the messenger, Fiona could bask in the glory of the invitation. It might go some way to mitigating the disaster of that awful date with Tony.

As she closed her eyes and massaged coconut shampoo into her scalp, Rob's face came back to her. Two versions of her ex-husband, old and young, separated by a huge question mark. The correct, self-preserving action would be to shred his business card and to stay away from him at any club events. But even as she was resolving to do this, Fiona knew she couldn't follow it through. There were too many questions. The only way to properly come to terms with the events of thirty years ago was to get everything out in the open. Rob's 'reparation' might be the key to doing that. And finding peace of mind over Amber would give the relationship with Joe a better chance.

Joe. She rinsed the shampoo and reached for the similarly tropically-scented conditioner. Joe. He'd sidestepped the question when she'd asked about his early arrival last night. Maybe this was how long-term, live-in relationships worked and she'd have to get used to factoring in the needs of another person in all her arrangements.

When Fiona went back into the bedroom, he was in his boxer shorts and hunting through the single drawer in her chest that she'd allocated to him. She pulled her towelling robe more tightly around her. "Why did you come early for me last night?" she tried the question again.

"I couldn't remember what time we agreed." He was still searching for something.

"It's not hard to remember a single instruction for a few hours."

"Maybe not for you, little Miss Organised." He paused in his hunt and looked up. "To be honest, I was tired after a long day *at work* being nice to patients who produce every excuse under the sun for not sticking to the exercises that would strengthen their knees, ease their spinal discomfort or increase the flexibility in their hips."

Fiona didn't like the emphasis on the words 'at work'. He was muddying the waters with resentment at her early-retired status. She'd saved to retire early and wasn't looking to him for financial support. If anything, it was the other way around.

"Did you allow Rose any freedom?" she snapped back at him. Then she was angry with herself for letting her confusion over Rob wind her up and make her react in this way.

Joe stared at her. "Rose wasn't like you. She enjoyed her family."

"Excuse me! You and Adele aren't actually my family and have only recently parachuted in." Fiona tried not to think about the family she might have had, if things had been different thirty years ago. She collected her clothes and went to get dressed in the bathroom.

* * *

Still angry, she rapped sharply on the front door of her mother's flat. Then she realised she had to tame her mood — none of this was her mother's fault. She took some deep breaths and listened for her mother's footsteps; usually she was at the door within seconds, either eager for company or ready with some admonishment for her only child. Today there was silence. Fiona knocked again. Nothing. The old lady must have gone out. Fiona hadn't responded to the early hours text to say that she was on her way — another little bit of organisation that had slipped through her fingers because there was too much other stuff going on in her life.

On the brink of walking away, she changed her mind. She'd come here to earn brownie points and get some positivity and goodwill into at least one of her relationships. The key to her mother's flat was on the ring with her own house keys. She unlocked the door. The hallway was as neat as ever but there were no slippers by the door and no sign of the old cardigan that her mother wore around the flat in the winter but always took off and hung by the door before she went anywhere public. The little backpack which served as a handbag was still on the hall table. Fiona suddenly felt cold.

"Mum?"

No response. There were four doors off the hallway: kitchen/lounge, bathroom, 'jigsaw' room and bedroom. All of them were ajar. Fiona wanted to run away, scared of what she might find. "Mum?"

The bed was neatly made. The bathroom was empty. That left only one room. Fiona steeled herself and walked into the open-plan kitchen/lounge. The breakfast washing-up was on the draining rack and her mum was in her usual armchair, eyes closed and head lolling to one side. Steeled for the worst, Fiona walked closer, eyes on her mum's chest. The old cardigan was rising and falling slowly. Fiona's own chest sagged as the breath she hadn't realised she was holding escaped her lungs. It was always at the back of her mind that one day she would find her mother's body. It was inevitable, as she was the person who visited most and had a key if the door wasn't answered. If the warden called and got no answer, Fiona suspected she would initially give her mother the benefit of the doubt and then, after a certain time period had elapsed, call

Fiona and ask her to go in and check. No one wants to find a dead person.

"Mum! Wakey-wakey." There was a smudge of saliva on the old lady's cheek. Fiona gently shook her mother's shoulder.

"Uuuh . . . what . . ." The older lady opened her eyes, blinked several times and then re-joined the world. Relief cascaded through Fiona. "I must have nodded off. I had a terrible night's sleep so I got up and had breakfast at five."

"You sent me a text, remember? Asking me to visit?"

Her mum sat up straight, picked up her glasses from the table and put them on. "So I did. I'll make tea." She pressed her hands into the arms of the chair, ready to push herself up.

"No, I'll do it."

In the kitchen Fiona breathed deeply. For a few seconds she'd thought this was the day she'd been dreading, and now a weird kind of elation had taken over. One day it would happen and perhaps it would be a blessing if her mother was taken overnight and quickly. But it would also be catastrophic — Dorothea's death would leave Fiona orphaned, childless and without siblings. For a few seconds she panicked. Then an image of Meeko with his twinkling eyes and dimples came into her head, followed by the thought of the other compartments which were slowly opening. Joe would be there. And Rob had offered a possible olive branch. Maybe she could even build a relationship with Adele when they weren't jostling under the same roof. All she had to do was stay open to the possibilities. But she still hoped her mum had a few more years yet.

Fiona warmed the teapot with scalding kettle water, spooned in tea leaves and flicked the switch to bring the water back up to the boil again. She popped a slice of bread in the toaster in case Dorothea was peckish again after such an early breakfast, and then spread it thickly with butter and marmalade. The pair of them rarely saw eye to eye but they were all each of them had.

Dorothea was back to her usual alert self when Fiona carried the tray into the lounge.

"Oh, you are a good girl!" Her mother went straight for the plate of toast and Fiona basked in the rare words of praise.

"I've come with an invitation, Mum." The older lady looked towards Fiona's handbag as if expecting an envelope to be handed over. "Not a formal one — that's not how young people do things nowadays. You remember I told you about Joe's daughter, Adele? She's having a baby shower for all her female friends and you are invited."

Dorothea's face had lit up at the mention of an invitation but now it frowned into confusion. "A baby shower — don't they have those plastic baths anymore? And why invite people to watch? The baby hasn't been born yet, has it?"

Fiona fought to keep a straight face. "No, Mum. Baby showers are American, like trick or treating and Black Friday. It's a party to celebrate the impending birth of the baby. It's an excuse for presents and frivolity. Sometimes it's used to announce the sex of the baby."

"And she wants me to come?"

"Yes." There was no need to say it had been Fiona's idea to invite Dorothea.

"I would like that very much. Should I write a note of acceptance? What present should I bring? Me and you will need to go shopping. And what should I wear? How formal is it?"

"Too many questions!" Fiona smiled at her mother's enthusiasm and imagined a gaggle of twenty-somethings writing out precise invitation acceptance cards in fountain pen 'a la Jane Austen'. "A note is not required. There'll be no formality. Wear whatever makes you feel comfortable in a room of strangers. I'll get gift vouchers for us to give her jointly." Fiona remembered the supermarket trip. "I bet her friends will go for cute little outfits but what she really needs is the practical stuff — like a plastic bath — but she hasn't thought about that yet." Fiona added an item to the list she'd started in her notepad app. Lists on the go, rather than pinned to the fridge, were new to her but were the only way to stop her head exploding with the baggage that Joe and Adele had brought.

Dorothea dabbed at the toast crumbs around her lips with the kitchen roll that Fiona had put beneath the plate on the tray. "A party to go to! And a new baby coming! And a granddaughter-by-proxy! I can hold my own at the coffee mornings now. I was thinking . . . for Christmas, could you get me one of those phones, like yours? I want to show photos around like everyone else."

"Absolutely."

Again her mother's face lit up with pleasure and, for once, Fiona felt that she was achieving her mother's high expectations of what a daughter should be.

CHAPTER 24

Fiona felt good when she got into the car to come home. That was one relationship back on an even keel. But there were a few more to go. Rob, for instance. She'd thought about it and had come to a decision: she needed to put him straight on the fact that he could expect nothing from her. Not reparation and not friendship. If Joe found out she was keeping secrets or had restarted communication with her ex-husband, it would threaten their companionable journey into old age. She pulled over in the car, and while she was still feeling confident, dialled the number on Rob's business card.

"Coffee? Great, I'm free now." His enthusiasm gave her cold feet. He was expecting more than she could give. But she had to see him as soon as possible and tell him face to face to avoid the expectations in his head growing to gargantuan proportions.

Twenty minutes later they were sitting in the window of One More Bean, the only independent coffee shop in the town. Having his full attention was like being back in the early days of their relationship when everything was positive and hopeful. His eyes were bright and dancing and she didn't want to quash his mood, so she found herself prattling while she plucked up the courage to say what she actually wanted to. "If we don't support places like this—" she gestured round at the tables, housed in cosy inglenooks and decorated with fresh flowers — "every high street in the country becomes the same homogenised blob. It's like the large numbers of us women over a certain age who dress in beige and brown — without individual colour, we become one invisible mass."

Rob sipped his coffee and ignored her words. He didn't seem to share her nerves. When he spoke, his voice was normal. "You never married again? Never tried for another baby?"

Fiona hoped he hadn't noticed her wince at the question. Counselling or no counselling, he didn't have the empathy to lead gently up to such a difficult subject. Or maybe that was the point of counselling, to get things out in the open. "No." She didn't have to justify her response but the words came out anyway. "I didn't have the capacity to trust anymore."

This time he winced. "I'm sorry. I never dreamed that my stupid actions would have such a long-lasting impact on you." His hand hovered over the table, as though he was about to place it on hers. She immediately put both hands around the tall latte glass in front of her and tried to take comfort from its warmth.

"How could you destroy our lives like that? And the life of an unborn child?"

"I was trying to do the opposite. I was trying to build a better life for all of us."

"By gambling our money away?" The conversation wasn't going to plan. She'd come here to tell him that she was in a steady relationship and didn't need ghosts from the past rocking the boat. She'd moved on from that terrible time and didn't want to be involved in his 'reparation'. She'd done nothing that required reparation. But now he was dragging her back.

"At first it was just a bit of fun — an office sweepstake, a night at the greyhounds, a tiny lottery win. Every time I tried, I won something. It was as though I had the Midas touch." He took a sip of black coffee.

Fiona sighed. He'd said all this three decades earlier in those black days at the end of December. Hearing the same words now didn't change how she felt about his actions back then.

"We were trying for a baby and I wanted to give you the option of being a stay-at-home mum. At that time, you were a perfectionist, maybe you still are, but I thought you would struggle to split yourself between home and work. I wanted to free you of that struggle. Given my unfailing luck, I thought that if I studied form and placed my bets judiciously, it would be easy to win enough money to allow you to take a year or two off work."

Back then she'd argued that he was trying to blame her by calling her a perfectionist; now, with the benefit of age and experience, she was able to let it go. It wasn't always an insult. Looking at his older face, creased with experience, his dark hair sprinkled with the silver of age and his eyes still with the same plea to understand, she actually believed that he had started his 'scheme' with the best intentions and out of love for her. Unexpectedly, and three decades too late, something started to thaw inside her.

"But it wasn't. My lucky streak collapsed. I tried to chase my losses. And it ended badly." He moved the sugar bowl from side to side on the table. "But you know this already."

Back then, with the pain of losing Amber acute and all-consuming, Fiona hadn't listened to him properly and hadn't tried to understand. Now, with her grief dulled by time, she began to comprehend. And to shoulder her own share of guilt. Back then, society had expected men to be the breadwinners, to put their women first and to keep their own emotions buttoned up. Fiona's younger self had judged and punished him unfairly. He was being as honest as he could with her and he deserved her honesty in return. "I'm not an innocent in this." There was a lump in her throat and she felt tears on her cheeks. "I was too wrapped up in my own misery. I was a bit of a diva — I expected all the sympathy and attention to be centred on me because I was the one who had physically lost Amber. I was the one going through the medical stuff." Emotion stopped her talking. Unconsciously, her hand had gone back to the table and now Rob was squeezing it and looking her in the eye. She wanted him to hug her, to forgive her and to make everything better. These were the same things she'd wanted back then; the things she had punished him for not providing. Now she realised that those things had to come from within her. To move forward she had to stop blaming others and learn to love herself.

"No — you were never a diva." There were tears in his eyes too. "I was the one to blame. For everything."

"They told me at the hospital . . . they said . . . losing Amber was probably not related to the bailiffs." She couldn't look at him. She'd never told anyone this before. "They said it would probably have happened anyway. And then they told me the statistics for how common miscarriage is. But I didn't believe them because I wanted to blame you. I was so angry about everything. It suited me to make it your fault. Over the years, blaming you made it easier. Don't ask why — it just helped me to move on by putting you in the baddy compartment and throwing away the key." There was an uncomfortable tension in her wrists; her hands were squeezing tightly against the rigid glass. This honesty made her vulnerable and open to attack — something the old Fiona avoided at any cost.

For a moment there was shock etched on his face and he looked almost angry. Then his features softened again and he handed her a napkin from the stainless-steel holder on the table. "I appreciate you being honest with me. I wasn't looking for this."

They both fell silent. Fiona blew her nose and then picked up her tall latte glass and, for a second, watched her hand tremble. Then she cradled it more gently in two hands. Rob stirred another spoonful of sugar into his coffee without seeming to realise what he was doing. She watched his face as he winced at the excessive sweetness. She slowed her breathing in an effort to regain control.

When the wave of emotion had subsided, she spoke again. "So, why are we here raking over the past?"

His turn to blow his nose. "My counsellor suggested reparation in order to bring closure and acceptance of what happened back then. I think she's right. And I think doing it together will be more effective."

Fiona could feel her guard rising again, like a metal barrier sliding into place. "What do you mean by *reparation*?"

"Trying to make amends for the wrong I did back then."

"And me too?" Now the moment of revelation was over, she was glad Rob knew the truth, but her stomach twisted at the thought of sharing this with anyone else.

"You have nothing to make amends for." He was still painting her as whiter than white, even though she'd treated him shabbily. "But I'd appreciate your help. I think it will make my own actions more powerful."

"What actions?"

"I'm going to talk to groups about the dangers of gambling. I've got the backing of the local gamblers' support group and they will get me into colleges, schools, young offenders' institutions, and possibly even prisons."

"I don't understand how I can help. I've never had a problem with gambling."

"You can explain the massive impact that me gambling away everything we owned had on you and . . . on our baby."

Fiona's hand went to the pendant around her neck. "Even though I lied to you? I'm not strong enough to admit to that."

"The fact that you lied adds weight to how badly I damaged you."

Fiona had arranged to meet her ex-husband with the intention of heading off any further direct contact and asking him to keep his distance at any future club events. Now it was snowballing into something else. She wanted to say 'yes' to his idea of putting others off gambling. She wanted to be strong enough to talk publicly about Amber and about how and why she hadn't told her then husband the whole truth. But wanting to and being tough enough to weren't the same thing. Plus, there were other difficult conversations to be had first; she couldn't talk about this in public if the people closest to her weren't aware of her past. It wasn't fair. Telling them would be more difficult than telling Rob because he had been part of it and, however he'd taken her confession, she'd had nothing to lose in that relationship. Meeko and Joe needed to know everything, and her mum needed to know how Fiona had concealed the medical truth. This latter conversation needed to happen sooner rather than later as Dorothea and Rob's mum were in contact. And how would this news go down? Dorothea would be angry at her daughter's dishonesty, Meeko would get the kid gloves out and treat her like a delicate china ornament, and Joe . . . Joe was unfathomable. "That is such a good thing to do," she said slowly. "But I need time to decide. It's delicate. I need to talk to . . . a few people."

She thought she detected a drop in the eagerness of Rob's expression. "Of course. Does your partner know everything? Sorry, stupid question, of course you will have told him about your reckless first husband."

"He knows I was married years ago and it didn't work out. That's all." Telling Joe that she'd been hoodwinked by a gambler and lost a baby would have revealed vulnerability. That's why keeping him at arm's length had suited her. She had control over how she presented herself and her past to him. Now, the relief and increased closeness she felt after finally being honest with Rob made her realise that holding information back from the significant people in her life had created the barricades and compartments. And these were stopping her relationships from flourishing to their full potential. And she included Meeko in that.

Rob nodded. "Call me when you've made a decision."

Fiona drained her coffee and pulled her jacket on. Rob followed her to the café door. "You're right," he said. "We do need to support these independents."

She smiled and, outside on the pavement, he pulled her into an unexpected hug. Then he took a step back and looked at her. "Has there been anyone over the years who you've trusted enough to tell everything?"

"I've come close to it." Rob had a way of looking at her that made her want to keep talking. There was no need to put up a front and nothing to lose. "I've thought about telling my best friend, Meeko. He would be sympathetic and he'd keep the information confidential. But I don't trust him not to start treating me differently. He'd probably wrap me in cotton wool. I don't want that. I don't want my revelation to change our relationship."

Rob reached out and gave her hands a squeeze. "I understand."

Then Rob turned right and Fiona went left. As she walked, she caught sight of Meeko a little way ahead. His gait looked awkward. She called to him and he glanced round, hesitating mid-step. She waved and called for him to wait but he turned forward again and increased his pace. It was impossible to know whether he was deliberately blanking her or hadn't realised who it was. Fiona stopped trying to catch him and gazed, unseeing, into the window of a women's budget fashion shop, trying to gather her thoughts. She turned her head in the direction taken by Rob, her mind in a turmoil.

CHAPTER 25

The worn lace in Meeko's left trainer had finally snapped as he jogged level with One More Bean. The reduction in tension across his foot made his heel start to move in the shoe. If he carried on, he'd either get a blister or trip up. He stopped just after the café door, crouched down and attempted to tie the two fraying ends together.

The sound of Fiona's voice behind him was a surprise and he was on the brink of standing up to greet her, when his brain started processing the snatches of her words that he could hear above the traffic. "I've thought about telling my . . . friend, Meeko." A lorry braked and then accelerated alongside them. "But I don't trust him . . ." A mother went past pushing a buggy containing a screaming toddler. "He'd probably . . . I don't want that . . . my revelation . . . relationship."

Fiona didn't trust him! Trust him with what? He thought they were best friends. How could he have got their relationship so wrong?

The words of a male voice were lost to the traffic.

He needed to get away. Fiona mustn't see his humiliation. Meeko's brain failed to instruct his hands how to join the ends of the laces. With his back still towards the café and his left toes tightly curled in an effort to keep his trainer on, he hurried away. He turned automatically when she called his name but then thought better of it and continued walking.

He'd thought that he and Fiona trusted each other completely. Whenever they touched accidentally there were sparks and tingles. He'd assumed she'd felt those too and had hoped there was a chance their friendship could develop into something more. These hopes had been the main reason he'd ended the relationship with Lynn. He'd been fond of Lynn and they got on well together but his feelings for her would never be as deep as those he had for Fiona. It hadn't been fair to keep Lynn hanging on.

He'd been waiting patiently for Fiona for two reasons. Firstly, if he made a move before she was ready, it would be a friendship ruined — and Meeko valued his friendship with Fiona more highly than any other relationship in his life.

Secondly, he was giving himself time to become someone that she would be proud to call her 'life partner'. Fiona moved in middle-class circles with people who had proper careers and pension pots. Her friends didn't live hand to mouth in rented flats. He would be an embarrassment at social events when people asked, "What do you do for a living?" Ad hoc yoga teacher with a temporary Father Christmas job wasn't good enough. He needed a salary and a job title and a pension. To that end he had applied for and failed to get all the Fitness Manager jobs that had come up at hotels within a fifteen-mile radius. Apparently, teaching great classes with a loyal clientele was not a qualification that helped when managing staff, timetabling classes, dealing with budgets and organising stuff. Meeko didn't want a Fitness Manager role, but he would have taken it to help his prospects with Fiona.

But now it seemed that Fiona didn't see him as unique and special at all. She didn't trust him. He wasn't good enough. The more he thought about it, the more devastated he felt. The only way forward was to pack up his hopes and dreams.

And he had to do it before he saw her again. That meant avoiding her until he'd got himself in check. He wouldn't let the pregnant girl down by cancelling his appearance at her baby shower, but, until the party, 'Fiona avoidance' was his tactic of choice. He constantly varied his hotel breakfast times, and on the couple of occasions when she arrived slightly ahead of him, he persuaded the staff to do him a takeaway coffee plus a paper bag filled with pastries and a couple of boiled eggs.

CHAPTER 26

By the morning of the baby shower, Adele still hadn't provided a proper list of confirmed guests.

"We're not in the Dark Ages now," she'd said when Fiona had pushed her on this point a few days before. "We're more laid-back than when you were young." Fiona had winced but Adele had been oblivious to her implied insult. "We go with the flow. Don't worry — if we run out of something on the day, I've an app that will get it delivered within thirty minutes." At an expensive premium, thought Fiona.

She had erred on the side of generosity with the food and drink. Only a couple of the bottles of prosecco actually fitted in the fridge, due to the amount of food ready for the buffet table. She'd managed to persuade Adele that takeaway pizzas weren't the best way to go and they'd decided on an 'adult' buffet menu together. The rest of the drink was assembled like a row of miniature soldiers in the December chill of the garage. Mid-afternoon, Fiona went to collect Dorothea plus a mountain of loaded cake tins. The old lady was dressed in the aquamarine skirt and jacket that she reserved for high days and holidays, plus a cream blouse with a little bow at the neck. Her shoes were silver with a little heel and she'd taken care with her hair and make-up.

"You look lovely, Mum."

"I should hope so. Meeting my granddaughter-by-proxy for the first time is an important occasion."

Fiona hoped Adele felt the same way. She carried the cake tins into the house and asked Adele to assist her mother out of the car. Both women were smiling when they came into the kitchen and Adele sported a scarlet splodge on her right cheek that matched her grandmother-by-proxy's lipstick. Fiona grinned.

Between the three of them, but with Fiona as chief labourer, given her mother's age and Adele's condition, food was laid out and furniture rearranged. With quarter of an hour to go before the guests were expected, there was still no sign of Meeko and his Father Christmas outfit. Fiona had assumed he'd arrive early, get changed upstairs and then make a grand ho-ho-ho entrance.

Adele was unconcerned. "Nobody else will be on time. There's a calculation we apply — add thirty minutes and then further five-minute chunks depending on how close you are to the host and how many other people you will know, et cetera, et cetera."

Fiona stared at the girl's serious face. Why hadn't she told her this earlier?

Adele's expression broke into a grin and she gave Fiona a gentle prod. "Got you!"

Fiona felt ancient and gullible. But it didn't matter because the teasing meant Adele was finally loosening up in her company.

"As long as he shows up before people start to leave, it will be fine," Adele said.

Urgent banging on the front door made the three of them jump to attention.

Fiona's heart lifted. "I knew he wouldn't let us down."

For a second, the three of them paused awkwardly in the hallway. Fiona was confused about who was the hostess, her or Adele.

"Don't leave them out in the cold." Dorothea opened the front door.

"Balloons!" Joe stepped inside, pulling his right hand downwards to navigate the doorframe. He held a ribbon attached to a white inflated stork carrying a pink bundle in its beak. In his other hand was a bulky, outsize, but obviously light, carrier bag. "You can't have a party without balloons — especially when it's a celebration for my very first grandchild."

Fiona hardly had the time to introduce Joe and Dorothea to each other before Adele butted in.

"Dad! You promised you'd stay away."

Joe turned back to the doorway. "And I will. I assume you want me to take these away as well?"

"No! Leave them."

Fiona was touched by Joe's thoughtfulness. Whatever his other faults, he definitely had his family's best interests at heart. She raised her eyebrows at Adele to indicate that she should thank her dad for the kind gesture and, at least, give him a peck on the cheek. Adele's eyes met hers for a split second.

"Thanks, Dad." She took the bag from him and Joe handed the stork to Dorothea. "Now go!"

He left with a cheery wave, a handshake for Dorothea and the order to send him lots of photos in real time because it was going to be a lonely evening by himself in the pub.

Dorothea was raising and lowering her arm and watching the stork bob up and down in response. She was like a toddler entranced by a helium balloon for the first time. She took a few steps and the giant bird followed like an obedient pet. She changed the ribbon from right to left hand and repeated her circular walk, the delight on her face growing with every movement. "These weren't invented when I was a child." She swapped arms again and gave short little jerks before stretching upwards, the stork almost reaching the ceiling. "Or, if they were, we couldn't afford them."

Adele untied the handles of the bulging carrier. It disgorged balloons like a mouth blowing bubbles through a hoop of soapy liquid. The hall ceiling became dotted with spheres of pink declaring 'It's a girl!' Dorothea giggled in a way that Fiona never remembered her doing before. Fiona put her arms around the older and younger generation. "It's going to be a good night!"

"Agreed!" Adele high-fived her.

Dorothea gave another smile of delight and held her raised palm towards the other two women. They both returned the palm-smacking gesture.

A second knock at the door brought them back to attention. Dorothea started to turn the handle.

"Wait — the balloons might escape in the wind!" Adele gave little jumps to pull the stray pink celebratory bubbles from the ceiling, pushed them into the lounge and closed the door.

Meeko was on the doorstep in plain clothes and he smiled at Dorothea gripping her balloon. "So, the rumour's true," he said to the old lady.

"What?"

"Babies really are delivered by storks."

Dorothea's face melted into another girlish giggle and she almost pulled Meeko inside. "We have to be careful of the breeze."

Fiona saw her best friend standing there in all his handsome, lithe glory and felt suddenly and confusingly proud. "Ladies," she announced, "let me present Meeko, our Father Christmas for the evening. Meeko, this is Adele, our star mum-to-be, and this is my mother, Dorothea."

"Also a star," said Adele, and then blushed when Fiona smiled appreciatively at her.

Meeko shook hands with each of the two women. When he reached Fiona she leaned slightly towards him, expecting their usual peck on the cheek and anticipating the clean, natural male smell that she loved about him. He seemed to hesitate for a second before kissing her briefly, and then he turned to Adele, pointing at the holdall in his right hand. "Where can

I get changed and what's the plan? Do you want me to stay hidden until a certain moment?"

Inexplicably, Fiona felt slighted, as though something had changed in their relationship. *Don't be silly. It's Adele's evening and Meeko is treating it as such. It's not personal.* The two of them went upstairs, with Adele leading the way in her lumbering baby elephant-style.

After that the guests started to arrive and there was no time to think, never mind dwell on some, possibly imagined, slight by Meeko. Fiona and Dorothea were in and out of the kitchen with drinks, plates and cups. Her mother was slow but careful. Fiona tried hard not to hurry the old lady when they both needed the same bottle of wine or tray of mini-Yorkshires keeping warm in the oven. Adele had selected all the supermarket party food advertised on TV for Christmas buffets.

"Why not?" she'd declared on their second joint shopping trip. "We've got Dad's credit card."

But still Fiona had worried about not having enough and, off her own bat, had done a pile of the derided 'children's party' food as well. Now it was being tackled enthusiastically and Adele was complimented on her 'retro' theme. The young woman was generous enough to explain each time that their family friend, Fiona, had created all the time-warp food.

The volume of chatter in the lounge rose and people spilled into the hallway and kitchen. Fiona had been anxious about too many people invading her space, standing in the nooks and crannies of her home and shedding crumbs, drips and dirt from outside. But now it was happening, the anxiety had been replaced by a pleasant feeling of warmth and joint enterprise. Since the divorce, she'd never thrown a party. Parties and guests couldn't be controlled. It was impossible to hand people a list of rules on arrival or to have twenty pairs of shoes lining the hallway to stop dirt being trodden in, or to ask people to keep still so that the flaky pastry vol-au-vent cases didn't do as their name suggested and fly off the plate at the slightest hint of a breeze. But those worries had fled through the door when the first guest arrived. It felt joyful to have such unbridled happiness and good wishes for Adele happening under her roof.

Her mother had helped herself to a large glass of red wine and taken a seat between two of Adele's school friends on the settee. The young women appeared enthralled by the old lady's description of their school nearly seventy years ago when Dorothea had been head girl. Fiona took the opportunity to slip upstairs and check on Meeko in case he needed help with his costume.

"How are you doing?" Adele had installed him in her own room. The door was ajar but Fiona stayed on the landing, waiting to be invited in, in case he wasn't decent. "Do you need any help?"

"I'm fine. You stay downstairs with your guests."

"They're not my guests, you are, and I appreciate you helping out."

"Don't forget you offered me money and I can't afford to turn that down."

There was a hardness in his voice that she hadn't heard before. She didn't know if it was meant for her or whether it was a reaction to his financial predicament. "I'll fetch the sack of presents," she said. It had taken her, Adele and Joe a whole evening to wrap thirty gifts for Santa to distribute. Adele had decided that she needed to be involved in buying the presents in case Fiona got it completely wrong by choosing cold cream or some other old-lady thing. She had spent ages on the internet trying to find something that would be a lasting reminder of the occasion and which the guests could take back to their respective far-flung unis. She'd decided on hinged silver-effect photo frames with space for two pictures, one either side of the central hinge. Santa would take a picture of the whole group and also a selfie of himself with each guest and Adele. The pictures would be printed and sent out in new year cards with instructions to place them in the frames and to carry them forward into the future with Adele's warmest wishes.

Meeko came out of the bedroom suddenly, bumping into Fiona with his extended belly. She staggered backwards into the bathroom.

"Sorry. I . . ." He looked as though he'd been about to say more, but instead he hoisted the sack onto his shoulder and went downstairs.

Fiona wanted to cry. Their relationship was out of kilter. Something had changed and she didn't know what or why. He began ho-ho-hoing as he reached the hallway. This was followed by excited laughter and a rise in the general volume from the party. Fiona swallowed, blinked, forced a smile and went down to observe.

She and Adele had set up a mini grotto against the far wall of the lounge. Two large pot plants framed the settee and Adele had strung multi-coloured tinsel from one to the other, like a fairyland washing line. She'd wrapped a string of tiny tree lights around the stem of each plant and these now twinkled in a magical fashion. Santa sat in the middle of the settee with Adele on his left and a slowly changing occupant on his right. There was much embarrassed giggling as he asked them what they wanted for Christmas and then pulled both girls in close for the selfie. When all the guests had received their gifts, there was one present left in the sack. Adele called Dorothea forward, introducing her as her new grandmother-by-proxy. The wine had gone to her mother's head and she was escorted to the settee in a wavering line. Fiona moved nearer to properly hear the interaction between Meeko and her mother.

"Now tell me, young lady, what would you like Santa to bring you for Christmas?"

Dorothea pondered for a moment, then she looked straight at Fiona and spoke decisively. "I want the right man to present himself to my daughter so that I can die happy. I want to know that she will have someone to love, care and worry about her even after I am gone. I don't want her to be alone in the world."

Everyone's eyes swivelled from Santa to Fiona. She turned away from the stares, wanting the ground to swallow her whole. Dorothea was drunk and maudlin. Why was she making such a request, and publicly, when she knew Fiona and Joe's relationship had become more serious with him moving in? The evening had suddenly taken a turn for the worse, especially coupled with Meeko's strange attitude towards her.

Santa seemed as taken aback at Dorothea's words as the rest of the guests. Fiona plucked up the courage to look at Adele. She wanted to signal to her that Dorothea was talking rubbish, but Adele's eyes were switching between Santa and her grandmother-by-proxy. Now the old lady was looking at Meeko, waiting for his answer to her gift request. He had to say something, everyone was waiting. Fiona started to sidle towards the hallway — she couldn't face any further embarrassment.

"Santa can't bring living things," he said eventually. "They are difficult to wrap and tend to suffocate when parcelled up for the long journey from the North Pole." A whisper of laughter went round the guests like a Mexican wave and the atmosphere eased. The tension in Fiona's shoulders subsided a little.

Then there were calls for Adele to open the shower of baby gifts provided by the guests and Fiona brought in the surprise cake she'd had specially made. The baker had decorated it with exquisitely formed pink roses and a tiny crib. There was a round of oohs and aahs as she set it on the table and, after everyone had finished capturing it for digital posterity, Fiona sliced it and Dorothea handed out the serviette-wrapped pieces of Victoria sandwich cake covered in thick icing. Meeko took the activity of cake eating as his cue to disappear back upstairs.

A plain-clothes version of Father Christmas, with a miraculously reduced and toned stomach and bum, re-emerged after the last guest had left. Fiona surreptitiously handed him an envelope holding his fee in cash.

"Thank you so much." Adele stood on tiptoe to kiss him on his now whisker-free cheek. "You were wonderful."

Meeko gave her a hug in return. "Good luck for all that is to come." Then he hugged Dorothea as well. Fiona was next in line. He looked at her sadly, gave her a polite hug, picked up his holdall and left. Fiona stared at the inside of her front door and felt she'd lost her best friend without having a clue as to what she'd done wrong.

CHAPTER 27

Fiona woke too early again the following morning. Still twenty minutes to go before Joe's alarm went off for work. She lay still to avoid waking him. He'd arrived home the previous evening just as Meeko left and he'd brought Indian food.

"I didn't want to sit at a table for one and eat alone," he'd explained, setting out what plates and cutlery hadn't already been used for the party. "And I reckoned you three would probably be hungry — buffet food never fills me up."

Fiona had been about to protest that they'd all had plenty, but once she smelled the Kashmir chicken and special fish balti she realised she'd done more serving than eating and was ravenous. After tucking in, Adele's eyelids drooped, she pushed her plate to one side and said she couldn't possibly eat another thing. Dorothea had fallen quiet after an excited, conversation-monopolising monologue about how wonderful the whole evening had been and what a good man Meeko was and how nice Adele's friends had been to her.

"I felt like a youngster again today," she said. "It was a shame Santa couldn't grant me my wish but I'm sure we'll make it happen somehow, won't we, Fiona?"

Joe looked up questioningly. Adele looked embarrassed. Fiona caught her mother's eye and shook her head. The old lady gave a little shrug. To shut the subject down, Fiona had suggested it was time she drove her mother home.

And now here she was, the morning after the night before, worrying about Meeko's coolness and remembering that the party clearing up was still waiting to be done downstairs. Last night's atmosphere had smothered her anxiety about mess, stains, crumbs and footprints, but now it sat in her mind with an evil grin and, coupled with Meeko's weird attitude, made the whole event seem a terrible mistake.

"You were brilliant last night." Joe was awake and whispering in her ear. "I am so grateful. And how wonderful to see three generations of women getting along together."

"It was good while it lasted." Fiona sat up. "But the clearing up is waiting. Even the smelly takeaway cartons didn't get put outside."

Joe failed to notice that the last sentence was a dig at him. "Adele will help."

No chance — she never surfaces before eleven. The house can't stay in a mess until then.

Fiona slipped out of bed and into the shower. Pounding hot water followed by caffeine and toast should energise her sufficiently for the task ahead. Downstairs she attempted to act like a blinkered horse, forbidding herself to look around until she'd eaten and drunk. But in the kitchen, she was forced to clear the sticky containers from the table to make room for breakfast. *Why didn't Joe do this while I was taking Mum home? He had the time — he wasn't in bed when I got back.* Her brain paused in mid-thought. No relationship was perfect and most of the time he was considerate. She thought of the pleasure his impromptu balloons had brought to her mother and how they'd given the house a party atmosphere. The ruby pendant proved his generosity. Perhaps she needed to cut him some slack, as she would expect him to do for her. How many times had her mother told her to stop treating life like a computer project with milestones and deadlines? Was that why the old lady had asked 'Santa' for such an embarrassing 'gift' — she was worried that her daughter's personality made her unlovable? Was Meeko's cold shoulder last night related to her controlling nature as well? But she couldn't recall any incident when she should have been more tolerant of Meeko or he of her. She loved the man.

Fiona was studying her toast crumbs as though they were tea leaves when Adele walked into the kitchen yawning. She was wearing an old tracksuit with the waistband pulled tight across her bump.

"Here she is." Joe, dressed in his work polo shirt, followed behind. "Ready and willing — but you might need to direct operations. Got to rush — I've slotted in an early patient."

"Eat first. And then we'll get started." Fiona didn't know whether Adele was going to be a help or a hindrance.

Adele did everything she was asked, but slowly. She operated at 'Dorothea speed', interspersed with intervals of examining the baby gifts and exclaiming over tiny sleeves, cute motifs and adorable teddies. Fiona powered away in the background with the vacuum cleaner, cloth and duster. At least doing things herself meant they got done properly.

"I told you nothing would be damaged, didn't I?"

Adele had been right and the house was almost back to normal. A thought grew at the back of Fiona's mind. The warm camaraderie of last night had been wonderful. And Adele would need a christening party, wouldn't she?

"What your mum asked for was odd." Adele broke into her thoughts. "About finding the right man? It was as though she'd completely forgotten about Dad and you living together."

"She gets funny ideas. It could have been her oblique way of hinting that she wants me and your dad to stay together long-term." Fiona didn't believe this but she wanted to skip over the subject until she'd got things clear in her own head.

"No. There was more to it than that." The girl's face was serious. "She's got Meeko in mind for you."

Fiona's heart missed a beat. "Mum barely knows the man. And anyway, he's sworn off all women after Lynn."

"Are you sure? I don't think Dad would have liked the way Meeko looked at you last night. As though he was hungry for you but cross with you at the same time." Adele paused and Fiona's brain circled like a fairground waltzer. "You're so different from Mum. Meeko's a better match for you than Dad."

Then Fiona realised what was going on. Adele was talking up the possibility of a relationship with Meeko so Joe would be free and ready for a reconciliation with his ex-wife. Meeko hadn't given out any signals about fancying Fiona, and he wouldn't. In fact the opposite was true; Meeko appeared to be cooling their friendship.

CHAPTER 28

The next day Rob followed up on his coffee shop promise to stay in touch about the two of them working together on gambling awareness talks. His text was straight to the point:

> *Have you had chance to check in with the people you needed to talk to? What about your other half? There's nothing for him to disapprove of, is there? Or do you want to introduce us so that he can see I'm harmless?*

Fiona had been trying to build up to the necessary conversations but it wasn't something that could be just dropped into small talk. A couple of times she'd jogged out to the hotel, all prepared to be honest with Meeko, but she'd missed him every single time. Proper conversation with Joe was almost impossible, he was either at work, out with his mates or Adele was floating around. The prospect of telling Dorothea was most scary but also the most urgent.

"I will do that today," she muttered to herself. Her fists were clenched tight. "After I've spoken to Rob."

Doing the talks would get her away from the increasingly claustrophobic situation at home and give her something to think about other than babies and second-guessing the men in her life. She sent a message back:

> No need for Joe to vet you. I'm up for it. Let's discuss details in One More Bean this afternoon.

Her ex-husband replied with a smiley face and a thumbs up emoji. She grinned — it felt good to be part of a team after losing the camaraderie of work. And she had a question to ask him about something that he did all those years ago.

If she was going to become part of this project it was only fair that she took something to the table and didn't expect Rob to do all the legwork. She opened her laptop and started researching gambling addiction. Fiona had done enough public speaking in her career to know it was essential to find an angle on her subject that enthused her and made her feel passionate, otherwise there'd be no fire in her words and what she had to say wouldn't hit home. There were many case histories online of middle-aged men whose home lives had fallen apart as their gambling losses mounted. Fiona felt for them and their families but she wasn't left brimming with enthusiasm to spread the word and prevent others following this same path. But her pulse quickened when she came across some articles about female gambling addiction. Women of all ages were risking their household's money for a quick thrill. It was a total contradiction that the 'homemaking' sex would stake everything in that home on the pull of a virtual fruit machine handle or the turn of a card.

There was a blog post about a female gambler in her early sixties. "My age," Fiona whispered. Suddenly this addiction felt closer to home and she needed to know more.

The anonymous blogger revealed that the only reason she wanted to win was to have the funds to carry on gambling — not to use the prize money to improve the life of her or her family, as one might expect. Sometimes this sexagenarian could keep herself away from gambling for a week or two, or even, more rarely, a whole month, before being sucked back into the vicious cycle. Elsewhere on the internet, younger women revealed how no one questioned why they were glued to their phones. "They don't suspect at all that I'm gambling," said one interviewee in her twenties. "In most people's heads, gamblers are male."

Another article described how the traditional gambling support groups are predominantly male, which puts women off attending and leaves them to battle the devil alone. Then Fiona discovered an interview with the founder of the first all-female gambling support group. "Women can be drawn into gambling when on maternity leave and struggling with the isolation and frustration of caring for a newborn. Existing support groups can be difficult for them to access because they make little allowance for women's responsibilities. Female support groups need to take a different route to those for their male counterparts."

Yes! This was it! This was Fiona's angle into speaking passionately about gambling addiction. She wouldn't be focusing solely on her experience as a victim of Rob's gambling, she would also be an advocate for increasing the help specifically targeted to women with a gambling problem.

"What do you think?" she asked Rob after telling him about the information she'd dug up. "Can part of what we do be aimed specifically at women? I don't want to be seen solely as a victim."

Rob sipped his black Americano. "It's so good to see you fired up about this, Fi."

Fi. That was his old nickname for her. His use of it simultaneously warmed her and put her on the alert.

"What you're suggesting is a brilliant idea. Let's get in touch with the organiser of this support group you've found and get some advice on how to initiate a similar group in this area."

Fiona nodded. "We'll need professionals on board, and funding and all sorts of other things." Her logical planning process kicked into gear and a surge of excitement raced through her body. "I think I've just found my retirement *raison d'être!*" Somewhere within Fiona was the sound of a door clicking open. It was louder and more echoey than the doors to those other compartments; this was the sound of the entrance to a long, dark tunnel clanging open. It would take time to clear out all the debris and cobwebs, but hope was already creeping inside. By bringing the hurt from thirty years ago into the light, there was a chance that Fiona could strengthen herself and her current relationships for the future. She felt a bubble of elation.

"The old twosome rides again, Fi!" Rob reached across the table and gave her a gentle punch on the shoulder. "We used to be good together, and we can be again."

Now added to that elation was a contradictory feeling of warmth and hyper-alertness. Rob was right, their relationship had been great, until his great big boot had crashed down on it. Having this feeling of partnership again *was* brilliant, but a leopard doesn't change its spots. Plus, there was Joe to think of . . . but Joe didn't need to get in the way of her and Rob working platonically together.

"Shall I concentrate on contacting that female group?" she suggested. "And you continue liaising with the existing support groups in this area about the best way for us to move forward?"

"Sounds like a plan, partner."

Then they switched to small talk about their mothers while finishing their coffee. Fiona took a breath. This brought things very nicely around to the question that she wanted to ask. "Why did you tell our parents about the miscarriage when I specifically asked you not to?"

Rob looked taken aback and paused before answering. "Selfish reasons. You were drowning in grief. I wanted to grieve as well but one of us had to keep a stiff upper lip in order to keep the show on the road and feed us and shop and wash and everything else. I didn't know how to cope with it all on my own."

168

"We would've managed somehow. You knew that my mother would try to take over and that she'd feel insulted that we hadn't announced the pregnancy earlier. You knew how deep their disappointment could be when anything went wrong in my life. That's the problem with being an only child, you are the sole focus of your parents' attention."

"Yes, I knew all of that. But I wanted *my* parents to know why I was upset, why I was acting out of character. I wanted *their* support. But I couldn't tell them without telling your parents as well."

Shame stopped Fiona raising her eyes from the table. How could she have been so self-centred? Was that part of the only-child legacy too? No. Blaming circumstance led nowhere. She looked at Rob. "I'm sorry. I should never have expected you to keep such a huge secret." She fiddled with her hands. "I realise now that sometimes we have to make welcoming gangways from one compartment to another for life to work properly."

"What?" He looked at her as though she was talking in riddles.

"Nothing. Just something I'm struggling with at the moment."

They parted on the pavement outside One More Bean. Again, Rob hugged her closely. Fiona shrugged it off as 'for old time's sake' and then decided belt and braces would be safer. "Just friends? Yes?"

He grinned and high-fived her. "Absolutely."

Before her determination could dissipate, she drove to her mother's flat.

"Fiona! What a lovely surprise. I've made scones. I'm not going to offer you one because I know you'll say no, but you will take a couple home for Adele and Joe, won't you? Tea?"

"That would be lovely, Mum. Thanks." Even though she'd just drunk coffee, Fiona knew this conversation would go better if they both had a cup of tea in front of them.

When her mother had stopped messing about with the milk jug and teapot, Fiona jumped straight in before courage deserted her. "I need to talk to you about my miscarriage."

"Oh!"

"I always blamed Rob and the arrival of the bailiffs for what happened. But that isn't the medical truth. The nurses told me it was probably just one of those things that would have happened with or without that event. And then they quoted statistics at me." The words tumbled out of her without pause.

"I see."

"I blamed Rob because I wanted him to suffer as much as me. And over time I almost started to believe my own lie."

"Come and sit here." Dorothea patted the empty seat next to her on the sofa.

Fiona moved over and her mother enveloped her in an embrace that smelled of baking, lemon soap, forgiveness and safety. "Thank you for telling me. But why now?"

Fiona explained about meeting Rob and his plans for them both to warn about the evils of gambling.

"That sounds good. Good for both of you."

"One more thing." This felt even harder to say. "Thank you. Thank you for looking after us when it all happened. I know I was surly, unwelcoming and downright rude, but you took no notice and stopped Rob and I sinking into a quagmire. Thank you."

Dorothea embraced her again. "I'm your mother. I don't need thanks."

Fiona's arms went tightly around her mum. When they pulled away, they were both crying and the old lady fetched a box of tissues.

Fiona went home with an old ice cream tub full of scones and the feeling that a massive barrier had come down. Going forward, mother and daughter would be closer and more honest with one another. And when Fiona thought about Rob, she felt energised. Having a project to get her teeth into was good. And it was helping her turn a life corner.

CHAPTER 29

There were only six days until Christmas. The festive season had always been Dorothea's favourite time of year. She had festooned the family home with holly, tinsel and at least two decorated trees, one indoors and one outside. What the Ormeroyd family lacked in size, it made up for in Dorothea's exuberance. Fiona and her parents always had a paper-chain-making evening the week before Christmas. It was these memories that were causing Fiona to blink hard as she wrote her final Christmas cards — a job that should have been accomplished at least a fortnight earlier.

On paper-chain day, Dorothea would retrieve the piles of used wrapping paper she'd neatly folded away from the previous year and the three of them would carefully cut the creased sheets into strips and then glue the ends of the strips together, interlocking each strip with another link in the chain. One year, she and her father had made a chain long enough to reach twice around the edge of the sitting room ceiling. As a child, Fiona had delighted in the magic and colour of it all, mixing up the different papers to produce the gaudiest, but to her the most beautiful chain of all. As a teenager, she'd tried and failed to look down her nose at the family tradition. But the designs of her chains became more sophisticated; she'd stick to hues of the same colour for each chain and had the motto that 'less is more', cutting tiny strips to create mini chains to hang around the pictures and to crown her mother's pot plants. In her father's eyes, whatever Fiona produced was wonderful but her mother was more critical, especially during Fiona's 'minimalist' phase when she tried to insist that all the chains should be made from old brown or white envelopes and the wrapping paper be reused for its original function.

The Ormeroyds had few extended family members but, once decorated, Dorothea filled the house with neighbours, friends and any waif or stray she heard about. There were always at least two pre-Christmas parties, another the day after Boxing Day — "It's a dead sort of day and people need it filled," her mother always used to say — and another on New Year's Eve. When Fiona and Rob married and moved into their own house, Fiona continued the traditions, becoming popular among her neighbours for her generosity, and among her uni friends for a New Year's Eve fixture for which they journeyed from all parts of the country, full of hope for what the next twelve months might bring.

The bailiffs, the divorce and the loss of Amber swept away Fiona's open-hearted spirit, like a volcanic eruption razes a town from the map. The house was gone, their savings were gone, her husband was lost and the most precious thing in the world had died. Every time December came around, the bleakest memories boiled up from their simmering point and burned Fiona again and again. She put a hand up to her face, as though she expected the skin to feel tender and blistered. For the last thirty years Christmas had merely been a series of lists, cards, presents to buy, a couple of Secret Santas at work, ensuring a pleasant day for both her parents, and then, for the last two years, just for her festive-loving Mum — duties to be fulfilled in order to conform to society's expectations, even though neither she nor most of her acquaintances set foot near religion during the whole of the holiday season.

"We need a tree." Adele stood in the doorway of the lounge with her hands in the small of her back and her bump straining against the confines of the maternity jeans. She looked matronly rather than like a girl at the start of her twenties. "At home the tree was always up by now."

"I've got a small artificial one with inbuilt lights in the loft." Joe had bought it the previous year, at the start of their relationship. He'd been horrified when she'd said there was no point bothering with decorations for only one person.

"No! It has to be real. Without the tree smell, it's not Christmas! And the presents need to go under the tree."

The prospect of full-on Christmas decor made Fiona want to curl up and cover her head with her hands. The day the bailiffs came, the house had been ready, with a real tree sheltering a pile of presents — expensive gifts (she'd even indulged in one for Amber — a CD of whale music that her daughter could enjoy *in utero* as Fiona practised relaxation in the months leading up to the birth) purchased on their joint credit card. She later learned they couldn't afford to pay the bill.

"All Mum's Christmas stuff is in our loft above the Airbnb people. Can we buy new, Fiona?" Fiona's face must have shown her lack of enthusiasm because Adele started to plead. "Please? This room looks more like a morgue than a home."

"Meeko's grotto is still there, and the balloons." She pointed at the ceiling where the pink blobs still tickled the white paint. "We can put the presents in a sack in the grotto."

"It's not enough. Please? Remember how good it felt when this place was full of people?"

Adele had chosen the right words. Fiona did want that warmth of feeling back. But that had been created by people, not trashy tinsel or gaudy baubles. But if they were what made the people in the house feel happy, maybe it was the right place to start. She was tempted to hand over money and send Adele on her own — the shops would be a nightmare.

But it wasn't fair to send a heavily pregnant girl on the bus to crowded shops.

The two of them shopped several times over the next few days. For decorations and for food. Fiona coped by persuading herself that, had Amber lived, she would have inherited her grandmother's love of the festive season. Adele insisted on plenty of cheeses and chocolates as well as the traditional turkey and pudding.

"The shops are only closed for *one* day," Fiona tried to argue. "We don't need to buy it all now."

"We do. Twixmas is hibernation time. That's when we hunker down at home, watch films and eat Quality Streets. And your Meeko will expect a good spread," Adele continued.

"He's not *my Meeko*."

"Body language rarely lies . . ."

"You are imagining things, Adele."

By the time Christmas Eve arrived both Joe and Adele seemed happy with the bulging fridge, crammed freezer, colourful fairyland lounge and the strings of tinsel adorning doorframes, banister, pictures and shelves around the house. Fiona had to admit that her home now looked warm and welcoming in the darkness of late afternoon. She crossed her fingers that she would receive help to put everything back to how it should be.

The physiotherapy practice was closed on Christmas Eve and, at lunchtime, Joe said he was heading out. "I'll be back late evening."

Adele had insisted Christmas was a big thing in their house so why would he go out? "Where are you going?"

"The boys. It's traditional. We always meet for a drink and a curry on Christmas Eve — the table's all booked and everything."

Adele was looking from her dad to Fiona and then back again, waiting for the next volley. Despite her recent mellowing, the girl was still bigging-up Meeko and would probably be glad if she and Joe split up, paving the way for a reconciliation with Rose. "You always do this — and Rose didn't mind?" His ex-wife must have been a saint.

"Yes. But if you feel strongly . . ."

"No, go ahead." To say anything else would make her possessive, and she was doing her utmost to make this relationship work and to be part of a family instead of waiting for a sea of sharks to consume her in the form of loneliness, old age, infirmity and empty days. Her career had to be replaced with another sort of belonging. And any belonging had to be worked at and earned.

Adele picked a romcom for her and Fiona to watch and filled a bowl with popcorn. They sat side by side with a brand-new Christmas blanket over their thighs. The festive woven crib scene had been chosen by Adele on one of their shopping sprees; she swore that Fiona would get years of good use out of it. And if Fiona didn't want it, Adele would take it with her when she got her own place. That last statement had been the deciding factor on the purchase for Fiona — her lodger was feathering her own nest for a departure at some point. Adele kicked off her slippers and put her feet on the low coffee table in front of them. Fiona stopped herself from criticising but refrained from following suit. From time to time Adele rubbed her belly with more vigour than usual. Then she shuffled her bottom and sat forward on the edge of the sofa, placing her hands in the small of her back and doing more rubbing.

"Are you OK?"

"Just some backache. I've had it all day, along with those pretend contractions. What do you call them?"

"Braxton Hicks?" Fiona could still remember every word of those baby books she'd devoured over the course of just a few weeks.

"I need the toilet again. The baby must have moved. Pause the film."

After using the bathroom Adele circled the room several times. Mostly she looked comfortable and then pain or discomfort kicked in and she paused in her perambulation, bent over and attempted to rub her own back. A lump of fear grew inside Fiona. She looked at her watch and was shocked to see only ninety minutes had elapsed since she'd poured the first of two large glasses of wine. It was out of character, but her way of sticking two fingers up at Joe and his Christmas Eve night out with the boys, and also a means of not thinking about the correlation between his current absence and Rob being late home all those years ago. She wouldn't dare get behind the wheel to drive Adele to hospital. "Should we call an ambulance? Or your dad?"

"No. It doesn't feel like it's for real — you know what I mean?"

Fiona nodded, but she didn't know what labour, real or not real, felt like. She only knew the agony, physical and mental, of losing a baby before she'd even had chance to meet it. "Why don't you have a bath?" It was something the books had recommended to ease the discomfort of the early pains.

Fiona ran the bath and gathered a couple of clean towels. She was about to add bubbles so that Adele could luxuriate for a while and then decided that might not be the right thing if the baby was imminent.

Downstairs Fiona stared at the frozen film image on the TV. It was part way through a Christmas party scene that had been about to throw together the two soon-to-be lovers who had proclaimed that they hated each other. Above her she could hear the noise of water sloshing in the bath as Adele shifted position. Fiona tried to use the time to mentally go through her checklist for the next day. Cooking Christmas dinner was an exercise in logistics as well as culinary skill and Fiona didn't know how she'd compare to the phantom of Rose. Even so, knowing Adele and Joe's liking for junk and takeaways, she'd decided to take the easier route and not do everything from scratch. The fridge was laden with packs of ready-prepared roast potatoes, pigs in blankets, bread sauce and red cabbage. The turkey breast joint was defrosting and would require a fraction of the faff and oven time of a full-size bird. Fingers crossed that her mother would still be so enamoured with her granddaughter-by-proxy and/or busy picking fault with Joe that she wouldn't notice what she was eating.

There was more sploshing from upstairs and then the sound of water draining down the plughole. A few minutes later Adele appeared wrapped in a towelling robe and her hair still wet.

"It's getting worse," she said weakly.

"Don't panic." This might have been an instruction to herself or to Adele. "I'll phone your dad to come home."

"He went in an Uber, remember? He'll have been drinking and be no use at all."

Fiona couldn't deal with the situation alone. "He's your father and he needs to know." She tried his mobile three times in quick succession. It went straight to voicemail each time. "Damn! He's switched it off." In her head she screamed expletives.

"The midwife said you're supposed to phone the hospital for advice."

"Then phone!" Adele's eyes widened at the sharpness in Fiona's voice and she immediately softened it. "Sorry, I didn't mean it to come out like that."

"You're more scared than I am." Adele took her mobile into the kitchen.

Fiona paced in the same way Adele had been doing. The younger woman was right — she was scared. Scared of being in this situation and failing another baby in the same way that she'd failed her own.

"They said I can go in if I want, but it sounds like only early stages of labour and I might be more comfortable at home. I said I'd stay put for a bit."

Fiona nodded, willing to be led by the person with the physical symptoms.

Adele started the film again. Every few minutes she got up and paced the room. Fiona watched her out of the corner of her eye, trying not to pass on her anxiety but aware some-one needed to watch the progress of Adele's labour objectively. The girl was getting up and down more frequently as the film reached its romantic climax: a church dressed for a winter wedding, surrounded by snow that was too white and pristine to be real.

"I've wet myself! Your carpet! Sorry." Adele lumbered from the room and up the stairs. Fiona heard the bathroom door shut and lock.

No! She ignored the carpet and ran after the girl. "Unlock!" she banged on the bathroom door. "We have to be able to get in if you get into trouble in there."

There was a shuffling noise and then another click of the lock. Fiona sank down onto the carpeted landing. "Shout if you want me to come in. Otherwise, I'll give you a few min-utes' privacy."

"I think that was my waters breaking . . ." The words disappeared into a loud groan which seemed to go on forever. "It's getting more painful."

Fiona's mind fixated on a section in one long-ago book about the increased risk of infection to mother and baby after the waters broke. "We need to get you to hospital. I'm going to phone an ambulance." She spoke loudly and slowly to pen-etrate the moans from within the bathroom. "And I'm going to open the bathroom door so that if you . . ." she was going to say 'collapse', but that might put the fear of God in the girl, ". . . so we can reach you easily. Back in two ticks."

She went downstairs to make the call so she could hear without the competition of Adele's moans. "No! That can't be right . . . she's in labour and it's Christmas Eve . . . and I've had too much to drink. A taxi? OK."

A six-hour wait for an ambulance! Fiona's brain felt suddenly sharp. She'd finished the last glass of wine at least an hour ago. She knew the route to the hospital like the back of her hand — she'd taken her mother to enough appointments there. But if something happened to Adele and the baby . . . She couldn't bear the responsibility of losing another baby.

Adele's groans were coming more frequently now, and with such a ferocious intensity that there might be a wild animal caged upstairs.

Fiona called all the local taxi firms. They either didn't answer or were fully booked. "Christmas Eve, sorry, love," was the stock answer if she tried to plead. The Uber app was on her phone but never used. At some point it had seemed the sensible thing to download in case she ever found herself stranded. She pressed it now and slowly worked her way through the prompts. Either she was doing it wrong or there was nothing to be had here either, or at least no takers for her requested journey.

Adele screamed and Fiona fumbled the phone. She pushed it into her jeans pocket and raced back up the stairs. Adele was on all fours and her fringe was stuck to her forehead with sweat. She didn't acknowledge Fiona's entrance. Her face was closed in, as though her entire being was concentrated on her belly. In between the harrowing cries, the silence felt deep and ominous, punctuated only by Adele's exaggerated deep breaths and panting. Eventually the younger woman managed to speak. "Are they coming? Please say they're coming."

"They're coming." Keep her calm and don't scare her any further. Fiona forced her own terror away and tried to pull her professional persona into play. "Give me a minute." She went back onto the landing to check her phone.

Still no message from Joe. Who else could she call late on Christmas Eve? Someone who wouldn't be deep within the bosom of their family? Meeko. The possible arrival of her best friend was like a mirage. He was the epitome of calm. When he hugged her, she felt as though she was in the safest place in the world, with someone who cared for her unconditionally and without judgement.

Except that Meeko had given her the cold shoulder at the baby shower, and in the week since then she'd received no communication from him at all. Whenever she'd turned up for breakfast at the hotel, he'd either been and gone or hadn't yet arrived. She'd messaged him twice and been blanked. In all the years they'd known each other, they'd never gone so long without some form of communication, most often instigated by Meeko. Something had happened to alienate him and she didn't have a clue what.

Adele screamed again. Fiona went back into the bathroom. The young woman had moved from hands and knees to a squatting position. "Push, push." Adele was talking to herself in an oblivion of natural urges.

"No! Don't push. Pant." If she pushed, the baby would arrive here, on the bathroom floor, and it would die. "Pant."

The message got through and Adele panted like a marathon runner. After thirty seconds she repositioned herself and looked like she was going in for the finale. "Can't hold it no more."

Fiona pressed the green telephone symbol next to Meeko's name and then flung her phone onto the landing while shouting, "The baby's here, please come!" Then too much happened all at once to think about the recent coldness of her best friend. She placed a clean, soft towel on the floor between Adele's feet just as the baby slithered into the world. Adele sank down like a deflated balloon and started to cry great huge, heaving sobs. She gently stroked the baby on her stomach. Excerpts from everything Fiona had ever heard about helping someone give birth danced in her head and formed a jumbled mental checklist. Right order, wrong order? Truth or old wives' tales? She had no way of knowing but tried to action them anyway.

Cord round the neck? She knelt close to Adele and lifted the baby. It was sticky with mucous and blood but the cord was definitely not strangling it.

Airways clear and breathing?

"Is it alive?" Adele whispered between sobs.

Fiona put her little finger in the baby's mouth and realised too late that she wasn't scrubbed up for doing such things. Tongue wasn't blocking throat. The baby still hadn't cried. Should she be checking anything else? In the old-fashioned films didn't they smack the baby? The umbilical cord still attached baby to mother, and Fiona managed to place the little girl face down on Adele's stomach and gently tap the tiny buttocks. And again, a little harder.

"Don't hurt her! Is it a girl?"

A tiny wail. And then another one, a little stronger. Fiona lifted the baby a little and showed her to Adele. Ineffective kicks and punches were now accompanying the wails.

Keep the baby warm. Fiona found yet another dry, clean towel and attempted to swaddle the infant like the Christmas card image of baby Jesus. Impossible to do it properly with the cord still attached.

Don't cut the cord. Infection and bleeding.

Check the mother. In what way? Adele was a picture of physical devastation. But the tears had stopped and as she leaned forward in her seated position on the floor, cradling her towel-clad baby, there was the hint of a smile. There was blood between her legs but it didn't appear to be flowing from her in torrents. It probably looked worse than it was. Fiona crossed her fingers behind her back.

Get mother and baby medical help. As if on cue, a faint tinny voice sounded from the discarded phone. "Are you still there, Fiona? I've been shouting for fifteen minutes." Was that how much time had elapsed? It simultaneously felt like seconds and days because the world had changed so profoundly; she had helped, for the first and probably last time, to bring a new life into it. "I'm in the car about five minutes away."

Meeko was nearly here. Relief flooded her. For a second she closed her eyes and exhaled. Then she pulled herself back into midwife mode.

She dampened a facecloth with warm water and cleaned Adele as best she could while the new mother sat there, shell-shocked. The bathroom looked like a murder scene. The baby was making snuffling noises. At the bottom of Fiona's checklist was something about putting the baby to the breast as soon as possible, but that looked too difficult, given the umbilical cord was still in place.

"One minute away!"

Fiona ran downstairs and opened the front door. When Meeko walked in, she pointed him straight upstairs.

CHAPTER 30

Meeko might have had a career as an ambulanceman. He was calm and kind and took charge as Fiona started to tremble now the immediate danger was over. In the hospital he sat with her in a corridor while Adele and the baby were checked over. He fetched her tea heavily laced with sugar to disguise the metallic machine taste and to soothe her constant trembling and little sobs. Only when she had drained two paper cups of the stuff did the shaking stop.

"Feeling better?" Meeko asked. "That was quite an experience."

Fiona took some breaths and nodded. "Especially for Adele. She was so brave. It happened so quickly."

They sat in silence. Waiting. Fiona tried calling Joe again and left another voice message. She watched the midnight minute tick over into the next day. "Happy Christmas, Meeko." She turned her face towards his and wondered what it would be like to be kissed properly by those lips.

"Happy Christmas, Fiona." He moved in his seat and she thought he was going to hug her like he'd often done before; a hug that was platonic on his part but which generated glorious, unrequited tingles within her.

He didn't hug her. Something unknown divided them, like a gauze curtain.

They were invited in to see a freshly cleaned-up mother and baby. Fiona was glad she'd had the foresight to grab Adele's ready-packed hospital bag as they went out to Meeko's car. The girl looked tired and dazed, but happy. She was attempting to latch the baby onto her breast with little success.

"Try again in a while, I think baby's just as tired as you are." The midwife turned to Meeko and Fiona. "Well done, Granny and Granddad!" The nurse beamed at them. "You did a good job with the home birth."

"We're not relations," Fiona said immediately.

"Oh!" The midwife glanced questioningly at Adele, as though asking whether she wanted them to be there. Adele nodded. "I'll leave you to it then."

Meeko tactfully kept his eyes averted from Adele's first attempts at feeding the baby until Fiona indicated that she was covered up and decent again. Then he disinfected his hands from the gel dispenser and went immediately to the side of the bed and stroked the downy, baby head. "She is gorgeous, Adele. You should be so proud."

Fiona's feet wouldn't carry her the few steps from the door to the baby. She felt shaky all over again. This time it wasn't the responsibility of managing the birth. It was a head full of regrets, of what might have been and what should have been.

"Fiona." Adele appeared to be offering the baby up to her. "Come and see what you helped bring into the world."

"You did all the work. I was a bystander."

"You were essential backstage crew and you stopped me going beyond panic and pain into a zone that might have harmed Natalie."

"What a lovely name." Meeko was besotted with the little mite. He glanced over at Fiona. "This is the closest I've ever been to a birth and a newborn baby. My nephews and nieces were all a few days old before I met them. Come and have a look. She's magical."

184

Fiona forced her legs to move. "It's the first time for me too."

The baby's eyes were closed and she looked like the most fragile thing in the world. But the tiny mite was also relaxed; baby Natalie had complete confidence that she would be kept safe. The infant hadn't yet closed off any part of herself to other people. She was open to being loved. Fiona was envious of her innocence.

Breaking down her self-built barriers against the love offered by others was tough. Barriers built because she believed a second betrayal would tip her into a bottomless abyss. This had even applied to her parents because they were almost guaranteed to abandon her through death. That was how she'd been able to function immediately after her dad's passing, propping Dorothea up through the funeral arrangements, admin and aftermath.

But the doors to some of those compartments were slipping ajar. The subsequent light was surprisingly pleasant, warm even. The baby shower hadn't been easy but it had left her glowing. Picking up with Rob had been scary but ultimately had left her feeling good. It had been painful to discover the extent of her mother's loneliness, caused in part by Fiona's control over their relationship. But now she could open that door wider too and do something about it. Fiona would never be as laid-back and open as baby Natalie, but she was making progress towards feeling pleasant warmth again. There was still a long way to go: she had to open up to Joe about the divorce and about Amber; there was the mystery of Meeko's coolness to solve, and much else, as yet unrecognised, to do before all those compartment doors were propped open on a permanent basis. But it seemed achievable.

"Do you want to hold her?" Adele asked.

"No, I might drop her or hurt her or squeeze her too tightly."

Meeko was frowning, a mixture of puzzlement and concern on his face. "You did none of those things when she was slippery and not breathing. You brought her to life. She's much easier to handle now she's bathed and dressed."

Adele was offering her the tiny mite.

Fiona's legs began to shake. "Let me sit down first." She sat in the black plastic-covered armchair at the side of the bed and Meeko passed Natalie over as though she was a parcel in a party game. Fiona's arms shook as she cradled the beautiful creature. She tried to be in the moment and focus on Adele's baby but, despite her positivity of a few moments ago, her mind kept turning tail and racing back through the years. She saw plainly the wrong decisions and roads not taken. She'd thought she was happy. She'd felt sorry for and superior to her colleagues who were trying to juggle stressful jobs, the needs of children, and often, to cap it all, the deterioration of the very relationships that had put them into that position in the first place. Now that compartments were creaking open, she recognised how wrong she'd been and how they'd probably been the ones feeling sorry for the emptiness and sterility of *her* life. She thought she'd had a life well lived and well directed, in which she'd achieved exactly what she wanted, when she wanted it. She'd kept all elements neat and tidy, but maybe things *had* to get messy in order to produce rewards that were worth having. She thought of the mess of blood, mucus and fluid in her bathroom, and the new life that had emerged there, and she started to cry.

"Hey." Meeko bent over and whispered gently in her ear. "I hope those are tears of happiness on Adele's part because it's not the done thing to rain on someone else's parade."

"Natalie is absolutely gorgeous, Adele." Fiona kissed the baby's velvety forehead. "But I think at this early stage in her life she needs to be with her mum."

There was a brief knock at the door and the midwife returned. "There's another man arrived, Adele. He says he's your father?"

"Dad! Yes, I want to see him."

This was the excuse Fiona needed. "We'll disappear. The last thing you need is a Piccadilly Circus in here." The nurse held the door open for them.

Outside Fiona zipped her thin jacket against the cold night air and realised in the mad rush to leave the house that she'd brought only her phone and door key, no handbag and no money. Meeko drove her home without being asked. Whatever the issue between them, his generosity hadn't changed.

"Thanks," she said when he stopped outside the house. The journey had been mostly in silence. Despite the momentous evening, Meeko seemed not to want to talk. Something still wasn't quite right between them.

"Are you going to be OK?" he asked as she undid her seat belt. "You got quite emotional over Natalie."

"I'll be fine." She couldn't look at him in case tears leaked out again. "She just reminded me of another time and another place." She was on the verge of flinging open the compartment door and telling him everything, but something about the coolness between them was warning her off. She took his hand from where it rested on the gear lever and squeezed it. "Thanks for everything you've done tonight. Without you, the end result could've been completely different." He gave a small smile but didn't return the pressure on her hand. He merely stared pointedly at the passenger door handle. "Don't forget Christmas lunch tomorrow, or should I say today?"

"I appreciate the offer, but I think it's better I don't come."

"Why?" Something was more wrong than she'd thought.

"You've got a lot on your plate, and . . ." He was glancing in the rear-view mirror now as though he was impatient for her to be out of the car and on her way.

"It's no trouble, honestly. Sleep on it and decide in the morning."

There was a non-committal shrug from Meeko but no words. Fiona went into the house. She was sure he'd show up — he never turned down free food. After they'd eaten, she'd find a way for them to be on their own. They both had things they needed to get off their chests.

She climbed into bed without brushing her teeth in order to avoid the bathroom. She'd stepped onto an emotional rollercoaster and couldn't get off. Beneath her eyelids scenes from the last six hours played on a continual loop: again and again she plummeted downwards when no taxi or ambulance was available and Adele was increasingly distressed, and then there was the slow rise of hope when Meeko turned up, and the highest plateau reached when mother and baby were both safe and well. And then downwards again as she realised that her suspicions at the baby shower were correct and there was an issue between her and Meeko. Something big that he wasn't going to share with her. Not knowing what had caused the problem between them put her out of control. There was no chance of sleep, despite the red digits of the alarm clock telling her it was 3.30 a.m.

Fiona got up, put on her oldest clothes and started the gargantuan task of cleaning up.

CHAPTER 31

Dawn was breaking as Fiona checked that she'd gathered together all of the towels and cloths and the bathmat that had become victim to either the process of giving birth or the process of cleaning up afterwards. She switched the dial on the washing machine to the hottest and longest wash and hoped that magic would be worked. The noise of the machine filling with water must have drowned the sound of Joe's key in the lock because as she turned to deal with the murky water in the mop bucket, he was standing in the kitchen doorway. He looked exhausted and elated at the same time.

"How is she?" Fiona had planned to get angry with him. What was the point of a mobile phone if he kept it switched off? But the physical exertion of cleaning and the strangely different atmosphere of Christmas morning had calmed her.

"Mother or baby?" He sank onto a chair. "They are both beautiful. Rose will be beside herself for missing these special early moments. She doesn't even know we are grandparents." Joe put his head in his hands and sobbed.

Fiona felt uncomfortable and fiddled with the mop. The shared histories of the ex-spouses, daughter and now grand-daughter were stronger than the single year shared at arm's

189

length by herself and Joe. Were the feelings of love he'd previously professed for Fiona genuine or, as her mother had suggested, was it a relationship of convenience on both their parts? She rinsed the mop bucket out at the sink. The sobbing became quieter but when she turned around his head was still in his hands.

Fiona stuck the mop in the corner by the back door and went over to Joe. She gently removed his hands from his face and helped him sit up straight. "Tell me exactly how they're both doing." She swallowed the lump in her throat. Joe didn't need all her emotional baggage brought to the situation. "Natalie is a poppet — it's the first time I've ever held a newborn baby. The first time I've ever seen a new life come into the world. It was magical." She didn't mention her own terror the previous evening or the wildness of Adele's screams. Let Joe have only the beautiful pictures in his head. She handed him the kitchen roll. He blew his nose and dabbed his eyes.

"She told me . . . you saved . . ." he spoke haltingly around the sobs, "both their . . . lives. And Meeko . . . apparently, he's a knight in shining armour . . . Thank you. I knew it was near her . . . time. I should have been contactable." Then he looked up at her and stroked her cheek. "You are a damn fine woman, Fiona."

His words made her glow. "Anyone would've done the same. And Meeko saved the day by getting us to hospital."

"Meeko." Joe stared down at the crumpled tissue in his hand. "The yoga teacher turned Santa turned demigod. His name keeps getting mentioned by you, and now by Adele." An edge had come into his voice.

"He's a friend." *At least he was until an invisible iceberg slid between us.* "A purely platonic friend."

Joe shrugged, as if dismissing the situation. Then he smiled and sat up straight. "Meeting your first grandchild is an instant cure for a hangover and it deserves a proper breakfast. I'll cook."

Later they made love. And that felt magical too. Fiona put it down to the emotional wringer they'd both travelled through. It was more than a physical act performed with the aim of pleasuring and self-indulgence. They clung to each other like a sailor with his lifebelt in a tumultuous sea, as though they each wanted to squeeze as much comfort and emotion from the act of placing naked flesh against naked flesh as possible. Afterwards they lay hand in hand and with their legs still wrapped around one another. Fiona was grateful for the privacy of Adele's absence.

The landline interrupted the sated feeling of togetherness.

"Fiona! I thought you were picking me up at ten?"

She glanced at her watch. Five past. "Mum! I'm so sorry. We overslept — it's been an exciting night."

"I don't want to know about the pair of you getting excited. When will you be here?"

"Thirty minutes. I promise." For once she didn't feel bowed by her mother's criticism. "And have I got news for you!" She kissed Joe's forehead in the same gentle way she'd kissed Natalie's hours earlier. "Read the turkey joint instructions while I'm gone and preheat the oven," she told him.

Dorothea was in seventh heaven when she learned about Natalie's birth and demanded they go straight to the hospital instead of back to Fiona's house.

"No. The nurse told Joe that they both need time to rest and get to know each other. She suggested visiting this evening."

Dorothea was happy to be plied with chocolates and sherry to make up for the late appearance of Christmas lunch. Fiona applied herself to warming, decanting and throwing away packaging. She felt both guilty and relieved for not adhering to her usual 'cook from first principles' rule. Joe helped Dorothea set up her new smartphone. The old lady came into the kitchen with it when the Yorkshire pudding box was still on the counter. Fiona held her breath, determined not to let whatever her mother said next spoil her Christmas.

"I can't wait until the next coffee morning! Brenda and Sonia will have to sit through these at least five times, and listen to my commentary." Her mother was beaming as she leaned in front of Fiona and slowly swiped through an album labelled 'Natalie'. Joe had obviously taken his proud grandfather role seriously. She and Meeko had been too shell-shocked by the whole event to take a single picture. "And by then I'll probably have even more — we must make sure to get one, or ten, of me nursing that little darling. After all the hours I've spent smiling, nodding and asking polite questions about other people's grandchildren, I deserve some air time of my own. Joe said he'll show me how to send the pictures to other people next." Her mother walked out of the kitchen without remarking on the Yorkshire pudding box.

Fiona grinned. It was unbelievable how much nicer her mother became when she had something to capture her attention and passion. Having something that mattered in life, be that a career, a relationship or a family, was truly important. The residents of Dorothea's block didn't know what was about to hit them, and it was likely the old lady would become a star turn because few of the others would have a great-granddaughter-*by-proxy*.

Lunch was ready to go on the table an hour later than originally planned but Meeko still hadn't arrived. Fiona was sure he would have had second thoughts about refusing her dinner invitation.

"How much longer?" Joe called from the lounge. "Our stomachs are beginning to think our throats have been cut."

"I was hanging on for Meeko." Her disappointment at his non-appearance was like a physical pain.

Joe walked into the kitchen and put his arms around her. "Is that really necessary? He'd be here by now if he was coming. I think your *best* friend has let you down."

Fiona tried to analyse Meeko's cool attitude when he'd dropped her off. Could his financial worries have caused something to sour between them? But how? If Joe and her mum weren't here, she would've gone round to Meeko's flat immediately to check on him and put right whatever had gone wrong between them.

Then her phone beeped with a message:

It's best I stay away. You've a lot going on. I'll let you concentrate on those you trust.

Meeko didn't even soften his words with a smiley face. And the last sentence was weird. Something cold settled in the pit of Fiona's stomach. This was a long-term rebuttal, not just a refusal of today's invitation. Losing your best friend on Christmas Day hurt like hell. And why was he talking about trust?

Fiona pasted on a bright smile and called her diners to the table. She buried her feelings beneath the excess jollity necessary to carry off a regal paper crown, a dire joke on a slip of paper and Dorothea demanding that they each have several turns with the flimsy, curling fortune fish from her cracker.

"It's a shame that nice young man with the Santa outfit couldn't make it." Dorothea sat back in her chair after managing to squeeze in a second helping of pudding. Unusually she hadn't had her annual moan about a homemade pudding giving far superior results than a bought one zapped in the microwave.

"Not much of a friend if he lets you down at the last minute on Christmas Day. It's been better just the three of us — all family, and that's what Christmas is about." Joe's antipathy, maybe even jealousy, towards Meeko was obvious. He looked at his watch. "I think it's time we went to see the newest addition to that family."

* * *

Adele looked as tired as Fiona felt after a night with negligible sleep. She'd been moved into a ward with five other women and babies, but her curtains were drawn along both sides of the bed and open only at the foot end. It made Fiona think of a blinkered horse. Natalie was sleeping in an opaque Perspex fishtank.

"Oooh! Let me at the little munchkin," Dorothea said excitedly as they approached the bed.

Fiona pulled on her mother's hand. "Wait. Let Joe and Adele have a couple of minutes together before we go barging in. It's tiring work being a new mum."

"In my experience mums always want as many people as possible to admire their offspring."

After giving his daughter a hug and a kiss, Joe turned and waved them over.

Dorothea stared into the fishtank with a mesmerised expression and gently stroked the baby's cheek with her forefinger.

"This is Natalie." Joe beamed at Fiona's mother.

"She is the most beautiful thing I ever saw. Can I hold her, Adele?"

Joe answered before his daughter could utter a word. "Of course you can. You're the nearest little Natalie will have to a great-grandparent." Dorothea sat down on one of the two plastic bedside chairs and Joe handed her the swaddled baby.

"Hello, Natalie. I am your great-grandma-by-proxy — how's that for a mouthful? We'll have to find a way of shortening it for you, won't we?" The old lady sat crooning and rocking as though she'd been transported to a better place.

Fiona studied the happiness radiating from her mother. Again it was obvious that the hours spent alone in her flat did not bring out the best in Dorothea. With nothing else to fill her mind she picked cantankerous fault with anything and everything. It was impossible for life to live up to how it had been in her mother's heyday. But giving the old lady a reason to get out of bed in the morning, and other people to interact with and care for, melted away that selfish, critical streak that hides somewhere inside all of us.

Joe was standing at Dorothea's shoulder, equally enraptured. Fiona pulled the second chair closer to the bedhead on the opposite side to her mother, relieved that this time she wasn't being forced into close physical proximity to Natalie before she was prepared emotionally. She spoke to Adele. "I'm sorry we've descended en masse like this when you're still exhausted and sore. Your dad hasn't stopped smiling all day. He is so proud of you, and as pleased as punch with little Natalie. He couldn't wait to bring Dorothea."

Adele gave a tight-lipped smile. "I just wish Mum could see her." A silent tear dripped down the pale cheek. Adele brushed it away with the back of her hand. "Sorry, you didn't come here to listen to me blub on Christmas Day."

"You cry all you want to." Fiona passed over a box of tissues from the bedside cabinet. "As well as a new baby, you're coping with the absence of someone close to you." She paused, not sure whether to say the next words, but if they were going to build any sort of relationship under the same roof, it would help to have everything out in the open. "Correction: with the absence of two people close to you, if you count the baby's father. Plus, you're still very young and have had to mature into a mother almost overnight."

Adele had her head turned away from her father and was trying simultaneously not to cry and to blow her nose silently. Fiona didn't know whether her words were helping the new mum or making the situation harder. "And you've done that last thing spectacularly well — as shown by the fact that you're worrying about upsetting *us* on Christmas Day, when in fact it's us that should be concerned about *you*. Less than twenty-four hours into motherhood and you are doing fine!"

Adele managed a smile. Natalie began to whimper and was trying to inject movement into her arms and legs beneath the blanket wrapper. Dorothea tried to calm her with little strokes to the head but the baby would have none of it and the noise level rose.

"She's hungry," Adele pronounced with the certainty of a mother already learning to interpret her infant's needs.

"We'll go for coffee and drop back in thirty minutes. OK?" Fiona hoped neither Joe nor her mother would put up an argument. "Do you want the curtains completely closed?" Adele nodded gratefully. Fiona hadn't suggested the cafeteria purely out of concern for a young mother who was still new to breastfeeding. After breaking down so publicly in the delivery room the previous evening, she felt on the verge again, and seeing that Madonna moment of a mother feeding her child would set her off. The thought of it made her blink hard.

Afterwards Adele looked brighter. Or maybe it was something to do with the recently applied lipstick and blusher. Her hospital bag had obviously been well planned.

"When can you both come home?" Joe was now cuddling Natalie, who was punch drunk on her mother's milk.

"A couple of days, I think. Something to do with my blood pressure and the lack of consultant rounds on the bank holidays."

Forty-eight hours of privacy for her and Joe, plus time to get a grip of herself emotionally. The moment these selfish thoughts surfaced, Fiona quashed them, but she couldn't help feeling grateful for the opportunity to regain and, hopefully, strengthen her relationship with Joe.

CHAPTER 32

Meeko glanced at the wrapped box of Belgian chocolates on the passenger seat of his car and hoped they were sufficient to make this call on Dorothea appear legitimate. He'd spent Christmas Day alone, trying to straighten out his feelings for Fiona and accept that she didn't trust him and, therefore, would never be interested in him romantically. But he couldn't just stop caring about her. And what terrible secret did she have that she couldn't share with him?

The obvious thing would be to ask her directly, but that meant admitting that he'd eavesdropped, albeit accidentally, and then he'd have to explain why he'd kept that eavesdropping secret for so long. Besides, if she didn't trust him, would he get a full and honest answer? Before he could even consider bringing up the subject he needed some background information.

He'd texted Fiona this morning and asked for her mother's address, on the pretext that the missed dinner invitation meant he still had a gift to present to the old lady. The chocolates had been given to him by a member of one of his classes and he had similarly sourced boxes of truffles for Fiona and Adele — purchasing Christmas presents had been beyond his means this year. He'd pulled back the sticky tape on one corner of each wrapped box in order to double-check the contents and then stuck it back down. These presents had been another reason for reneging on yesterday's invitation — the value of his gifts wasn't sufficient to warrant the hospitality that was being offered to him. The Fiona whom he thought he knew wouldn't do comparisons, but it bothered Meeko.

"Meeko!" Dorothea looked genuinely pleased to see him. She sat him down in an armchair, turned off the blaring rerun of the original *Willy Wonka and the Chocolate Factory* film and served him tea and mince pies from bone china crockery. Then she settled in the chair opposite him. "It's so lovely to have company," she said. "After all the excitement of yesterday and meeting baby Natalie and learning all about this." She waved a mobile phone at him. "Everything has fallen very flat today. But it's still family time, isn't it? There's nothing going on in the lounge here and I daren't knock on anybody's door in case I'm interrupting a thing with relatives. You are a godsend." She reached out her arm and squeezed his hand. "And we missed you yesterday."

The warmth of the welcome made tears prick at the back of Meeko's eyes. He swallowed them away. "I came to bring you this. It's not much."

"You shouldn't have! Fiona said things weren't going well at work for you." The old lady pulled back the strips of sticky tape and unwrapped the box without tearing the paper, which she then folded neatly. "But I'm so glad you did. I love an extravagant sort of chocolate in the evening when I'm watching the soaps. Let's have one now!" Dorothea grinned and flashed her eyes at him wickedly.

For a couple of minutes they savoured the richness of the chocolates in silence. Then the old lady dabbed at her lips with one of the paper serviettes she'd put on the tray with the mince pies. "Now tell me the real reason you didn't come yesterday. Fiona said something about you not wanting to intrude when there was so much going on. But it wasn't just to do with Natalie being born, was it?" she asked.

Meeko pretended to still have some chocolate in his mouth while he played for time. He'd expected to be able to bring the subject of Fiona up gradually and to not be asked such a question outright. He wasn't sure of the answer himself. "Fiona," he said eventually.

"Ah . . . my daughter isn't the most perfect person in the world. She can be annoyingly self-centred at times. It's too many years living alone and doing as she pleases. What has she done to alienate you?"

Articulating the words was going to be more difficult than he'd anticipated without showing Dorothea he had romantic feelings for her daughter. Feelings that refused to be quashed, no matter how unrealistic they now were. "Something's gone wrong with our friendship. Or maybe my version of that friendship never matched Fiona's in the first place. She doesn't trust me." Meeko let his words fade away as a frown of confusion passed over the old lady's face followed by the brightness of realisation.

"Is this something to do with Joe? You're suspecting, like me, that he's only moved in out of convenience, not true love. She's being used and, given half a chance, he'll go back to the ex-wife, you mark my words. And Adele being a single mother — that's not perfect, is it?" She gave his arm a reassuring pat. "You are lovely and traditional, Meeko. It's just a shame that you're not . . . interested in Fiona."

His own words tumbled over themselves in his rush to make Dorothea understand. "I didn't approve of Joe but then he moved in and I knew I had to accept that as a 'proper relationship'." He added the air quotation marks. "Adele — that's just one of those things, although something to do with the baby is putting a strain on Fiona. But it's not just Joe. It's Fiona herself. She's keeping things from me. Things that must be important to her." He paused as the old lady's final sentence suddenly registered with him. "What do you mean, I'm not interested?"

Dorothea poured milk for a second cup of tea and gestured with the jug at Meeko. He nodded and she poured his milk and then tea for both of them. "Fiona told me." She was rearranging the remaining mince pies. "She told me that you and Lynn had split up and that you wanted some time on your own before even contemplating another relationship." She sat back in her armchair and looked him in the eye. "But it's Fiona's supposed secrets that we're talking about."

It was true he had told Fiona that. But he'd been talking about relationships with women whom he didn't yet know. He had not mentally included Fiona in that sweeping statement.

"You said she doesn't trust you. That she's keeping secrets," Dorothea prompted.

"Yes. She was outside One More Bean with a man. They didn't see me and I accidentally overheard Fiona say that she hadn't told me something because she didn't trust me." He looked across the table for a reaction to his confession of eavesdropping. Dorothea looked puzzled so Meeko continued. "Is she keeping secrets?"

The old lady's face closed up. "I don't know who she's told what. Who was the man?"

"I don't know."

"He's unlikely to be a relative. Fiona is an only child and both her father and me are only children. What did he look like?"

"They were behind me. I didn't get a proper look. Perhaps a couple of inches taller than Fiona. Dark hair. Stockier than me but still slim."

"Overly confident?"

"Couldn't say because I didn't speak to him. But Fiona obviously thinks he's more trustworthy than me."

"It might be Rob. I know that she did meet him recently."

"Rob?" An innocent explanation was coming and it felt like the anticipation of stepping into a warm bath when every single muscle aches from exertion.

"Her husband."

"Husband!" The icing-sugar-dusted pastry of his second mince pie suddenly stuck in his throat and made him cough. Meeko reached for the paper serviette again.

"Sorry, ex-husband. It must be about . . ." She paused. ". . . thirty years ago. I'm surprised she hasn't told you."

"I know she was divorced. A long time ago." There was a tightness in his stomach as he contemplated Fiona getting back together with her ex-husband. He hardly dared to ask the next question. "Is there more that I need to know?"

Dorothea hesitated and her eyes roamed the room. "It's not for me to say. You need to ask her yourself."

"Could there be something going on between Rob and Fiona now?" He hoped his voice didn't sound as shaky as he felt.

"Doubtful. Until very recently Fiona hadn't mentioned him for years, and whenever she did, it was always in the role of the Antichrist."

"How do we find out what their relationship is now? Can you talk to her?"

Dorothea shook her head. "Absolutely not. Our relationship has the ups and downs of a mountain range as it is. If I start prying, she'll close me off completely, and that can't happen when I've just met my granddaughter- and great-granddaughter-by-proxy. I've got pictures!"

Meeko sat politely as the old lady scrolled slowly through the images of her newly found non-blood relatives. As he was about to leave, she placed a hand on his arm. "It's in my best interests to find out what's going on with Rob, isn't it? If Fiona gets side-tracked by him and boots Joe out, I might lose access to Adele and Natalie. I don't care about Joe but I do love them lasses, especially since the mother has run off — they need me."

Meeko nodded. Whatever reason brought Dorothea onto his side was fine by him. But he would prefer it if Joe didn't stick around long-term.

"I will put out feelers." She gave him a wink. "As I told Santa at the party: I want to see my daughter settled down with a good man before I go to my grave. And, putting my selfish grandma reasons aside, I don't think that man is Joe.

No proper man would have been happy with that arm's-length relationship she instigated."

"Thank you."

"Put your number in my new phone. We might need to be in touch." Dorothea's eyes were alight now, as though she was looking forward to some cloak-and-dagger espionage. "It's subterfuge, like on the TV, isn't it?"

He tapped the screen of the phone to add his number to the meagre few already in there.

"Thank you. One question for you." Dorothea paused. "Are you available as a long-term partner for my daughter?" Her face was deadly serious.

CHAPTER 33

It was 29 December before mother and baby were given a clean bill of health to come home. Joe was beside himself with excitement and Fiona tried but failed to elevate herself to his level of anticipation. She was growing fond of Adele — there was a lot of herself in the girl, in particular the way Adele was adamant there was no place in her or Natalie's life for the baby's father. It reminded Fiona of the way she had dropped Rob and become totally self-reliant. Women learn from the adversity that men inflict upon them. They learn that you should trust no one but yourself.

During their daily visits to the hospital, she had come to tolerate short periods of holding Natalie without tears falling. And she was loving the newly animated version of Dorothea — rejuvenated by her new relatives-by-proxy. But all of this was tempered by the realities to come when Adele and Natalie were in her space twenty-four hours a day.

It would be goodbye to the privacy she and Joe had just enjoyed, from their emotional lovemaking on Christmas morning to both of them being able to walk around the house only half-dressed, to Joe not constantly criticising his daughter's behaviour, to not having to think about Adele's preference for convenience foods. All of those freedoms would be replaced by a house full of new baby chaos. She'd visited friends with babies and their domestic life went out of control: mess, toys, and everything focused around that one tiny being. It was probably acceptable when that tiny being was your own flesh and blood, but when it was an uninvited guest, was it possible to put up with it?

She and Joe had spent the previous day reorganising Adele's room to accommodate the newly purchased cot in one corner and a changing unit with storage cupboard underneath in the other. The steam steriliser was left boxed in the garage — with luck Adele would breastfeed for a while, meaning it might be a few months before this would have to come out and clutter up the kitchen counter. And she might have moved out by then.

"Do you think we've missed anything? Are there enough packs of nappies? Are you sure we don't need one of those baby gym toys?" The new grandfather was like a cat on a hot tin roof.

"It will be fine. More nappies can be bought at the drop of a hat, and Adele might like a hand in choosing things herself." Fiona remembered the girl's independent streak.

"Perhaps we should have a Welcome Home party this evening and invite Dan? Since he went to see her, he's been posting 'proud uncle' photos all over social media."

"No party today. Let Adele settle and Dan can pop round soon."

Joe had followed the instructions for fitting the car seat. He had got Fiona to double-check it and then he had again compared its positioning and fastening with the illustrations in the leaflet. Fiona refused when he asked her to give it a fourth look-over. "We are both intelligent people. You followed the instructions and we've checked it. Off you go and do the honours."

"Will you come with me?"

"Why? This is a once-in-a-lifetime family thing — Adele won't want me there cluttering up the scene." I*t will be emotional* *and I don't want to have to fight tears of regret that bringing a baby home from hospital was something I deliberately turned my back on forever.*

"It feels like it needs a woman's touch. And, well, Rose . . . she's not here . . . so . . . I don't know anything about babies."

You know more than me — you've been involved in bringing up two of them, and I am not and never will be a Rose replacement, in either Adele's life or yours. "OK." Joe was acting like a small child who needed his hand holding, and she eventually agreed to go with him for Adele's sake rather than his. "We need to go now or Adele will worry that we've abandoned her."

* * *

Adele was sitting in the small lobby of the ward when they arrived, Natalie in her arms and her overnight bag at her feet. "You're late and they needed the bed for somebody else. I didn't know whether to call a taxi or not." There were dark circles under the girl's eyes and a frown across her forehead.

Joe bent and kissed the cranky young mother and the peaceful baby. "I'm sorry, love, but I wanted to make sure that the baby seat was properly fitted in the car."

Adele looked puzzled. "Where is it?"

"What?"

"Where's the car seat, Dad?"

"In the car."

The point of this question-and-answer session hit home quicker for Fiona than Joe as a young couple walked towards them. The man was holding the car seat by the handle. The baby was fastened securely in place.

"That—" Adele pointed at the seat as it swung gently in the man's grip — "is how they are used."

It took a few moments for Joe to grasp the meaning of his daughter's comment. "Are you telling me that we carry Natalie around in the seat and then for every journey we have to fit and refit it in the car?"

"Yes, exactly that, Dad."

"I can't go through the stress of doing it wrong on every journey."

"It can't be rocket science, Dad. Thousands of people of ordinary intelligence do it every single day."

The argument was not auguring well for them playing happy families at home, but it had swept away any emotion that Fiona had feared might overcome her.

"Are you able to carry Natalie to the car in your arms, Adele? I'll carry your bag." Fiona broke the antagonism between father and daughter. "With a little time, your dad will get used to everything. It's brand new to all of us at the moment."

Adele harrumphed but acquiesced.

At home Fiona made Joe leave Adele to her own devices with Natalie upstairs. "Let her settle them both in. She is in charge of Natalie, not us."

"But while I've got time off work I could help."

"We'll help when we're asked, but she's got to grow her own confidence."

"You are so wise." Joe kissed her on the cheek. "You are just as good as Rose would have been at all this, *and* you're not even related to Adele, *and* you've never had children. Unless you've got a closet full that you've never told me about?"

That statement is hurtful to me in so many ways. But I'll let you off because you know not what you say. But I will only be able to let comparisons to Rose go so far and then I will have to put my foot down.

Fiona cooked the evening meal and Joe watched football on TV, but every few minutes she heard him walk to the foot of the stairs and listen. Adele came downstairs alone when the food was ready. All remained calm and silent as the three of them started to eat the shepherd's pie, carrots and broccoli. Adele devoured it with gusto and made no reference to when they might have pizza or a takeaway.

"Fiona's food is better than what they gave you in hospital then?" Joe said.

Fiona frowned. He had to treat his daughter like an adult otherwise this whole arrangement would go to pot.

Adele merely shrugged. She'd placed the baby monitor in the middle of the table and kept glancing at it. They'd nearly finished the main course when the first cries came simultaneously through the baby monitor and the open door into the hallway. Adele looked at her watch. "It's only two hours since I fed and changed her."

"Babies need a lot of looking after."

Well done on stating both the obvious and the unnecessary, Joe. "I can put your plate in the oven and hold the pudding back, if you like? Or shall I check on her while you finish?"

"No, I should go. She'll want her mum." Adele disappeared, leaving her fork fully loaded with the next mouthful. Fiona put the plate in the still-warm oven.

Fiona and Joe ate their bananas and yoghurt to the backdrop of Adele's one-sided conversation with her daughter sounding through the monitor. The attempted feed wasn't successful and Adele's voice changed from gentle cooing to tighter pleas for Natalie to go to sleep. There were several deep silences followed by squawks. Fiona assumed these were failed attempts to get Natalie to remain calm once she was out of her mother's arms and in the cot. Joe was glancing edgily from Fiona to the stairs and back.

"I'll go see how she's doing, shall I?" Relief washed over his face as she took his unspoken hint.

Upstairs there were tears on Adele's cheeks. "I should know what to do. Maternal instinct should tell me what she wants. But I don't know. She isn't even a week old and I've failed as her mother."

"You haven't failed and you won't fail." Fiona spoke firmly, even though she felt as much at sea as Adele looked — and just as emotional. Adele was bowed down by brand-new parental responsibility, society's expectations and the feeling that, because giving birth was a natural process, looking after the newborn should come automatically too.

"I *am* a failure." The anguish of Adele's voice made Fiona realise she was being selfish by not taking the lead when the young woman was obviously mentally and physically exhausted.

"Let me take her." Fiona held out her arms, not wanting to take Natalie because of the emotion that handling the tiny infant generated, but knowing it was the only fair and reasonable thing to do. "You can finish your dinner and Natalie and I will sit at the table with you so that she can see you." *Did babies recognise their mothers by sight at this age? It didn't matter, she was saying this for Fiona's benefit only.* "And later you can try feeding and changing her again."

The dirty dishes were still on the table and Joe was on the settee scrolling through his phone. Fiona felt a bud of tension elongate and run across her shoulders. "Joe, please could you get Adele's dinner from the oven and chop her a banana for pudding?" She glanced over at the wan girl taking her seat at the table. "And add a good splodge of golden syrup to the banana — energy is needed here."

Adele gave her a grateful grin and Joe sighed exaggeratedly before moving his stockinged feet from settee to floor and going into the kitchen. Natalie remained calm in Fiona's arms while Adele ate. The baby stared up into Fiona's face, her clear blue eyes wide open in wonder. Fiona felt herself beaming back at the tiny bundle but also blinking hard to hold back her emotion. In another life she might have been holding her actual, related granddaughter. "Joe, would you like to hold her? She's lovely and alert."

Joe put down his phone and looked over Fiona's shoulder. At the same time Natalie's fists curled into tiny balls, her feet started to kick and the cries came loud and strong. Fiona thought about how much she'd willed this baby to cry after she was born; now she equally strongly wanted her to remain silent to give her mother a chance to eat and recuperate.

"That's your fault, Dad." Adele was spooning yoghurt, banana and golden syrup into her mouth as quickly as she could. "She was fine until she saw you. Maybe she doesn't like men. You best stay away."

There was hurt in Joe's expression as he put his hands up in surrender. Fiona remained silent. She wasn't going to mediate. It was up to Joe to sort that relationship. Adele took Natalie back upstairs to feed her. When she hadn't reappeared an hour later Fiona went upstairs to check. The baby was asleep on her back in the cot and Adele was fast asleep, fully clothed on the top of her bed. When Joe switched on the TV again, she made him keep the volume low to avoid disturbing them.

CHAPTER 34

The next couple of days went by in a claustrophobic blur of tears — mostly Natalie's but a fair few from Adele and a lot blinked and swallowed away by Fiona, plus one lot that she had to rush to the bathroom and let out with a towel stuffed in her mouth. The latter wasn't just caused by her coming to terms with the life choices she'd made, but also the increasing hurt and confusion she was feeling around Joe's continued comments about Rose.

"I know you're doing what you think best, Fiona," he'd said when Adele got upset over the difficulties of supporting a crying baby in a bath of warm water with one arm and trying to gently wash her with the other hand.

"I can't do it without drowning her," Adele was wailing.

Fiona had stood in the doorway of the small bathroom. There wasn't room for two of them to kneel over the baby bath, which Adele had placed in the middle of the floor. Adele had requested that Fiona help with the procedure, but working as a double act wasn't practical.

"Can you do it for me? I don't want to kill her."

"You won't kill her. And I'm right here if anything does go wrong. But it won't."

Joe had been standing at the top of the stairs, from where he could whisper in Fiona's ear. Adele was too wrapped up in her own difficulties to be aware of what was going on behind her. "If Rose was here, she wouldn't be putting her daughter through this hell. She would be doing the bathing until Adele was over the birth, calmer and able to do it herself more objectively."

Fiona had bristled. "How many times do I have to point out that I am *not* Rose. And my relationship with both you and your daughter is completely different to the relationship which the two of you had, or still have, with her."

"I get that. But you're the nearest thing to a Rose replacement we have."

"I am *not* a Rose replacement." There'd been a twitch across Adele's back and Fiona hoped the girl hadn't heard them. The last thing she needed was strife between her father and the woman who was giving both of them a roof over their heads. She lowered her voice. "And me doing the bathing instead of Adele is merely kicking the can down the road. It's better that she is pushed to fly safely without stabilisers now, otherwise she will end up scared of handling Natalie and it will be me bonding with the baby rather than her mother."

"I think you're wrong."

Fiona had refused to argue any further, but she'd stuck to her guns of making Adele do as much of the baby-care as possible and only stepped in occasionally to allow Adele to rest.

These ongoing stresses meant New Year's Eve didn't have any special feel about it. Fiona couldn't dredge up any optimism for the new start that would be heralded by the midnight chimes of Big Ben.

"Are we doing anything special this evening?" Joe asked her after lunch. "I could ring round and see if there's anywhere with a table free."

"Two problems with that. Is it fair to abandon your struggling daughter and her new baby on one of the most emotive nights of the year? Secondly, going out at New Year costs an arm and a leg."

"But it's our first New Year together as a proper couple. I want people to see us. To know we are together."

Fiona let his shallow sentiment go. It was becoming increasingly obvious that Joe wasn't the man she'd thought he was and that scared her. It was more fun to miss him for most of the week than to have him living in her house. And now she was cornered without an easy way to ask him to leave.

"I could invite Mum and Meeko over," she offered. "To make it a bit different to the other nights." Dorothea would jump at the chance but Meeko would probably say 'no'. She'd sent him some light-hearted quips and a couple of photos of Natalie since Christmas Day but had had nothing back bar a few thumbs up emojis indicating he'd seen her messages.

"Not Meeko."

Fiona sensed an edge to his voice. "Oh?" Did Joe know something about Meeko's distancing himself from her?

"I don't know him properly and it would be weird having him here. We're a couple and he'd be the odd one out."

"He probably saved your granddaughter's life; he could never be the odd one out in this house. And he's the nicest man you could imagine. In fact, it would be lovely to have him here tonight, and my mum—"

"Adele told me about the way he looks at you."

Her heart missed a beat. "What do you mean?"

"Like he fancies you! His eyes follow you round the room. He stands a little bit too close when he's speaking to you. He touches you more than a normal person would."

Joe was talking rubbish, and Adele was stirring things up to pave the way for a reconciliation between her parents. "Meeko is warm, affectionate and touchy-feely. But he's like that with everyone."

"Adele says he's different with you."

Joe's jealousy of Meeko's close friendship with her was misplaced and, by voicing it, he was spoiling what might remain of her relationship with her best friend. "On second thoughts, with all this rubbish in your head, having him here tonight wouldn't be a good idea. You'd read things into him giving me a new year kiss or us holding hands for *Auld Lang Syne*. And I don't want Mum here either if there's these horrible undercurrents of tension between us."

No visitors were invited and an unhealthy, claustrophobic atmosphere hung over the three adults and one baby as the light faded and the last evening of the year began. Fiona felt it was her responsibility to elevate the mood — this was her house and Joe and Adele were guests rather than permanent residents. She suggested ordering a Chinese and a bottle of prosecco to open at midnight.

"Yes to the food," said Adele, pacing the floor with a restless Natalie, "but, fingers crossed, I'll be asleep by midnight. And it says in the book that fizz and alcohol don't agree with babies."

"Fiona wasn't offering it to Natalie." Joe's voice was sharp following their earlier disagreement over Meeko.

"Duh! Put your brain in, Dad. I'm talking about Natalie getting it second-hand through my milk."

"Food for three but maybe a bottle of red for two?" Fiona looked at Joe, willing his attitude to settle so that, once mother and baby had gone to bed, they could cosy up on the sofa and salvage something of their previous relationship, now lost or buried through too much domesticity.

Joe shrugged.

Why did men so rarely admit when they were wrong? He was still smarting over Adele's comment about the milk and probably would do all evening.

Joe went to collect a set meal for three because nobody had the brain power to think about individual dishes. Fiona warmed plates and set the table. As a nod to the date on the calendar, she added a couple of candles and dimmed the lights just enough to make it feel like an occasion, but not enough to make Adele feel like an intruder at a dinner for two. Then, before she could overthink it, she sent a message to Meeko wishing him a pleasant evening whatever he was doing, and hoping they could arrange to breakfast together in the next few days because she'd timed it wrong and missed him every morning for ages. She hoped this wasn't because the hotel had dispensed with his services completely but she didn't articulate that in the message.

Adele had soothed Natalie to sleep in the cot ten minutes before Joe arrived back with the white plastic carriers of food. But she started wailing again before they'd finished the starter of Peking duck with pancakes. The coloured lights on the monitor flashed in synch with the noise. Adele groaned and pretended to bang her head on the table.

"I'll go," Fiona said.

Adele mouthed a silent thank you and Fiona caught the sigh of relief that Joe unconsciously released. Upstairs, Natalie calmed as soon as she was picked up.

"I think you like to be in company, don't you? Like any other person," Fiona crooned gently. "But my dinner's going cold downstairs and I'm hungry." Natalie's eyes closed in response to Fiona's gentle noises and the rocking movement of continuously taking the four steps between the spare room's door and its window. "Now I'm going to lie you down again and you're going to stay asleep, aren't you?"

Fiona hadn't even reached the landing before the infant started crying again. She sighed and returned to the cot. "I'm going to have to take you downstairs with me, aren't I?" Natalie stared at her with wide, innocent eyes and Fiona thought she detected the slightest of nods. She grinned at the infant's audacity. She held the baby closer and showered her downy head with kisses. Then she stopped suddenly — the usual sadness she felt when holding Natalie was gone. Fiona was falling in love and bonding with a baby that wasn't hers, and who, depending on the longevity of the relationship between her and Joe, or on what happened when Rose returned, might be snatched away. Adele's circumstances would change in the next few months. For the young woman's own sake, Fiona wanted her to live independently, or at least somewhere with more space, and at that point their shaky relationship might crack and Natalie would no longer be in her life. Fiona couldn't get close to this child and then lose her. Once in a lifetime was enough. She put Natalie in the car seat to carry her downstairs — close physical contact with the infant was dangerous.

She deliberately placed the seat on the floor next to Joe, who had finished his starter and was scrolling through his phone. Adele had finished as well. She'd pushed the plate to one side and had her head on the table with her eyes closed. The duck pancakes in front of Fiona were cold now. She pushed her plate away too. Joe put his phone down and looked at her and then across at Adele and then he rolled his eyes. Fiona got the message — he was trying to tell her they could've gone out for the evening after all. Fiona shook her head and indicated the carry-seat. As if on cue, Natalie started crying. Adele's head immediately jolted upwards. Fiona passed the infant over to her mother. "Cuddle her for a few minutes while your dad clears the starters and gets the mains from the oven." Joe grunted and groaned as he stood up. "I've got the warming tray heating up in the kitchen as well," Fiona continued. "Bring that in first and then at least we can keep everything hot if Natalie slows down proceedings."

Proceedings didn't just slow down, they ground to a halt. Leisurely eating and a bit of fun with the chopsticks Fiona had found at the back of her cutlery drawer were abandoned. Natalie was the most unsettled she'd been since they'd brought her home two days earlier. Joe kept his head focused on his plate, but the whites of his knuckles could be seen in the grip on his cutlery. Adele and Fiona switched the baby between them at regular intervals, Adele shovelling food into her mouth in between turns while constantly glancing at her daughter. When it was Fiona's turn to eat, she tried to force her knotted stomach to relax and take food. She ate small mouthfuls so she might remember something of what she ate. And all the time in the background were Natalie's wails.

"For heaven's sake! Can't one of you shut her up!" For a few seconds Joe got silence as all three female heads swivelled towards his outburst. "I can't sit in this uproar all night." He levered himself up to standing.

It was like discovering that Santa Claus is a myth, that the tooth fairy is a lie and that there never was such a thing as the Easter Bunny — all in the same split second. In small doses, and without the baggage of his domestic needs, whims and foibles, Joe had been the perfect occasional companion — the significant other who made her feel good about herself and her life choices, and who didn't need to undergo the public scrutiny of others or live up to anyone else's expectations. Now she saw his true colours and how he reacted when the chips were down. And it wasn't good. It was unforgivably awful. Maybe his attitude to Natalie seemed worse because she still carried Amber in her heart. But Joe had raised two of his own children, he had a wealth of experience that neither she nor Adele had, but, apart from his absolute besottedness and photography session on first meeting his granddaughter, he had kept well back from the front line. "If Rose was here, we wouldn't be trying to enjoy a nice meal and a bottle of wine—" he gestured at the bottle of red, which so far had only made its way into his glass — "with this cacophony in the background."

Adele joined in with Natalie's sobs.

"And what exactly would Rose have done in this situation?" If humans had hackles, Fiona's were raised.

He shrugged. "Don't ask me the details. I'm not a woman. But she always advocated that if the parent is relaxed then the baby will be too. Put Natalie down and take ten minutes to have a drink and finish your food. Both of you." He had calmed his voice a little but the last sentence came out like an order. Fiona expected him to step forward and take his granddaughter, but he sat back down, topped up his wine and then poured some for both Fiona and his daughter.

Adele looked close to tears as she strapped Natalie back into the car seat. She ignored the wine her father pushed towards her — *Well done you, Adele. Stick to your guns* — and concentrated on her food. Joe handed a glass filled too full to Fiona. To avoid a messy accident on her virgin white tablecloth she was forced to take it and start sipping before it slopped over the edges. She closed her eyes and tried to savour the richness trickling down her throat. She drank some more. Maybe it was psychological but the tight band of tension across her shoulders and the ball that had been in her stomach since the meal began eased. Maybe there was something in Rose's philosophy. When she opened her eyes, she was surprised to find only a centimetre of liquid left in the glass. Joe was smiling at her.

"What did I tell you? Even from a distance, Rose knows best."

"Please stop mentioning Rose." Fiona spoke sharply.

"Fiona's right, Dad. It's not helpful to praise your ex-wife in front of your current girlfriend."

Wow! Thank you, Adele. She shot her daughter-by-proxy a grateful glance.

Natalie was still crying but it didn't seem to penetrate Fiona's brain quite so much. She put a hand over the sudden growl of her empty stomach and understood the sudden effect of the wine.

"Now eat." Joe spoke without acknowledging the remarks of either Fiona or Adele.

Fiona obeyed. She spooned egg-fried rice, lemon chicken, garlic vegetables and beef in black bean sauce onto her plate. Joe refilled her glass and then brandished the bottle. "I'll fetch another — it is New Year's Eve after all."

"Dad . . ." Adele was frowning and blowing her nose. "I might need some help, and if you're both—"

"Nonsense. You're doing brilliantly."

Another realisation hit Fiona. Joe said whatever suited him at that moment in time. When Adele had been struggling to bathe Natalie it had suited his needs to ask Fiona to take over and thus silence the anguished cries of his daughter. Now he didn't want to drink alone, plus he wanted some built-in insulation from the baby's cries, and so he told Adele that she was more than capable, thus encouraging Fiona to let herself go on the alcohol front.

In the meantime, Natalie had fallen silent and was staring directly at Joe as he raised the new bottle over Fiona's glass. As soon as he started pouring, she screamed as though she'd been stabbed. Adele was on her feet immediately, unbuckling and taking the infant in her arms. Pacing backwards and forwards reduced the ferocity of the noise but it was still constant, in the background, like tinnitus.

"I'll try feeding and changing her again." The anguished girl and baby disappeared upstairs.

"Thank goodness for that." She hoped Joe's words emanated from the bottle and not his heart. He headed for the sofa.

"We should clear up." Fiona gestured at the table with its litter of plates and cartons.

"It'll go straight in the bin." He was fiddling with the remote now.

"It may have escaped your notice but we didn't use disposable plates, cutlery or glasses." Despite all her wonderful maternal and domestic skills, Rose had been a complete failure at housetraining her husband. Or maybe she'd wanted to keep him dependent on her? No. No woman would want to wait on her man like this.

Joe failed to respond to the sarcasm in her voice. Maybe he didn't even notice it. Fiona was past caring. She cleared the table and washed up.

Thirty minutes later Adele was back downstairs with Natalie just as noisy as when they'd left. "She's had a feed and I've changed her nappy but still she won't settle. And I'm soooo tired."

Fiona wanted to offer to take the infant while Adele caught a couple of hours sleep but, after her realisation that the Joe she'd previously enjoyed in small doses was slipping between the cracks, she was afraid to get too close to his grand-daughter. A granddaughter who may be out of bounds very soon.

"Dad! I don't know what to do with her."

Joe looked surprised at this direct appeal for help. "We could take her for a drive — that makes babies nod off, doesn't it?"

"And who would drive? You've had far too much, plus you encouraged Fiona."

Fiona thought guiltily about her second glass, which she'd finished without thinking. Now she had to make the offer. "Let me take her and you get your head down for a couple of hours. We'll manage this if we take it in shifts." Adele looked at her with relief. Joe shook his head as if he couldn't believe the drama they were making out of caring for this tiny being.

After the departure of her mother, Natalie grew even more vocal and restless. Pacing up and down the room had no effect. Swinging her gently in the car seat didn't quieten her. After a while Joe put his hands over his ears. Fiona ignored him.

Finally, he spoke. "OK, let me take her." His tone implied that he'd given Fiona her opportunity to prove herself and she'd failed so now he'd show her how it was done.

He cradled Natalie's head in one hand and held her upright against his shoulder in the other. To start with, he swayed from side to side, then he walked, then he tried jig-gling, attempted some gentle crooning and, finally, after a whole five minutes, handed her back to Fiona. "She must be ill," he said confidently. "There's no other explanation."

"Ill! No, please no!" Adele was back in the room and rushing towards Fiona and her daughter.

"He's probably wrong." Fiona glared at Joe and then back to Adele. "And you're supposed to be asleep."

"I can't sleep while I can hear her crying."

"That means you are definitely a good mum," Fiona whispered to the increasingly distraught young woman. Then she spoke more normally. "I don't think she's ill. There's no sign of a temperature or floppiness or anything else the books tell you about."

"You've read books about babies?" Adele's eyes were wide.

It would be so easy to share Amber with Adele. After the girl's support of Fiona over Joe's mentions of Rose, it felt possible even. But she couldn't do it now, with Joe there. His behaviour tonight had removed the last scales from her eyes. He wouldn't understand. "Friends had babies. I did the odd spot of babysitting for them and tried to keep abreast of things."

"I can't take this stress for much longer. We need someone who knows about babies." Joe's voice was impatient.

You've supposedly brought up two yourself.

"What about Dorothea?" Adele's face brightened a little as she spoke. "We could phone her. It's not too late."

Fiona put the old lady on speakerphone. Her mother was delighted to be approached for expert advice but could offer no suggestions other than what they'd already tried. "Sometimes it needs a person to hold her who's not so emotionally invested," she said finally. "You three are stressed and at your wits' end. Little Natalie might have sensed that. If you could fetch me over, it might make a difference. No guarantees, but it could be worth a try."

"That would be great, Dorothea." The younger woman's shoulders were visibly dropping back a little from their hunched position.

"But neither Joe nor I are fit to drive."

"I'm sorting an Uber right now." Adele's fingers moved fast over the screen of her smartphone. "We're in luck! Everyone who's going out has gone, but there's still a couple of hours until midnight and the massive rush."

220

CHAPTER 35

Thirty minutes later Dorothea arrived. As soon as she had her coat off and the slippers that she'd brought with her on, she plonked herself in an armchair and almost snatched Natalie into her arms when Adele offered her. "You've no idea how lovely it is to hold new life close when you are as old as me." The old lady shut her eyes for a moment and appeared to be breathing in great lungfuls of Natalie's sweet milky smell. "This makes me feel like a solid cog in the circle of life rather than a spare part that's not needed anymore. Natalie's heart beating so close to mine is better than a rejuvenation drug."

Joe rolled his eyes to the ceiling. Fiona swallowed tears and wondered if it would have been an even more potent drug if the baby were an actual blood relation.

"That's a really lovely thing to say." Adele paused for a couple of seconds before adding, "Gran."

Dorothea's eyes opened wide and a huge smile made her look like the young woman that Fiona remembered from her childhood. Fiona wanted to hug the tableau in front of her and never let it go: her mother nursing her great-granddaughter-by-proxy, whose startling screams were now replaced by gentle snuffles, and the baby's mother, who was staring at the old lady in wonder, as though she had woven a magic spell to calm and quieten the infant. But she also wanted to wade in and urge her mum-to-be cautious with her feelings because these were not blood relatives and liable to slip away like sand through an egg timer.

"Thank goodness for that." Joe picked up the TV remote.

Fiona took it from him. "No. Let's just enjoy some quiet time."

Adele indicated that she was going to bed for a little while. The three adults sat in silence until it became obvious that Natalie was sleeping the sleep of the exhausted.

"Shall I transfer her to the car seat," Fiona asked, "to give you a break?"

"No. Let's not take the risk of disturbing her. And, like I said, it's really nice having the heart of another living thing beating so close to my own." Then she looked pointedly at Joe. "A cup of tea would be nice right now."

Dorothea spoke in an urgent whisper as soon as Joe was out of the room. "Have you spoken to Meeko?"

"No. I think . . ." She might as well be honest since their estrangement now seemed permanent. "I think I've done something to upset him but I don't know what."

"He came round on Boxing Day. With a present. Well, I think the chocolates were just an excuse — he'd forgotten to remove a gift tag addressed to him that was hidden in the folds of the wrapping paper, so he was regifting — and really he wanted to talk about you." Dorothea paused, as if for dramatic effect. "I think he is available — to you, anyway. And please trust him with your . . . history. He's a good man."

"What?" Fiona's brain cartwheeled.

Dorothea spoke again before Fiona could engage logic. "Meeko saw you and Rob together and he heard something he didn't like."

Her mother's accusatory tone put Fiona on the defensive about her brief encounters with her ex-husband. She felt like a little girl caught with her hand in the biscuit tin. She tried to channel her inner grown-up. She'd done nothing wrong. She remembered her sighting of Meeko walking away from One More Bean. "And what did he hear?"

"Something about you not trusting him."

Fiona felt like a skittle caught full-on by a bowling ball. "Of course I trust him." Then Dorothea's other declaration hit home. "And how is Meeko available? He told me he'd sworn off meeting women for the time being."

"He has designs on you."

"He actually said that?" Now the skittle was horizontal and skimming across a highly polished surface towards oblivion. This wasn't making sense. The words circled in her head — *He is available. He has designs on you. He thinks you don't trust him.*

There was a thud as Joe kicked open the lounge door. Both women jumped. Dorothea's sudden wide-eyed expression made Fiona confident that her mother wouldn't breathe a word of this in Joe's presence. He carried in three mugs held in two fists, slopping brown liquid as he bent to put them on the coffee table. Dorothea placed a protective hand over the baby still sleeping in the crook of her other arm. Joe disappeared again and came back with a small red cardboard box. "I managed to find the last of the mince pies." He pulled a moulded plastic tray from the box and offered the pies, in their foil cups, to Fiona and Dorothea.

"I'll swap you," said the old lady, looking fixedly at Joe. "You take Natalie while I eat and drink."

"No. Let me go first. I eat quicker than you." After licking the pastry crumbs from his fingers with satisfaction, he spoke again. "Rose was always anti shop-bought mince pies but they're nearly as good as homemade, aren't they?"

Turn the knife a little further in the Rose v. Fiona scorecard, why don't you? Or did you overhear the talk about Meeko from the kitchen and now you're getting your own back?

"My daughter is perfectly capable of making mince pies that are a hundred times better than these." Dorothea's voice was strong and she was staring defiantly at Joe. "But she's been rather busy with house guests lately."

Fiona found herself sitting up straighter and grinning at her mother. These rare words of praise would sit in her mind like pearls. What had she done to earn both Adele and Dorothea on her side?

Just before midnight Joe insisted on opening the prosecco. "We can't let the moment go unmarked. Shall I wake Adele?"

"No!" Fiona and Dorothea spoke in unison.

Joe gave an exaggerated performance of being cowed by the majority verdict. "Resolutions?" he asked as Big Ben stopped chiming from the TV and the fireworks started, both on screen and with huge bangs outside. The sudden loud noises made Fiona glance apprehensively at Natalie but she slept on.

"To get out more," declared Dorothea. "I'm going to check whether there's an age limit on volunteering on the children's or maternity wards. Being with Adele and Natalie is doing me a power of good. Young people keep you young." Fiona was silently impressed.

Joe took his turn next. "I guess I should say, be a good granddad. But I want to build on *all* the important relationships in my life, and especially with my significant other." He put down his glass, took Fiona's from her as well and kissed her passionately and embarrassingly in front of her mother. If Dorothea had been a ten-year-old boy instead of an octogenarian, she would have been sticking two fingers in her mouth and making gagging noises. After everything Fiona had recently witnessed from Joe, she felt like doing that herself. She pulled away from him. He frowned and then asked about her resolutions.

"Making the most of my time now I'm retired," she said lamely, while mentally quaking at what the events of the evening had actually made her want to do: get to the bottom of the Meeko bombshell her mother had dropped and ask Joe to leave. She crossed her fingers that the latter could be achieved without destroying her links to Adele and Natalie.

CHAPTER 36

Christmas and New Year's Eve had been the bleakest Meeko had ever known. Except for his Boxing Day visit to Dorothea, he had spoken to no one. In previous years Lynn had been there and there'd been classes to teach. This year the hotel had taken the penny-pinching action of making all classes in Christmas week virtual online recordings supplied by head office. And Fiona had been out of bounds.

There were three reasons why he hadn't accepted her Christmas Day invitation. Firstly, Joe's presence meant there was no Meeko-sized hole for him. Joe had barged in permanently, albeit as the consequence of a flood rather than a positive move on his part, and Fiona had accepted him. Secondly, Fiona had told her ex-husband that she didn't trust Meeko. Thirdly, he couldn't accept festive hospitality while giving only second-hand chocolates in return. Adding all of that to his job problems meant this was going to be one of the worst years ever.

Over the last few days, he'd attempted to learn more about Tarot from books and the internet and he'd asked it about his future — several times, in order to get a conclusive view. To his untrained eye, the cards' verdict indicated he should talk honestly with people. That had become his new year's resolution, to be carried out today.

On Boxing Day, Dorothea had intimated that there were things about Fiona's divorce from Rob that she wasn't at liberty to tell him. Things that he ought to know in order to fully understand his best friend, but Fiona had to be the one to tell him those things. Following the cards' direction to talk honestly, he had to ask her about the past in order to fix the future and to sort out her lack of trust in him.

He'd texted Fiona to invite her to run with him. Apparently, it was easier to talk when side by side rather than face to face, which was why strangers on trains so frequently exchanged life stories. Meeko thought that was also helped by knowing the other person would never be seen again, but it was worth a try. Fiona had replied almost instantaneously, which made him think she'd been waiting for his message and hadn't needed to give his invitation any consideration. He wasn't sure whether this was good or bad. He wasn't sure about anything in their relationship anymore.

They'd agreed to meet at the park, five minutes from Fiona's house. The nerves kicked in as he saw her approach out of the murk of the wintry morning. She stopped a couple of feet away and neither took a step closer to go in for their usual hug.

"Happy New Year," she said.

"And to you." They were speaking with the formality of strangers.

She rubbed her arms vigorously and gave a little jog on the spot. "Shall we start?"

It was the first time they'd actually run together rather than meeting for breakfast afterwards. Meeko tried to match his pace to her slightly slower one. He wondered if she was also trying to match him, and if, gradually, they'd be reduced to a snail crawl as neither felt brave enough to take the lead.

"How are mother and baby?" The atmosphere between them needed relaxing if he was going to bring up the difficult subjects of Rob and Joe.

"Healthwise — fine. Coping-wise — not so good." She described Adele's exhaustion, Natalie's constant crying, and how Dorothea had had to be taxied over the previous evening. "It was the New Year's Eve from hell. And, though it pains me to say it, Mum was right. Natalie was picking up on all the tension and nervousness surrounding her. When Mum arrived Natalie imbibed her relaxed demeanour and went out like a light."

"And Joe?" He kept his voice deliberately light, not even glancing at Fiona. Let her think it was the most casual of small-talk questions.

"Joe is . . ." Fiona paused, breathing heavily as she got into their running rhythm. Meeko slowed in case he was pushing her too hard. She wouldn't complain or give in but he wanted to keep the pace suitable for conversation. ". . . Joe."

"That tells me nothing." From the corner of his eye, he saw her glance over at him. He kept his gaze forward, watching their matching streams of breath cloud in the cold air.

"I thought I knew him but I didn't really. In hindsight, I enjoyed his absence more than his presence." This time Meeko couldn't stop his head from turning towards her, but her eyes were fixed forward and then down on the ground as they entered the wooded area with tree roots to negotiate.

"And now you do know him?"

"Different situations reveal different personality aspects. He's probably having the same thoughts about me."

Meeko let the silence hang between them until they came back out onto damp grass at the other side of the small copse. He didn't want to fire a series of questions that might make her clam up.

"Want to talk about it?"

"Before he moved in, we were always on our best behaviour with each other. Like a series of dates that we wanted to make special because they were just once a week. We always wanted to leave the other with positive memories — so there was something good to hold on to until next time." Talking made her breathe more heavily and she paused before picking up the thread again. "Living together makes keeping up that perfection difficult. And when you add in the stress of Adele and Natalie, our true colours have started to leak out." She continued running without talking and Meeko wondered if that was all he was going to get. Then she spoke again, almost under her breath, as if she might be ashamed of it. "And I don't like the true Joe."

Meeko's heart filled with shocked relief. They had to stop and look both ways to cross the main road. Was Fiona exaggerating the side-to-side movements of her head so she didn't have to look at him?

Running became easier along the tarmac path. "Is there anybody else?"

"Anybody else?" She repeated the words as though she didn't understand the question.

"For you. I just wondered . . ." She was throwing him weird looks. He kept his head forward, remembering it was supposed to be easier to talk like that. "I saw you come out of One More Bean about ten days before the baby shower with a man. You were . . . confiding in him."

The only sound was their feet and their breathing. Bedroom curtains were still closed. A dog walker said 'Happy New Year' as he passed them going in the opposite direction. Meeko gave him an acknowledging nod.

"That was Rob. My ex-husband."

"Are you getting back together?" He couldn't stop the questions coming out like an inquisition now.

Her head swivelled towards him and, at the last moment, she was forced into some fancy footwork to avoid tripping over a protruding manhole cover. "I can't talk about this while I'm running. Can we cut it short and go straight for breakfast?"

Meeko was struggling as well. Without eye contact, body language or facial expressions, half of the conversation was lost. So much for the philosophy of having a deep conversation side by side while carrying out another activity. They upped the pace and took a shortcut directly to the hotel.

* * *

"... and that's the story. He basically gambled away everything we had." Fiona pushed away the plate loaded with scrambled eggs and beans. She added sugar to her coffee and stirred for a long time. Fiona didn't normally take sugar. When she lifted the cup, it trembled slightly. She took a tiny sip before returning it to the saucer with an uncontrolled clunk.

Meeko didn't speak for a long time. Her story had been a shock. He was torn between taking her in his arms and protecting her forever from the big, bad world, and admonishing her for keeping such a significant part of her life secret from her supposed best friend. Jigsaw pieces were slotting into place. The reason she needed relationships that could be controlled, plus the source of her lack of trust, was now crystal clear. But he still didn't understand why she deemed him untrustworthy. And he got the sense that Fiona was still holding something back.

"I'm sorry that you had to go through that," he said. He reached across the table and touched her hand, the fingers of which were agitating the tablecloth. As the bolt of electricity hit, his eyes went to hers. "But why didn't you trust me before?"

She pursed and unpursed her lips and then gave him a wry smile. "I know I should've told you — and I nearly did, several times. But I thought the knowledge would change how you saw me. You would feel sorry for me — exactly like you do now. And I didn't want that to happen."

Her hand had calmed beneath his. He did feel sorry for her. But he had to be worthy of her trust and react in the right way, without drowning her in sympathy and without building up or belittling what had happened to her.

"Why have you told me now?"

She turned her hand over so that their palms were in contact and gently squeezed his hand. The gesture was tiny but it felt significant. "When I met Rob, we completely cleared the air between us. And it felt good. It felt good to be with someone who knew absolutely everything. But clearing the air with him was low risk — there was no ongoing relationship to damage."

Now their fingers were interlaced. "That good feeling showed me what is to be gained by properly trusting someone. It made me realise that the benefits of opening up to you would be even greater. And I wanted those benefits." She looked him directly in the eye and squeezed his hand again.

He sensed there was more of the story to come, but now wasn't the time to push her. Instead, he returned to the present. "So why, after all those years and after what he did to you, are you back in communication with him?"

Fiona slowly stretched her fingers and slipped her hand from his. Meeko felt oddly bereft and busied himself by spreading butter and then marmalade on his toast. He tried to pretend that he wasn't invested in what she might say next.

Fiona looked like she was struggling internally.

Please don't tell me you want to give him another chance.

She took another sip of coffee, her hand still shaking. She added even more sugar and stirred for longer. Then she looked him straight in the eye. "I lost my unborn daughter on that evening. Initially I believed it was the shock of those men turning up, that it was Rob's fault our baby died." Meeko was thrown off kilter. "A miscarriage. Twelve weeks into the pregnancy." Her voice was tight as she delivered these basic facts. "For all of those three months I had a very strong feeling I was carrying a girl. I called her Amber. We were going to announce the pregnancy on New Year's Day." Her eyes filled with tears. "Thirty years ago today, both sets of parents were supposed to come to lunch. Rob and I were so excited about having made it through the first three months and finally being able to tell them and the rest of the world. Instead, it was the second worst day of my life. Our parents helped us work out the finances and how we might manage going forward through all the debt. Mum and Dad brought us an old TV and video from their loft. It was humiliating. I was still wobbly from losing the baby and felt awful dumping all the gambling and debt stuff on them. I was trying to be strong and do the right thing because I felt I should support Rob through his addiction and keep my marriage vows. But in the following months I found I couldn't live in a constant state of suspicion about what he was doing when he was out of my sight. He'd broken the financial trust I'd put in him — we'd pooled all our money when we got married because it was easier than watching who paid for what all the time. My view was that we were emotionally and physically bound together and therefore our finances should be joint too. I can't believe how naive I was."

Fiona paused. Blew her nose. Breathed deeply. Made coffee stains on the white cloth as she removed the teaspoon from the saucer and started to fiddle with it.

"You don't have to carry on . . ." He tried to calm her fiddling hand with his own. "I shouldn't have . . ." Watching her pain as she told him what had happened was far worse than thinking that she didn't trust him. And he was causing the pain by asking her to relive it. It was the last thing he wanted to do.

"In April of that year I told him I couldn't live like that anymore. He didn't put up a fight. He knew I could never forgive him for the loss of Amber. I think he understood that he'd lost my trust too. That was the end of the marriage and the point at which I realised that relationships requiring trust weren't for me. I decided I would never lay myself open like that to anyone ever again. I would rely solely on myself. Because I am the only person I can truly trust."

So much of Fiona's personality and lifestyle was now dropping into place for Meeko. He squeezed her hand again and she gave him a tiny apologetic smile as she pulled away to get her tissue. Apart from such quiet gestures, he didn't know how else to respond to the terrible trauma she'd been through. He wanted to scoop her up and protect her forever from any further horrors. But he recognised that what she needed now was the time and space to get used to having shared such a key piece of her past. She did not need the claustrophobia of being wrapped in cotton wool. She needed him to continue being her friend.

"Does seeing Rob again help in some way?" he asked.

She swallowed and then blinked her eyes a couple of times. "We met by accident at a Christmas do a few weeks back. He said he wanted to do something to make amends. 'Reparation', he called it. He's been a member of an ex-gamblers' support unit for years and done well for himself in business. He wants to give talks to warn others of the dangers of gambling and he wants me to put across how the families suffer. We've met a couple of times to discuss that."

"Keeping all that pain to yourself for three decades must have been so hard."

"At least now I've had the chance to come clean and ease his guilt over Amber's death."

"How do you mean?"

Her voice dropped to almost a whisper. "The hospital staff told me that the miscarriage was probably 'just one of those things' and not caused by the bailiffs turning up. But I wanted to make Rob suffer. So I never told him, until just recently."

Meeko could only imagine the depth of grief that had caused Fiona to act this way. Frustratingly, there was nothing he could do to make her feel better. If only it was as easy as taking a cloth and wiping away the suffering. Her face was anguished but, beneath the emotion, he noticed something else: a more relaxed, open expression, as though finally unburdening herself had broken a barrier in their relationship and built a new bridge of trust.

She blew her nose. "If we're being open with each other, I've got a question for you. Are you still sworn off romantic relationships?"

The question took him by surprise. "Why do you ask?"

She blushed, looked down and started shredding her paper serviette. "After Lynn, you said you were. And then Adele said . . . and Mum said something in passing."

"I don't want a *new* woman in my life." he said slowly, looking directly at her and taking care to emphasise the word 'new'.

Fiona's cheeks coloured and she dropped her eyes to the table and the remains of her serviette.

Meeko willed her to say something. He'd been as obvious as he dared without actually declaring how he felt — if he did that, and the feeling wasn't mutual, their friendship would be destroyed forever. She looked up at him. There was no smile, just a confused frown. His heart sank a little.

The waitresses were clearing up around them but Meeko didn't want to leave. They'd both had assumptions about the other knocked away and the boundaries of their relationship had blurred — but into what, he wasn't sure either of them knew.

"I'd better go." Fiona stood up. "I don't know what catastrophe will have happened at home while I've been out."

"Can't Joe deal with it?"

"I'm learning he's not good at that sort of thing."

CHAPTER 37

Fiona felt wrung out when she left the hotel. Emotionally exhausted. But there was a swirl of relief as well. Relief that Meeko now knew everything. Relief that she no longer had to keep secrets from her closest friend. And relief that he hadn't over-reacted. He hadn't tried to comfort her or tell her all the things in life she should be grateful for. He hadn't suffocated her with pity. She'd been worried the revelation would change their relationship for the worse. Now there was the possibility it might have changed it for the better. Deepened it.

And there was the weird way that Meeko had looked at her when he'd said that he didn't want a *new* woman in his life. Dangerous but attractive possibilities erupted. But if they boiled over, she'd lose her closest friend as well as a chance at love. Had Meeko considered that? Better to grow old without a life partner but with a close friend, than to grow old without a partner but with a ruined close friendship.

"What's for lunch?" Joe's voice tugged her back to reality as soon as she got home. "That was a long run," he added as an afterthought.

"Lunch is whatever you make for Adele and yourself. I've just had brunch and now I'm going to have a long bath."

Fiona needed to shut herself away and think. Think about Joe and their possibly not-future together. Think about Meeko and the implications of him being 'available'. The reality of that prospect sent tingles down her spine. Think about Rob and whether she should go ahead with the talks — would that be cathartic or playing with fire?

The hot water was balm for her soul, easing the tension that had built in her shoulders and neck. She was in a relationship with a physio, and she knew how strong and clever his fingers were, but never had she asked for, or had he offered to give her, a massage. Was that because, right from the start, he had decided not to mix business with pleasure? Or simply that he didn't want to use his skills unless it was for financial gain?

Natalie squalled. Fiona leaned over the edge of the bath to turn up the small radio she'd placed on the bathroom floor. A Radio 4 current affairs programme provided white noise to shut out the crying and facilitate the thinking.

After forty-five minutes and several top-ups from the hot tap, her skin resembled a prune. Joe knocked on the door demanding to know how long she was going to be because they couldn't find the tomato ketchup. Fiona simply smiled: she had decided her future.

She stepped out of the bath and wrapped herself in a soft pink towel. "In the door of the fridge!" she shouted. Then she took another twenty minutes to apply body lotion and loosely blow dry her hair. It was the longest time she'd spent pampering herself since Joe had turned up with his suitcases. It was the first time she'd fully relaxed since retiring and she'd enjoyed every minute. The real Fiona had been rescued from drowning in the domestic demands of others. She hoped Rose was feeling exactly the same way wherever she was. In an odd way, they were like sisters.

Downstairs, lunch, with tomato ketchup, was finished. Joe was on the settee flicking between football and a film on TV. Adele was feeding Natalie, having got the hang of doing it discreetly so she didn't mind her father being in the room. In the kitchen, the breakfast things had been pushed to one end of the table and the lunch plates remained in situ. The sandwich toaster had been left switched on and was surrounded by crumbs and the innards of a couple of tomatoes. The cheese was warming nicely, right next to the kettle. Fiona started to put her kitchen to rights. This time she didn't feel resentful; all of this vindicated her decision. It would have been more difficult to be sure she was doing the right thing if the room had been left pristine.

Later, Adele and Natalie went upstairs for a nap. Fiona closed the lounge door, took the remote from Joe and turned the TV off. She was done with being compared to Rose, with Joe not clearing up after himself, with the way he continued to treat his adult daughter like a child, and with him always putting himself first.

"Hey! I was watching that."

"We need to talk and we need to do it before things go any further."

Joe sat up straight and eyed her suspiciously. "You sound like Rose when she brought up the subject of divorce."

"I'm not surprised."

"She had it all cut and dried in her head. But I didn't want to throw in the towel until I was sure that she was sure it was what she wanted."

"You mean you didn't want to fend for yourself for the first time in your life." Joe had the decency to colour and look away. "After just one month together I can understand why Rose needed to get away. The only thing I don't understand is why she took so long to do it." Now she had Joe's full attention.

"What are you trying to say? Rose loved me. She devoted her life to me and the family. The divorce and this 'trip' of hers are some mid-life crisis thing. She'll be back when she's got it out of her system."

"That will be convenient because you'll be needing her."

"Adele will be needing her." Joe spoke like a teacher correcting a pupil. "And that will give us the space to reconnect." He glanced at the lounge door, saw it was closed, and patted his lap.

Fiona shook her head. Sitting on his knee was the last thing she wanted to do. "Joe, there is no 'us' anymore. I shouldn't have let this domestic charade continue as long as I have. Right back when you wanted to choose what I wore to your works do, I didn't feel comfortable about how you were treating me, but you wouldn't listen and made me feel that I was making a mountain out of a molehill. I gave you another chance. And then one of your boomerangs returned."

Joe was frowning at her onslaught and there was confusion in his eyes. "Don't bring Adele into this. There was no option but to let her stay."

"Agreed. And I've grown fond of her and Natalie. But you've made a difficult situation harder by consistently treating her like a child, going AWOL when you're most needed and, this is the bit that really hurts, continually telling me how much better Rose would've handled things. Even though I am not a Rose replacement — I am not your wife and not Adele's mother. Plus, you seem to think I am your domestic drudge. Even when Adele moves out, I can't see you cleaning or cooking."

"What do you expect? I'm working full-time but you're retired with nothing else to do."

Fiona resisted the urge to slap his face. "I didn't work hard all my life to retire at sixty and attend to all your washing, meals and cleaning." She watched his hands curl and uncurl. He pursed and unpursed his lips. She'd expected to have a lump in her throat by now and to be wondering if she was being hasty and would regret this decision. She'd even put a sheet of kitchen roll in her pocket so that, if necessary, she could easily turn her head, blow her nose and regain some equilibrium. It wasn't needed. His responses had made it easy for her to fire the final salvo. "Joe, I'd like you to move out as soon as possible."

For a moment he was shocked into silence. Then he glared at her. "Where am I supposed to go with a daughter and her newborn baby in tow, a flooded house and a landlord who can't seem to get it fixed?"

"Adele can stay until either Rose returns or you find somewhere suitable." Fiona hoped Adele would stay. It would be better for the young woman than living with Joe and, despite her best intentions, Fiona had become attached to both mother and daughter.

"What do we do until I can find somewhere?" It hurt that he didn't put up a fight to try to save their relationship. For him it was obviously a relationship of convenience rather than love.

"Adele is using my spare room. My office is too tiny to fit a bed. But the sofa is free every night." She pointed and his glare became evil. "What about your brother with a four-bedroomed house on the other side of town? The one that dropped in to see Adele in hospital. That will be nearer work for you as well. It's your choice. Sofa here or a bedroom there."

Joe walked out of the room. Fiona started to tremble. She was proud of the way she'd remained calm, but now it was over she couldn't stop shaking. For twelve months she'd believed she and Joe had the perfect relationship. It had taken just a few short weeks to realise that only seeing each other when on their best behaviour equated to building a castle on sand. Even if Adele found her own place, or if Fiona and Joe had made the conscious decision to live together instead of having it thrust upon them — neither of these things would have made them any more compatible. Joe wanted a Rose replacement, not someone who was used to her own independence and was unwilling to look after a man who thought that was still the woman's role.

A few minutes later he walked to his car with his two suitcases and drove away. Upstairs she opened the wardrobe and shuffled her clothes along the rail to refill the slice of space she'd been forced to clear for him. A little more tension left her.

"Dad!" Adele's voice called from the spare room.

He hadn't told her or said goodbye.

Fiona gave a gentle knock and walked in. "It's me, not your dad."

The young mum was in the middle of a feed. "Oh. I just wondered if someone could refill this glass with water for me, please? I swear she's drinking more now and I forget how thirsty it makes me until we're part way through and I can't move."

Fiona refilled the glass from the bathroom and then perched on the edge of the bed. There was no easy way to say this without causing anxiety. "I've asked your dad to move out. He's gone to stay with your uncle."

Adele sat up straighter and the sudden movement made Natalie lose her grip on the nipple and she screamed. "Shit!" Adele glanced across at Fiona. "Sorry." Very gently, she cradled her baby's head and redirected it towards her breast.

"No, I'm sorry. I should've waited until you'd finished."

"Why?" The younger woman's face was an expression of panic. "Is it because of me? Do you want me to go? And you do know that Uncle Tom and Dad have never been the best of friends?"

It felt like a diluted version of explaining to a child that their parents were divorcing. "Me and your dad have discovered we're not the best of friends either." *Tread carefully, don't assign blame — even though he deserves it.* "We're one of those couples that worked fine when we saw each other once a week, but we can't actually live *with* each other."

"Are you still a couple?"

"No. But don't worry, there is no need for you and Natalie to move out until you are absolutely ready."

The girl smiled gratefully. "I don't think Uncle Tom could cope with us in the way that you have." She paused, and Fiona could tell that she was thinking how to phrase the next part of what she wanted to say. "Will Dad be allowed to visit us here? I haven't got transport, and it's two buses . . ."

Fiona hadn't anticipated this. She didn't want Joe back in the house. She now knew he was the type to hold a grudge and he wouldn't hold back on letting her know. But he was still Adele's father and Fiona couldn't expect her to lug tiny Natalie across town on two buses in the freezing January weather. "Yes. But please give me warning so that I can arrange to be out. I don't want to sour the atmosphere for you."

For a minute they both watched the contented infant suckle. Then Fiona spoke again. "I was pregnant once."

"What?"

"I had a miscarriage." She hadn't planned this moment of revelation. It just seemed the natural next step in her relationship with Adele. "I never told your dad."

"I can keep a secret."

"It's not a secret anymore. Telling people feels like letting the sunshine in." Then Fiona told her daughter-by-proxy the whole story. At the end, they both had a little cry and a hug.

After that, Fiona was too tired for any further new year, life-changing decisions. Thoughts about Meeko would have to wait. She was looking forward to a good night's sleep with the whole of the bed to herself. This anticipation confirmed just how much she had given up and moulded herself in order to accommodate Joe.

Adele tiptoed out of the spare room with a finger over her lips. "She's asleep. Would you like me to cook tea for a change? If you tell me what you had in mind."

"That would be lovely! There's haddock in the freezer — how about fish pie? I'll get you the recipe."

Adele cooked. Natalie slept. Fiona stripped her bed, turned the mattress and flung the bedroom windows open despite the freezing temperatures. Then she dusted and vacuumed away all traces of Joe from her bedroom. Beneath the bed she found an odd sock and a screwed-up pair of used boxers. They went straight in the wheelie bin black bag. The bed was remade with her favourite dusky pink bedding. It felt like a brand-new life chapter, but she wasn't yet sure of the plot or its characters. The need to talk to Meeko almost overwhelmed her. But, despite that new bond of trust, he might think it weird if she asked to see him without a specific reason. She needed an excuse that would explain why it was him she was contacting to discuss her future.

CHAPTER 38

Meeko was surprised when Fiona asked if he would give her a proper Tarot reading; she'd appeared unimpressed by the cartomancy before Christmas.

"Joe's gone," she'd told him on the phone. "And I've got to create my next chapter from a blank sheet. Your cards might not help but I need options. I'll pay the going rate."

He punched the air. The toad was gone! Hopefully it had been a positive choice by Fiona to throw him out and not the toad leaving of his own free will. Then rational thought and memories of their conversation the previous day crept in. It had been impossible to discern for certain whether, like him, she felt they could be more than just friends, and if she too tingled with electricity whenever they touched. Plus, there was that big red danger sign in his head, warning there could be no way back to a solid friendship from an unworkable romance. After his loneliness over Christmas, Meeko didn't want to lose Fiona forever. It would be best to sit tight and be there for her as she worked through things herself.

The immediate problem was the Tarot. He had the cards and he had the books but he hadn't properly put them together to learn how to read the cards. Having to make every penny count had taken all his brain power. Plus, research had shown him that the internet was awash with Tarot readers — the chances of him making any meaningful money was low. He glanced at his watch: thirty minutes until she arrived. He fed coins into the meter and put the gas fire on full blast. There was only one solution: he would make up the reading to be suitably vague. She wouldn't believe it anyway — her brain was too logical.

Meeko zoomed around his kitchen and living area, dusting and putting stuff away. He bleached the toilet and wished he had air freshener because now the tiny room smelled like a hospital. He stuffed the used tea towel in the bag for the launderette and put out his slightly smarter spare one. At the same time, he was trying to guess if there was specific advice that Fiona might want.

"Come in." He'd run down the stairs at the sound of the doorbell. Once in the flat, Fiona seemed about to take her coat off, but then twitched her shoulders and changed her mind. It was obviously colder than she was used to. "We'll sit by the fire," Meeko said quickly. "It's the warmest spot. Keep your coat on until you acclimatise."

He had the cards out ready. When Fiona was settled with a mug of coffee, he turned over three cards.

"I'm at a turning point in my life." She looked him in the eye. "There are choices and I don't know which way to jump." There was an unspoken plea for guidance. As her friend, he should fabricate a neutral reading to encourage her to consider all options carefully.

Fiona's gaze was intense, moving between his face and the cards. He tried to formulate a narrative to give meaning to what he saw before him. From his initial reading on the subject, he had an inkling that the three cards were supposed to represent past, present and future. He looked up at her and picked on the left-most card, which showed a ladder of swords. "The Nine of Swords shows that things in the home aren't running as smoothly as they might."

"We already know that."

"But that sets the context for moving forward." He was working hard to keep his voice confident and believable. The next card along was captioned 'The Lovers' and was illustrated with a naked man and woman, plus an angel hovering above them. "This one indicates you are at a fork in your close relationships and decisions must be made, for your own peace of mind as well as those near to you." He dared to glance up.

She was looking intently at the cards. "What guidance are they giving?"

Meeko took a breath and bent over the pictures again. Now their heads were almost touching. He could smell her perfume, something spicy with a fruity undertone. He hoped it wasn't a present from Joe.

"The cards can't be exact. They deal in hints and generalisations. You must interpret them according to your own situation."

She frowned and sat back in her chair.

The final card was captioned the 'Ace of Cups' and appeared to show an overflowing fountain with the excess water playing into a woman's hand. He took a gamble. "This shows that there is a relationship to be had which will make you very happy." He couldn't meet her eye. "And that person is close by."

"Do you mean long-lasting romantic love or platonic friendship?" Her voice faltered over the last two words and then picked up. "Or perhaps a maternal, caring kind of love for a younger person, or the love that one might feel for a parent? Or someone I was close to years ago?"

He knew exactly who she meant in each of those scenarios but it wasn't fair to point her specifically in his direction. Changing the nature of their relationship carried a huge risk. "It could be any one of those, or more than one."

She bit her lip and frowned. "This isn't helping. I need more direct advice."

Meeko's mouth went dry and there was a fluttery feeling in his stomach. This opportunity wouldn't come again. And Fiona still had the free will to make her own decision. "If I was doing this reading for me." He spoke slowly, wanting to get every word right. "I would interpret it as pertaining to a relationship in my life that has the potential to change and grow." He held the edges of the table to steady his hands and his heart thumped as he put his case as plainly as he dared.

Fiona met his eyes, blushed and looked down again. "I . . ."

Meeko was certain she'd understood his subtext. He felt the angular wood of the table edges dig into his hands. Both their futures hung between them.

"I . . ." she repeated. There was a silence and then she looked directly at him again. "I . . . I don't want to jeopardise the most valuable thing in my life."

Meeko's heart contracted painfully. His shoulders slumped. The disappointment was huge. She had decided to obey that red danger sign. A second later he hitched his shoulders, relaxed his hands into the middle of the table and attempted to smile. Earlier he'd decided to be neutral and let her work through her options. That was still the fairest policy. "Other relationships?"

Fiona looked relieved at the change of focus. "There are several people that could apply to. I've held everybody at arm's length for so long. Including my mum. With her I automatically revert to the role of awkward teenager because that was our relationship when I last lived at home. But when I see her with Adele and other adults, I see she is an interesting person in her own right, and if I could change our relationship then I could benefit from knowing that person too."

"Improve that relationship if you can, but I don't think it's that that the cards are alluding to." He had to tread carefully; he wasn't ready to give up completely on the belief that they had a future together.

"And there's Rob. In the early part of our marriage, we were as thick as thieves. I didn't think any couple could be closer, or happier, than us. Neither of us have successfully found another partner since." She paused. Meeko hoped she couldn't hear the pounding of his heart. Rob was available and Fiona was available. "We need to work on that relationship and become friends if I'm to become part of his 'reparations tour'." Her hands added air quotation marks and she emphasised the word *tour* as though she was a rock singer with a huge live audience.

He said nothing.

"The arm's-length relationship with Joe worked because it was all I thought I needed. In the last month I've wised up. The two of us always showing our polished side, and me being in control of everything, was a house of cards. And now it's come tumbling down."

Again Meeko said nothing. Fiona stopped speaking and looked directly at him. His heart leaped. His shoulders tensed and he felt his cheeks warm. The gas fire hissed as it tried and failed to send its heat across the room. His cheeks continued to burn.

The hope still deep within him meant he couldn't stay silent any longer. "Sometimes the safest thing isn't always the best thing." He gripped the table again so the shaking of his hands wasn't visible. "Sometimes we have to take a chance." It was up to Fiona now and he would accept her verdict.

"I can't afford to gamble and lose the thing I treasure the most." Her eyes were speaking louder than her voice. "I thought I'd lost it recently and I was devastated. I can't take that risk again."

Meeko wanted to pull her close and reassure her it wasn't a gamble. But that wasn't true — they would be taking a huge risk that could end in catastrophe. That didn't stop him wanting to kiss her neck, her throat, her face. He wanted to kiss her deeply on the mouth. He wanted to tell her that the two of them being happy together was a dead cert. It was odds-on to be a success. But there were no guarantees and so he didn't speak and he didn't move.

After a silence that felt interminable, Meeko looked at the cards and then across the table to Fiona. "Have the cards helped?"

"Talking to you has helped."

"I'm glad. You're welcome anytime for another reading, a chat or . . . whatever. But bring your own hot water bottle next time." He gave a mock shiver and she had the decency to laugh.

Their drinks had gone cold and Meeko made more coffee.

"It's not fair," Fiona said when he sat back down.

"What's not fair?"

"The way the hotel is treating you. You are the most popular instructor in that place, yet they are cutting your classes. Surely your boss is slitting his own throat?"

"That's not how he sees it. Believe me — I have tried to plead my case with Frank. The lovely ladies that come to my classes are regulars, some of them come every day. Which is marvellous for me, but not so good for the hotel. They are clogging up the changing rooms and using the facilities but not bringing in any extra income because they use their membership to the full. Head office is pressurising Frank to bring in more cash, which means attracting more members, preferably working people who have less time to exercise and therefore won't monopolise the place as much as my ladies, but will still bring in the same amount of cash per head. And because they attend less frequently, we'll have space for more of them. Working people are younger and less interested in my holistic classes — they want an instant hit of calorie-burning, fat-shedding, heart-rate-rising, muscle-strengthening exercise. That way they feel attending only two or three times a week is beneficial. Does any of that make sense to you?"

"Yes and no. I understand that members who attend less frequently are more profitable. But I don't fully agree with the way your boss is going about it. I'm sure lateral thinking could come up with a better solution."

"Frank doesn't do lateral thinking. He does what the bosses from on high tell him." Meeko shrugged. "I guess that's life."

"You are too nice and too amenable, Meeko. Don't let people take advantage of that. How much do I owe you for the reading?"

"Nothing." He stopped her hand reaching for her purse, but the sudden surge of electricity from the skin-to-skin contact made him drop it immediately. They stared at each other.

CHAPTER 39

Fiona stopped the car part way home, at the picnic place by the river. She needed space to think before heading back to the demands of tiny Natalie. The cards hadn't given her answers and she was feeling strange; emotionally trembly. She'd been naive to think something as airy-fairy as Tarot would give her a direct life path to follow. And her logical mind didn't believe in it anyway. But speaking to Meeko had helped clarify some of her feelings, as well as emphasising the scary one that grew in strength every time she thought of him.

She couldn't deny that she hadn't wondered what it would be like to get back together with Rob. He knew that he owed her big time and therefore his best behaviour was guaranteed. But now she knew that best behaviour wasn't a strong enough foundation for a relationship. Had she expected perfection from Rob in the early days of their marriage, before she knew about the gambling? No. Definitely not. She had clear memories of the mess he'd left in the kitchen after his attempt at making her a birthday cake. But she also remembered him clearing up when morning sickness overcame her and she couldn't reach the toilet in time. It had been different with Joe; he hadn't seen the need to help when she was struggling. She pulled her mind back to Rob. Did he still have feelings for her? Since they'd resumed contact Fiona had begun to feel a vague sisterly concern for him but nothing romantic. That bond of trust could never be rebuilt, and he would forever have to be an arm's-length relationship. Nothing more than their joint activity with the anti-gambling talks.

Meeko. Her heart lurched again — a sensation that had never happened when she thought of either Joe or Rob. An accidental glance in the rear-view mirror caught her smiling. He was her closest friend. She hadn't been aware of him showing any interest in her as a woman until he'd announced his break-up with Lynn. But now there was no mistaking, he was throwing his cap into the ring. And, despite her reciprocal feelings towards him, she was pushing him back. Why? It was impossible to ignore those sparks of electricity. And close friends could become lovers. Often they made the best life partners — you had to be friends with someone in order to live together. But when that relationship didn't last, the close friends bit was gone too. It was a high-stakes gamble. And gambling didn't sit well with Fiona. She didn't want to take the risk. She wanted things to go safely back to how they were before. But that wasn't possible.

Pull yourself together. Look at this rationally. Tackle it like a work feasibility study.

How would you feel if he introduced you to a new girlfriend?

Gutted.

Would you be worried that she would impinge on your 'close friendship'?

Absolutely. Meeko and Lynn were already an item when he and I first met. So the issue of romance between us never arose and our friendship worked because Lynn was easy-going and understood. A new girlfriend might see me as a threat and would need tiptoeing around.

Is there a major risk of this happening?

250

Yes. He's the nicest guy I know and when he walks his hips move in a way that is incredibly sexy.

How can you mitigate this risk?

Alternative 1: Sabotage any relationship that develops. Not fair on Meeko.

Alternative 2: String him along with the excuse that I need some time to get over Joe before embarking on something new. Not fair to put the brakes on Meeko's life. I might never feel brave enough to take the plunge.

Alternative 3: Take a massive risk, pick his cap out of the ring and see what happens. Fair to Meeko but incredibly scary. Failure would be as devastating as Rob's gambling and the loss of Amber. If our romance broke down, I wouldn't be able to climb out of another big black, lonely hole. There is no way out of this mess.

Fiona's mind switched to the final part of their conversation and the drastic reduction in Meeko's classes at the hotel. Then the penny dropped and she was seized with a sudden rush of enthusiasm. He was a brilliant teacher. She was a good organiser. Together they could be a great team. This was something she could do with Meeko but without taking that step over the edge into oblivion. Something that would test their ability to work together.

"You look like a cat that's got the cream," Adele said when Fiona arrived home.

"I have a plan."

"A plan?" Adele was sporting a muslin cloth over her shoulder, holding Natalie against it and tapping her daughter gently on the back. Fiona felt proud of how the young woman's maternal confidence was developing on a daily basis.

"Project Meeko. *We* are going to make the hotel change its mind and reinstate his classes, so that he doesn't have to live like a pauper or hire himself out dressed in silly costumes or pretend to be a fortune teller."

"He did excellently as Father Christmas — all my friends said so."

"But it's not an all-year job, is it? He needs a reliable, reasonable income for the next seven years, until he can draw his state pension."

"And how do we go about doing that?"

"I haven't thought that far forward. I'll be in my office if you need me."

CHAPTER 40

Fiona turned on her laptop, created a new folder called 'Project Meeko' and, within that, a spreadsheet. Focusing on a concrete task offered a blissful release from somersaulting over and over the romantic relationship problem. She needed a list of required steps to get her friend where he wanted to be with his career.

'*Fiona to talk to Frank, hotel leisure club manager,*' she typed on Row One. But Meeko had already pleaded his case. What good would an outsider like Fiona do turning up and telling this Frank how to run his hotel? She needed a legitimate interest in what classes were available and her friendship with Meeko shouldn't be obvious to Frank, otherwise she would be ignored — and Meeko might be branded a troublemaker.

Fiona inserted three rows above Row One and typed, '*Adele to Join Hotel Leisure Club.*' Beneath that she wrote, '*Adele to request post-natal/baby yoga sessions (need to research whether these exist and whether Meeko can teach them).*' Row Three became, '*When Frank says there isn't the demand, Adele canvasses other new mums and shows the positive result to Frank.*'

Then she changed Row Four (originally Row One) to read: '*Fiona to talk to manager of Dorothea's sheltered flats about*

253

using Meeko to deliver chair/elder yoga (need to research whether these exist and whether Meeko can teach them).'

Then she went to put her ideas to Adele.

"I love the idea of doing something to help flatten my baby bump." The young woman patted the small bulge that had once nurtured Natalie. "But there are two obstacles to my involvement in this plan. Firstly, membership of that hotel leisure club is way more than I can afford. Secondly, I don't know any other new mums — I parachuted in here a month ago without the chance to attend any antenatal classes or anything."

"First point easily solved. I didn't get you a proper Christmas present, so I'll pay your membership. And I had anticipated your second point. There is a local Facebook group where people trade, advertise, offer services and so on. Put a post in there asking if anyone can recommend a post-natal or mothers and babies group you could join. That would be a big benefit to you anyway, wouldn't it?"

Adele nodded. "You've noticed that I'm going a bit stir crazy in the house all the time? But won't they think it odd if I'm trying to get support for this yoga thing at my very first meeting?"

"No, people like it when others take the lead and get things started. It benefits them without any work or organisation involved. People are inherently lazy."

"But aren't you jumping the gun by not running this past Meeko first — especially since you don't know anything about yoga?"

Fiona was doing what she'd promised herself she wouldn't do in retirement — be over-controlling. One of the points of Project Meeko was to see if she and Meeko could still get along when working together, therefore she had to bring him in on this now. She called and invited him around the next morning, after he'd taught his one and only class for the day. When he arrived, they were alone in the hallway and he looked questioningly at her. He was obviously thinking about their conversation the previous day. Fiona gave a slight shake of her head to indicate that now was not the time and directed him into the lounge.

"Post-natal yoga is definitely a thing," he confirmed. "I'd have to create a routine and gen up on the health and safety warnings for a class of new mums. But I can do it. And, for everyone's peace of mind, I'll investigate whether I need a DBS check — or whatever certificate is needed for working with potentially vulnerable people. The elderly people in Dorothea's flats might fall into that category."

"What would we do with the babies during the class?" asked Adele.

"Ah!" Why hadn't she thought of this problem? Because she'd never been a mother.

"A crèche? Meaning more money for the hotel and thus pleasing Frank?" Meeko suggested.

"A lot of us might not be able to afford it."

"Or we could have pushchairs and car seats around the edge of the room — my yoga music would be soothing for babies."

"And most of them would sleep through the class," Adele added, "if they'd been fed and pushed or driven there. And if we're all mums together it won't matter if some cry and have to be attended to."

"We'll offer both options to Frank." Fiona felt like she was leading a band of musketeers.

A couple of hours later Meeko and Fiona were sitting in Dorothea's flat watching her reaction as they explained the plan to save Meeko's career and, in the process, introduce some gentle yoga into the lives of her fellow residents. The old lady had a half-smile on her face as she looked from one to the other of them.

"What do you think?" Fiona asked as she finished explaining.

"I think," Dorothea paused and sat back with a self-satisfied expression, "I think something has changed between the two of you."

Fiona glanced at Meeko and found him looking at her. There was a flash of electricity and a feeling she'd never had before, not even in the early days of being married to Rob; that ability of couples who are close to know what the other is thinking. She felt herself flush and tried to change the subject. "The communal lounge would be perfect for classes. Meeko could get here early to push the armchairs to one side."

"I know what I'm seeing pass between you," Dorothea persisted. "Even if you two won't admit it to yourselves yet. And it has my blessing."

"The yoga . . ." Meeko said. His cheeks had gone pink and he seemed as much thrown off course as she was. "The yoga," he repeated. "Is it something you'd take part in, Dorothea? Would your neighbours be interested?"

"I'd take swinging trapeze lessons, Meeko, if it would help cement things between the pair of you. Just get me the sparkly leotard and tassels. Fiona needs someone like you to make her later years a pleasure. Arthur and I were married for fifty-five years and the ones we shared in retirement were the best."

"Mum! Meeko needs to be able to say there is a definite interest among the residents."

"I can't force them to attend but I guarantee that if you advertise there will be tea and biscuits at the end, they will be there in droves. And don't worry, I'll make the tea while Meeko finishes up his dead dog or curled cat or whatever the names of those positions are."

"Would you come with me, Dorothea? To see Mrs Fairchild?"

Fiona smiled inside; this was a good idea. It had taken a great act of will earlier not to argue when Meeko had said he wanted to see the sheltered housing manager on his own. As usual, she'd wanted to be in on whatever was happening but Meeko had put his foot down. "It's my career, my self-employment. You have the best intentions but I have to do some of the fighting on my own."

"I intended seeing her alone but that will look like me touting for business."

"Which you are," Dorothea said pointedly.

"Which I am. But I want it to look like this request is coming, at least partly, from the residents. Otherwise, it's likely to be refused because 'there is no demand'." Meeko added the air quotes and mimicked an official voice.

"I'll come. We get precious little in the way of entertainment for all the money we pay in service charges."

They had to wait until Mrs Fairchild was back from her extended Christmas break the following Monday in order to get an appointment with her. During that time Fiona continued to meet Meeko for breakfast. Neither of them mentioned their relationship, either obliquely or openly. Meeko was less generous with his hugs and she wondered whether he'd decided that platonic was best. That thought planted an unexpected kernel of disappointment in her heart.

Fiona was waiting with her mother when Meeko arrived for the meeting.

As Dorothea stood to switch from slippers to shoes, her eyes were ablaze and she was full of suffragette-like enthusiasm to fight tooth and nail for the yoga class. Meeko placed his hands on the old lady's shoulders. "Stay calm. We don't want to get this woman's back up before we've even started. Be complimentary and nice to her."

Dorothea harrumphed.

Fiona waited in the quiet of her mother's flat, the fingers of her left hand crossed tightly. Since she'd explained Project Meeko to him, Meeko had regained some of the confidence that had been slowly eaten away as he lost class after class and had to scratch around for other bits of piecemeal work. He'd been fired with a new zest for life — which was attractive. The kernel of disappointment grew and pointed itself towards her and her inability to take risks as its cause.

She loosened her fingers and picked the topmost issue from a pile of women's magazines by her mother's armchair. It was mostly filled with adverts for fashion and 'healthy' convenience foods and pages of celebrity gossip. Towards the back a problem page headline caught her eye: '*When one pal wants more than friendship'*. The reader's letter outlining the dilemma was almost a carbon copy of what was happening between her and Meeko. The senders of the letters were identified by their initials and town only. This one was written by D.O. from their very own town. A line of tension strung itself between Fiona's shoulders. Would her mother have dared write a letter like this and then leave the magazine for Fiona to read? She looked at the date on the front cover: mid-December. To allow for journalistic deadlines, the letter must have been written weeks before Joe moved in. Had her mother been wishing her and Meeko together for a very long time? Fiona read the advice of the agony aunt:

> *Close contact with a person of the opposite (or same) sex such as a working relationship, neighbour or a close 'platonic' friendship can often lead to the growth of an attraction. Often this attraction is merely fleeting and not acted upon because one or both parties is already in a relationship or because workplace affairs are not allowed or because whatever has brought the people close disappears, for example a particular project, and with no longer anything in common, the attraction and thoughts of the other person disappear. This is not the case for the daughter of D.O. The friendship is long-standing. There is a well-known risk of a friendship being lost if a subsequent romantic relationship between the pair fails. But what is often overlooked is the fact that the friendship may also be lost if one or both of the pair can't tolerate the constant unfulfilled nature of the relationship. Situations like this always lead to a situation where the people involved must take a gamble. My advice to these friends is to talk, Talk, TALK and then talk some more. Heartbreak will be minimised if the lines of communication are kept open in this way.*

No definite advice. It seemed that no one could light the way forward through this mess other than her and Meeko. She closed the magazine and put it back where she found it, trying to make it look as though it had never been touched.

Fiona jumped at the sound of a key in the lock. "Well?" Within a second, she was in the hallway greeting them. Their expressions were solemn. She'd built Meeko up for success — please don't let everything crash down now.

"She talked about the cost-of-living crisis."

"And inflation and the difficulty in getting staff."

"I pointed out that residents were getting antsy about the lack of entertainment."

"And I told her I'd had interest from some of the other retirement complexes."

"And I reminded her about next week's visit from the head office bigwigs to run a members' forum."

It was like watching a game of tennis as Meeko and Dorothea recounted the conversation without getting to the point.

"She drives a hard bargain."

"But I think she was definitely swayed by me being there on behalf of the residents."

"So, she's hired you?"

"Not hired me, exactly."

"She's given him three unpaid trial sessions. If they are well attended then he can continue — and be paid from then on."

"And for me that counts as a success." Meeko raised his hand, Dorothea followed suit and their palms met in self-congratulation.

Fiona pulled them both towards her in a hug. Things were on the up.

When Fiona got home Adele was flapping around trying to put on make-up at the same time as rocking Natalie's car seat with one foot. "I was trying to take her out for the first time but it's too difficult."

"I'll take her while you get ready. And have I got success news for you! Meeko has got three trial sessions at Mum's flat complex."

Adele turned round from the mirror. "You really like him, don't you? When Dad was here you were trying to quash it but it's written all over your face now. And when I say 'like' I don't mean any of that platonic best friend stuff either."

Fiona was mortified. She was sure she'd kept her feelings well hidden, especially when Joe was around. Even though Adele had previously voiced suspicions, she didn't want her to think she'd been fancying other men when her father was still in the picture. "I'm just pleased for him. Like I would be pleased for anyone who achieved the success they deserved."

"Yeah, right." Adele turned back to the mirror and began brushing mascara onto her lashes.

"Where are you off to?" She'd been so full of Meeko she hadn't properly registered what Adele had said about going out.

"I'm following your orders. I joined a couple of online neighbourhood groups and asked about stuff for new mums and babies. There's a group that meets at St Michael's church hall at two p.m. I believe my instructions from you are to infiltrate and then brainwash them into marching on the hotel to demand post-natal yoga sessions."

"You are a star, Adele. I'll give you a lift, it's already almost two."

"Thanks. And don't worry, I won't let lover boy down. For what it's worth, I don't think you and Dad were a good fit anyway."

Fiona couldn't meet the young woman's eyes. Adele's perspicacity made her feel like a teenager caught with an illicit boyfriend in her bedroom — even though it was unlikely she and Meeko would get that far.

"Now I'm seeing you properly in action," Adele continued, "rather than merely reacting to the awkward position that me and Dad bamboozled you into, it's obvious that you're too independent and go-getting for him. Dad's a staid traditionalist. I thought Mum was as well, but now I'm not sure."

After dropping her at the hall, Fiona drove to the hotel and enquired about Adele joining the club, specifically questioning the availability of post-natal yoga classes. The woman on the desk had the joining form out in a split second but became less positive when pushed on the specialised yoga classes. Instead, she talked broadly about how the club was constantly innovating, and perhaps Fiona's friend could put in a formal request once she was a member.

"Oh, she'll definitely be doing that," Fiona said with a smile as she swiped her debit card for Adele's membership.

An hour later, Fiona helped Adele fasten Natalie's seat back into the car. "Well?" she asked. "Were there any takers for Meeko's yoga?"

"Well and truly smitten. There is no other verdict."

"What?"

"You! You are well and truly smitten with Meeko and his future. Or, dare I say it more specifically, with *your joint* future. You haven't asked me how I enjoyed it or did Natalie behave."

"Sorry." Damn! She gave Adele a tight hug by way of apology. She was falling back into her old habit of obsessing over one train of thought and forgetting that other people had their own concerns too. It came from living alone and not needing to consider anyone else. It had made her good at her job — she could follow projects through without going off at tangents — but she'd often been criticised for excluding the opinions of others, thus missing beneficial ideas and failing to give the members of her team room to grow. "How was it for you? Tell me all!"

"Weird but reassuring. Full-on baby talk, but it made me feel better that I'm not the only one struggling and feeling a failure and sometimes wanting to go and dump Natalie on the doorstep of the hospital and demand they take her back."

"Tell me you don't really feel that way!" Still standing beside the open passenger door, Fiona held both of Adele's hands and squeezed them. She had never wanted this girl to cross her threshold; two months ago, she was happy for her to be a nameless blur somewhere in Joe's invisible 'other' life. Now, what she felt for her could only be described as love and respect. An infinite amount of respect for a girl who had found herself accidentally pregnant by a boyfriend who didn't want to know, with a mother who'd scarpered without a word to 'find herself', and a father who'd been forced to move in with his reluctant girlfriend. Yet Adele had pulled herself together, matured at the speed of light and was becoming confident in her new maternal role. "Please say you don't really want to abandon Natalie?" Fiona had tried not to love the baby. Then circumstances had given her no option but to get involved. Still she'd tried to hold back because she knew having Adele under her roof could only be temporary and any attachment that grew would eventually be torn apart. Temporary for all the right reasons: Adele needed to be independent, Fiona needed her own space, and maybe, subconsciously, she'd always felt her relationship with Joe wouldn't last. However, despite her best efforts, Fiona did love the baby and the thought of her being dumped somewhere was abhorrent.

"Don't look so shocked, Fiona. Yes, I have felt that way several times. Just like all the other new mums in there — and a couple of them are *over forty* — but none of us would ever do it. And I especially wouldn't do it now I know I'm not the only one feeling that way — they've put me in the WhatsApp group and we can sound off in there whenever we need to."

Over forty — Adele said it like it was a terminal disease. If Fiona hadn't wasted her forties still laser focused on keeping any male emotional attachment at bay, she might have sat in a church hall and felt the support of other women around her. Women who, through that shared experience, might have become lifelong friends and still be supporting each other into their sixties. Suddenly she was aware of Adele speaking to her again.

"Calling planet Fiona! Calling planet Fiona!"

"What?"

"You're hurting my wrists. Please can we get in the car and go home? It's cold standing here."

Adele's words flicked Fiona back to reality. She immediately loosened her hands, stamped her feet and pulled her jacket closer across her body, trying to appear nonchalant instead of embarrassed.

Once they were on the main road, Adele picked up the conversation again. "Eventually I brought up the subject of post-natal yoga. Don't forget it was my first time in a room of strangers and a brand-new environment — I couldn't do it straight away."

"No, of course not. What did they say?"

"They all patted their flab and moaned about the lack of time to fit in an exercise class and the lack of money for gym fees. And, well, how difficult making it to the hotel leisure club would be for various reasons."

It was a blow. But Fiona had weathered greater storms at work. All it would take was another brain dump.

"Then I had an idea!" There was excitement in Adele's voice now and, in response, Fiona could feel her heart lifting with anticipation. "If they can't get to the yoga, why doesn't Meeko bring the yoga to them. He wouldn't have the security of a regular payment by the hotel — but that security has turned out to be worthless anyway — and we could only pay him according to how many people turned up. The church lets the group use the room for free and each time you attend you put a pound in the kitty to cover tea and biscuits, and any excess buys toys for the older babies to play with. It was agreed that if a yoga class was included, people would be happy to pay five pounds for the session. Meeko would get four pounds per person and attendance can be anywhere between ten and fifteen people."

Fiona tried to compute the practicalities. "That sounds like an outcome with possibilities. And the potential to grow."

"You sound like an estate agent describing a property 'in need of modernisation'."

"Let's get Meeko round tomorrow to discuss. This evening's job is taking down the tree — I've just realised it's Epiphany today."

CHAPTER 41

Rob had found it an exercise in self-control to stay away from Fiona over Christmas, but breaking into her festive period didn't seem right. At this time of year everyone burrowed down for at least a fortnight and family took priority. He'd done a lot of thinking since their last meeting and now he understood why he'd never found another life partner. Fiona was special. Unique. Passionate (in all senses of the word). The decades hadn't dimmed her physical attraction and they had sharpened her personal qualities, which he realised he'd been unconsciously searching for in every woman since. Some people were absolutely meant to be together. His actions of thirty years earlier had scuppered any chance of him and Fiona getting back together, but he still valued having her back in his life.

They hadn't been in touch since before Christmas and it was now 6 January. A casual phone call, ostensibly to see if she'd made any progress in contacting the female gambling support group, wouldn't be out of place. Just when he thought the answering service on her mobile would kick in, Fiona picked up.

"Hello Rob."

"Fiona. I hope you've had a good Christmas and New Year?"

A big sigh. "Yes. No. Let's call it eventful." There was a mewling sound which could have been a very angry cat . . . or possibly a baby?!

"Is now a good time to talk about the anti-gambling stuff?"

"We're just taking the tree down. And Natalie's playing up. Hold on." The sound of a whispered conversation with a woman. "Give me an hour to finish up here and I'll meet you at the Golden Lion."

"Great. See you soon." It was a good omen that she wanted to meet face to face.

* * *

Fiona was flushed when she arrived and came in from the cold. Rosy cheeks and bright eyes suited her. Rob stood up and waved. Her face broke into a grin as she spotted him. For a second the years shifted away and they were meeting after work so they could travel home together. As she sat down, he pushed a glass of wine towards her. "I hope you don't mind. I noticed at the club Christmas dinner that you still drink red wine."

Fiona took a sip and gave a deep sigh. "That's just what I need. My head's spinning with everything that's going on." She took another sip and smiled at him. "I just need a few minutes to ground myself and gather my thoughts."

"Want to talk about it?"

She shook her head. "Not right now. It would take too long to explain. Focusing on the anti-gambling project is what I need to get me outside of my own head and off my constant merry-go-round of thoughts."

"OK." He took a mouthful of the beer in front of him. "I'll go first with my progress. I contacted all the gambling support groups within a twenty-mile radius. With it being

265

Christmas, I've only heard from a handful of them but I have managed to set up a meeting with Colin, the chairperson of the group nearest to us, for a week today. It would really help if you could come with me." Her wine was almost half-gone. He watched her check the calendar on her phone.

She looked up at him and smiled. "Not a problem."

He watched her type in the time and location. "Colin asked, in advance of the meeting, if you could draft what you might say about being the partner of someone with a gambling problem? It needs to be something that will make potential gamblers think twice before putting their partners through that anguish."

Fiona nodded. "I'll try to give it some thought in between childcare and masterminding yoga classes."

He raised an eyebrow.

"In a nutshell: Joe has moved out, leaving behind his daughter and her new baby, which I had to help deliver in my bathroom on Christmas Eve. In addition, my friend has had his yoga classes cut at the fitness club in the Birnside Hotel and I'm trying to get some private classes started for him."

"If you want something doing, ask a busy person . . ."

"It was easier when I was at work. At least I could go home and leave it behind. It's impossible to do that when it's all happening at home."

"Anytime you want a listening ear, give me a shout." He hoped he'd spoken in a throw-away manner but with enough sentiment that Fiona would feel able to take him up on it. "Another drink?" He pointed at her almost empty glass. "Or are you driving?"

"Yes, please. This place is only a ten-minute walk from my house."

With both drinks refilled, he asked how she'd got on with the all-female gambling groups.

"I'm sorry. It was only on the way here that I remembered I was supposed to do that. Life totally got in the way." She smiled ruefully.

"No problem. But could you do it before we see Colin. Or would you like me to—"

"No." There wasn't a moment's hesitation. "I'll do it. I don't want any accusations of me not pulling my weight."

"There's never been any danger of that."

"It used to annoy me when people gave that excuse about life getting in the way. I thought if people were properly organised, like I believed I was, then nothing, barring death or serious illness, should derail things." She took a drink of the fresh wine. "But now I understand how easy it is to get knocked off course. I wish I could go back and apologise to everyone I've ever rolled my eyes at. It's nothing to do with not being organised and everything to do with actually having a life, with real, fallible people in it."

"Tell me more about this friend with the yoga classes."

"His name's Meeko." There was no mistaking the fondness in her voice as she described the impecunious yoga teacher and the efforts that both she and the young woman, Adele, were making to generate more classes for him. "I want to see his confidence and pride in himself back to their old levels. He's too old to be barely scratching a living. And he's got that gift of making people feel good about themselves. Including me. And I don't want to lose that."

It was difficult to tell whether her fondness for Meeko was platonic or if there was something else lurking in the background. He suspected there was, but Meeko didn't sound like the kind of ambitious male that would attract Fiona.

She drank the second glass of wine more slowly and told him about Natalie's birth and then summoning Meeko, who turned up like a knight on a white charger, to get them safely to hospital. The attraction of this man was obviously in his hidden depths.

Afterwards, it seemed only natural that Rob walked her home. They paused at the end of her drive and he gave her a hug. He deeply regretted the big black, life-destroying hole he'd dragged them both into decades ago. Discovering her secrecy over the nurse saying that the miscarriage would've happened anyway, regardless of the bailiffs turning up, had shocked him. But, mulling it over, he realised that even if he had known, he was in such a downward spiral back then that he would've blamed himself anyway. However, now that they were talking again and working together, he had a shiny feeling of hope that they could pull each other towards a bright new future.

CHAPTER 42

Fiona made herself sit back and let Adele explain the Mother and Baby group proposition to Meeko. That was easier to do if she was busy with something else, but she didn't want to lose the reins completely by leaving the room; one of them might get hold of the wrong end of the stick or make assumptions that led them up a blind alley. She was the one with the most knowledge of money, organising and running a business. So she stayed in the lounge and busied herself setting up the new multi-coloured, all-singing, all-dancing baby gym that Joe had dropped off on his way to work. He was keeping strictly to scheduled visits when Fiona was absent, but she could tolerate a few minutes of his presence if it was a visit with a brief but definite purpose. Adele had asked if he could come for a couple of hours on the coming Saturday afternoon. Fiona had agreed but hadn't yet got a plan about where she would disappear to. At the moment it was a choice between visiting Dorothea or a late visit to the sales.

Natalie was lying on the floor gazing up at the red, blue and green elephants dangling a little way above her head. She gave a kick and a barely perceptible arm wave. Fiona gazed down into the huge wide blue eyes, her heart suddenly feeling so full that she wanted to cry. It wasn't the tearful sadness and regret she'd had the first few times she'd been forced to hold Natalie. These were feelings of genuine happiness and gratitude that Adele, Natalie and Meeko were here in her house. The atmosphere had been too sterile and too controlled for too long. The previous jealousy that it wasn't her baby lying on the rug in front of her had dissipated. The last time she could remember feeling this way was when the blue line on the pregnancy test appeared, confirming Amber's existence. At that point her life and the world and the universe had felt rich with promise. She felt the same way now, except that she couldn't define what that promise was. Only that it was something to do with letting herself feel emotion and be close to other people, sharing their hopes and dreams for the future.

"Sounds like a good plan. What do you think, Fiona?"

She'd managed to tune out of the conversation that she'd planned to listen in on. In work meetings, even over Teams in lockdown, she'd been careful to stay engaged, and even to prompt people to get to the point when they drifted around the houses repeating what everyone else had already said. To lose focus would have been a disaster and involve much backtracking through emails later to try and pick up anything important. But now she actually felt pleased that she'd managed to disassociate herself and let Meeko have his head in a discussion that would impact him rather than her. "Sorry. I missed that. I'm sure you've got it all sorted. What's the conclusion?"

"You are turning into a besotted granny-by-proxy." Meeko spoke in a playful voice and poked her back gently with his stockinged foot. Instead of making her tense and out of control, the teasing felt good. "I'm going to the next Mother and Baby group to introduce myself and explain what yoga can do to help new mums get back into shape. I'll do a thirty-minute trial session. No charge. If they enjoy the session, the group will ask the vicar if they can have the hall for an extra hour so that a yoga session can be included in the meeting. And I will be paid four pounds per participant."

"I'll volunteer to collect the money," Adele said. "No one else will want the hassle. Not sure yet whether it will be bank transfer or a payment app. We might need to experiment."

"And once it's established, I'm going to look at the ins and outs of running my own general public yoga class in the hall. I like the idea of relying more on myself and flexing to the needs of the community rather than having to constantly kowtow to Frank."

"Public liability insurance!" She'd meant to hold back on interfering but that had just hit her in the head like an arrow. Meeko would be ruined if anyone sued him.

He raised a palm to calm her. "It's in hand. I've been googling and there are specialist companies that can provide this for yoga teachers."

Natalie lost interest in the parade of elephants and started to whimper.

"Time for a nappy change and a feed." Adele moved the baby gym out of the way and scooped up her daughter. Leaving the room, she looked over her shoulder, caught Fiona's eye and winked. "I'm sure you two will get along just fine without me hanging around here and making it an odd number."

"Actually," said Meeko after Adele had finished making a big show of closing the door properly behind her, "I have got something to ask you."

Fiona flinched and felt her stomach go rock hard. *Please, no. Don't put into words what the two of us are feeling for each other. Don't make it real. Don't make me have to decide whether or not to take that risk. Don't make me have to choose between throwing myself off a cliff in the hope of a soft and forever landing, or carrying on in this sweet little friendship rut that may or may not hit a blockage further down the path. I don't do gambling.*

Meeko stood up and wriggled an envelope out of his trouser pocket. Fiona sagged back in her chair — it wasn't a small black box embossed with the name of a jeweller. Instead, he handed her a piece of stiff white card with silver writing. "I've been invited to a wedding and it includes a 'plus one'." He paused. "It would be nice if the person I take with me . . . is you."

Meeko's voice was serious and his eyes reinforced the message that he wanted her to say yes. She half expected him to go down on one knee and reiterate his invitation, such was the amount of feeling behind it. "It's this coming Saturday," he added. "Sorry about the short notice but I didn't dare invite you when Joe was still the man in your life." He seemed to realise what he'd implied and added quickly, "Not that I'm presuming to be the new man in your life. But since we get on well and you've got all this Project Meeko stuff off the ground for me, I wanted to take you somewhere nice as a treat. And this will be a very good do — my cousin is marrying into an investment banking family with squillions of pounds. He's fallen on his feet and the rest of our family are keen to make the most of whatever crumbs are thrown our way, for example wedding invites," he paused again, "with overnight accommodation included." Then he named a London hotel well known for its celebrity and royal clientele.

Opportunities like this didn't grow on trees, and who better to enjoy it with than Meeko. Her head was sending out warning signals but at the same time reminding her that she did need somewhere to go on Saturday to avoid Joe. Her heart was saying, yes please! Yes please! Her head was saying, ask about the accommodation. Her heart was saying, let's stick with our resolution to not be controlling and to go with the flow and see what happens.

Meeko stood up again to put the invitation away. "Don't worry, I should've guessed that you'd already have something on at this short notice. It's not that important." He was looking over her left shoulder now rather than directly meeting her gaze.

"Yes," she said. "I'd like to go with you."

"You would?" She'd given Meeko the answer he'd least expected. "That's fabulous! I'll add you onto my RSVP this very minute." He picked up his phone and started swiping and typing as though she would change her mind if he didn't immediately make her response official.

"What's the dress code?" Her heart was thumping at what she'd just agreed to do — spend a whole day in Meeko's company, meet other members of his family (what would he introduce her as?) and potentially share a very posh hotel room with him. "Should I buy a gift?" Organisational questions grounded her mind and stopped panic taking over.

"Dress code?" Meeko looked at her as though she was talking another language.

"Let me see the invitation." He stood again and handed the envelope over.

"Morning dress. Have you got a morning suit?"

Meeko looked at her blankly. "I don't ever wear a suit — I thought my navy trousers plus my one and only jacket would do. They don't quite match but I do own a tie and that's blue too, although it passes for black if the lighting in the crematorium is sufficiently dim. Shoes might be a problem because I only ever wear trainers. There's a brown pair at the back of my wardrobe. I could polish them up."

"Morning dress," she repeated. "Like you're wearing in the wedding photo in your flat."

"Oh, that! The happy couple provided that for me and whisked it away again at the end of the day."

"You cannot go to a wedding at the best hotel in London wearing mismatched clothes. Even if everyone is too polite to comment it will be captured in the photos and be there as evidence — *forever*." She deliberately emphasised the last word.

"I'm not buying some poncey suit to wear just once. I'm broke, remember?"

"A suit maketh a man. Not poncey at all. Most women adore a man wearing any sort of smart suit — it has a similar effect to a uniform."

"Oh?" Now he appeared to be giving it some consideration.

Fiona pictured him in a tailcoat with pressed trousers, shiny black shoes and a carnation in his buttonhole. Warmth flooded her body and she knew it would take a concentrated effort to keep things on a platonic footing if he scrubbed up as well as she expected.

"How much do these magic suits cost?" he continued.

"Too much. But," she paused, wanting to word this correctly so he didn't feel she was offering charity, "I'll hire one for you. It's cheaper and I want to thank you for including me in this posh outing."

He squeezed her hand and a shot of electricity darted up it. "No thanks are necessary. I absolutely want you there."

A fierce heat was burning inside her. "I think we can order online and hopefully get it delivered by Saturday morning."

"I need it by Friday. The accommodation is the night before the wedding *and* the night of the wedding."

Fiona wasn't sure her self-control was up to the challenge of two nights alone with Meeko, but still she didn't have the guts to question the sleeping arrangements in detail. "It's Tuesday now!"

They found a hire site offering expedited delivery for a fee. Fiona located her tape measure to check Meeko's sizing. Adele appeared just as Fiona was wondering how she was going to manage the inside leg manoeuvre. "Adele! Would you do the honours please? I'm too old to be kneeling down or bending over."

Adele caught her eye and winked. "Too embarrassed, you mean. You had no trouble getting down on the floor earlier to sort out Natalie's baby gym." But she took the tape that Fiona was thrusting at her.

Fiona completed the order form, added her credit card details and pressed 'Pay'. She was promised delivery to Meeko's flat before 7 p.m. the following day.

CHAPTER 43

The next morning Fiona's phone pinged with a task reminder: *Contact female gambling support group ready for Monday 13th meeting with Rob.* It gave her a surge of positivity. She was learning that to safeguard her mental health and satisfy her craving for purpose, external projects were essential. She was discovering the joy in friends and family, even 'by proxy' family, but she would always need something outside of that to continue functioning happily as Fiona Ormeroyd.

A quick search on the internet brought up the charity's website and a range of 'contact us' options. Fiona glanced at her watch: it was only 7.30 a.m. and the chances of anyone picking up the phone were slim. She composed an email outlining what she and Rob were trying to achieve via their proposed talks, how they'd also like to campaign and raise funds for a female-only support group in their local area, and how grateful they'd be to receive any advice on the way forward.

After pressing 'send' she heard the floorboards creak into life in Adele's bedroom above the kitchen. Then there were footsteps on the stairs before a crumpled Adele came into the kitchen and picked up the kettle. "Miracles do happen! She only woke me once during the night and I managed to get her straight back down after feeding and changing her. It feels like I've had the best, deepest sleep ever." She paused while water pounded from the tap into the kettle. "And twelve months ago, I never thought I would say that after waking up just before eight a.m."

Fiona passed her mug when Adele indicated she was offering tea. "You've done brilliantly," she said, and then realised they hadn't yet broached the subject of Adele's half-finished degree, student loans, accommodation and all the other baggage that comes with abandoning a degree course. She watched Adele swirl teabags and add milk to mugs. "Talking about uni . . . And I'm not trying to throw you out by mentioning this," Fiona added hurriedly. "But what happens next?"

Adele gave a rueful smile and pointed to the ceiling with an upside-down teaspoon. "The earliest I could go back is the autumn term. There is an onsite crèche and I could get a flat. But all that needs money. If I don't finish my degree, I'm potentially ruining our futures. So . . . I've found a couple of bursaries to apply for and I'm investigating whether I qualify for an increased student loan or even a grant. Depending on childcare here, I might be able to get a casual job for a couple of months before September. If I can raise the finances, I'm going back in September, with Natalie, to retake my second year and then do the final year."

Fiona was impressed. "I can help with childcare on a casual, ad hoc basis," she said slowly. She wanted to help but she didn't want to commit vast amounts of time to something that would only fulfil a small part of her current needs.

Adele finished her mug of tea and ate a bowl of cereal before the squawks started from above. She took care to rinse her bowl out before going upstairs to her daughter. Fiona turned back to her laptop; there was already a reply from the gambling support group inviting her and Rob to visit them to find out more. A research visit — again she experienced a ripple of excitement. She had a purpose, and someone to share that purpose. And the new Rob was surprisingly easy to be with. She'd expected him to bring out the negativity within her but the opposite was happening. Plus, there was Meeko and the wedding to come, and the unspoken but mutual attraction between them. And the big risk attached to that.

CHAPTER 44

They travelled down to London by train, arriving mid-afternoon Friday, and checked straight into the hotel. The room was the largest Fiona had ever seen; the bathroom was more than twice the size of her own at home and boasted two sinks.

"Why?" she said to Meeko. "Washing isn't a team sport."

He pointed to the elephant in the room: the one king-size bed.

She swallowed hard and tried to keep her face expressionless. *Don't moan. Meeko wants you to enjoy this and someone else is paying for it. Go with the flow, that was your intention when you accepted the invitation. It's too late to change things.*

"I could ask at reception," Meeko said. "Sometimes these can be split into twin beds. Would that be more comfortable?"

She wanted to say yes but she didn't want him to feel humiliated or awkward asking for something different to what they'd very kindly been given. It would be embarrassing if one of his family overheard or saw what was going on. "No. It will be fine. The bed is huge anyway." A look of relief whispered over his face.

There was a family dinner that evening. They were placed on a table with several of Meeko's cousins and their partners.

Fiona immediately felt comfortable among them and they didn't question Meeko's introduction of her as 'Fiona — my best friend'. It was a good label. The cousins lived across all areas of the UK, in a variety of occupations, and caught up with each other rarely, except during lockdown it seemed — there was much talk of a Zoom quiz league they'd set up to help beat the boredom. Someone suggested they breakfast together the next day and then take a boat trip down the Thames, arriving back at the hotel for a quick lunch before donning their glad rags for the ceremony, which was due to happen in the hotel ballroom.

"Is lunch here included?" someone asked.

"Don't think so."

"Think arm and a leg," Meeko warned.

"Then we'll pick up a Subway on the way back from the river," someone else suggested.

Fiona had only one glass of wine with dinner, even though Meeko kept reminding her it was free and she wasn't driving. She didn't explain that the thought of the one bed was looming and she wanted to be sober enough to not do anything either of them might regret. She'd brought her most puritan, long-length, long-sleeved and high-necked nightdress with her. It wasn't the most comfortable of her nightwear options, and definitely not the most attractive, but the aim wasn't to portray herself as a sexual being. She washed, brushed her teeth and changed in the privacy of the giant bathroom. When she came out Meeko had already shed his one pair of good chinos and best shirt and was wearing a style of blue and red paisley pyjamas that a grandfather might choose. He was fiddling with the huge teal sofa that sat beneath the bedroom window. "This converts into a sofa bed," he said. "And there's spare bedding in the top of the wardrobe. It would save us any . . . embarrassment."

He turned his back and ran his fingers along the floor edge of the settee, as though searching for a magic catch that would spring the whole thing open. This was what she'd wanted, separate sleeping arrangements so they each knew where the line was drawn. But now that Meeko was trying to make it happen, it felt like an insult. Did he not want to be near her? Had she misread the signs? Neither of them had openly voiced their attraction. Perhaps it wasn't mutual. She tried not to be disappointed that the thing she'd previously been hoping for was happening. She was over-tired and things were getting warped in her brain. It was gone midnight and they'd agreed to meet the others for breakfast at 7.30. Plus, she'd started the day exhausted after a night listening to Natalie crying and finally getting up herself to offer moral support to Adele before the poor girl cracked, ordered an Uber and abandoned her baby on the steps of the hospital. Meeko was making no progress with the bed-settee.

"Leave it, Meeko," she said. "This is a huge bed. We can manage for a couple of nights."

He jumped up immediately. "If you're sure?"

She nodded and then watched as he took the four spare pillows from the wardrobe and built a cushioned wall down the centre of the bed. She loved and hated him for it at the same time. Then she surprised herself by closing her eyes and being aware of nothing else until Meeko gently tapped her on the shoulder at 6.45 and asked if she'd like to use the shower first.

"I'm not trying to say that you need to shower," his face coloured. "But I thought you might like first go. And I've made coffee."

They pussyfooted around each other until they reached the dining room and were waved over to a table full of the cousins they'd sat with the previous evening. Family in-jokes were batted around along with reminiscences of previous reunions and comments on family members who had been lost. Fiona was finding it increasingly difficult to pretend active involvement and keep a smile on her face.

"You go on the boat trip without me," she said to him afterwards. "We're both feeling awkward, let's give each other some space and then reconvene to dress for the ceremony."

"Will you be OK on your own?"

She nodded. It wasn't her ideal weekend in London, but she didn't want to be an interloper in a family who rarely had a chance to catch up with each other.

Meeko kept his expression blank so she couldn't tell if it was what he wanted. She suspected it was and, from his actions last night, that he was also happy with a purely platonic friendship between the two of them. This thought made her mood descend even lower than when Joe was comparing her to Rose and finding her wanting. She had to make herself more positive before the wedding this afternoon. After the boat trip party had gone, Fiona went off to indulge herself in history at the British Museum.

On her way back to the hotel she picked up a prawn sandwich and a banana from the M&S food hall. The empty packet was in the bin and Fiona was stepping out of the shower when she heard Meeko return. Her fitted, gold knee-length dress was laid out across the bed and she had only the thick, fluffy bath towel to protect her from prying eyes. Fiona cursed his return; she'd been hoping to have a relaxed session getting ready without the need to hide away in the now steamy bathroom.

"Hi," she called through the bathroom door. "Won't be a minute. Just getting dry." She towelled her arms and legs again and tried to think of a plan. Her deodorant, body lotion, moisturiser, in fact everything she needed to make her sixty-year-old self presentable, were in her overnight bag which sat in the corner of the bedroom. She could ask Meeko to pass the case and her dress and the fresh underwear which she'd unpacked into the top drawer, and just open the bathroom door a few inches for him to do so. Or she could brazen it out by appearing before him in her towel and then attempting to get dressed behind it, like she used to do in the school changing rooms after PE. Then she had a better plan.

"Meeko? Will you be showering next?"

"Yes. Even I know putting a brand-new shirt and freshly hired suit over a slightly sweaty body is not the best thing."

"Why don't you slip into the bathroom as I slip out so that we both get some privacy to paper over the cracks of age?"

There was the sound of fumbling and a suitcase opening. "Can you throw me a fresh towel out."

It was only after she'd tossed a large dry towel into the main part of the room that Fiona realised Meeko hadn't properly understood what she meant. She had wanted him to enter the bathroom fully clothed carrying all his wedding stuff while she slipped out.

Too late. "I'm ready if you are!" he called.

She opened the bathroom door slowly. He was immediately in front of her wearing only a matching towel tied around his waist. She remembered the two robes in the wardrobe, which would have offered both of them better protection, but they'd ignored them. He was standing too close. She turned sideways to edge past. He misread her movements and stepped the wrong way. They collided. Bare arm against bare arm. Fiona jumped as though a red-hot iron had branded her skin. Meeko's eyes were wide and he was rooted to the spot. *Move!* she wanted to urge him. *Lock yourself away and keep that body of yours out of my sight.* But she couldn't speak. He stepped forward again and this time his skin lingered slightly longer against hers, giving strength to the ensuing heat that travelled to her groin. She wavered, wanting to stride away from danger but also wanting to stay and find out what might happen.

"Just testing," said Meeko. His eyes bored directly into hers.

"Testing what?" Her words came out little louder than a whisper.

"That the magical feeling was real and that you felt it too. You did, didn't you?"

"Yes." A squeak was all she could manage. There it was, their mutual attraction openly acknowledged. Neither of them moved. She'd never been a daredevil wanting to jump out of a plane with only a flimsy parachute between her and a horrific death. But now they'd both taken this massive leap of faith without knowing the landing place.

Meeko stepped away first and shut the bathroom door behind him. Was that good or bad? Was he shutting the door permanently on what might come next?

Concentrate on the wedding. In thirty minutes, we have to be seated in the extremely posh ballroom of this incredibly expensive hotel looking smarter than we've ever looked in our lives. We need to appear relaxed and at ease with each other in the way that only best friends can.

She moisturised from head to toe and applied extra deodorant — anxiety made her armpits continually damp. When she heard the shower switch off, she wriggled hurriedly into her dress to avoid Meeko marching straight out of the bathroom and catching her in bra and pants. Her best bra and pants, bought just before Joe moved in and never worn — which sort of made them virgin. When Meeko emerged a couple of minutes later in morning trousers and shirt, she was spraying perfume on her neck and stepping into heels that would give her blisters within the hour.

"Ten minutes before we need to head downstairs." He paused and she felt her cheeks grow hot as he made it obvious that he was inspecting her from top to toe. "You look fabulous."

"Thank you. Do you need a hand with your tie or cuff links?"

"Cuff links? Didn't they go out with the ark?"

"Sorry. Childhood memory — I would sit on the landing and watch Mum and Dad get ready for a dinner dance and she always asked him that question." She prattled nonsensically when she was nervous.

Meeko knotted his gold tie. He'd chosen it when she'd told him the colour of her dress. He looked more handsome than ever.

Fiona checked the contents of her evening bag while Meeko put on his tailcoat and black patent shoes. "I feel like I'm on *Strictly*," he complained.

"Good, because the invitation said there would be dancing until midnight."

The ballroom was spectacular. Huge crystal chandeliers hung from gold chains, the walls were unblemished buttermilk with occasional alcoves housing claret-coloured velvet sofas. The rows of chairs had thick seat pads covered in the same dark fabric, and the chair backs were decorated in wispy netting which matched the pink silk dresses of the eight bridesmaids: four adult and four cute, tiny ones. The bride wore a figure-hugging cream sheath with a huge train and carried a bouquet of red roses and greenery. The groom, his best man and groomsmen were in top hat and tails with scarlet ties plus single red roses in their buttonholes. The whole ceremony and the dinner that followed felt to Fiona like a fantasy filmset. The real world had receded and she was playing a part in a fiction or a dream. The best part was being on the arm of the most handsome man in the room. Finally, she was the princess in all those fairytales her mother had read to her decades earlier. With Meeko as her Prince Charming.

All the family reminiscing was done, his relatives were friendly, fun and fantastic to be with. The champagne flowed, the food was top notch and, as the evening progressed, the dance floor was never empty. At 11 p.m. the best man organised a gangway through the throng of guests for the bride and groom to take their leave. Meeko squeezed the two of them into a gap near the end of the guard of honour of waving hands. He positioned Fiona immediately in front of him and wrapped his arms around her waist. She leaned back into him, completely relaxed by the continuous topping up of her fizz, the dancing and the convivial storybook atmosphere. She was happily tired and content in a way she couldn't remember feeling since her own wedding to Rob — but today felt even better than that. There was much clapping, cheering and shouts of good wishes. Fiona raised both arms and waved and applauded as the couple passed in front of her, smiling as though they were on a royal walkabout. In the ballroom's grand doorway, the bride, with her back to the throng, lifted her right hand and tossed her bouquet over her head towards the guests. Fiona's brain had lost logical thought somewhere around the dessert course hours earlier and she'd been acting on instinct ever since. Something flew through the air and reflex made her step forward to catch it, just as she would have done long ago in the rounders or netball team.

There was a moment of hush and then more cheering. Fiona looked down; she was holding the bride's bouquet of scarlet roses and green fronds. The implication made her stumble slightly and she looked around for a chair. Instead, she found Meeko's face wearing a mask of shock.

"I . . . I didn't realise what I was doing," she said quietly. "What a waste when someone young and in love could have made wonderful things happen."

"Does that mean that someone slightly older but still in love can't make wonderful things happen?"

"I . . ." It was impossible to formulate words when she couldn't move her eyes from his deep gaze. The green pools pulled with an irresistible magnetism. Now Fiona didn't want to speak. She was done with words. She placed her free hand on Meeko's waist and stepped into his personal space. Their mouths were inches apart and Fiona was desperate for that gap between them to disappear.

And then Meeko kissed her.

Fiona melted inside. Despite the blisters from dancing in ill-fitting heels, her toes curled. A sweet warmth travelled rapidly through her body, settling in her groin and breasts. Meeko's arms felt safe, secure and immensely strong. She felt one of his hands travel down her back and rest suggestively on her right bum cheek. Forgetting the people around them, she pressed herself up against him, noticing that he was feeling the same way as her.

She was dimly aware that the DJ had taken back control of the evening and the next track was from those ancient days of the 1980s when she'd been experiencing the heady independence of student life. 'Don't You Want

Me' by The Human League. It was impossible to disobey its magnetic force. She gently led Meeko into the crowd of dancers and kicked off her shoes. Meeko picked her up and whirled her around. They danced until they failed to recognise a splurge of more recent tunes. Fiona retrieved her shoes and mouthed the word 'bed' at him. He nodded. Manners wouldn't allow them to simply evaporate from the party. Breakfast arrangements had to be made with the cousins via shouting and hand signals because the music volume had risen. The bride's parents had to be thanked. And then they were free to go.

The hotel corridors and lift were deserted except for a couple of uniformed bellboys collecting room-service breakfast orders from door handles. Meeko held her hand all the way into their room. Inside he reluctantly released it when she insisted on finding a vase for the bouquet. She had to make do with a pint glass located in the minibar.

"They won't charge us for using that, will they?" All day money had been irrelevant but now she wanted to protect Meeko from any possible criticism or bill.

"Not as long as we don't fill it from their store of alcohol. Kiss me again. I always knew that kissing you would be perfection, but it was one hundred times better."

He was right. It was an experience better than any other. Better than Joe, better than Rob. The heat returned to her body. She kicked off her shoes again while their lips were still melded. Meeko had to pause briefly to undo his laces, remove his tie and toss his tailcoat over the chair. Still entwined, they sat down and then half reclined on the bed. Meeko put his hand on the gold silk of the dress covering her breast. Fiona shivered with anticipation and then sat up slowly, allowing in part of the logic battering at her brain — the part that would limit immediate physical damage to expensive clothing. The logic that would limit long-term emotional damage to vulnerable people and a best-friendship, she quashed. Or perhaps it was the champagne or the hazy veil of unreality that quashed it. "Shall we . . . I could do with some help with the zip. And . . . your shirt and trousers . . . they're hired."

Meeko was sitting up as well, staring at her with a serious but tender look on his face. She'd overstepped some invisible line. She'd misread the signals. But how? He'd drawn her into that kiss downstairs. He thought she wasn't too old to catch a wedding bouquet. The feel of his body against hers had advertised his physical interest in her.

"What?" she said. "What?"

"I love you, Fiona." His words were a great wave of warmth. "But I can't make love to you."

He wasn't making sense. She stood up and walked away. When she reached the failed sofa bed, her legs would hold her up no longer. She sat down. "Why?" she whispered. "I thought . . ."

"I don't want to become another Joe, kept in a little box on the periphery of your life."

"But Joe moved in."

"Not through your choice. You never wanted him there. I don't want to be another man who is rationed because it's more fun that way."

He was making her sound cheap and heartless. He sat next to her on the sofa. She inched away until her thigh hit the armrest. He took her hand. She didn't know whether to pull away. She wanted to grab the mocking wedding bouquet from its pint glass and decimate it.

Meeko squeezed her hand, then fetched the bouquet, the stalk now dripping with water. Had she spoken aloud?

"I don't want to be in one of your little time-controlled boxes." He slipped off the sofa and knelt in front of her, the wet bouquet held out towards her. "Fiona Ormeroyd, please will you do the honour of becoming my wife as well as my best friend."

Fiona's heart hammered in her chest. Her emotions were on a fairground waltzer. This moment was important. Whatever came out of her mouth next would make or break her relationship with Meeko as well as her own future. Her heart wanted to shout 'Yes' from the rooftops. But the logical-thinking part of her was recovering from the shock and was repeating 'No' louder and louder. She had been down the marriage route before and it would require absolute trust in Meeko. The last time she'd placed that trust in a man it had been abused in a life-destroying manner. She couldn't do that again. But what she felt for Meeko was bigger, deeper and scarier than anything she'd ever felt for any man before.

"Meeko, I love you." Now she understood that when she'd uttered those words first to Rob, and then to Joe, her feelings had been lukewarm, and that she'd hoped saying those words would make the feeling come true. Saying them to Meeko, she was speaking an absolute truth.

His lips curled into a huge smile and his eyes danced in anticipation. His whole face was illuminated.

"But it's too soon. Too fast. Too scary. We haven't even become 'an item'."

His expression crumpled and was replaced by confusion and frowning. "But not too soon to stick me in a sealed compartment?"

"It wouldn't be like that. We'd be a normal couple — a 'courting' couple, to use my grandmother's words."

"I don't want to be used at your convenience as Joe was. I want to give myself properly to you, hook, line and sinker. Or not at all. We've had years of being friends. There is no need for us to 'court' — we already know everything about each other. Unless there are more secrets that you're keeping from me?" There was a crack in his voice as he stopped speaking.

"No. No secrets. You know everything." Tears were pricking behind her eyes and it felt as though her world was tumbling in. They'd tried to move beyond friendship and failed because they had different expectations from a romantic relationship. This had always been the risk and now it was a reality. Unlike most of the other people she knew, Meeko had never tried to change her outlook or view on life. But could she expect him to compromise on what he wanted from their changed relationship?

"What do we do now?" He stood up, swallowed and blinked hard, putting the bouquet back in the pint glass. "Agree to disagree?"

"Can we go back to being friends until . . . there might be a time . . . ?"

"We can try. But I love you as a woman, Fiona. I always will. And that is different to loving a friend. I will try to pretend tonight never happened but I can't guarantee how things will turn out. Sometimes broken hearts don't mend."

Fiona reached for the hotel box of tissues and blew her nose. She was trembling and felt slightly sick.

"I'll sleep on the settee tonight."

"There's no need." She tried to bar the way to stop him fiddling with the hidden lever that would perform the magic act of turning the settee into a bed. "We managed together last night." She was crying now.

"Last night was different. We hadn't blurred the line."

Hardly able to see for the tears, she grabbed her nightdress and went into the bathroom. When she came out, he was already in his pyjamas and the sofa had become a bed. Meeko was tucking in sheets.

After they'd turned out the lights, he spoke gently into the darkness. "Everything you've done since losing Amber has been built around never trusting anyone ever again. Is that how she would have wanted her mother to live? Would you have wanted her to live in this artificial prison cell you've created for yourself? Stop making yourself suffer for something that was nobody's fault."

He was right but she could think of no reply. The following morning they were polite to one another and managed to appear as 'best friends' in front of his cousins at breakfast.

They said little on the train journey home. Fiona tried to imagine a future without even his friendship. He had taken the risk of trying to move their platonic relationship, which had worked fantastically well for years, into the unchartered waters of marriage. It was a risk that hadn't paid off and now they were both adrift without a lifebelt. Both wanting the same thing but in different ways. Was it possible to find some middle ground?

CHAPTER 45

"Take her, please! Before I get on that bus and dump her outside the maternity ward."

"The hospital bus doesn't run on a Sunday." Fiona held her arms out to receive Natalie.

"In that case I'll spend my last pennies on an Uber."

"Has it been that bad without me?" Fiona planted kisses all over the baby's face and then breathed in the sweet, sweet smell of her. A little of the Meeko tension eased. She felt needed on her home ground.

"Scary, knowing there was no one to call on."

"Your dad's not far away. Didn't he come on Saturday?"

"He came but he had one eye on his phone all the time, checking the football scores. We both know that domesticity and practical childrearing aren't his strong subjects. Don't get me wrong — he adores Natalie, and me as well, but he doesn't have a clue and doesn't want to learn about nappies and burping and all that stuff. He doesn't understand what it's like being responsible for keeping a tiny human alive 24-7. Now your Meeko on the other hand — he'd be willing to help with anything."

"He's not *my* Meeko," Fiona whispered into the down on Natalie's head.

"I thought you just had a dirty weekend together? Did you bother turning up to the wedding or did you spend the whole time in that massive posh bedroom? The pictures you sent were unbelievable. That one room was the size of our student flat."

The whole occasion felt like a fairytale gone wrong. "The wedding was good."

"Good? That's all you can say about two nights away at the poshest do that we plebs can only dream about?"

"I'm tired, Adele. Make me a cup of tea and then I'll watch Natalie while you get your head down for a few hours."

"It's a deal."

Nuzzling Natalie was the best stress reliever. Pacing the floor with her upright and burping was even better. It stopped the mind from doubting, questioning and second-guessing. Natalie was comfort and solace personified. After a shaky start, the longer Fiona's house guests stayed, the better.

On Monday morning reality stampeded back. Fiona's habitual jog to the hotel and breakfast with her best friend would be too awkward. Instead, she sat at the kitchen table and ate a bowl of porridge with a giant spoonful of golden syrup (who cared if she broke her own healthy eating rules — her life was a train crash anyway) and far too many slices of toast loaded with marmalade.

"Incredibly, she's still asleep." Adele crept into the kitchen and filled a dish with cornflakes. "There were a couple of episodes in the night but she quietened after a feed." She swiped at her phone as she ate. "Oh my God!"

"What?"

"Mum is back in communication. She's on a plane home. No, that's wrong. She sent that message in the middle of the night. She'll now be on a train from London. She says she'll get a taxi straight to your house."

"Here? How does she know?"

"She must have picked up the message I sent when I first arrived here."

"But she doesn't know about . . . ?" Fiona pointed at the ceiling. "Or about me and Joe splitting up?"

"Not unless Dad's told her, which I doubt."

Life was spooling even further out of control — like the brown tape that spewed out of broken cassettes when she was a teenager. A pencil could get the tape wound back in, but sorting out Fiona's life would take infinitely more effort than twisting a pencil round and round. "I need to clean the house. Buy food, plan what to feed her." *Get in control of the situation and then the appearance of your ex-boyfriend's wife won't faze you.* "Should I go out and stay out? Give you time to introduce Natalie to her proper grandma?" Where to? Not Meeko's; there'd been no word from him since they'd parted at the station. He'd even refused her offer to order him an Uber. There was only Dorothea, who'd want chapter and verse on the wedding and then lament the imminent loss of her grand-daughter- and great-granddaughter-by-proxy. Fiona wouldn't be able to talk about either without crying.

Adele looked surprised. "Why should you care about making things easier for Mum? Even though they were divorced, she was sort of your rival."

Good question. Until Joe had started citing her domestic inadequacies compared to his ex-wife, Fiona had never seen Rose as a rival; merely someone from his past who would become increasingly insignificant as time went on. But his constant harping back to Rose had been one of the key factors in Fiona ending their relationship. Now she felt grateful to Rose for saving her from wasting any more time on a man who would never be her soulmate. And, for reasons she couldn't understand, Fiona wanted Rose to like her. That unruly brown tape had just unwound a bit more.

She couldn't give either of these explanations to Rose's daughter and so she just shrugged.

Fiona had barely got back from the supermarket with the ingredients for a chicken casserole plus an expensive box of granola because Rose would have to be offered somewhere to stay for the night, when the doorbell rang.

"Take Natalie and answer it," Fiona urged. "I'll stay upstairs until you signal that you've got all the explaining out of the way."

"Where do I start?" The girl looked terrified, and then a flash of hope passed across her face. "Perhaps it's someone else at the door?"

Meeko? Don't even go there, Fiona. That relationship is now an official mess.

The doorbell rang again. "Answer it!" Fiona hissed from the top step. She heard the door open and an unfamiliar female voice. She went into her office, closed the door and waited. The indecipherable conversation in the room below ebbed and flowed like waves in the ocean. Fiona tried to put herself in Rose's shoes. If Amber had lived, Fiona would never have run away and left her without a single word. She'd often visualised Amber as she passed through the major milestones of life: starting school, becoming a teenager, leaving for university. When Adele had given birth, the emotion of how it might have been for Amber had been unbearable. Now Fiona tried to spool back to that moment in her imagination and panicked. She no longer saw the familiar image she had fabricated of her daughter in adulthood — instead it was a hazy female face that could fit any one of a million people. She rewound further in her mind, but as the versions of Amber grew younger, so did their genericness. Fiona gripped the edge of her office desk. She was losing the Amber of her imagination.

She lost track of how long she sat there, staring at the black screen of her laptop. No one had understood the depth of her grief over the miscarriage. And she couldn't tell anyone about this devastating second loss, of the imagined face of her daughter. They'd think she was mad. Except . . . Meeko. She looked at her mobile. Would he even take the call? She'd implied that she only wanted him for sex, not a total emotional commitment, and yet here she was wanting to unburden a deep fear. But even that wasn't the same as handing over her whole self to someone and trusting them to take care of it. A light of understanding came on as the indistinguishable multi-age images of Amber faded completely. The very fact that she wanted to talk to Meeko about her fear that these imagined images of her daughter were receding forever showed the level of trust she had in him. She trusted him, and only him, enough to reveal this vulnerability. From this point it was only a small step to trusting him with her whole future.

A knock made her jump and the office door opened.

"Fiona! I've been calling up the stairs. I'm putting the kettle on. Will you join Mum and I for coffee?"

"What? Are you sure you're ready for me? How's it going? Get the best chocolate biscuits — they're at the back of the cupboard." All introspection fled from Fiona's head as she tried to read Adele's face.

"It's OK. I'll introduce you."

Rose stood up, holding her granddaughter, when Fiona and Adele entered the lounge. Fiona felt a stab of jealousy as she saw blood-related grandmother and granddaughter together. How would Dorothea take to their own much-diluted, if any, presence in the baby's life?

"I'll leave you two to talk." Adele disappeared into the kitchen.

The two women sat awkwardly, looking anywhere but at each other. The mysterious domestic angel, Rose, looked tired, tanned and travel weary. She wore no make-up, or if she did it had disappeared during the long hours on the plane and the train. She was ordinary, not saintly.

Rose spoke first. "Thank you very much for all you've done for Adele." She paused and smiled. "I never thought I'd have cause to be grateful to my ex-husband's girlfriend."

"Ex-girlfriend, we split up." He'd only been gone a few days but already his previous importance in Fiona's life had slipped away. She felt nothing: no regret, love or longing for him, and no negativity towards Rose. Meeko was right: she'd put Joe in one of her life's compartments without emotional ties. Now she understood why Meeko didn't want to bend himself into a similar sealed box. He wanted to be, and deserved to be, centre stage in her life. "Didn't Adele tell you that it's over? That I asked him to leave? He's staying with his brother."

"In that case, I'm even more grateful to you for continuing to let Adele and Natalie—" Rose's expression softened as she glanced down at the baby — "stay here. Tom isn't well known for his hospitality."

"I don't need gratitude. And Joe living here just didn't work out."

Rose nodded. "My friends think he's Mr Wonderful because they only see him on his best behaviour, pouring wine and entertaining. Ingratiating himself, I call it. The rest of the time he has a habit of assuming the stuff in the house, or even the people, don't need his input. I tolerated it because I loved him and I didn't want to work outside the home and I wanted Adele and her brother to have a stable background and . . . I don't know, sometimes marriages just work even though outsiders might struggle to understand why. But then ours stopped working as the children moved out. I'm not sure exactly why. I still miss him in an odd sort of way. When I'm over the jetlag I'm going to surprise him. Can we keep my arrival here a secret for now?"

"Are you going to take him back?" *Please don't, Rose. You can do much better than Joe.*

Rose shrugged. "Sometimes what our soul craves is a purpose in life — feeling needed by other living beings. My family gave me that feeling. And, although he would never admit it, I think Joe needed me too."

Fiona thought of Dorothea and how she'd come back to life thanks to the recent demands placed on her: Natalie, the yoga class campaign, the baby shower . . .

"You're right." But who needed Fiona? Her mother? Meeko? Rob? Adele and Natalie had done. Did she enjoy the feeling? Yes. But only when she loosened the steel band around her emotions and threw her whole self into it.

"Joe's very malleable — I may have appeared downtrodden but actually I was in complete control of our lives, financially, domestically and socially. Everything. And that made it work. Until we became empty nesters and then, somehow, we lost ourselves in the increased space of our lives. Certainly I lost some of that feeling of being needed and thought the grass might be greener elsewhere. But I think it might work again."

Fiona was warming to Rose's honesty. "Did you find yourself in India?"

Rose coloured, looked down and planted a kiss on the smooth forehead of the sleeping baby. "It was an impulse decision and the first time I'd left the country alone. With hindsight, I should have done more research. But once I was there, I needed to prove to myself that I had the strength of character to stick it out."

Adele put a tray loaded with three mugs of black coffee, milk jug, sugar bowl and the best chocolate biscuits on the low table. There was also a plate of what looked like homemade chocolate brownies. Fiona glanced questioningly at her housemate.

"Beetroot chocolate brownies made with ground almonds. They're supposed to be healthy. I made them on Sunday morning while you were away. A sort of thank you."

Fiona pulled the girl into a hug. "You are wonderful!"

Rose was staring at her daughter open-mouthed. "Discovering I had a granddaughter was a shock. And now I learn that you are turning into a chef." She turned to Fiona. "I should hate you but I can't."

Fiona tried nonchalantly to shake off the praise but her heart was swelling in an unfamiliar way. These two women had been in need and, somehow, she'd found her way to doing the right thing instead of deciding they didn't fit any of her labelled compartments and discarding them. She wanted more of this feeling of being needed. The sensation held faint reminders of coming up trumps for her team at work when they hit an obstacle or deadline and being bought a drink, clapped on the back or receiving a bonus. Only this was more important and the feeling of satisfaction a million times better.

"You were telling me about finding yourself?" Fiona turned the spotlight away from herself and bit into one of the brownies with a grand, and genuine, gesture of enjoyment.

"Conditions at the retreat were primitive: cold communal showers, outside toilets, dodgy electricity supply. The food was basic and didn't always agree with me, or I didn't agree with it. There was lots of solitude, yoga and mindfulness training. I don't think I found myself. Maybe I got to know myself a tiny bit better but not completely — we shy away from our bad bits and pretend they don't exist, don't we?"

Fiona nodded. "It takes courage to recognise our weaknesses but we can't move forward without doing that." She was thinking how much she'd learned about herself over the previous six weeks, and the lovely feeling of those compartments inching open.

"Exactly — we are all selfish, have temper triggers and prejudices, but it takes a strong person to openly admit to them." Rose paused and took a sip of coffee. "Ooh! That's got a kick — we had no stimulants on the retreat." She swallowed. "No, I didn't find myself, whatever that means, but I did discover what is important in my life. And that is my family." She smiled at Adele. "Whatever they've done." She glanced down at Natalie. "I missed them like hell. More than I missed my comfortable bathroom or food that didn't wreck my insides or working light switches." Rose let out a sigh of contentment. "I want to gather them around me and have what we had before. But this time I hope all of us will appreciate it so much more."

Adele reached over and squeezed her mother's hand. "It's lovely to have you back, Mum, and Natalie is pleased to meet her grandma. She's never been this quiet for such a long time." As if on cue the baby's arms and legs started to curl and straighten as if preparing for a big crying session. "But . . . is it OK if we include Natalie's grandmother- and great-grandmother-by-proxy in our extended family? You'll love Dorothea when you meet her."

"Absolutely. One thing I observed out there is that even a family knee-deep in poverty has love in abundance for all its extended relatives. It adds richness and perspective to their lives. And it takes a village to raise a child, as they say."

Another layer of tension lifted from Fiona's shoulders; neither she nor her mother were going to lose this fledgling relationship with Adele and Natalie. The sudden feeling of belonging made her feel calm and loved. Rose might not have found herself but she'd found a way forward with her life.

Rose handed the hungry baby back to her daughter. "I need to find a hotel and get some sleep. The current Airbnb let doesn't finish for another week."

"There's a bed for you here until the house is available," Fiona offered.

Adele looked at her as if to say, where? All beds are taken.

"My mum's got a spare room that she won't mind me filling." Dorothea would be ecstatic to have her daughter as a house guest for a few days. "You two have got a lot to catch up on without me hanging around. And, without me here, you can have Joe over as well. And Dan, too."

CHAPTER 46

Fiona left the three female generations of the Ferguson family to get to know each other in private, and told Dorothea that she was on her way to claim a bed for the night. But before that there were plans to discuss with Rob. The anti-gambling project was a welcome distraction from the mess-up she'd made with Meeko, and it made her feel useful too.

Rob was in the pub before her and Fiona found herself apologising for being late, even though she'd actually arrived with two minutes to spare.

He shrugged away her words. "I deliberately came early — I didn't want you sitting alone in a pub waiting for me. You'd have had every local lech trying to hit on you."

"I doubt that." Fiona had often waited for female friends to arrive without any problems, but she appreciated Rob's actions.

Rob handed her a menu. "Let's eat and make an evening of it. Unless you've got other plans?"

Fiona felt suddenly hungry; with all that had happened she'd forgotten to factor in an evening meal for herself. She remembered the chicken casserole ingredients and wondered whether Adele or Rose would make use of them. "No plans." After completely messing up with Meeko, rediscovering her increasingly easy connection with Rob felt like balm to the soul.

300

"Tell me how you got on contacting the female support group?" Rob asked once his steak pie and chips and Fiona's salmon and new potatoes had arrived.

She explained about the invitation to visit the group and observe a session as well as spending time with the small staff and volunteers to find out exactly what was required.

"It's a three-hour drive to Norfolk," Rob said when she'd finished. "And it's an evening meeting. We'll have to stay over."

How could she have missed that detail? Too much stuff on her plate domestically.

"I can book us a hotel," Rob continued. "Are you OK with that?"

No. She wasn't OK with that. She'd just spent a disastrous weekend in a hotel with a man.

"I . . ."

"Separate rooms." The speed at which the words tumbled out meant he'd read the doubt on her face. She hoped her relief wasn't equally as obvious.

She finished the last of the salmon, put her knife and fork together and smiled at him. "I'm glad you made contact. This project is just what I needed to get away from everything else that's going on. It's given me a new purpose."

He looked her directly in the eye. "I've got good memories of our marriage, but we've been a lifetime apart and we've both changed."

"I think we'll work together well."

"Absolutely. I'm passionate about this project and you're the perfect partner in crime."

Fiona paused before speaking again. "Being with you and talking about what happened is cathartic for me. It's definitely helping."

"It's the same for me. Bringing the skeletons out of the cupboard and into broad daylight makes the past finally seem manageable."

"You hit the nail on the head."

CHAPTER 47

Dorothea had cleared away her latest jigsaw and dropped the leaves of the table. Fiona had opened the camp bed and added the bedding. A dining chair acted as a makeshift bedside table, holding an old desk lamp and acting as a resting place for glasses and a book. It was a tight squeeze.

The following morning Fiona was surprised to discover that she had slept well. It may have been the brandy her mother had insisted on as a nightcap.

"I don't drink alone — because of our genes," the old lady had said as she set up a couple of small tumblers. "So, when people are here, which is too rare, I take every opportunity." As soon as their glasses were half-empty, she topped them up and then put the bottle away.

"What do you mean 'our genes'?"

"I had an uncle with an alcohol problem and another who couldn't go an hour without a nicotine hit. Lung cancer got him." Then Dorothea's voice softened. "And it looks like that same gene, coupled with Rob and the miscarriage, led to your need to be in control all the time." Her mother put an arm around Fiona and hugged her tight. "But now I'm so proud of the way you're letting people into your life and helping them: Adele, Meeko, Rob, and even me." She kissed her daughter. "There was a time you wouldn't have dreamed of leaving two almost-strangers plus a puking baby alone in your house for a week."

"You say I'm helping other people, Mum. But it's actually them, and you, who are helping me." It really did feel like any aid she'd given was coming back to her in more generous dollops than she had offered.

"Now you're making me all emotional. Tell me about that big posh wedding."

Fiona had shown her mum the photos of the happy couple on her phone and the selfies she'd taken at the table early in the evening.

"And did all that romance wrap itself around you and Meeko?"

"I've told you, Mum, we're just good friends." Maybe they weren't even that now.

"Hmmm. There is much meaning behind that phrase, 'just good friends'."

Fiona said nothing about how everything had gone horribly wrong and that she didn't know if there was a way back. Then her mother switched to asking about Rose. She got the brandy out again and poured them another glass. By the time Fiona had turned out the desk lamp her anxiety about Meeko had been swept away by the alcohol and her heart was warm from telling Dorothea about the gratitude that both Rose and Adele had expressed in their different ways. Her mother's face had beamed after learning that she could continue to be a great-grandmother-by-proxy.

"Porridge is ready!" her mother called.

Fiona pulled on her dressing gown and found her mother sitting at the small table in the window alcove of the lounge. Having someone else prepare food for her resurrected that same warm feeling of belonging as she'd had from Adele's chocolate brownies. Was it small gestures like these that made marriages work? Would mornings with Meeko create a feeling of mutual support or would she tar him with the same brush as Rob and wonder if he was telling the truth about his activities? She was being ridiculous. She had to draw a line under Meeko. They were incompatible — he wouldn't trust her not to put him in a steel box unless they had rings on their fingers, and she didn't trust him sufficiently to accept one of those rings and all the 'jointness' that went with it.

"Help yourself." Dorothea pushed the squeezy golden syrup bottle across the table. Fiona was about to ignore it and plough on with a plain but healthy breakfast when her mother spoke again. "You haven't forgotten it's Meeko's first trial yoga class this morning? At ten thirty, so there's time for this to go down first — we won't be exercising on a full stomach."

"We?" She had remembered and had brought biscuits for her mother to take for the refreshments, but she couldn't face Meeko herself. And it wasn't fair to throw him off balance by turning up unexpectedly when this was his very first class and he was trying to impress. The manager of the complex might be there and he couldn't afford to get distracted by any implications, real or in his imagination, of her being there. "I'm not old enough — better to leave the space for someone else."

"Nonsense. There's plenty of room in the lounge and Meeko will be grateful for a friendly face. Plus, there are lots of chairs to move out and then put back — he'll need the help of another able-bodied person."

"I should really check on Adele and—"

"Nonsense. You'll be good for Meeko, plus I want to show my daughter off — I get precious little opportunity to do that, even though you're retired now. Eat your porridge before it gets cold."

Fiona squirted the sweet syrup over her breakfast. If she had to face Meeko, she needed energy.

Her running gear was in the small suitcase she'd brought to her mother's, and those leggings and T-shirt would do for the class. She didn't have her mat but the room was carpeted and most of the action would take place seated. Dorothea insisted they get to the lounge early to help Meeko arrange things. He was surveying the area when they arrived.

"You tell Fiona what you need moving. She is your slave. I'll sit and watch." The old lady took on the role of captain of the ship.

"Fiona. Hi." It was a half-hearted greeting.

She shrugged at him and inclined her head towards the old lady to convey to him that her presence at the class wasn't her own idea. Impossible to say whether the message was received.

"There's not much furniture moving to do," he said. "I'm focusing on chair yoga today so I can assess the level of fitness and mobility. I don't want people doing themselves an injury getting down on the floor. But everyone will need to be able to stick their arms out at shoulder height, so we need to space the chairs out appropriately. And we want chairs without arms if possible."

They worked in silence, elongating the existing rows of chairs, which looked as though they'd last been used for a film show. As they finished, a couple of Dorothea's fellow residents entered, one on a walking frame and one with a stick. Meeko seemed to be silently assessing them, while her mother rushed over and made introductions, her words falling over each other in her pride. "Barbara, Alice, this is my daughter Fiona and her . . ." there was a slight hesitation before she pronounced the next word with a peculiar emphasis, ". . . *friend*, Meeko, our new yoga teacher." Dorothea repeated this exercise until there were eight participants, plus Mrs Fairchild, the manager, and the clock said 10.30 a.m. Not as many as Fiona had hoped — she wondered if Mrs Fairchild had a mental cut-off figure which must be reached before the complex would agree to fund the classes beyond the three trial sessions. Please don't let another part of Meeko's future come crashing down — it would be her fault for encouraging him to believe he could improve on the hand that fate had dealt him. Fiona took a seat at the back so she could easily put the kettle on ten minutes before the end and arrange the promised biscuits on a plate.

"Hello and welcome!" An energised Meeko introduced himself with open arms and welcoming smile. "This first session is experimental to find out your baseline starting position with yoga. Going forward, the classes will be adapted to suit you. It will be easier with shoes off. Give me a wave if you need a hand?"

A murmur of conversation as Meeko made sure that everyone who needed help removing their shoes got it. Fiona helped the lady nearest to her.

"Let's start by sitting tall with our feet on the floor." There was a general shuffling of bottoms on seats as comfortable positions were found. Meeko was watching carefully. "If you can't quite get your feet flat on the floor, don't worry for this week. Next time I'll bring some blocks you can use as foot rests. Now, inhale and lengthen through the spine. Imagine you are a puppet with piece of string pulling you up from the crown of your head."

Fiona watched shoulders move back and the women appeared to grow taller in their chairs.

"Inhale deeply as you lift your heart and exhale as you move your shoulders backwards and down. We are going to find mobility in a way that's soft and gentle. We'll start by lifting the toes, keeping heels on the floor, and then lowering the toes. Let's do that a few times."

Meeko's words were gentle and soothing as he ran through a range of easy stretches. Fiona imagined the bliss of hearing that voice every day. Stress, bitterness or anger couldn't thrive in the presence of such calm. The daydream transported her away from the residents' lounge. When she tuned back in to Meeko's instructions, he was bringing the ladies into a seated twist. "Bring your right hand to your outer left thigh and, if possible, move your left hand onto the chair back."

She followed the rest of the movements along with the residents until he talked them into how to fold the top half of their bodies over their knees and to breathe deeply. Fiona glanced at the clock; the session was coming to a close. Meeko was bringing the energy in the room down. She crept over to the lounge's tiny kitchenette area, put the kettle on and started putting out mugs and arranging the custard creams she'd brought onto a plate. When she looked up, several faces were looking through the glass of the lounge doors, like zoo visitors staring into the lion enclosure. Some ducked when they realised they'd been spotted, others brazenly continued peeping. In the background Meeko was talking the ladies through bringing themselves back up to sitting by placing hands on thighs and gently pushing.

"Thank you, ladies . . . and gentleman." Meeko gave a respectful nod towards the only man in the room. "It's been a pleasure to have you here today and I hope you've enjoyed it." There was a smattering of applause among the group, who looked half-asleep after the end-of-class relaxation session. "I will definitely be here for the next two weeks. If those classes are well attended then Mrs Fairchild will consider funding these sessions — unfortunately I do need to pay my rent and buy food. Any questions, please give me a wave and I'll come and have a word with you." A couple of hands went up. *That had to be a good sign — it meant people were taking an interest in what was going on.*

Suddenly there was a throng of people around Fiona and the urn. And the custard cream plate was empty. There were significantly more than eight people now. A lady, who Fiona recognised as her mother's neighbour, whispered to Fiona, "Didn't you see them gathering outside the door? Vultures they are whenever the word 'biscuits' appears on a poster. They should be banned — they haven't earned their refreshments like we have." Fiona thought she'd left petty politics and snide remarks behind when she retired but they obviously existed in all areas of life. From her bag, she retrieved her second 'in case of a mammoth class attendance' pack of biscuits and refilled the plate.

"Custard creams." The voice was derogatory and made Fiona feel like a failed staff member rather than a volunteer giving her own time and biscuits free of charge. The lady was wearing a silky blouse with a bow at the neck and a close-fitting skirt. She had definitely not been in the class. "I was hoping for a dark chocolate digestive. That's what they put out during the film club interval."

It was too late to say the refreshments were for yoga participants only, but Fiona wasn't going to let these hangers-on get away with snaffling biscuits when Meeko was desperate for class members. "Apologies. I am taking biscuit requests from session participants. Let me make a note against your name." She picked up a piece of A4 paper on which Meeko had jotted the running order of his class. "What name is it?"

Even beneath the woman's heavy make-up, Fiona could see her cheeks redden. "No need. A custard cream will do just as well." The woman grabbed a mug and biscuit and disappeared into a huddle of similarly dressed ladies.

The volume of chat in the room was a reward in itself — even if at least half of them hadn't participated in the yoga. Knowing how lonely and frustrated Dorothea became in the prison of her own four walls, this happy atmosphere, with so many keen to get a slice of the action, would surely please Mrs Fairchild. And the cost to the residential complex could be justified by the myriad of health benefits, both physical and mental, emanating from yoga. Meeko was an expert at explaining those. She could see him now, deep in conversation with the manager, and was tempted to rush over and interrupt to make sure that Mrs Fairchild took on board the additional benefit of the after-class refreshments in reducing social isolation. No. She held back. Meeko's future was his own. She'd given him a little push, like a teenager leaving for university, and now it was up to him. Neither of them wanted to accept the terms offered for being involved as a partner in the other's life, and so they each had to go it alone from now on.

Afterwards, when she realised Dorothea had invited Meeko back to her flat for a debrief, Fiona tried to slip away on the pretext of a dental appointment.

"Balderdash! I can read you like a book, Fiona Ormeroyd, and that is a lie." The old lady opened her front door and ushered them both in ahead of her. "If you check the fridge, you will see that I'm not lying when I say I am out of milk. You two have thirty minutes to slay the elephant in the room while I go to the shop."

"It's a ploy on her behalf," Fiona said when she was alone with Meeko. "Look." She slid back the door of the cupboard under the sink to reveal a two-litre plastic container of milk, which was almost full. "I remember seeing it at breakfast. And under the sink is where she always used to hide sweets when I was a kid."

Meeko managed a smile. "Mrs Fairchild was pleased with the turnout. Apparently, it needs fifteen to make any activity eligible for funds, but she said we had one of the main resident personalities there. If she enjoyed it then it's likely she will corral her acolytes into attending next time."

"That's good — I wish you well with it. And with the post-natal group — but that will be fine; Adele's got your back there. If you need help with the refreshments again here, drop me a text — I'm happy to come and boil a kettle and do some washing up." And at least we will still have some contact with each other, however tenuous.

"I'd love that. Thanks." Did his swift response mean Meeko wanted to rebuild the 'best friends' thing?

"I'll put the kettle on ready for when Mum gets back."

"Can we search her shopping to make sure she actually has bought more milk?" Meeko was grinning at her. The dimples that made her toes curl were there but his eyes were missing their dancing feet. She wanted that happiness back for him. For both of them. She missed their camaraderie, his calming supportive nature, the way he was so good with Dorothea and the way he understood her own needs. Everything had been so easy when she'd thought he was out of reach. She'd been able to say to herself that, *if* she was looking for a committed partnership, she would choose Meeko. Now she knew he was available, she still thought that. And he wanted that. *But was she looking for a committed partnership?* Trust. Absolute trust in another person. Her lack of trust was the elephant that Dorothea was talking about. But he'd been the person her mind had flitted to when she'd panicked about her disappearing imaginings of Amber.

"Mum will let you delve in her bag but not me!" They were mildly flirting with each other. It wasn't what best friends did. She took a breath. "We do need to clear the air, don't we?"

He nodded. For several moments they looked at each other. Words wouldn't come and so she touched his hand. The shock of their mutual attraction made her pull away. Trust. Other people managed it. That trust sometimes got broken or misused but they found a way back. She thought about Rose's ability to weigh up what really mattered to her and then consider starting again with her ex-husband. She thought about Adele and the misplaced trust she'd put in the boyfriend who'd dropped her as soon as she announced her pregnancy. The girl had been shattered but she was coming out of what might be considered a catastrophe, as a stronger, more mature person — with no regrets about bringing baby Natalie into the world. And she thought about Dorothea and that failed attempt at dating — her mother had gone into that knowing she was never going to re-create the closeness of her long marriage with Fiona's dad, but she still thought it worth the gamble. Better to have loved and lost than never to have loved at all — wasn't that the old adage?

Fiona was broken when she lost Amber but she didn't regret having become pregnant with her. She'd been catastrophically bruised by Rob's abuse of her financial trust, but was that reason never to let anyone else become close to her — ever? Was she cutting off her nose to spite her face? If you looked hard enough, it was possible to find a positive in every experience, no matter how bad it had seemed at the time. In their brief meetings, she'd started to see the old Rob, the one she'd chosen to marry, and now he was intent on giving back to society. And helping him was giving purpose to her post-work life. Their marriage had ended in a bad way but she couldn't regret taking those vows.

Fiona looked at Meeko. He'd created within her a strength of feeling that she'd never had for any other man. And it frightened her. It was turning out impossible for them to be 'best friends' again. It didn't work because this fierce emotion, now it had been acknowledged, was growing by the day. She had to act or regret it forever.

"I've been thinking." Their words collided in mid-air.

"You first," he said.

She wanted him to speak first, before she said the wrong thing. Perhaps he'd decided marriage wasn't an essential back-drop to an intimate relationship between them. Perhaps he'd realised he could trust her not to drop him into a steel com-partment. But in either or both of those cases, she knew she was only offering a chunk of herself rather than the whole package, as he was prepared to do. Fiona had too much respect for him to not give equally of herself.

This time it had to be her who went down on one knee. "Michael Woods, please will you do me the honour of becom-ing my lawful, legally wedded, official, public-facing and non-compartmentalised husband?" From his initial shocked expression, the biggest smile she had ever seen erupted.

"I will." Then he was on the floor beside her, pulling her into his arms. They were still wrapped in a kiss when Fiona became aware of her mother standing over them.

"I see you chased the elephant away."

CHAPTER 48

Snowdrops were emerging in the garden, darkness was no longer cutting the afternoons brutally short, and everywhere had the smell of new beginnings. New beginnings. Fiona rolled the phrase around her mind. New beginnings. For the first time in her adult life she had no idea where the coming months would take her, what she would achieve by the end of the year, or whether she would even be the same person by then. Something inside her still wanted to grab the reins, impose a structure on the coming weeks, days, hours, and to control those around her. But the last three months had taught her there were great benefits to be had by going with the flow and following the lead of others

Fiona's eyes drifted back from the lounge window to the rows and columns on her laptop screen. Most of the steps on the 'Naming Ceremony' spreadsheet had been completed. Invitations had gone out and been returned. The function room at the Birnside Hotel had been secured. Several of Meeko's classes had been reinstated following vocal protests and a sit-in at the hotel reception by his long-standing class attendees. This had increased his profile and he'd got a staff discount on the room hire as his contribution to the party.

Rose had arranged outside caterers to provide a savoury finger buffet and there would be two glasses of sparkling wine for each of the forty guests. She was adamant there would be plenty of toasts because, although baby Natalie would be centre stage, the occasion wasn't just to celebrate the beginning of life for her first granddaughter. It was to mark new beginnings across the lives of so many of the guests and to thank them for their support of Adele and Natalie over the last few months.

Rose hadn't been allowed to push the boat out on her own; everyone wanted to help and be a part of things. Dorothea had been baking cakes for the last week and sticking them in her freezer and those of her neighbours, to ensure they were all at the peak of freshness on the day. Adele and Natalie had been regular visitors to the old lady's flat as Adele learned the ancient art of scone making — finally she'd found perfection and the last four batches would be served with jam and cream after the sandwiches and sausage rolls but before the cakes. "I've also done some more of those healthy flapjacks," she'd told Fiona. "We'll hide them behind everything else — just for you. And Mum's asked the caterers to do some salad options alongside all the sandwiches and stuff — you've done so much for me that I don't want you to be forced to eat things you'd prefer not to."

Words had failed Fiona and she'd felt tears pricking her eyes. She'd hugged her daughter-by-proxy and swallowed the lump in her throat. She didn't regret one minute of her relationship with Joe or all the upheaval of Christmas and New Year. Those events had catapulted her out of her comfort zone into an unknown galaxy. And navigating that difficult time had brought her this whole new family and freed her from the addiction of controlling her life into specific, sterile compartments.

She closed the laptop and opened her wardrobe. The beige suit she'd planned to wear hung in front of her beneath its transparent dry cleaner's wrapper. Both the skirt and jacket were fitted and the best effect came from having the jacket buttoned almost to the top. Previously the suit had clothed Fiona in confidence as she'd stalked around christenings and weddings; an outsider peeking in at scenes of togetherness. She'd always felt like an observer rather than part of the celebrations. But now things were different. She wasn't going to be centre stage at the naming ceremony, but she did feel that she belonged and that her life was now flowing naturally rather than being carefully choreographed and channelled. Buttoned-up jackets weren't part of her life anymore. At the back of her wardrobe was an unworn cream dress. She'd bought it in a sale, on a whim, straight after her first-ever yoga class with Meeko. Fiona never bought things on a whim but the class had made her feel lithe, flowing and young. The dress had stayed in her wardrobe because, until now, social occasions had always made her crave a feeling of control. Cap sleeves, a full knee-length skirt and a collarbone-revealing neckline whispered 'relaxed and flowing' not 'I must be in control'. She put the dress on and positioned the amber pendant in full view. She twirled and the skirt spun outwards 'a la Marilyn Monroe'. This was a party she was going to enjoy.

The ceremony went like a dream. Afterwards there was the food and getting to know the other guests. Adele and Rose introduced her and Meeko as 'close family friends' — the relationship with Joe was never mentioned. Joe himself kept his distance but Fiona spotted him on at least a couple of occasions catching hold of his ex-wife's hands and whispering in her ear; she rewarded him with a broad smile. Fiona smiled too; all's well that ends well — and she now knew from experience that temporarily losing something could make it better than before.

"He's grown a foot taller since that diamond went on your finger." Dorothea was at Fiona's shoulder, pointing at Meeko, who was fiddling with the microphone attached to the sound system. He'd volunteered to act as MC for the speeches.

"One, two. One, two."

"A couple of months ago he'd never have willingly made announcements," the old lady continued.

Fiona looked over at her fiancé with pride. Then she turned back to her mother and took the old lady's hand. "I think I might have changed too, Mum."

Dorothea beamed. "You have blossomed, my love. It's like someone reached inside you and turned the sunshine on."

Fiona's heart swelled. "I could say the same about you. That smile is rarely off your face and you tackle everything with such gusto, from yoga to organising coffee mornings, or simply cuddling Natalie."

"Fiona, we've had unrealistic expectations of each other in the past. And might do in the future. But now we know how it feels to be actual friends — and I know we'll hold on to that in the future."

They hugged each other until Meeko's first announcement interrupted them.

"Ladies and gentlemen, please find a seat, Adele and her supporters would like to say a few words."

There was a rise in volume as everyone shuffled around. Fiona guided her mother to a chair and sat down beside her. She looked over at Meeko who was gently shepherding people and then beckoning Adele, Rose and Joe over to him. It felt so special that this gentle, caring man had seen something attractive within her, even though she often faced the world with longer prickles than a porcupine. Joe spoke first. He talked about his pride in his daughter and new granddaughter and how he loved seeing the family likeness cascade down the generations. Rose spoke about the joy of being a grandmother, which she'd never understood until she met baby Natalie for the first time and thought her heart might burst with all the love she felt. Adele took the microphone, her voice shaky with nerves, and she kept glancing sideways at Meeko, as though he were invisibly feeding her confidence and reassurance. She talked about the deep debt of gratitude she owed to the people who had been on this difficult, yet joyous, journey to motherhood with her.

"Circumstances weren't in my favour and I was forced into a corner not of my choosing. At first, I resented the woman who eventually became my saviour." Adele looked up from her sheet of A4 paper and glanced at Fiona. "She gave me a roof over my head, she masterminded my baby shower and . . ." Gaining confidence at the microphone, Adele paused and let her eyes scan the audience for dramatic effect. "And she delivered my baby and made sure we got to hospital on the busiest night of the year and stayed there with me until my dad could arrive." Another pause. Even though her name hadn't yet been mentioned, heads were turning towards Fiona and she could feel her cheeks burning. "Over two thousand years ago there was no room at the inn. But just a couple of months ago, there was ample room in Fiona's heart for a pregnant young woman." Adele turned to one side, where her brother was manhandling a huge bouquet of flowers out of a bucket of water. "Fiona, please will you come forward?"

Fiona was rooted to her seat by embarrassment and emotion. If she moved, she would cry. As part of her career, she'd given presentations to large audiences and been completely unfazed. Now she was terrified to stand up in a room of friendly faces. She didn't deserve these accolades.

"Go on!" She felt a nudge from her mother and, turning, saw the old lady's face was a picture of pride and love. "You deserve this, plus all the thanks and praise in the world." Suddenly Fiona recognised that her mother's previous criticisms hadn't come from a dark place to hurt her only child. On the contrary, they'd come from a place of love and hope, a place that wanted Fiona to live the happiest and most rewarding life that she could. She grabbed her mother, kissed her on the cheek again and hugged her tight. "You daft ha'peth! Go on — they're waiting. The flowers are dripping down Adele's lovely new dress." Fiona looked up towards the front of the room. She noticed that Rose and Joe had stepped into the background and were now holding hands — she was happy for them. Both Meeko and Adele were beckoning her forward. Fiona stood up.

"Nobody can replace the love of an actual mother," Adele said, looking over to her parents. "But some people come within a hair's breadth of doing that, turning their own life upside down in the process. Fiona — I can never thank you enough for what you have done for Natalie and I." Fiona received the dripping bouquet, not caring about water stains on her new dress. Adele kissed her on both cheeks. "I hope both you and Dorothea will continue in our lives as grandma- and great-grandma-by-proxy to Natalie." Then she handed the microphone to Fiona.

Fiona willed the tears and the tightness in her chest to dissipate so she didn't embarrass herself or anyone else. Then she took a breath as another inspirational truth hit her. "The benefits of showing kindness are rarely one-sided. I didn't offer Adele a place under my roof *because* I thought I would gain from it. But gain from it I have — many times over. Adele, Natalie and all the events surrounding them taught me that life is like a river — if you try to control it by building a dam in one place, the torrent will insist on finding a way through in another." Fiona glanced across at Meeko, who was grinning widely at her. "And Adele has given back generously. Thanks to her, my *fiancé*," Fiona paused, still enjoying the novelty of that word, "has a thriving post-natal yoga class, plus not one but *two* Hatha yoga classes at the same venue. If you're interested, catch him afterwards for his business card — also designed by Adele." There was a ripple of laughter and then applause as Fiona went back to her seat. Meeko introduced the DJ and then seats were being moved to the edges of the room in order to create a dance floor.

"I never thought we'd have a baby to coo over," Dorothea said. "Adele's taking me shopping next week so she can choose a couple of patterns and some wool for me to knit up for Natalie. There's only a couple of coldish months to go so I'll have to get cracking." Her mother sounded energised by the prospect of a project with a deadline. "I think I'll offer to do a cotton, short-sleeved top for the summer for Adele, too. And I forgot to tell you, now that Meeko's chair yoga sessions are in full swing, Mrs Fairchild has put me in charge of organising volunteers for the tea rota, checking the biscuit stock and making sure that only those attending the class get the refreshments. You can never be too busy, can you?"

"No, Mum." Fiona smiled. There'd been no more of the distraught, lonely and panicky telephone calls that Dorothea had been making at the end of the previous year. Fiona no longer worried that her mother was on the cusp of dementia — all the old lady had needed was a purpose in life and someone to love. Now she had both.

Then Joe was tapping Fiona on the shoulder. Dorothea frowned. Fiona went tense — she didn't want a scene. Everything they had to say to each other had already been said. The relationship was finished. "Can I have a word?" She shrugged and followed him. "I'm sorry I used you," he said. "I thought I loved you. I thought we had something better than my old relationship with Rose."

Fiona gave a small smile; she hadn't been expecting him to speak to her at all, and especially not to apologise for something that wasn't exclusively his fault. "It takes two to tango. I thought I loved you too. But if I truly had, I wouldn't have been happy to see you only once a week. No apology necessary." She offered him her hand and they shook. Another layer of a difficult past had been shed and she was a step nearer a brighter future.

Dorothea was swaying gently to the music on the edge of the dance floor with a couple of Adele's friends. Meeko joined Fiona. "OK?" he asked. She nodded. He took her left hand and squeezed it. She looked down and felt warmed by the sight of her hand in his and the tiny gem stone on her fourth finger. He'd promised her something bigger just as soon as his new endeavours started turning a profit, but Fiona didn't want anything bigger — both the ring and Meeko were absolutely perfect as they were.

THE END

ACKNOWLEDGEMENTS

I would like to thank the Romantic Novelists' Association for providing the inspiration for this book via their 2023 Elizabeth Goudge Award. This competition is run alongside each RNA conference. The brief for the 2023 competition was to write a 1,000-word opening chapter on the theme *Absence Makes the Heart Grow Fonder*. My brain whirred and I created Fiona, a mature woman who loves her once-a-week meetings with her manfriend Joe because she avoids all the inconvenience and messiness of living with a man full-time. I introduced jeopardy into the situation by Joe turning up on her doorstep with his suitcases, needing somewhere to live. I was astonished and proud when my competition entry was announced as the winner. Filled with enthusiasm, I completed the whole of Fiona's story, and that 1,000-word competition entry formed the basis of chapter two of the novel you've just read.

Also deserving thanks is the wonderful editorial team at Choc Lit/Joffe Books. I received great advice on how to knock the rough edges off my initial draft manuscript and turn it into a smooth, well-rounded read. I couldn't have done it without them!

Finally, a big shout-out for all my family and friends, who continue to listen patiently to me chuntering on about my writing, plot difficulties and general literary angst, without rolling their eyes or telling me to shut up. You are all stars!

READING GROUP QUESTIONS

1. What did you think of Fiona's once-a-week relationship with Joe? Is it something you would like? Could such a relationship ever last over the long-term?

2. Rob's gambling had a massive impact on the whole of Fiona's life. Do you think she over-reacted or can you empathise with her?

3. Has the internet spawned a new type of gambler? Should gambling be banned? Are some gambling activities, such as raffles, bingo and lotteries, more acceptable than others?

4. For thirty years, Fiona let Rob believe the arrival of the bailiffs was the cause of her miscarriage, even though she had been told it would probably have happened anyway. Did the keeping of that secret change your feelings towards Fiona?

5. What did you think about the relationship between Joe and Adele? Would it have been better or worse if Rose had been there?

6. In the early part of the book, Dorothea is lonely, even though she lives in sheltered accommodation alongside others in a similar situation to her. Do you think retirement complexes are a good thing or are we better living among people of all ages?

7. Fiona marks her visiting schedule on her mother's calendar in orange circles. What do you think about this fixed schedule?

8. Meeko and Fiona have very different personalities. Do you think their relationship will last? Why?

9. What do you think attracts Fiona to Meeko and vice versa?

10. What did you think about Rose? Can you understand why she disappeared to India or why she might give Joe a second chance?

THE CHOC LIT STORY

Established in 2009, Choc Lit is an independent, award-winning publisher dedicated to creating a delicious selection of quality women's fiction.

We have won 18 awards, including Publisher of the Year and the Romantic Novel of the Year, and have been shortlisted for countless others. In 2023, we were shortlisted for Publisher of the Year by the Romantic Novelists' Association.

All our novels are selected by genuine readers. We are proud to publish talented first-time authors, as well as established writers whose books we love introducing to a new generation of readers.

In 2023, we became a Joffe Books company. Best known for publishing a wide range of commercial fiction, Joffe Books has its roots in women's fiction. Today it is one of the largest independent publishers in the UK.

We love to hear from you, so please email us about absolutely anything bookish at choc-lit@joffebooks.com.

If you want to receive free books every Friday and hear about all our new releases, join our mailing list here: www.joffebooks.com/freebooks.